This book should be returned to any branch of the
Lancashire County Library on or before the date shown

ENE

− 5 NOV 2018

2 6 NOV 2019

Lancashire County Library,
County Hall Complex,
1st floor Christ Church Precinct,
Preston, PR1 8XJ

Lancashire
County
Council

www.lancashire.gov.uk/libraries

LL1(A)

THE MAGIC OF RAMBLINGS

THE MAGIC OF RAMBLINGS

by

Kate Field

Magna Large Print Books
Long Preston, North Yorkshire,
BD23 4ND, England.

British Library Cataloguing in Publication Data.

_____

A catalogue record of this book is
available from the British Library

ISBN   978-0-7505-4433-7

First published in Great Britain by Accent Press 2016

Published in Large Print 2017 by arrangement with
Accent Press Ltd.

Magna Large Print is an imprint of Library Magna Books Ltd.

Printed and bound in Great Britain by
T.J. (International) Ltd., Cornwall, PL28 8RW

135349193

Dedication

To Mum and Dad, for everything.

CHAPTER ONE

As soon as she saw the advert, in one of the magazines she was paid to dust, not read, Cassie knew it had been written for her.

'WANTED: Female live-in companion for independent lady in isolated Lancashire village. Own room provided. <u>Must not chatter</u>. References required.'

Isolation and silence – *underlined* silence. It was perfect. Carrying the magazine to the study, careful not to crease any pages, Cassie found a scrap of paper and copied out the advert.

Her pen hovered over the final two words. References? How was she going to manage that? Then her gaze landed on the computer, and the letterheaded notepaper lying beside it. No one would notice one missing sheet. The password for the computer was taped on the inside of the desk drawer: she hadn't cleaned here three times a week for the last three months without finding that out. It would take barely five minutes to conjure something suitable. And surely her boss at the cleaning company, who had employed her without references and without questioning why she had no ID in the name she'd given him, wouldn't scruple to give her a reference in any name she wanted?

Her conscience protested, but conscience was

11

one of the many luxuries that Cassie could no longer afford. Her fingers trembling, she switched on the laptop and typed out a letter, recommending herself as an employee in terms she hoped were too good to refuse. She had to get this job. It was time to move on.

Two weeks later, Cassie tramped along a twisting Lancashire lane, knees buckling under the weight of an Army-style backpack. Exhaustion made every step feel like ten, and her feet would have ached if the February chill hadn't numbed them. But her heart was lighter than it had been in months. Glorious countryside stretched around her, unbroken by any sign of human life. It was almost as good as home. This was exactly the isolation she needed.

She let her backpack slide to the ground, rolled her shoulders to ease the tension and stepped forward for a closer look at a lamb in the field on the opposite side of the road.

A horn blared. Cassie felt a rush of air as a vehicle swerved around her and came to a halt in the hedge. The mother sheep started to run, her muddy brown bottom bobbing up and down, her lamb close behind.

'What the hell were you doing leaping out into the road?'

Cassie stared up into a face of darkness and bristles. Black eyebrows met over furious brown eyes, and she could just about detect lips set in a cross line inside an unruly beard.

'You scared the sheep,' she said, watching as the animals halted at the far side of the field.

'What?' The man briefly followed her gaze, then swung back. 'Stupid woman. I could have killed you! Cars rocket along this road.'

Stupid woman... A different voice fogged Cassie's brain. She stepped back.

A strong tug on her arm jerked her forwards again just as another car shot round the bend of the road.

'What's the matter with you? Do you have a death wish?'

The man looked even more cross and bristly.

'Sorry.' Cassie began to rub the knuckle at the base of her right thumb, willing him to leave.

'Where are you going? Are you heading for Ribblemill?'

'Yes.'

'I'll give you a lift.' He picked up Cassie's bag and slung it in the back of his pick-up truck. He opened the passenger door and a brown Border Collie jumped down. It ran over to sniff Cassie and she bent to stroke it, letting her fingers sink into the soft fur. The dog licked her hand, its tongue rough and warm. It was the most affectionate touch she had felt for months.

'Gin, here girl.'

The dog abandoned Cassie and returned to the man, who lifted her into the back of the truck. He looked across at Cassie.

'Come on. It's too cold to hang about.' When Cassie didn't move, he sighed and scratched his nails along his beard. 'You'll be perfectly safe. I'm sorry I shouted, OK? A local girl was knocked down on this road last year. I don't want it to happen again.'

His tone was gentler than it had been, and concern diluted the crossness in his eyes: undoubtedly genuine concern, surprising and disconcerting in equal measure. It took less than a moment for Cassie to make her mind up and climb into the truck. What had she to lose? All she had left was in her backpack, and he had already taken that.

After five minutes of silence, they pulled up just past a substantial stone bus shelter, in what Cassie assumed was the heart of the village. The road split in two before joining a third road, creating a triangular village green in the centre. For a place in the middle of nowhere, the village was surprisingly well-equipped. A pub, its exterior blackened with age, dominated one side of the triangle, and she could see a Post Office and general store, a butcher's, and a hardware shop that had an extensive jumble of brushes, mops, buckets and other paraphernalia cluttering the pavement outside.

'This is Ribblemill,' the man said, cutting the engine and interrupting Cassie's inspection of what she hoped would be her new home. 'Do you know where you're going?'

Cassie peered through the windscreen. None of the roads had names. She shook her head.

'Which is Wood End Road?'

'That one.' He pointed to the road that disappeared to the left, at the opposite point of the triangle from the Post Office. 'There's not much that way. Have you been here before?'

'No,' Cassie admitted. 'I'm looking for a house called Ramblings. Do you know it?'

There was a definite shift in atmosphere inside the truck. The man turned towards Cassie.

'What are you going there for?'

'I have a meeting with the owner, Mrs Smallwood.'

'What about?'

'Is that any of your business?'

'Why don't you tell me? Is it really *Mrs* Smallwood you want?'

Cassie wondered why he was looking at her with such suspicion, when he was the one acting oddly. She reached for the door handle.

'Wait! I'm on my way to Ramblings now. I can take you there.'

This seemed a remarkable coincidence, but it was impossible to know what he was thinking under all that hair.

'It's no problem. I can walk.'

'It's a mile and a half away.'

Cassie let go of the door handle. She was already feeling the effects of pushing herself too far today. If the interview wasn't successful, she had no idea how she would find her way back to public transport or, more to the point, where she would go once she did. For the first time she regretted the impulse that had led her to give up her job and her room to come here.

'I've a couple of errands in the village, then we'll go. I'll be five minutes. Wait there.'

The man was halfway out of the truck before Cassie realised that he was talking to her, not the dog. The dog was allowed to go with him, and she watched them cross the road and head into the hardware shop. A few minutes later they emerged and walked over the green to the pub. Errands! Cassie snorted to herself. A swift pint, more like. Her eyes flicked across to the general store. If he was having a drink, she could easily pop over there and be back before he knew she'd moved. She climbed out, grabbed her bag, and headed to the shop.

Five minutes later, Cassie left the store and inwardly groaned as she saw the man standing at the side of his truck, looking up and down the road. She could sense waves of bristling irritation flooding her way.

'Where did you go?' he demanded, as soon as she was within shouting distance. 'I told you to wait.'

'I went to the shop.'

'What for? Have you been asking questions about me?'

'No. I needed some tablets,' she said, thinking that this lie must surely end the interrogation. She wished she had asked about him while she was there. Was he actually mad, or just good at behaving like it?

'What tablets? Are you ill?'

'Period pain,' she improvised, confident this would be the perfect full stop to the conversation. She put her bag into the back of the truck with the dog, and climbed into the passenger seat. The man started the engine, but didn't set off.

'What tablets did you get?'

'Ibuprofen.'

'Don't take them on an empty stomach. Have you any food?' Cassie shook her head. He reached across and opened the glove box. It was stashed full of chocolate bars. It was possible he blushed under Cassie's astonished gaze, but it was hard to be sure, what with the beard. 'Help yourself.'

'I don't eat chocolate.'

He snapped the glove box shut again, and pulled an apple from the door pocket. He polished it on his jeans and tossed it to Cassie. She crunched into it, preferring his germs to his questions.

The road out of the village passed a couple of cottages and then there was nothing but undulating fields on either side. They approached a copse, and the truck swung abruptly through a pair of elaborate stone gateposts and along a well-kept drive. Cassie sat up. This wasn't right.

'I thought you were taking me to Ramblings.'

'I am.'

'But...'

Cassie's words fell away as they pulled onto a gravel forecourt in front of a house of stately home proportions. Built of a pale grey stone, elaborate turrets and towers propped up the corners and huge chimneys burst through the roof. There was no symmetry or order. It looked like someone had thrown every fantasy together in one building – and yet it worked. It was beautiful.

'This is Ramblings?'

'Yes. What were you expecting?'

Cassie gave a vague shrug, which was as good as a lie, because after one brief conversation with Frances Smallwood, she'd had a clear idea of what to expect. She'd imagined a detached house, possibly Edwardian, neat gardens outside and inside a riot of ornamental china displayed on lace doilies.

17

Never in a million years had she imagined *this*.

Her companion was beetling his brows again.

'Surely you looked it up before you came?'

'I don't have a computer.' She hadn't dared use the ones in the houses she cleaned in case she left a search history. On finding out the address, Cassie had gone into the nearest WH Smiths and looked on a road map to see where the village was, and which was the closest railway station. The house itself had been irrelevant. The advert had promised her own room, and as she'd learnt over the past few months, ultimately she didn't need more than that.

The man continued to stare at her, clearly unconvinced.

'Why are you here?'

'I told you. I'm here to see Mrs Smallwood.' She opened the door. 'Thanks for the lift.'

She hopped down, but before she could reach into the back for her bag, he had come round and picked it up himself, swinging it over one shoulder as if it contained nothing more than cobwebs.

'I'll introduce you,' he said, and led the way under an ornate entrance canopy that reminded Cassie of a four-poster bed. He flung open one half of the massive oak door, without ringing the bell, and walked into a hall the size of a tennis court. The walls were wood-panelled, carved into arches that echoed the windows, the door frames and the fireplace.

'Frances!' he shouted. There was no answer. 'She's probably in the morning room.'

He marched off and Cassie hurried after him, through an over-sized archway and down a corridor until he burst through a door.

'There you are,' Cassie heard him say as she dawdled behind, unsure whether she should have followed him or waited in the hall. 'Why have you got your feet up? Are you feeling ill?'

It was a softer version of the inquisitive tone he had used on Cassie.

'Barney! I did not expect you to be here today.' The answering voice was female, elderly, and querulous. 'I was simply resting my legs. Stop fussing and get off to your office.'

'What's the hurry? Am I interrupting something?'

'Nothing that concerns you. I am expecting a visitor.'

'Then it does concern me, because I've brought you one. Or I thought I had. Has she done a runner already?' Cassie heard footsteps and then the man, Barney, peered round the door. 'It appears you were telling the truth – about your meeting, at least. You'd better come in.'

Cassie pushed open the door and went into a large but surprisingly cosy room, decorated in a soothing shade of blue, with squashy sofas and chairs scattered around and not a single doily in sight.

An old lady rose from a chair. She was immaculate in an A-line wool skirt, silk blouse and cardigan, her grey hair set into a softer version of the Queen's style.

'Miss Bancroft? It is very good of you to come. I am Frances Smallwood.'

She swept a sharp, assessing look over Cassie, who gazed back, helplessly aware that if she was going to be judged on appearance, the job was as good as lost.

'Do sit down. You look exhausted. Was it a bad journey?'

'Not really, until the last few miles...'

'Until she ran me off the road,' Barney interrupted. 'She jumped out of the hedge like a rabbit.'

'Are you still here?' Frances cast an irritated glance at him before turning back to Cassie. 'Why were you in the road? Where was your car?'

'I don't have one.'

'No car? But I assumed...' Frances trailed off.

'Is it a problem? I don't mind the isolation. There's nowhere I want to go.'

Out of the corner of her eye, Cassie noticed Barney shift nearer Frances. She looked up as she felt his gaze land on her, cool and appraising. It was worse than Frances' scrutiny, and Cassie shrank back into her seat.

'What's going on here, Frances? Is she here about me? Have the journalists started again?'

Frances smoothed her skirt out with a small huff of resignation.

'It has nothing to do with you. Miss Bancroft has applied to be my companion.'

'Your what?'

Barney's expression of stupefaction might have been amusing, if Cassie's lips could remember how to smile.

'My companion.' Frances cradled her hands in her lap. 'Someone to keep me company. To be another presence in the house.'

'I'm in and out of the house all day!'

'Working,' Frances replied. 'And you are not here at night.'

'I can be. I'll move in.'

'I hardly think that would be appropriate. I have no wish to find a parade of strange ladies wandering round my house in their smalls.'

'Then why have you invited one to live with you!'

Cassie moved a cushion on to her knee, trying to fade into the sofa. She glanced at Barney, who stared back at her, eyebrows drawn in obvious challenge. For the first time since she'd encountered him on the road, she considered him properly. He was younger than she'd thought, perhaps mid thirties, a similar age to her; his hair was thick and conker brown, though rather wild, and his eyes, when he stopped frowning long enough to reveal them, were large and expressive. Objectively he was an attractive man, notwithstanding the beard. Perhaps it wasn't so unlikely that he had streams of ladies visiting him, if they blocked their ears and didn't listen to him shouting. And if they could stand the intense scrutiny: he had a gaze that could strip away skin and bone, and see straight into the soul. Cassie gripped the cushion tighter.

'There is nothing strange about Miss Bancroft. You only need look at her to see how utterly normal she is.'

Two pairs of eyes now scrutinised her: a faint shadow of doubt in one set and frank disbelief in the other. Cassie stared silently back, soaking in the unintended compliment. Normal! She hadn't felt normal for months, years maybe.

'This is the first time you've met. You don't know

anything about her. Which agency is she from?'

'Agency? I want a companion, not an escort.'

'I mean a care agency.' Barney crouched down by Frances. A look passed between them, loud with words that Cassie could see but not hear. 'If you're set on this, you need someone who knows what they are doing – what to expect. This isn't right.'

Cassie tossed aside her cushion. All her polished interview phrases vanished from her head.

'I can do this,' she said. 'Please give me a chance. I need this job.'

Frances met her gaze, with an expression so stern that Cassie thought she had blown it. But then she gave a slight but definite nod, a gesture that somehow seemed to convey understanding as well as agreement.

'I think I am the best judge of what I need,' Frances said, turning to Barney. 'I will not be bullied: not again, not in my own home, and certainly not now. I am employing Miss Bancroft as my companion, and you, Barnaby Smallwood, will have to get used to that.'

CHAPTER TWO

'We should discuss the practicalities, Miss Bancroft, now that is settled,' Frances said.

It was a curious definition of settled, given that Barney had just stormed out, trailing fury in his wake.

'Call me Cassie.'

The name Miss Bancroft was still alien. She felt like a bride acclimatising to a new surname – although it was hard to imagine a less fitting analogy.

'Very well, and I suppose you ought to call me Frances.' It seemed a grudging concession. 'Would you collect the notebook and pen from the top left drawer of the desk?'

Cassie brought the items back to Frances.

'No, you keep them. My arthritis is bad today. I would like you to make a list of what needs to be done.' Cassie noticed as she sat down again that Frances was cradling her right hand. 'Firstly, your hair. Is it a wig?'

'My hair?' Cassie's eyes jerked up from the pad, where she had been preparing to write. 'It's real.' She touched it, freshly self-conscious. She didn't need to ask what was wrong with it. There was good reason why she'd stopped poring over mirrors.

'Surely not the colour?' Frances persisted. 'You cannot be a natural blonde. No one could naturally be that colour. You look common. A girl from the village comes here to set my hair every week. She is due tomorrow and can tidy you up.'

'I can't afford it.'

'I will pay. It is for my benefit,' Frances insisted, as Cassie opened her mouth to protest. 'I cannot bear to look at whatever you have done. You might be pretty if one could see past the monstrosity on your head. Write it on the list. I will telephone Melanie later and tell her to bring her colours.'

Cassie obediently wrote 'Hair by Melanie' on

23

the top of a blank page of the notebook.

'The second point is the car. I assume that you drive. I like to make a regular appearance at church. Barney usually drives me but his heathen huffing is most unsettling. I can see that you will be a more restful presence. There is an old Volvo estate in the garage. Barney will arrange for you to be added to the insurance. Put it on the list.'

Cassie did, hoping that Frances was going to broach that with Barney herself.

'We have not yet discussed what you should be paid. I understand that £350 per week should be an adequate wage.'

Adequate? It was more than double what Cassie had earned from her cleaning work, where the minimum wage had referred to the minimum her boss could get away with paying.

'I'm happy with that,' Cassie said, writing it down before Frances could change her mind. 'Would you mind paying in cash?'

'I had thought a cheque.'

'I don't have a bank account at the moment.' Not in the name Bancroft; and not one, in any name, that she would dare to access.

'As you wish. Write it down. Barney can arrange to bring me the cash each week. But I think that we can go through any other matters later. I would like to have a rest for a little while.'

'Of course. Do you want me to stay or go?'

'There is no need for you to be with me all the time. We should have a pager, so that I can call you if I need you. Put it on the list. Barney will know of something suitable.'

Of course he would. Cassie was beginning to

think that there was nothing he didn't know, or couldn't turn his hand to. She had understood from the advert, and from talking to Frances, that it would be the two of them: a female household. That had been half the attraction. She didn't want a man to intrude. But what choice did she have? She had nowhere else to go. And surely their paths needn't cross that often?

'I expect you would like to see your room,' Frances said, interrupting Cassie's thoughts. 'Press the red button on the telephone on the desk and you will get through to Barney's office. He can show you up.'

'I'm sure I can find the way.'

'It took me two months to get my bearings when I first moved in. Stop making a fuss and ring Barney.'

Reluctantly Cassie picked up the phone and pressed the red button. It was answered immediately.

'Frances?' A growl came from the other end. 'I hope you're ringing to tell me you've seen sense and she's gone.'

'It's Cassie.'

A fine example of what Frances would probably have called a heathen huff blew down the line. It didn't sound apologetic.

'Where's Frances?'

'In her chair. She's asked if you could show me to my room.'

'Your what? I'm coming round.'

The phone slammed down. Cassie replaced the receiver, and turned back to Frances, who tilted her head in enquiry.

'He's on his way.'

It was less than a minute before the door crashed open and Barney thundered in. He had taken off his coat and boots, and looked slightly more human in a grey Arran jumper and walking socks. His big toe poked through the end of the left sock. The imperfection offered Cassie a morsel of comfort, despite the irritation evidenced by his knitted brows.

'She's staying?' he asked, striding over to Frances without so much as a glance at Cassie.

'Of course.' Frances remained unruffled by the abrupt entrance and question. Perhaps this was his usual way of behaving, Cassie reflected. It wasn't an appealing idea. 'I explained that I wanted a companion at night.'

'Yes, but why tonight? How do you know that she is who she says she is? Don't you think you should at least take some references first? If she can even provide references,' he muttered, turning that angry brow to bristle in Cassie's direction.

'Cassie has already provided some excellent references. I am more than satisfied with them.' It was hard to say whether Barney or Cassie was more surprised by Frances' pronouncement. When had Frances spoken to her referees? She couldn't have spoken to the one she'd made up. 'Barney, could you show Cassie the way to the bedrooms? And carry her bags. Are they still in the hall?'

'No, it's there.' Cassie pointed at the scruffy backpack, which was sitting on the floor where Barney had dumped it when they first arrived.

'Are the rest of your belongings following on?'

26

'That's all I have.'

And then, as Frances and Barney stared at her, with surprise, curiosity and – in his case – suspicion, a brutal sense of the shabbiness of her life descended over Cassie like freezing fog. She saw how she must appear in their eyes, in the grandeur of this house – the sallow skin, tired eyes, jaundiced hair; the old clothes that had grown baggy while she had shrunk; the battered rucksack which contained her life. What was she doing here, and how could she hope to get away with it? Frances would soon discover that she was nothing, totally worthless, and send her on her way.

'Stop it!' Barney pulled her hands apart, and inspected the knuckle of her right thumb. 'You'll break the skin.'

Cassie took her hand away but didn't reply. Barney was so close now that she felt as much as heard his huff.

'Which room?' he said, moving away and picking up Cassie's rucksack. 'The attic?'

'Vienna.'

'Vienna? But...'

'Don't make such a fuss, Barney. Cassie is my companion, not a servant.' Frances smiled at Cassie. 'Perhaps you could find your way back here in a couple of hours, and we can carry on? Feel free to explore the rest of the house. Would you mind switching on the wireless before you go?'

Following the feeble flap of Frances' arm, Cassie noticed an old-fashioned radio on the table and switched it on. Classical music drifted into the room, and Frances closed her eyes. Barney, still carrying the rucksack, held the door open

27

for Cassie.

'I can manage the bag,' she said, hurrying to keep up with his quick pace down the corridor.

'It's no problem.'

They reached the hall again and Barney started to climb the stairs.

'If you tell me where to go, I'll find my own way.'

'Don't tempt me.'

He continued at his record-breaking pace up the stairs, along a gallery with an ornate painted ceiling, and through a door that led into a plainer corridor, thickly carpeted and crammed with paintings and display cases. As she scampered along, Cassie just had time to read some of the names on the doors, written in Copperplate script on paper yellowed with age: Lisbon, Berne, Amsterdam and, oddly, Ribblemill.

'Are all the rooms named after capital cities?' she asked, when she caught up with Barney outside Vienna.

'The bedrooms, yes.'

'But there's one down there that's called Ribble-mill.'

'The master bedroom. A joke by the Smallwood who built the house. He said that Ribblemill was the most capital place on earth.'

'Really?' Cassie would have liked to hear more, but Barney's scowl didn't suggest he was in the mood for a history lesson.

'Is Frances your mum?' she asked instead, as he pushed the door open.

'Aunt.'

Cassie scarcely heard him. The room was

exquisite. The size alone would have been enough to impress: the bed, an enormous wooden half tester, filled barely a fifth of the space. The walls were covered in pale wallpaper, scattered with giant sprigs of blue flowers with lush green foliage. The same shade of blue was picked out in the silk curtains at each of the three windows, and in paintwork along a picture rail and on the carved plasterwork of the ceiling. A large rug, edged with a green border and woven with small flowers, covered almost all of the polished wooden floorboards. The original colours had faded, but that only added to the charm. There was no damp, no mould, no noise, no unsavoury neighbours, and no terror about who might burst in at any moment. It was so much more than she had expected, and so much more than she deserved.

'Are all the windows in the house arched?' she asked, going over to the bay of the largest window.

'Most of them.'

'It's very Gothic, isn't it?'

When no answer came, Cassie turned back into the room. Barney had dropped her bag, and was standing near the door, arms and eyebrows folded.

'If you're trying to win me round with all these questions, don't bother. Once I've spoken to Frances you won't be staying long.'

'Win you round?' Cassie couldn't disguise her horror. 'I've no interest in doing anything to you, except saying goodbye and never seeing you again.'

'Easily arranged. I'll drive you back to Clitheroe.'

Cassie rested her head against the cool glass of the window, letting the chill slowly numb her skin, and gazed out. Down below she could see a terrace, with steps leading down to a well-groomed lawn. In the distance, the cultivated garden gave way to a copse, and then fields as far as she could see. She had missed a rural view, and her heart fluttered with the sense of contentment that reminders of home can bring – reminders of a happy home, she silently corrected herself. And she felt she might be happy, if only Barney wasn't here, polluting the place with his masculinity and threatening to send her away.

'It's musty in here. The room hasn't been used for a while.'

Barney reached past her and thrust open the window. An icy blast of February air invaded the room, and Cassie stepped back. She was conscious that Barney was looking at her again. He pulled a tissue from the box beside the bed, and held it out. She took it and wiped her eyes and cheeks, embarrassed that he had witnessed her weakness.

'Don't use the fire yet. I'll have the sweep come out to look at it tomorrow.'

His voice was gentler than at any time since they had met. Cassie gave a slight nod, and sat down on the edge of a chaise longue, not moving until she heard the door close behind him.

It took less than ten minutes to unpack her meagre belongings, and the only obvious signs of her occupation were her hairbrush on the dressing table and the mobile at the side of her bed.

She picked up the phone and stared at the single name in the contacts list. She hadn't intended to ring so soon after the last call, but the pull of home she had felt earlier was too hard to resist.

'Cassie? Is that you?'

Hearing her sister's voice was like curling under a duvet on a cold afternoon, and Cassie closed her eyes and wallowed in the warmth and comfort of it.

'Cass? Are you OK?'

'Yes. I needed to hear a friendly voice, that's all. Sorry to interrupt.'

'Don't be silly. You know I wish you would ring more often. In fact, you know I wish you would come here...'

Cassie didn't reply. She never did when Vicky suggested that. She longed to go there, but it was too obvious a place to hide. Still she couldn't bring herself to say the 'no' out loud.

'So where are you?' Vicky laughed, an anxious rather than amused sound. 'I don't suppose you'll tell me, will you?'

'No.' Cassie wandered over to the windows, closed the casement and looked out. 'I'm in the countryside. I can see fields, and trees, and sheep. It's good.'

'The next best thing to being here, then. I don't suppose they are Devon Longwool?'

'No, I think they might be Blackface, but I've only seen them from a distance so far.'

'You're never wrong about sheep.'

Unlike men. Cassie could have finished Vicky's thought for her. It used to be a joke between them. It wasn't so funny now.

'How is everyone? Stu and the boys?'

'Stu's busy with lambing. You know what it's like. The boys are great. Stanley is Stu's right hand man, and thinks he can deliver all the lambs himself. Alfie is driving us all bananas practising his whistling, and the dogs are running round in utter confusion. So it's pretty much the usual chaos.'

'Give them all my love, won't you? And force a big cuddle on Stanley and Alfie from me.' Cassie's throat seized up with unshed tears as she pictured her sister's family, the farm that was once her home and was now theirs, and she felt the accumulated agony of every day that had passed since she had seen them. The farm might be utter chaos, but it was also utter bliss. It was everything she had always wished for Vicky; and everything she had always wished for herself. At least one of them had found their perfect happiness. It had to be enough. 'I miss you.'

'And we miss you. Alfie never stops asking when you're going to come back and take him for a ride in the tractor. Apparently Stu is too boring because he's never got stuck in a ditch.' Vicky laughed again. 'Do you have everything you need, wherever you are? You're not too remote are you? Is there a doctor, at least?'

'I don't know. I haven't investigated the village yet.'

'Cass...'

'I know. I will.' Cassie clung to the phone, hating this moment, knowing that the call would have to end, and she would be plunged back into a world where no one cared for her. Or worse, she reflected as Barney Smallwood's bristling face flashed into her mind, back into a world where someone seemed to positively detest her.

'Are you sure you can't come back to us?' Vicky asked, easily translating Cassie's silence. 'Do you really think Mike's still looking?'

'Yes.'

'But there's been no contact for a few weeks now. And what can he do? He can't drag you back if you don't want to go.'

'I know.' She had told herself the same thing, many times. 'It's the risk that he'll persuade me to go back that worries me most. I don't know if I'm strong enough to resist it. And until I am, I can't let him find me.'

CHAPTER THREE

The silence woke Cassie the next morning. She lay on dry, unstained sheets that smelt faintly of floral laundry powder, listening to the lack of traffic, of sirens, of thudding footsteps and hardly dared to open her eyes, in case the reality was so much less than she remembered.

But when she did open her eyes, there it was: the pretty, feminine bedroom, the delicate furniture, light streaming in through the three large windows. Light! Cassie sat up. It must be later than she thought. She dashed down the corridor to the bathroom, was woken even more thoroughly by a chilly shower, dressed and managed to find her way down to the kitchen.

She pushed open the kitchen door on to the aroma of coffee and toast, and the sight of a rotund lady wearing an apron, her smiling face hovering over a cartoon image of a buxom female body squeezed into a bikini.

'Hello, my love, you must be Cassie. How do you take your coffee? Milk and sugar?'

'No sugar, thanks.'

'And what can I get you for breakfast?' the lady asked, as she poured a mug of steaming coffee from a cafetière. 'Full English? You look like you could do with fattening up. Look at the size of your wrist!' she exclaimed, as Cassie reached out for the mug and her sleeve rolled back. 'Mine must be twice the thickness of yours.' She held up her arm next to Cassie's to prove the point. 'I daren't compare our ankles. You'd be hard pressed to even find mine.'

She waggled a foot at Cassie, displaying a woolly stocking and fluffy slipper.

'Do you live here?' Cassie asked, noting the slipper, and wondering why no one had thought to mention it yesterday, and why she was even needed with this lady in the house.

'Bless you no. Has no one explained who I am? Mrs Aldred. Call me Ruth. Mrs S calls me her housekeeper, but I'm nowt as grand as that. I come in three days a week and do a bit of cooking, and a bit of cleaning. I do the supermarket run for Mrs S on Friday, so if you want any bits and bobs add them to the list over there.' She waved at a piece of paper pinned to a corkboard. 'I see Barney has scribbled on it again. His writing's dreadful, as you'd expect, so I just bring a selection of chocolate bars, biscuits and cakes. Lucky he's easily pleased.'

Cassie wondered if Ruth was talking about the same man she had met yesterday. She glanced at the list. It was mainly basic supplies and household goods, written in slanted capitals by Ruth, probably, but at the bottom there were several lines of thick black scrawl. It was possible, if she screwed up her eyes enough, to believe that one of the words may have been 'Twix'.

'Is that for Frances?' Cassie asked, as Ruth put a full packet of bacon in the frying pan.

'No, Mrs S doesn't get up until nine, and she never has bacon. This is yours.'

'That's too much! I don't usually eat a fried breakfast.'

'Not a veggie, are you?'

Cassie shook her head.

'Nothing to stop you, then, is there? You'll never convince me you're on a diet. Besides, it's not all for you. I'll make a bacon butty for Barney. It must be a couple of hours since he had breakfast.'

'Can I smell bacon?'

The kitchen door crashed open and the man himself walked in. He pulled up short at the sight of Cassie, as if he had forgotten she existed.

'Don't worry, there's some for you,' Ruth said, sticking a couple of slices of bread under the grill. 'I'm making a fry-up for Cassie, but she's not keen. You can tell her how healthy it is. Look at her, she's as thin as a lath!'

'I wouldn't say healthy...' Barney murmured, doing an excellent job of looking everywhere

35

except at Cassie's body.

'We'll soon build you up,' Ruth carried on, ignoring Barney's lack of enthusiasm, and turning the bacon just as it crisped. Despite her earlier refusal, Cassie's mouth watered at the sight of it. 'You'll feel better after a good breakfast and a haircut. Mel is coming over to do you later, isn't she?'

Cassie nodded, wishing that bacon and a haircut was all it took to make everything better. And why had Ruth assumed she needed to feel better? Did she give off vibes of misery?

'Perhaps Mel could fit you in too, Barney. Do a job lot,' Ruth said, applying thick helpings of butter to the toast.

'What for?' Barney stroked his thumb along his jawline, making an awful scratching noise as nail met bristles. 'I'm fine.'

'Fine if you want to look like a Yeti.' Ruth laughed. 'There might still be a handsome man under all that hair. What do you say, Cassie?'

Cassie made a noise which she hoped sounded noncommittal, and tried as hard not to look at Barney's face as he had not to look at her body. She heard a thundering huff, and then the very welcome sound of the kitchen door slamming as Barney made his usual stormy exit.

Mel turned out to be a short, buxom lady in her mid forties, with a mass of curly brown hair piled on her head like a pineapple top, and good legs.

'Crikey,' she said, pulling a critical face as she examined Cassie's hair. 'What colour did that say on the bottle? I'm assuming you did this to yourself. What were you thinking?'

'I wanted a change.'

'A change?' Mel snorted. 'You're changing back now I'm here. You look like an egg custard, with a burnt skin on top,' she added, standing on tip-toes to inspect Cassie's roots.

'Can you make her look normal?' Frances asked. She had insisted on supervising Mel's work, as if she didn't trust Cassie to give proper instructions.

'*More* normal, but it will help if I cut a good chunk off. Do you mind going to shoulder length?'

'I'd rather not.'

Mel poked her upper arm.

'This is the lowest I'll go. The ends are in a terrible state. It'll soon grow back if you want it longer. What about this shade?' she asked, waving a file at Cassie and pointing at a tuft of fake hair. 'I think this might be closest to your own colour.'

'I don't want to go back to my own colour.'

'Of course you do. You make a terrible blonde. You have a lovely voice, don't you? Very husky. Sexy, like that woman off the telly. Don't you think so, Mrs S?' Mel asked, raising her voice as she addressed Frances.

'I have no idea whom you mean. I only watch the news.'

This was news to Cassie. She hadn't seen a tele-vision on her initial exploration yesterday, and she had spent last evening in the morning room with Frances, listening to Classic FM. She had man-aged for the last six months without a television. Doing double shifts for the cleaning company had filled most of her waking hours, and any spare minutes had been spent devouring the books she had bought at charity shops.

'Where is the nearest library?' Cassie asked, as Mel combed through her hair after the final wash. There wasn't a mirror in the room, so Cassie had no idea what colour it was now. She had a horrible suspicion that Mel was building up to a big 'ta da!' reveal, and knew already that her reaction would be a disappointment.

'Clitheroe, I should think, but I'm not a big reader,' Mel said. 'I think I've seen a mobile library van a few times in the next village. We did once talk about setting up our own library in the village hall, but no one wanted to take on the responsibility of running it.'

It was a shame the idea had never taken off, Cassie thought, trying to distract herself while Mel bustled around her and horrifyingly large chunks of hair fell to the ground. She had hoped a small village library might allow her to join without ID. An informal arrangement in a village hall would have been perfect. She slumped in her chair, the attractions of the job diminishing if she didn't have the luxury – the necessity – of a book to escape into.

'There's no chance of you being bored in this village,' Mel said, as she pulled down strands of hair on either side of Cassie's face. 'There's always something going on. There's bound to be a club or society that would interest you. And if all else fails, you can join everyone else in the No Name.'

'The No Name?'

'The pub. I'm the landlady. You'll have to come down and meet everyone. What do you say, Mrs S?' Mel bellowed next to Cassie's ear. 'Shouldn't

Cassie come to the No Name and meet everyone?'

'I don't think so,' Cassie said.

'I suppose you have a point, Melanie,' Frances conceded. 'I do not need you under my feet every second, Cassie. You should get involved in the village life, now you look presentable, and the No Name is a sensible place to start.' She held up a hand as Cassie continued to protest. 'You can go there tonight. I will ring Barney later and tell him to take you. I am sure he will not mind.'

CHAPTER FOUR

Cassie heard the scratch of dog's claws against a wooden floor as she neared the bottom of the stairs, and Gin skittered into view. The dog stood with her front paws on the first step, tongue lolling and tail wagging, until Cassie reached the bottom. Cassie bent down and buried her face in Gin's fur.

'Hey! What are you doing in here?'

Gin immediately dropped down at the sound of Barney's voice, but stayed at Cassie's feet.

'Sorry,' Cassie said, straightening up. 'I didn't realise she wasn't allowed...'

Barney performed a double take that would have been the envy of comedy actors everywhere, and stared at Cassie.

'I didn't mean Gin. Of course she's allowed in the house. I didn't recognise you. You look...' He paused, grappling for suitable words. 'Less weird.'

'Mel's been,' Cassie replied, passing over the less than glowing compliment. 'Less weird' was probably one of the better things a man had called her over the last couple of years. And she didn't care about the lack of a compliment: she had no wish to be noticed by men, never mind to attract them.

'Oh yes, Mel,' Barney replied, shoving his hands in his pockets and frowning. 'I believe we have her interference to thank for tonight's ordeal. Thinking only of profit, not what people actually want to do with their evening...'

'Let's forget it. I don't want to go to the pub any more than you do.'

'And defy Frances? I wouldn't dare.'

'I won't tell her we didn't go.'

'Lying comes easily to you, does it?' Cassie blushed under his suspicious gaze. 'You're clearly not used to living in a village. It will be news, whether we go or don't go. Mel will make sure of that.' He looked at his watch. 'Are you ready? We may as well get it over with.'

Without another word, Cassie followed Barney through the hall and out of the front door, Gin close on her heels. Barney's truck was parked at the front of the house. He opened the passenger door for Cassie, and Gin jumped in beside her. They travelled to the village in silence broken only by the rustling of Barney's waxed jacket and the occasional snort from Gin.

The pub was a long, sprawling building made from stone that had long since blackened. A weathered metal sign hung outside, declaring it was 'The House with No Name'. Barney led Cassie into a large room with a log fire in a central chimney breast. Mismatched chairs and tables were scattered around the flagged floor. Everyone seemed to know each other, and one conversation flowed between the groups. It was far busier than Cassie had expected on a Thursday night.

There was a definite hiatus in the hum of chatter as the door slammed shut behind Barney. Cassie stepped behind him, sheltering from what felt like a thousand eyes.

'What do you want to drink?' Barney addressed the question to the gap at his side, and frowned as he had to rotate to find her.

'You don't have to...' Cassie faltered under his stare. 'Sparkling mineral water, please.'

Spotting an empty table slightly away from the others, she headed towards it, horribly conscious of continuing interest as she passed, despite having her eyes fixed firmly on the floor. She perched on the narrow windowseat at the table, and glanced over at the bar. Barney was standing to one side, engrossed in conversation with an attractive blonde in her forties. As Cassie watched, he took hold of the blonde's hand and ran his fingers up her arm.

Ten minutes must have passed before Barney joined her, banging her glass of water down on the table so hard some spilled over the side. He put his pint down more gently, and flopped into a chair, tossing a floral cushion over to Cassie's windowseat with a wrinkle of his nose.

'Thanks for the drink,' Cassie said, 'but I'm sure we don't need to go as far as sitting together. Feel free to join your girlfriend.'

'Girlfriend?' He turned to see where Cassie was

41

looking, and let out a definite snort, enough to shake his whiskers. 'Don't be ridiculous. She's married. Her husband's at the next table.'

Conversation lapsed until Cassie picked up her glass. 'Are you an alcoholic?'

'Of course not!' Cassie lost more water as she slammed down her drink. 'Why would you think that?'

'The water. No one drinks water here. Mel probably hasn't sold a bottle for years. There's definitely something going on.' Barney broke his trademark stare with a sudden, slow blink. 'Are you pregnant?'

'No.' There was no comfort in being able to give a wholly honest answer for once, not on that question. She reached out for her glass, and started to spin it round and round on the table. Barney prised away her hand and yanked it towards him, examining the base of her thumb.

'What have you done? I warned you about breaking the skin.'

He pushed his chair back, the wooden legs scraping against the flags, and marched through the crowd and out of the door. Cassie tried to fade into the curtain beside her head, wondering where Barney had gone, and whether he intended to come back. What had she done to upset him now? She was about to give up, and walk back to the house, when he stormed into the pub, Gin dancing round his feet.

He took a few long strides in her direction, but halfway across the room he was waylaid by an elderly man. Then – and Cassie wouldn't have believed it if she wasn't seeing it for herself – Barney

42

laughed: a proper gust of delight that swept through his whole body and transformed him, revealing an engaging, warm-hearted, attractive man. The smile still hadn't entirely faded from his lips when he fell back into his chair.

One glance at Cassie – who knew she was staring at him, but couldn't seem to stop – was enough to blow away the dust of the smile.

'Give me your hand.'

She held it out, too dazed to object, and Barney took from his pocket a small tube of cream and squeezed some onto her thumb. Cassie closed her eyes as the antiseptic smell whisked her back through the years, to the happy days running around the farm with Vicky, and the constant scrapes and grazes they had suffered. Tears hovered behind her eyelids as she imagined she could feel her mother's gentle touch as she rubbed in the cream.

Cassie opened her eyes. This wasn't in her imagination: the touch was real. Barney was rubbing the ointment into the wound with a gentleness she had hardly thought he possessed. That brief moment of tenderness, so unexpected and so mundane, made her heart ache for what she was missing. His eyes met hers, and temporarily the frown gave way to a flash of curiosity; and then it was gone, and he moved his hand away.

'Hello, what's going on here then?' An Indian man with a protruding belly and a strong Yorkshire accent stopped at their table, and looked from Cassie to Barney with a lively grin.

'Nothing.' It would surely have been impossible for Barney to answer more quickly or more vehemently. 'Blame your wife. She forced us into this drink.'

'Aye, there's nowt you can do when she gets an idea in her head.' The man smiled with apparent pride at this pronouncement. 'So you're Cassie? Shame. I was hoping Barney might have found himself a proper girlfriend at last. You looked a fine pair when you walked in. Still, it's early days. Plenty of time for more to develop, isn't there?'

'Never.' Cassie's emphatic answer produced an awkward silence. Her usual need to appease kicked in. 'Sorry, I mean...'

'Don't be concerned on my account,' Barney interrupted. He pushed his chair back with another excruciating squeal, and stretched out his long legs, crossed at the ankle. 'I couldn't agree more.'

The other man's easy smile was faltering by this point. He brightened when Mel arrived at his side, and his arm shot round her as if to ensure she didn't leave without him.

'Hello,' Mel said to Cassie. 'Glad you could make it.'

'As if we had a choice...' Barney muttered. Mel ignored him.

'I see you've met my husband, Akram. A fine hunk of a man, isn't he?' She laughed, and wobbled Akram's stomach. 'I hope you've admired Cassie's hair. I slaved for hours over that.'

'She's a proper bonny lass,' Akram agreed. 'I would never have recognised her from your description.'

A glimmer of a smile peeped through Barney's beard as Cassie was damned with this faint praise.

44

'Are you coming to the meeting?' Mel asked Barney.

'What meeting?'

'About the village hall. Surely you hadn't forgotten? It starts in a few minutes, that's why everyone is here.'

'Is that tonight? I wondered why it was so busy. But I can hardly come now, can I?' He flapped his hand towards Cassie, letting the full draught of his irritation waft her way.

'It's fine. I'll walk back.'

'In the dark? With your road sense? You'll kill yourself.' Barney gulped down some beer. 'I probably have time to run you back first.'

'Cassie can come to the meeting,' Mel said. 'She's hardly met anyone yet, and she should get involved now she's living here.'

'It's not settled that she's staying,' Barney grumbled, but for Mel the discussion was closed.

'Never mind Mr Grouchy,' she said to Cassie. 'He may have a handsome smile and a heart of gold, but Gin has better manners.'

Cassie thought Gin was probably the winner when it came to the smile and the heart as well, but said nothing, and allowed Mel to bundle her into her coat. She lost sight of Barney as Mel led her behind the bar, talking nineteen to the dozen.

'The village hall is only a couple of hundred metres down the road, near the church,' Mel explained. 'We're trying to raise money to mend the roof. Well, we're always trying to raise money to repair something, but since a storm in November, the roof has become the priority. There's usually a good turn-out.'

45

Cassie could see this for herself, as they left the pub through a back door, and crossed the car park to the street. Torches illuminated a stream of villagers arriving from all directions to converge on the plain brick building, lit up like a lighthouse by powerful outside lights.

'These lights were last year's big project,' Mel said, as they skirted round some parked cars and joined the crowd going in through the double doors. 'The hall is used by all the village groups. Now the Rainbows and Cubs can see where they're going, not to mention the oldies on bingo night. I'll have to leave you here. I'm up at the top. Find a seat and I'll catch up with you later.'

Cassie couldn't see either Akram or Ruth, and knowing no one else, perched on the end of a row near the back, wondering why she had let herself be railroaded into this. She watched Mel make her way onto the stage at the far end of the hall, and join a tall, distinguished man in his seventies, who now stood up and addressed the crowd.

'Attention!' The manner in which he said the word, and the way it produced instant silence, confirmed Cassie's impression that he must have a military background. 'Welcome to the first meeting this year of the Ribblemill Village Hall Committee. Are the November minutes approved? Any matters arising? Good. Then let's get down to business.'

There followed a succinct but dull account of the committee's financial performance over the last year, and the likely cost of repairs to the roof. It sounded a staggering amount for a relatively small building, and induced a chorus of gasps and mutterings from the floor. And then it was Mel's turn to take over the stage, in her role as chief fundraiser. She looked in her element as she launched into a rallying cry for money.

'All the local shops have agreed to have a loose change jar on the counter, and we'll have one at the No Name too. This is the biggest sum we've had to find, and so every penny really will help. We're going to hold the usual events through the year: the summer barbecue, the bonfire and the Christmas party. But I think we need to squeeze in another event before the barbecue. Does any-one have any ideas?'

There was an awkward silence, punctuated by the rustle of clothing as people shifted in their seats and avoided making eye contact with Mel.

'Come on,' Mel said. 'We must be able to come up with something. We need an idea that we haven't tried before, to get everyone involved and excited.'

'What about a sponsored knit?' an old lady near the front suggested.

Mel's face showed a definite lack of excitement, but at least it sparked off a few more ideas.

'A jumble sale?'

'A line dance?'

'How about a beer festival?'

That suggestion certainly got the male section of the audience excited.

'Great ideas, guys. Anyone else? Let's have a few more and then we can take a vote.' Mel was looking increasingly desperate. She seemed to be scanning the crowd, as if she was searching for someone. Her gaze landed on Cassie.

'Cassie!' Mel said, with a beaming smile. 'You're new to the village. I bet you have some ideas that we might not have tried before.'

Mel's gaze picked her out like a spotlight. Even if she'd had an idea, Cassie couldn't have uttered it. Her cheeks burned and her throat seized as the crowd swivelled to inspect her.

'Don't be so unfair, Mel.' Cassie recognised Barney's voice, though she couldn't see him. 'What is she supposed to say? She didn't even know the place existed twenty minutes ago. Pick on someone else.'

Cassie waited for him to add that she wouldn't be around long enough to be part of any event – surely he wouldn't resist such a prize opportunity – but the words didn't come. The villagers in front of her shifted, as they switched their attention to Barney, and Cassie saw him in the middle of the opposite block. His steady, unblinking stare was focused on her. Then something snapped. She was fed up of being written off, of being thought too worthless to have an opinion. What had been the point of getting away, if she was still letting herself be treated like that?

'I was once...' She coughed; her throat was dry. 'We once held an auction of talents.' She faltered as heads turned back her way. She could still see Barney. 'People put their names down to offer a skill or service, and others bid for it. It costs next to nothing to organise, so it makes a good profit.'

'Exactly what sort of service are you suggesting?' A woman in front cast a frosty glare at Cassie. 'This is a respectable village.'

'It can be anything, from mowing lawns, or

cooking a meal, to a more professional service.'

'If you offer to read a bedtime story, with that voice of yours, I'll put in a bid or two.' Cassie couldn't see the man who spoke, but everyone laughed and Mel took over the reins again.

'It's a fantastic idea. We haven't done anything like that before. Shall we vote on the suggestions we've had?'

She went through a show of hands, and there was overwhelming support for the auction.

'That's settled. I'll try to find a date in April or May, so all get thinking about what service you can offer. Cassie, you can help me and the Colonel organise it as you've been involved in one before.'

She gave Cassie no chance to refuse. The rest of the meeting passed quickly. Cassie tried to escape as soon as it finished, but found herself surrounded by people keen to introduce them-selves and welcome her to the village.

'I'm Ethel,' said a short lady with a steel-grey pudding-bowl haircut. Cassie recognised her from the village shop. 'I hear you've moved in with Barney. He brought you up yesterday, didn't he?'

'No!' Cassie replied quickly. 'I mean, yes he did, but I'm staying with Frances at Ramblings.'

'Good for you. There's too much living in sin these days. I'm glad to see some young people exercise restraint.'

'I'm not...' Cassie stopped. It seemed rude to point out that no restraint was required. Besides, it wasn't personal. Barney was a man. She wanted nothing to do with the entire breed. 'Frances has employed me as her companion.'

'She's paying you money for that? She could

have as much company as she wanted, if she made more effort to leave that house, or invited people to it,' Ethel said. 'I know there was a lot of trouble between her husband and the village, when he tried to build houses on the Ramblings land, but that was years ago. We all know it was his fault not hers. I bet she has no idea what she's missing. She'd enjoy the bingo with the other senior citizens. You'll tell her about it, won't you?'

Cassie promised she would, but without much hope of persuading Frances to join in.

'I'd better stock up on Jelly Babies if you're stopping around,' Ethel said. She smiled at a few other people who had wandered over. 'She bought six bags yesterday! Cleared out the shelf!'

Amid the laughter, Cassie caught sight of Barney towering over the rest of the group. His face was expressionless. Cassie excused herself and walked to the door.

'I'll drive you back if you're ready.'

Barney had materialised at her side.

'No, it's fine, I don't want to spoil your evening.'

'Too late for that,' he replied bluntly. 'I've had enough. I'd forgotten what a factory of gossip this place can be.'

'Leaving together won't help.'

'I know, but nor will leaving separately. At least this way I can be sure you make it back safely, without jumping in front of any cars.'

He led a silent walk back to the pub car park and held open the truck door while Cassie climbed in.

'Six bags of Jelly Babies,' he said, his eyes glittering in the muted light shining from the windows of the pub. 'I didn't know they'd started making them with ibuprofen.'

Before Cassie could respond, he slammed the door and stalked round to the driver's side. They drove back to Ramblings without speaking. Barney pulled up in front of the entrance and switched off the engine.

'Are you coming in?' Cassie's question rose from surprise, not invitation. Surely they'd spent enough time together for one night? For one lifetime, she thought, as he opened the door without a glance in her direction.

'I check on Frances every night, and make sure the house is locked up.'

Cassie jumped down from the truck and hurried after him into the halt.

'You don't have to do that now I'm here.'

'Yes I do.' He turned to face her. 'Look, you may be a perfectly pleasant woman, but that's not what Frances needs. You're out of your depth. If she persists in wanting a companion, I'll find her one who's suitably qualified.'

'I am suitably qualified,' Cassie protested, hoping as she spoke that he wouldn't ask her how. What was a companion other than a glorified servant? And hadn't she spent the last few years perfecting that role? Although never perfecting it quite enough.

'How? What experience do you have of looking after the elderly? Visiting your parents?'

'They're dead.'

'Not a great reference then, is it?'

An uncomfortable silence hovered between them.

51

'They died twelve years ago in a car accident,' Cassie said.

'Sorry.' Barney scratched his beard. 'That was crass. I shouldn't have said it. But it doesn't change my point. You don't know what you're dealing with here.'

'Presumably Frances does, so as long as she wants me here, I'm staying. And I'll check on her, so you can go home.'

'Why don't you tell me where she is, then?'

'What?'

'Tell me where you're going to go to check on her.'

'The morning room.' It was where Frances had been last night, when she had sent Cassie off to bed, but a twitch around Barney's eyebrows suggested it might be the wrong answer. Ignoring him, Cassie turned and walked down the corridor towards the morning room. It was empty.

'It's ten o'clock,' Barney said, close behind her. 'She'll be watching the news.'

'Of course.' Cassie could feel his eyes boring into her back, waiting for her to ask the inevitable question. 'And where would she do that?'

'Where the television is. In the television room.'

Television room? Cassie hadn't even known there was such a thing. It didn't sound very Gothic.

'Follow me.'

She had no choice but to do as he said, and Barney led her through a hidden door in the wall, down a narrow corridor covered in carpet tiles. This brought them to an inner hall, where a series of servants' bells hung over a plain wide staircase. A stairlift ran up the side of the stairs.

'Is that for Frances?'

'Yes. These stairs shortcut to the bedrooms. The kitchen wing is along there.' He pointed to the left. 'And here,' he continued, opening a door on the right, 'is the TV room.'

Cassie stepped into the most modern room she had so far seen in the house, with a low ceiling, magnolia walls, beige carpet and floral curtains, which hid the windows. A large television set, broadcasting the news, stood on a mahogany cabinet in one corner. The bars of an old-fashioned gas fire glowed red. The room could have been in any house, anywhere.

'Frances?' Cassie approached the chair in front of the television. Frances' eyes were closed, her mouth open, and a line of spittle was drying on her chin. Cassie was about to touch her hand when Barney put his arm out to stop her.

'Wait.' He covered Frances' hand with his own, then put two fingers against her neck, feeling for a pulse.

'Is she...?' Cassie couldn't bring herself to finish the question.

'No.' As he couldn't have known if she was going to say dead or alive, Barney's answer didn't help. Frances opened her eyes and recoiled at the sight of Barney bending over her.

'Barney!' she said, her voice sounding dry with sleep. 'What are you doing, poking at me like that? Take your hand away.'

'I was making sure you weren't dead.' He straightened up, and took a step back, colliding with Cassie, who had been hovering anxiously behind him. He automatically put his hands on her arms to steady her.

'You can take your hands off Cassie as well,' Frances ordered. 'She does not look like she is enjoying it any more than I did. You are not adding her to your victory parade.'

'I don't have...' Barney looked from Frances to Cassie, and finished his sentence with an exasperated sigh. 'You were asleep. Aren't you feeling well?'

'Stop making a fuss. I am perfectly well – only tired. You know I have never approved of the BBC moving the news to ten o'clock. It was much better at nine. I wrote and told them but they paid no notice.'

'Surely you have News 24?' Taking a wide berth round Barney, Cassie approached Frances and picked up the remote control. She pressed the buttons, and BBC News 24 appeared on screen. 'You can watch the news at any time of day. You don't need to wait up. Has no one told you?'

'No. When this new television arrived, I assumed I had the same four channels as before. So I can go back to watching the nine o'clock news on this channel?'

'You can watch the news at any o'clock you want,' Cassie confirmed. 'It never stops.' She pressed some more buttons on the remote control. 'I've set it as a favourite, so you can find it whenever you want by pushing this blue button.'

'Thank you. I wish someone had thought to tell me that before.' For a moment, Cassie thought she saw Frances' usual stern composure slip, before it was quickly donned again. 'You see, Barney, what a difference Cassie has made already. I cannot think what I would do without her.'

Barney's only response was a frustrated slam of the door as he walked out.

CHAPTER FIVE

Cassie's first week passed more easily than she could have hoped. But after a lifetime spent working, it still didn't feel right to have hours in the day when she had nothing to do but sit with Frances and listen to the radio, which was how Frances spent most of her afternoons. Cassie was no fan of classical music, and the hours dragged by – especially as, remembering Frances' original stipulation of no chatter, she hardly dared speak.

'Is there nothing you can do to occupy yourself?' Frances asked one afternoon, when Cassie shifted in her chair for about the hundredth time that hour. 'Do you not sew, or knit? What do you normally do to relax?'

As both 'normal' and 'relax' had been foreign concepts to Cassie for some time, she struggled for an answer.

'I love to read,' she said at last. It had been almost two weeks since she last touched a book. It felt longer.

'Have you not investigated the library?'

'I think Mel said the nearest one was in Clitheroe.'

'The one in Clitheroe is a public library.'

Frances flapped a dismissive hand. 'I was referring to the house library.'

'I didn't know there was one!' Cassie tried not to sound too frustrated that Frances hadn't thought to mention it when they had been discussing libraries before. 'Where is it?'

'In the north wing. What sort of books do you enjoy?'

'Anything – as long as it's fiction.' Anything that offered her an escape from reality. The shrewd look that Frances sent her made Cassie wonder whether she'd voiced that thought aloud.

'I doubt you will find anything to suit you in the library then,' Frances said. 'The collection was built for education, not pleasure.' She stopped and studied Cassie, her expression as piercing and as astute as that of a woman half her age. 'Come with me,' she continued, rising from her chair.

Cassie jumped up.

'Can I get you something?'

'No, I want you to come to my sitting room.'

Sitting room? It was the first Cassie had heard of it, though it was hardly a surprise that there were still huge areas of the house she hadn't discovered. She had barely scratched the surface on her first day. The place needed a guidebook and map, like a National Trust house, and Cassie was determined to ask Frances whether one existed.

Frances led the way up the back stairs, gliding up on the stairlift in stately fashion, back straight and hands folded neatly on her lap. She collected her walking stick – at Cassie's suggestion, she now had one for upstairs and one for downstairs – and headed in the direction of her bedroom, stopping at an unmarked door before the one labelled Ribblemill.

Cassie had never been in here before, nor in Frances' bedroom, and could hardly hide her curiosity when Frances pushed open the door and revealed a small, cosy room, decorated in shades of soft green and gold. There wasn't space for much furniture, beyond two armchairs in front of the fireplace, and – Cassie's heart soared – a bookcase that filled an entire wall, jammed full of books. She examined the spines: Elizabeth Taylor, Daphne du Maurier, the Mitfords, Elizabeth Bowen... It was a collection of some of the greatest female fiction of the last century, some that Cassie was familiar with and others that she didn't know, and her fingers itched to pluck them from the shelves.

'You will not find anything modern,' Frances said. 'Very little beyond the 1970s. I had less time for books than I would have liked.'

'It's wonderful,' Cassie said. Her fingers trailed reverentially over what looked like a complete set of hardcover Georgette Heyers. 'I love Georgette Heyer. I have all the Regency romances. Had them all,' she corrected herself.

Who knew where they might be now? Had Mike disposed of them, along with every other reminder of her? He was spiteful enough to have done so. Cassie glanced over her shoulder to check if Frances had noticed her slip. Of course she had. Her body may be faded, but her mind retained all the agility of an Olympic athlete.

'They have always been my favourites,' Frances said. 'It has been a while since I read them. The arthritis makes it too difficult to hold books now, especially the heavier hard covers.'

Cassie pulled out *April Lady*, wiping off the dust with the edge of her hand, and tenderly opened the pages.

'What if I read it to you?' she asked. When Frances didn't immediately reply, she closed the book again. 'Sorry. Of course you wouldn't want to listen to me. I shouldn't have...'

'It is an excellent idea,' Frances interrupted. 'Will you take the book downstairs?'

'Or we could read it here?' Cassie suggested. She felt more comfortable here than in the formal rooms downstairs, perhaps because it was more a size she was used to. 'If you don't mind.'

'Very well.'

Frances sat down in one chair, and motioned to Cassie to take the other. Cassie began to read, losing herself at once in the delicious words and floating off into another life. She had no idea how long she'd been reading for – she was firmly established two centuries ago – when she sensed Frances' attention shift, and looked up to see Barney in the doorway, staring at her with in-explicable surprise. The words stilled on Cassie's tongue, and she let the book drop.

'What are you doing in here?' Barney asked. He turned to Frances. 'You don't let anyone else in this room.'

'*You* are in here,' Frances pointed out.

'I've been all around the house looking for you. You left a message that you wanted to see me.'

'I did, several hours ago. But now that you are finally here, you can make yourself useful. I need

58

you to add Cassie to the car insurance. I suppose she will be able to drive the Volvo?'

'No reason why not, if she has a licence.'

Cassie nodded, but Barney still looked suspicious.

'Where are you going?'

'I've no plans to go anywhere,' Cassie replied, suspecting that Barney was hoping that wherever it was, she would be making a one-way journey.

'I need Cassie to be able to drive me about,' Frances said. 'It will spare you the trouble.'

'It's no trouble.'

'I need you to make the arrangements before Sunday. There is a visiting preacher I would like to hear. I expect you will be glad to be spared God's scrutiny of all you have been up to for the last fortnight.'

And there it came again, the momentary flash of a smile almost but not quite obscured by the beard, exposing the depth of affection that Barney held for Frances.

'It wouldn't be so bad if all I had to worry about was God's scrutiny.' He turned back to Cassie, all trace of the smile gone. 'You'd better give me your full name and date of birth.'

'Cassandra Jane Bar...' Cassie stopped short, muted by a spasm of panic. She had answered automatically, without thought, and without caution. She tried to disguise the error in a cough, but it didn't uproot the suspicion on Barney's face. 'Cassandra Jane Bancroft,' she repeated firmly, and gave him her date of birth.

Barney tapped the information into his iPhone. It seemed an incongruously modern gadget for someone who looked like a half-groomed tramp.

'You're thirty-three?'

'Yes. Does that matter?'

'No. Only it seems odd that someone your age would give up their life to live with a stranger, bringing nothing more than a rucksack.'

It wouldn't seem odd at all, if he knew the life Cassie was giving up. It wasn't a life at all; yet it had taken her days, months, years to recognise that – years of being ground down, of being played to believe that all she had was all she deserved. Barney could stare at her all he wanted, with that unblinking gaze, which seemed as if it could draw out the truth whether she liked it or not. She wasn't going to tell him, or anyone, what had happened to bring her here.

It was over two weeks before Cassie felt that she was beginning to make something of her role of companion, and, she hoped, to make a difference to Frances.

'She's looking better since you came,' Ruth said, as Cassie prepared Frances' afternoon tea: Earl Grey served in a china teapot, with proper cups and saucers. 'So are you. You've lost that haunted look you had. Although, I wish Mrs S didn't insist on that uniform. Black isn't your colour.'

'This isn't a uniform.' Cassie glanced down at herself: black trousers, black jersey top and black shoes. It was dull, but that was the point. She dressed plainly so she would be overlooked, and these cheap, easy-care clothes had been perfect when she was working as a cleaner. She was under no illusion that they flattered her. 'These are my clothes.'

'You never chose those for yourself!' Ruth looked up from her ironing, a pair of men's boxer shorts dangling from her hand. Cassie didn't want to contemplate whose bottom they belonged to. 'You need to meet my daughter, Becca. She works in a clothes shop in Clitheroe. She'll sort you out.'

'I can't afford any new clothes.'

'Don't worry about that. She can use her staff discount. You can't come to the party dressed like that. You're dressed for a funeral, not an engagement.'

'What party?' Cassie sloshed hot water round the teapot to warm it up, and glanced over at Ruth.

'Haven't I mentioned it? Becca's having an engagement do in a few weeks in the village hall. The whole village is invited.'

Cassie spooned tea into the pot.

'I don't think that includes me.'

'Of course it does. You're one of us now. And it's a ceilidh! You can't miss that.'

Cassie thought she easily could miss that, but Ruth wouldn't listen, however many times she said no.

'Come to the No Name one night and I'll introduce you to Becca. You can make plans for your shopping trip.' Ruth winced and rubbed her back as she bent to pick up the next item from the laundry basket. 'I hope this isn't another bout of sciatica. I need to be fit for dancing. I'd better have a word with Barney.'

'Barney? What can he do?' Cassie laid out a selection of biscuits on a plate. 'You should see a doctor. Is there one nearby?'

She hadn't expected Ruth to answer the question with a gust of laughter.

'Down the corridor, third door on the left. You can't get much nearer.'

'Third door on the left?' Cassie repeated, failing to see why this was such a joke. 'But isn't that Barney's office?'

'Yes. Surely you know?' Ruth beamed widely. 'He is a doctor! Or perhaps a "Mister". I'm never sure how that works.'

'Barney's a doctor? Of medicine?' Even though she asked the question, Cassie couldn't doubt the answer. So much of his behaviour now made sense: his bizarre curiosity over her fictional period pain at their first meeting; his fussing over her hand; and his evident concern over Frances. His caring attitude had been there all along, if hidden by the worst bedside manner she had ever seen.

'He worked in the hospital, until a couple of years ago,' Ruth said, steam rising around her from the iron. 'Until there was that bit of bother. Not that we ever believed he did anything wrong, whatever the papers said. You could tour ten hospitals and not find a doctor so caring or so committed. We all go to him first with our aches and pains, and he tells us whether it's worth troubling the doctor in the next village. Half the time he spots that something's amiss before we know ourselves.'

Did he? Cassie was glad of the warning. All the more reason for her to stay out of his way before he could spot all that was amiss with her.

CHAPTER SIX

The phone rang while Cassie was waiting for Frances to return from the bathroom. After only a second's hesitation, she answered it with a wary hello.

'Hello? Mother? Mother?' A tut and a sigh followed the word. 'Mother, you need to speak into the telephone.'

'I think you must have the wrong number,' Cassie said.

'That's impossible. The number is saved to my phone. Who are you? And where is my mother? Has something happened to her? Why must I always be the last to know? Are you the cleaner? You don't sound like her.'

'I'm Cassie.' Cassie picked the easiest out of the woman's barrage of questions, and answered that. 'Who are you trying to ring?'

'My mother, Frances Smallwood. What have you done with her? Why are you answering her phone?'

Cassie couldn't believe it. Frances had a daughter? She hadn't mentioned her since Cassie's arrival, and there weren't any photographs of her around the house, as far as Cassie had seen.

'Frances is in the bathroom,' she explained, deciding that it would be better to cooperate than antagonise another member of Frances' family. 'I'm her companion.'

'Her what?' The screech of outrage told Cassie that her attempt not to antagonise had failed. 'You mean you work for her? She's paying you? How much?'

'I don't think...'

'This is outrageous! Do my brothers know? Tell Mother to ring me back at once.'

The line went dead just as Frances returned. She was leaning more heavily on her stick today, and she looked weary, her eyelids drooping, and her mouth twitching restlessly, even when she wasn't trying to speak. Frances lowered herself into her chair.

'Did I hear the telephone?'

'Yes.' Cassie sat down. 'It was your daughter.'

'Was it? What did she want?'

'Nothing. She asked if you could ring her back.'

'Oh, she will certainly want something.' Frances threaded her hands together in her lap. She plucked at her chunky gold wedding ring. 'Diana only ever gets in touch when she wants something.'

'I didn't know you had any children,' Cassie said, treading carefully, in case this was exactly the sort of chatter that Frances had warned against. For a moment she thought she might have crossed the line, as Frances' lips pursed in what could equally have been displeasure at Cassie or at whatever she was thinking.

'I have three children,' Frances said. 'Hugh, Diana and Guy. Also two ex-daughters-in-law, a current son-in-law, and five grandchildren.'

It was a decent haul and begged the question why, when Frances was so relatively rich, there had been no obvious contact from them since Cassie arrived, and why Frances had to pay someone to keep her company. But that would definitely be a question too far; and it would hardly be in Cassie's interests to raise it.

'Shall I pass you the telephone?' she asked instead.

'No, Diana must learn to wait.' Frances looked across at Cassie. 'Did you tell her who you were?'

'Yes. Sorry. Should I not have done? When she said she was your daughter, I assumed she knew already.'

'And so she would have done, if she had made any effort to get in touch since Christmas. How did she react?'

'Not well,' Cassie admitted. 'She screeched. I'm sorry, I...'

'There is no need for you to apologise. They were bound to find out eventually.'

Curiously, Frances was smiling and appeared brighter than she had done all day.

'I expect we will hear from Diana and the others soon.'

When the telephone rang again a couple of hours later, Cassie was in the hall. She assumed it would be Diana, and let it ring on, hoping that Frances would pick it up in the morning room. But when it went on and on, she gave in and answered with an even warier hello than last time.

'Ah! You must be Cassie, the evil interloper who is trying to steal our inheritance.'

It wasn't the greeting Cassie had been expecting, nor the voice: far from Diana's angry screech, this one was male, cultured and amused.

'I'll agree to the Cassie part of the sentence,' she said.

'Quite right.' The man on the other end of the line laughed. 'I see you've learnt already never to agree with anything my sister says. It took me years to work that out. I'm Guy Smallwood.'

'Would you like me to put you through to Frances? It might be easier if I ask her to call you back. I'm not sure where she is.'

'Have you mislaid her? Surely the main duty of a companion is to keep an eye on your charge?' Guy laughed. 'Should I be concerned over whether my mother is wasting her money?'

The laugh didn't stop Cassie feeling immediately guilty. She rushed to reassure him.

'It's not costing much for me to be here, and I promise it will be worth it.'

Barney chose the exact moment she said that to stalk through the hall. It was quite clear from the pause in his tread and the scratch of the beard that he was putting his own interpretation on her words. Cassie sat down on the hard wooden chair beside the telephone table, and watched as he yanked open the heavy oak door and disappeared.

'I think whatever she's paying would be a small price for the pleasure of listening to your voice.' Guy paused. Cassie wondered if she was supposed to be flattered by that comment. She wasn't. 'You certainly don't sound like a scheming whatnot. I won't repeat Diana's word. She always has had an overactive imagination. How are you finding life at Ramblings? It's a beautiful place, isn't it?'

'Yes, it is.'

'It's always belonged to the Smallwoods. We're very lucky.'

'Shall I go and find your mum now?'

'No, I don't want to put you to any trouble. If she's busy, she won't thank you for disturbing her. I can't imagine she's the easiest person to work for. Are you getting on well so far?'

'I think so.'

'I'm glad to hear it.' So he said; yet something in Guy's voice made Cassie wary. Even after he had ended the call, with warm wishes that they might meet soon, Cassie felt that if they ever did meet, she would need to be on her guard. Charm was a cheap veneer, and could cover all sorts of problems. She hardly needed to be told that a second time.

Cassie had worked at Ramblings for a month before she was told to take an afternoon off by Frances, who suddenly seemed to become aware of employment rights, and insisted that from now on Cassie had to take off two hours every day and one full afternoon each week. She spent her first free afternoon driving round in the Volvo, getting her bearings in the local area.

She ended her day at the No Name. Without a laptop or a smartphone, Cassie had no access to the internet; and though she assumed that one person at Ramblings did, she had no intention of asking him. Mel had offered to let her borrow her laptop, and so Cassie settled down in the small snug off the main bar, to begin some research into an idea that had occurred to her when she had been reading to Frances yesterday. The bar was surprisingly busy for late afternoon, but the snug, with only a couple of tables and an ancient wing-backed chair, was deserted, and Mel assured her it was likely to stay that way.

Cassie had set up a new email account in the name Cassie Bancroft, and was engrossed in the pages of a website, when heavy footsteps warned her someone was coming. Barney was frozen in the snug entrance, a pint in one hand and a newspaper in the other.

It was too late for him to reverse without appearing rude, and while he hadn't avoided rudeness up till now, he must have thought better of it on this occasion. He took a couple of steps forward. Cassie instinctively angled the laptop screen away from him. That proved to be a mistake.

'What are you doing with that computer?' Barney put down his glass and paper. 'I knew it! You're a bloody journalist, aren't you? I can't believe I fell for that innocent act. Was that what you were doing on the phone the other day, promising your editor a good story? What rubbish are you concocting now?'

'I'm not...'

He gave her no time to finish.

'How dare you involve Frances in this? How can any story justify worming your way into someone's home? You're the worst one yet. Never mind me, don't you care what this will do to her? She trusted you.'

'I don't know what you're talking about.'

But Barney didn't listen.

'What more is there to say? Is there really so little news that you have to drag this up again?

For God's sake, when are you people going to leave me alone?'

He sounded angry, but Cassie saw only pain and frustration in his eyes.

'I'm not a journalist,' she said. 'Look.'

She pushed the laptop across the table to show him what was on the screen. As she did, something fell to the floor. Barney swooped and picked it up.

'What's this?'

The question was redundant. They both knew what he held in his hand. It was Frances' credit card.

'I can...' Cassie began at once.

'Oh, I'm sure you can,' Barney interrupted. 'I'm sure you're very good at explaining, thinking that voice of yours and those big eyes will get you out of all sorts of trouble. They won't wash with me. So you're a thief? And the worst sort: preying on vulnerable old ladies. It's despicable.' He rummaged in his pockets and pulled out his phone. 'You're not going to do this to anyone else. I'm ringing the police.'

Cassie rubbed her eyes, as the vision of Barney's angry features blurred. She reached into her bag, pulled out some Jelly Babies, and stuffed a couple into her mouth.

'Hello Smiler, are you hungry?' Akram wandered in, filling the small room. 'I said you should have had some cake with that coffee. You're looking right pale.'

Barney's gaze flickered over Cassie. In the momentary distraction, Akram plucked the phone from Barney's hand before he could make the call.

'No need for that, Barney mate. We can all hear you shouting from the bar. You're acting like a pillock.'

'Stay out of this, Akram. I've caught her using Frances' credit card. God knows how much she's already taken. I need to call the police. And all she can do is eat sweets. Talk about hard-nosed...'

Cassie wiped her sweaty, sugary fingers on her leg. It was ridiculous. She was innocent, so why did she feel so guilty? She'd been this way since childhood, always the one blushing in vicarious shame at school, if a teacher had asked for an anonymous culprit to own up. It was no wonder she had grown into such an easy victim. The horror of the current accusation froze her tongue and prevented her from defending herself.

'She's shopping for Frances,' Akram said. 'She told Mel about it. Was that website Mel suggested any good? Audible, wasn't it?'

Akram's encouraging smile loosened Cassie's tongue. She concentrated her attention on him. 'I think so. I was just checking the different packages when...'

The rest of her sentence spoke for itself. Barney spun the laptop round to face him.

'Audible?' he said, peering at the screen. 'What's that?'

'They sell audiobooks.'

'Why would Frances need that? I thought you were reading to her.'

'I am, during the day. She wanted something to listen to at night, in bed. I said I'd have a look, but I'm not sure if this would be any good,' Cassie said, still looking only at Akram. 'It seems to work by downloading books onto a computer or tablet. We need to have it on CD.'

Barney was still poring over the computer.

'It says you can burn the downloads onto a disc. I'll do it for you.' Cassie looked at him in surprise. 'For Frances,' he corrected himself, standing up, rubbing his nail along the bristles on his chin.

'Is it safe to leave you two alone now?' Akram asked, slapping Barney on the shoulder. 'It's no wonder we've never seen Cassie smile if you go about shouting at her like this.'

'I don't shout.'

Akram snorted. 'I've got a pub full of customers who can contradict you on that, unless you've driven them all out. Now, are you going to kiss and make up?' He laughed.

Cassie kept her eyes very firmly away from Barney, certain that for once they were in complete agreement about how horrifying that idea was. Yet, she felt a prickling sensation creep along the inside of her skin, making her wonder if he was looking at her.

Akram returned to the main bar and before the floor of the snug could sink under the weight of the uncomfortable silence left behind, Ethel bustled in.

'I heard you were in here,' she said, going over to Cassie. Ethel's disapproving sniff in Barney's direction suggested she'd heard everything. 'Your order's arrived, so I thought I might as well bob round with it.'

She handed over a large carrier bag to Cassie. Conscious that Barney's eyes were on her, Cassie pulled out a box.

'Upwords?' Barney frowned. 'What's that?'

'It's a board game. It's similar to Scrabble, but you can build on top of existing words.'

Cassie had remembered playing it years ago, and had thought Frances might enjoy it as a change from Scrabble. They had tried card games, but sometimes Frances found it difficult to hold the cards.

'It was harder to track down than I expected,' Ethel said. 'A bit dearer too. It was £36. Is that OK?'

'Yes, of course,' Cassie said, blanching. She couldn't pay for this with Frances' card. The game had been entirely Cassie's idea and was intended as a surprise. But it was a much bigger chunk of her wages than she'd expected to pay. She reached down into her handbag and pulled out her purse.

'Is that your money?' Barney asked, as she took out two twenty-pound notes and held them towards Ethel.

'Yes! I haven't stolen it, if that's what you're thinking.'

'Is the game for Frances?'

'Yes.'

'Then you shouldn't be paying for it. I will.' He dived into his pocket and withdrew a handful of crumpled notes, and offered them to Ethel.

'It's a gift,' Cassie insisted, stretching her arm out further towards Ethel.

'One you don't need to make.' Barney stretched his arm out too, but his eyes were on Cassie's. Instead of the coldness and domination she had expected, his brown eyes were warm and... Her immediate thought was kind. But how could that be right? And how could she even remember what kindness looked like?

Ethel looked from one to the other.

'I'll take his money, love,' she said to Cassie, accepting the handful of notes from Barney. 'It's the least he can do. A thief, indeed!' She shook her head. 'Shame on you, Barney Smallwood. Whatever would your mother think? She didn't bring you up to be so rude, or so stupid. I don't blame Cassie for not wanting to live with you!'

On this bewildering note, Ethel walked out. The silence she left behind was even more un-comfortable than before. Cassie closed down the computer, and gathered up her belongings to leave. She was almost at the doorway before Barney spoke.

'Cassie?'

She didn't think she'd heard him use her name before. It sounded odd, too intimate following the conversation they'd just had, and considering the relationship they'd established until now. She paused, but didn't turn round, until his hand connected with her arm. That was an intimacy too far. She stepped back, crashing her thigh painfully into a table. She saw a questioning look hover across Barney's face. He let go, and took a couple of paces back into the snug, giving her some room.

'I'm sorry,' he said. He plucked at his beard. He meant it, Cassie didn't doubt that. She had become a master in the art of apologising over the years, and knew when one was real and one was not. It was a novelty to be on the receiving end of one. 'I was an idiot and overreacted. The last couple of years have been tough. I have a bad habit of assuming the worst about everyone.'

'You're not the only one with a tough past,' she said. 'It's no excuse for rudeness. But I don't care what you call me. I've heard much worse, from people who matter much more. Your opinion means nothing to me at all.'

CHAPTER SEVEN

As she'd predicted, Frances' children were coming to visit her. It was unwelcome news to Cassie in many ways and presented a practical problem.

'Do you want me to go away for the weekend?' she asked, when Frances told her that they would be coming on Saturday – only two days away – and staying the night. Cassie had no idea what she would do if Frances said yes: where would she go? Unless the No Name did B&B, she might end up under a hedge in the garden which, given the bone-chilling March weather they were currently enduring, wasn't an attractive prospect.

'Is there somewhere you need to go?'

Cassie shook her head under Frances' shrewd scrutiny.

'Then of course you must stay. This is your home. And I need you to cook our meal on Saturday night. I thought your cidered pork casserole. Perhaps you could ask Ruth to make a syrup sponge pudding? It was always Guy's favourite.'

Ruth was happy to oblige.

'It's a proper treat for her, isn't it?' Ruth said, when Cassie remarked how pleased Frances was about the visit. 'I can't remember when they were last all here together. Or separately, come to that.'

'Not even at Christmas?'

'No, it was Mrs S and Barney sharing a chicken on Christmas Day. He stayed here instead of visiting his parents so she wouldn't be on her own. Guy popped in on New Year's Day, on his way back from a party, but that's been it for months.'

It sounded better than Cassie's Christmas, but she felt a pang for Frances, with none of her children bothering to see her on such a special day.

'So why are they all descending now?'

'Beats me. There must be something going on. Why don't you ask Barney? He's more likely to know.'

Cassie had no intention of asking him, and had done her best to avoid him altogether after the incident in the pub. He had left a message with Ruth one day that he would be out so Cassie could use his computer in the office. She had gone in, joined Audible, and chosen the first download for Frances. It had been odd sitting at his desk. The office had a different feel from the rest of the house: it was a masculine room, lived in, worked in, and full of individuality, although the only personal item in the room was a graduation photo on the desk of a handsome young man sandwiched between a couple whose pride could hardly be contained within the edges of the frame. The next day Cassie had found a CD of the audiobook waiting for her in the kitchen when she came down for breakfast. But she hadn't seen anything of Barney.

The imminent arrival of the family meant that more rooms would be put to use. Cassie had only been in the dining room once. It was magnificent but neglected and she suspected that the bedrooms would be the same. There was no way Ruth could get everything ready in time, so Cassie volunteered to help with the cleaning. Ruth lent her a voluminous pink housecoat 'to protect her clothes' – as if she were wearing Prada, not Primark – and they split up, with Cassie taking on the downstairs.

She walked into the dining room, carrying her housekeeper's bucket, and her heart sank. The room was vast. The wood-panelled walls formed perfect hollows and ridges for the dust to gather: and the ornate carving on the ceiling and around the fireplace made an ideal playground for spiders, who had spun webs from one feature to another. This room alone would take hours.

The dining chairs looked far too valuable to stand on, so Cassie went to find a stepladder and a long-handled duster. She manoeuvred back to the dining room with some difficulty, and was standing behind the door, wondering where to start, when she heard an unwelcome voice in the corridor calling for Ruth, and the next thing she knew, the dining room door was slammed into her back. She stumbled forward, hitting her face on the metal edge of the ladder with such force that tears leapt to her eyes.

'Cassie?' Barney took the ladder out of her hands and leant it against the wall, then dragged out a chair for her to sit on. He studied her face, tipping it up with gentle fingers under her chin. His face was closer than it had ever been. Cassie could see every eyelash, surprisingly thick and glossy, and the small frown line between his eyebrows. He smelt of soap and fresh air. His fingers prodded her cheek with such tenderness that she yearned for more. She had been wrong. His bedside manner was excellent.

'You're going to have a bruise,' he said, withdrawing his fingers. 'But there's no underlying damage. I'm sorry. I saw the pink housecoat and thought Ruth had come in here.'

'You wanted to do this to Ruth?'

Cassie touched her cheek, although whether it was to assess the damage, or to make a connection with where Barney had been, she hardly knew.

'No, I...' He stopped and his eyes met hers, widened slightly and softened at the edges as a glimmer of humour washed over them. It faded as quickly as it had appeared, and Barney stepped back, taking several strides away from Cassie. 'What do you need the stepladder for?'

'I'm cleaning the room.'

'Cleaning it? Why? No one comes in here.'

'But I thought it would be used this weekend, when Frances' children are here.'

'Frances' children? They're coming here? All of them?'

Cassie nodded. Judging by his expression, Barney didn't welcome the news any more than she did.

'What are they coming for?'

'I don't know. It has nothing to do with me.'

'I wouldn't be so sure of that. I'd better speak to Frances.'

He was halfway out of the door when he looked back.

'Do you need a hand?' he asked. 'This is a massive room, and there are proportionately sized spiders up there.'

'I've noticed.'

They didn't bother Cassie – or not as much as having to spend several hours with Barney. Her cheek was stinging, and hurt when she spoke, but she couldn't forget how tenderly Barney had examined her. It was only the shock of the accident, she was sure, but it would be much better if he would go, and let her lose herself in her work.

'Spiders don't scare me,' she said. 'What's the worst they can do? Crawl over my skin? It's the things that get under it that are the problem.'

Barney's lips parted, as though he intended to reply, but he must have thought better of it, because he left without another word.

Hugh was the first to arrive. He was tall, bronzed and wearing indigo jeans, a black leather jacket and brown shoes, all of which looked too pristine, and as if they had been designed for a man half his age. A vapid blonde, younger than Cassie, wafted round at his side. Diana came next, looking as if she had been firmly embedded in her late forties for all her life, and had every intention of staying there. An air of exasperation and a whiff of horse hung over her. She had brought along her husband, James, who was too browbeaten or too stupid to do anything but smile blandly at everyone.

Cassie had offered to make and serve the meal, hoping that would mean she could hide in the kitchen for most of the day. The family were already seated when she came up to the dining room, and there were two new arrivals: Barney, and a handsome man with thick golden hair, who was in his late thirties. He cast a sunny smile on her as she walked in. She put the plates down on the table with a clumsy rattle. Barney stood up and handed them round.

'Cassie dear, we are a place setting short,' Frances said, as Barney laid the final plate in front of his chair.

'Are we?' Cassie looked round, but couldn't work out who was missing. Perhaps Guy had brought a date, or even Barney; although if it was Barney, he hadn't dressed to impress, Cassie thought, as she took in the jeans that were frayed at the hem where he stood on them, and the sloppy fisherman's jumper. He caught her looking and she turned back to Frances. 'Is someone else coming?'

'No. You have not set a place for yourself.'

'I'll just have something in the kitchen,' Cassie said, although it was tempting to sit down just to see if Diana could look even more outraged.

'You are not hiding in the kitchen. I am quite sure that everyone would like to get to know you.'

'Mother, you know the staff don't sit at the table with us. It's not the way things are done,' Hugh said slowly.

'How would you know how things are done

79

here? Cassie is not staff. She is as good as one of the family.'

It turned out that Diana could look more outraged. Cassie hovered by the sideboard, wondering what Frances was up to. There was a definite glint in her eye.

Hugh sighed and leaned across his girlfriend to speak to Barney.

'How long has she been like this?'

'Like what?' Barney asked.

'Senile.'

'I am neither senile or deaf.'

'But Mother,' Hugh protested, using his slow voice again. 'Think what Father would say. He wouldn't condone this.'

Frances studied Hugh.

'You are quite right,' she said.

Hugh sat back in his chair, a satisfied smirk on his lips.

'He would not like it at all.' Frances gestured at Cassie. 'Hurry up and set yourself a place, Cassie. Our plates are growing cold.'

A sound suspiciously like a chuckle escaped Barney, and he went over to the sideboard and took out another set of cutlery. Cassie held out her hand to take it off him, but he brushed past her and laid them in the place next to his.

'Need a hand bringing the food up?' he asked.

Cassie nodded, but as they were heading to the door, Guy pushed back his chair.

'I'll help. You're a guest in the house, Barney.' He stood in front of Cassie and held out his hand. 'Guy Smallwood. It's good to put a face to the voice.' His handshake was enthusiastic, and was accompanied by a dazzling smile. Cassie stepped back. 'So you're the famous Cassie. Don't tell me you're a boxer as well as a companion?' He gestured at her face.

'I had an accident,' Cassie said, and her eyes flickered involuntarily to Barney. Guy didn't miss it.

'Oh yes?' His smile widened. 'What have you been up to, Barney? Are you having to resort to brute force to get a woman now?'

'He's not got me,' Cassie said, but neither of the men were listening to her. They were having a private conversation in body language, Barney's punctuated with frowns and Guy's with smirks.

'Is that another reason why Nessa left?' Guy laughed though Barney seemed distinctly unamused. 'Worried about becoming a battered wife?'

Barney was married? Cassie couldn't explain why she was so surprised, except that the hair, the beard and the clothes – his sheer grumpiness – screamed that he was a single man. Then she remembered the way he had rubbed cream into her hand, and how his fingers had stroked her cheek. Heat prickled along her chest, and she slipped out of the dining room.

'Cassie!' With a few long strides, Guy caught her up. 'I suppose you're used to turning a blind eye to family bickering. Have you come across people as bad as us in your previous posts?'

'No family is perfect,' Cassie replied, pushing open the kitchen door, and letting that reference to previous posts go uncorrected. She wondered, misery balling in her throat, whether she would

81

ever get back her simple, honest life again.

'An admirably tactful response.' Guy smiled. 'I can see why you're good at your job. Mum certainly seems to think highly of you.'

'I hope so.'

She hoped she was proving indispensable. She didn't want to move on again yet. In fact, the more time she spent at Ramblings, the less she wanted to move on at all. Cassie had taken to wandering round the garden and the fields near the house in her free hours. She hadn't felt so connected to a place since she had left the farm in Devon.

'I'm glad she has someone to look after her,' Guy said, watching as Cassie took several large dishes out of the oven. He opened a cupboard, and brought out an old but serviceable trolley. 'I've often worried about her being alone out here. Hugh lives too far away, and frankly Diana is only interested if something has four legs, a mane and a tail. My work prevents me coming as often as I'd like to.'

'What do you do?' Cassie asked, loading up the trolley.

'Land management.'

'Like Barney?' She hadn't appreciated what Barney did until she had seen all the books and papers in his office. 'He manages the estate here, doesn't he?'

'I wouldn't go that far. I don't think he does anything much, does he?' Guy pushed the trolley out into the corridor and headed for the dining room. 'Mum took him in when he messed up at being a doctor, and had nowhere else to go. He's never going to get a real job again. Killing a patient is hardly something employers look for on a CV.'

Killing a patient? Cassie stared at him, but Guy laughed and trundled past her into the dining room before she could ask what he meant. Barney glanced up and straight at her. She broke the eye contact at once, convinced that he knew exactly what they had been talking about, and struck by a twist of guilt. But she couldn't dismiss Guy's words from her head. How could Barney have killed a patient? She had seen gentleness in his eyes, and felt it in his touch. It couldn't be true, could it?

Cassie kept her head down during the meal, even when Hugh complained about the food. Criticism hardly registered any more.

'I find it delicious,' Frances said. 'So much easier to eat than a tough roast.'

Barney leaned forward. 'Is your arthritis getting worse? Are you struggling to eat? I can...'

'There is no need to make a fuss. Cassie has devised a very clever menu, and mealtimes are much easier now. She is an absolute treasure.'

Cassie thought this was higher praise than she deserved, but before she could object, Barney turned to her with something that looked distractingly like a smile. She dropped her gaze to the table, and it landed on his left hand. There was no ring on his finger, but she was well aware how little that proved. She looked up again, straight into Diana's frosty glare.

'Don't your own family miss you, if you're such a treasure?' she asked. 'Do you have a home of your own?'

'I inherited a house with my sister. She lives

there with her family.' After months of lies and deception, this one snippet of truth felt like honey rolling over her tongue.

'It is a difficult situation where there is one home and several children,' Frances said, putting down her knife and fork. It sounded an innocuous remark to Cassie, but Hugh, Diana and Guy all froze and turned to their mother. Even Barney looked towards Frances.

'Thankfully not something we need to worry about,' Hugh said. 'This house has always passed to the first-born son. It's what Father would have wanted.'

'I am sure he would. Fortunately he is not here to put in place such an antiquated idea. Even the Royal Family has moved on. I could sell the whole estate tomorrow, or leave it to the local dogs' home – or even to Cassie – if that is what I choose to do.'

Frances smiled. She was the only one at the table who did.

'But I would be interested to know how each of you would use the estate if you inherited it. Let us see if one of you can come up with a magnificent solution as to how it can benefit you all.'

CHAPTER EIGHT

A storm like nothing Cassie had ever experienced before had blown up outside. The wind screamed through invisible cracks in the windows, and rushed down the chimney, sending ash flying onto the rug. An occasional change in its direction sent rain hurling against the glass panes like bullets. The blackness surrounding the house was absolute, until a slice of lightning, far too close for Cassie's comfort, lit up the garden like a floodlight, revealing bushes and trees swaying as if they were giving their final bow. Cassie felt chilled inside, in a way that no amount of jumpers or huddling against radiators could cure. The house creaked and rattled around her. How could Frances have lived here on her own?

Cassie shrieked as another blast of rain battered against the window. That was it. She didn't care what time it was. She was going to follow Frances' example, and retreat to bed, with the duvet pulled up round her ears, and stay there until this was over. She had reached the door when the telephone rang, a jarring sound against the noise of nature that was filling the house.

'Hello?'

'Cassie? How are things at the house?'

It was Barney, though he clearly saw no need for niceties.

'Everything's fine.' Yet another lie on the charge sheet. Everything was terrifying, but she wasn't going to admit that to him.

'According to the radio, the wind is averaging 100 mph, and this rain could go on for hours. Some houses in the village have lost power.'

'Have they? The lights flickered a couple of times, but they're still on.'

Of course, the moment she said the words, the lights flickered again, at the same time as the wind flung a stray twig or branch against the window.

Cassie thought she'd managed a silent gasp, but Barney's ears were as sharp as his eyes.

'I'll come over.'

'There's no need.'

'I'm passing anyway. A couple of trees in the village are wobbling, and one will hit a power line if it falls. We're going to see if we can tether it. Have you found the emergency torches in case the lights go out?'

'No. I don't know where they are.'

'Frances could have told you. There's a small torch in every room, but the main ones are in the storeroom next to my office. Go and get a couple so you each have one. How is Frances?'

'She's in bed.'

'What?'

'She's in bed,' Cassie shouted. She felt as much as heard the huff down the telephone.

'I heard you. Why didn't you ring me? Is she feeling unwell?'

'No, she was cold and tired, and wanted to go to bed.'

'Have you given her an extra blanket?'

'Yes.'

'What about a hotwater bottle? There's a stack...'

'I know. I made her one.' Cassie was tempted to borrow Frances' line, and tell him to stop fussing.

'How was her breathing?'

'Fine. Normal. Why shouldn't it be?'

'No reason. That's good. Keep an eye on her, won't you?'

'Of course. It's what I'm paid for.'

Honestly, Cassie thought, as she put down the

phone, how fickle could one man be? One minute he was objecting to her appointment, the next he was demanding she did the job he hadn't wanted her to have. And now he was on his way to check up on her and interfere. There was no way he was going to find anything to criticise. She ran to the storage room and took out the torches, then went upstairs to see Frances.

Ten minutes later, swamped in a borrowed coat and wellington boots, Cassie dashed out from the shelter of the entrance canopy, shining her torch at Barney's truck as it pulled up at the front of the house. The window opened and he leaned out.

'For God's sake!' Barney shouted, drawing his head back in as a gust of rain slapped against his cheek. 'If you're going to make a habit of jumping rabbit impressions, can't you at least wait for better weather?'

Cassie ignored him, opened the passenger door and hopped in. Gin clambered onto Barney's knee to make way for her.

'What are you doing?' Barney asked.

'I'm coming to help in the village,' she said, pushing back her hood. It hadn't served much purpose: her hair was plastered to her cheeks and forehead, so she probably did look more animal than human. Not that Barney could talk. If she was a rabbit, he was definitely doing his usual wild bear impression.

'We're trying to tether a tree,' he said slowly, in a similar tone to the one Hugh had used with Frances. 'What help do you think you can be?'

'I've brought flasks of tea.' Cassie indicated the Tesco bag she had just stowed in the footwell. The interior light switched off, but Cassie could feel the heat of the Barney stare through the darkness. Something battered against the windscreen, and Cassie heard Gin whimper. Except it didn't sound like a canine noise. It sounded human. It sounded like her. Barney switched the light back on.

'Are you scared of the dark?'

'No. I'm scared of not being able to see.'

He frowned, as if considering the difference, but didn't pursue it.

'You'd be better staying with Frances.'

'I know. But when she heard there was trouble in the village, she decided it was her duty to help. That means sending me. She said that if I wanted to make a fuss I could do it there instead. Frances is fine,' she added. 'I've given her a torch, and the phone is beside her bed.'

Cassie thought she detected a sigh of resignation. It was all the encouragement she needed. She fastened her seatbelt.

'I don't have much choice then, do I?' Barney grumbled, but he pushed Gin over to Cassie and set off. He crawled down the drive, hunched forward over the steering wheel to peer through the windscreen. Even with the wipers on their fastest setting, the window was drenched in rain, as if buckets of water were being thrown at it between each wipe. The full beam of the headlights picked out trees rocking at the edges of the drive, and Cassie clung to Gin, unable to tell whether the trembles in her arms came from her or the dog.

'Thank God,' she muttered, relaxing back in her seat as they pulled up outside the pub. Lights blazed from the windows, and a few figures were running round carrying torches and lanterns.

'I told you to stay behind,' Barney said, but there was relief in his voice too. He pulled a beanie hat out of his pocket and put it on. 'Wait there. I don't want either of you getting underfoot. If anyone wants tea I'll send them your way.' He opened the door and slid out, letting in rain and wind. Cassie shrank into her coat, and kept a tight hold on Gin.

It probably took a minute – a dark, terrifying minute that felt like a year – for Cassie to decide that she didn't like waiting in the truck. With the wipers off, rain coursed down all the windows, and she could see nothing but the occasional blurred light up ahead. She felt like a sitting target, waiting for that extra strong gust that would knock the truck over, or lift her into the air and then drop her back down. The more she thought about it, the more convinced she became that in fact the truck was the most dangerous place in the whole village. The warm, solid pub was at her side. Surely she would be safer in there? At least she would be with other people, and not in the dark. A crowd had never seemed so desirable.

A few seconds later, Cassie pushed open the pub door with her body, the bag of flasks in one hand and Gin's collar in the other. She looked round the pub. It wasn't as busy as she had expected. There were only three other people there: Mel and Ethel by the bar, and an elderly man sitting at a table. His head dropped down in erratic jerks, then shot back up as he tried to stay awake.

'Cassie?' Mel sounded as if she doubted her eyes. 'What are you doing here?'

'I came with Barney.'

'Oh yes?' Mel grinned. 'I'll want to hear all about that later.'

'Where is everyone?' Cassie asked, ignoring the glint of gossip in Mel's face. She let go of Gin's collar, and the dog immediately ran over to the fire and shook herself. Cassie followed. 'I thought there was an emergency, and help was needed.'

'Akram phoned Barney because of the weak tree near the village hall. We thought it might hit the power line, so they're all out seeing if it can be tethered until it can be cut down. But there's a new problem now. The old bus shelter has blown down, and there's stone all across the road into the village. No one can get in or out.'

'Can't the stones be moved?'

'That's what we've been discussing. The stones are heavy, and there are loads of them. We could probably only manage one at a time, and in this weather it will take hours.'

'You need a digger with a bucket, or a tractor,' Cassie said. 'Surely there must be a farm round here?'

'There's no answer from Green Farm,' Ethel replied. 'And our other local farmer is here.' She gave the man in the chair a prod. 'He's sozzled. His tractor is in the car park, but it's no use without a driver.'

'Can no one else drive it?' Cassie asked. Her conscience had grown feet, and she could feel it trying to kick her into action.

'Barney could, but he'll be needed by the tree-tethering team.' Mel sighed. 'We've no choice, have we? We'll have to start shifting them by

90

hand. You stay here, Ethel. No offence, but you can't go out humping stones at your age.'

'Of course I can!' Ethel was already looking round for her coat. 'I'm not dead yet. We all muck in together; it's what we've always done in this village.'

It was no use. Loath as she was to draw attention to herself, Cassie looked at Ethel, in her fluorescent sou'wester and Hotter shoes, and knew she couldn't allow an elderly woman to go out moving heavy stones in this weather.

'I could drive the tractor,' she said. Mel laughed.

'Frances' Volvo might feel like a juddery old tractor, but it's different from driving a real one, or else I'd give it a go myself.'

'I've driven tractors before. I grew up on a farm. My sister still lives there. It's been a couple of years, but...'

Mel wasn't waiting to hear any but. She gave the sleeping man a hearty shake.

'Joe? Where are your keys?'

'What?' Joe jerked awake, but his eyelids were fluttering dangerously low. 'What keys?'

'Your tractor keys. Come on, hand them over.'

Joe patted his pockets and deposited a set of keys and a dirty tissue onto Mel's outstretched hand.

'Wasn't planning to drive,' he muttered. 'Needn't pinch the keys.'

'I'm not pinching them. You can have them back later. Cassie needs to borrow your tractor for a while.'

Drunken eyes tried and failed to focus on Cassie.

'She's a girl.'

'Well spotted. But you don't need a willy to operate the tractor, do you?' Mel handed the keys over to Cassie. 'Are you sure about this? We can see if the men can spare Barney.'

Cassie wasn't the slightest bit sure, bearing in mind that last time she'd driven a tractor she'd ended up in a ditch, but the reference to Barney stiffened her resolve. She didn't need him to come to her rescue. So she nodded at Mel, put up her hood, and went back outside.

The weather hadn't improved in the few minutes she'd been in the pub. As soon as Cassie stepped outside, she was attacked by a faceful of rain, and the wind swirled around and inside her over-sized clothes, inflating her coat so that she felt she might take off at any moment. She was propelled into a strange half-run as she headed for the tractor at the far side of the car park. She could hear shouts from the men working down the road, and see shaky torch beams lighting up one of the trees, but she ignored all the activity and concentrated. The tractor was a John Deere, so at least it was familiar, though it was older than the ones she'd driven before. The cab was closed, but one of the doors was missing and the driver's seat was wet. Cassie climbed in, and pulled down her coat to cover her bottom.

She looked round the cab, adjusted her seat and reacquainted herself with all the controls. Taking a deep breath, she pressed down on the clutch with her left foot, then the brake pedal with her right foot, turned the key and as the engine roared into life, she dropped the throttle. The tractor shuddered and stalled.

Cassie sat back in her seat and felt the cold prickle along the underside of her thighs as dampness penetrated her trousers. She couldn't do this. What had she been thinking, to push herself forward and volunteer for this? *Neither use nor ornament:* Mike's voice, in that special sneering tone he saved for her, sliced through her head, leaving despair behind. She should go back to the pub, admit defeat, and return to hiding away at Ramblings.

But as she looked out at the rain, bracing herself to run to the pub, the feel of the steering wheel beneath her hand and the earthy smell filling the cab combined to revive happier memories of the past. She remembered riding in a tractor with her father, and her delight when he had finally agreed to teach her to drive one. She thought back to the last summer she had spent with Vicky, driving her nephews around, at a time when she had still clung onto a sliver of hope that one day it might be her own child at her side. The memories fought back against the despair.

This was her chance to set aside the secrets and deception. The real her was here, sitting in a tractor, ready to work. She could do this.

Cassie tried the tractor again, and this time the engine came to life and stayed alive, each vibration increasing her confidence. She released the clutch slowly, took her foot off the brake and the tractor inched forward across the car park. It was a slow, jerky ride at first, but as she pulled out on to the empty road and picked up speed, familiarity chased away any lingering nerves. She saw Mel and Ethel enthusiastically waving from the front

93

door of the No Name, raised a quick hand back, and headed down past the village green to where the road was blocked.

It took a few minutes to get the hang of operating the loader, and Cassie's confidence wobbled again as she crawled backwards and forwards, trying to get the angle right for the first scoop. The nearest streetlamp was some way behind her, and even the headlights of the tractor were of limited use when rain continued to lash against the front of the cab and in through the open door. But at last she did it. The first pile of stone was in the loader, and with a few more manoeuvres she deposited it on the village green.

Cassie had no idea how long it took to move the complete pile: probably not much more than twenty minutes; but it felt like hours had passed. Her arms, back and shoulders ached from the effort of controlling the tractor, and every inch of her was drenched, from sweat as much as rain. She climbed down from the cab to check the road, no longer bothering to put up her hood, welcoming the water that ran over her face and slid down her neck. She picked up a couple of stones the tractor had missed, kicked the small debris to the side of the road, and finally drove back to the pub.

'Oh my God, you've really done it, haven't you? You're a complete star.' Mel threw herself on Cassie as soon as she staggered into the pub. 'Urgh, you're completely soaked. Come over to the fire and I'll get you a towel.'

Ethel had pulled up a chair in front of the fire, but stood up when Cassie wandered over. She took Cassie's hand and shook it in both of hers.

'We were watching you from the window. You were like one of those land girls from the war! I didn't think a slip of a thing like you would be able to handle Joe's old tractor. He's always complaining how temperamental it is. Well, we've shown the men what we're made of tonight, haven't we?'

'Are they back?' Cassie pushed wet hair away from her face and looked round, horrified by the idea that the whole village might have been standing in the windows watching her efforts.

'No, they're still out fiddling with the tree, unless they've found another problem now.'

'Where's Gin?' Cassie's sweep of the pub had shown her a lack of men, but also no dog. She walked round to the other side of the fireplace, and peered into the snug. Gin wasn't there. 'Ethel, have you seen Gin?' Cassie's voice felt raw in her throat. She ran behind the bar. It was empty. 'Where's Gin?' she repeated.

'Cassie?' Mel came back. 'What's the matter?'

'I've lost Gin.' She ignored the towel that Mel was attempting to thrust into her hand. 'He told me to wait in the truck with Gin. Now I've lost her. Where has she gone? She can't have got out, can she?'

'No,' Mel said. 'No one has been in or out since you left.'

'Well,' Ethel admitted. 'I had a peek outside five minutes ago to see what was going on down the road...'

Five minutes ago? How far might Gin have gone in five minutes? She could be anywhere. But then Cassie realised she wouldn't be just anywhere. She was devoted to Barney. She would be looking for

95

him. Cassie zipped up her coat again, and disregarding Mel's protests, ventured back outside.

Lights blazed around the village hall and the torch lights confirmed that it was still busy down there. Cassie ran in that direction, scanning the sides of the road and calling for Gin, though the wind tossed her words straight back at her. She reached the hall without finding the dog, and to her dismay the first person she saw was Barney, standing in the open doorway.

'There's more rope in the storeroom,' she heard him shout. 'I'll go and get it.'

He disappeared into the hall, and seconds later Cassie heard a bark, and saw a furry form slink through the door behind him.

'Gin!' she called. 'Gin! Come back!'

But her words were drowned out by an almighty crack that she would never forget, and she watched in helpless, hopeless horror as a tree crashed down through the roof of the village hall.

CHAPTER NINE

Cassie was vaguely aware of activity around her, of shouts, and moving lights, and people running. Her eyes and ears absorbed the commotion, passing information to her brain that help was on the way. But the message didn't reach her legs. They started to run, straight through the door and into the hall.

The tree had knocked out all lights inside.

Enough light spilled through the windows for Cassie to see that several huge branches filled the hall, having crushed the roof and the rafters. The trunk was caught on the side wall. Debris fell like snow, and now the wind found its way in, exploring its new playground and shaking the dangling branches. It was eerily silent. Apart from Cassie's own ragged breathing, there was no sound of life – from dog or man.

An ominous crack from overhead shattered the silence, and the tree dropped down another few inches, bringing with it a shower of roof tiles. It shook Cassie into action.

'Gin!' she shrieked, hardly recognising the strained voice as her own. She shuffled forwards. 'Gin! Barney! Where are you?'

Cassie nearly cried when she heard an answering bark. It sounded close by, and she squeezed past a branch. Gin was on the other side, unharmed as far as Cassie could tell in the gloom, although as she hugged the dog she felt bits of grit and dirt caught in her fur.

Another creak echoed over their heads.

'Gin, where's Barney?' Cassie asked, hooking her fingers in Gin's collar. 'Show me where Barney is.'

Gin pulled her forwards, heading towards an open door in the corner of the room. Cassie saw that the largest branch, as thick as her waist, was hanging through the ceiling here – and then her stomach lurched as she noticed Barney slumped on the floor, his back against the wall. A torch lay near him. Cassie picked it up and turned it on, pointing it towards Barney. The beam wavered up and down in her shaking hand, but travelled over his face long enough for her to see that his eyes were open and staring.

The torch dropped to the floor. Cassie took a step back. Was he dead? How could he be dead? She had seen him striding into the village hall only a few minutes ago. How could all that life, all that energy, be gone? What would Frances do without him? What would happen to Gin? She couldn't let this happen.

'Barney!' She leaned forwards and slapped him on the face. His beard was rough under her hand. His cheek was still warm. 'Barney!' she shouted, hitting him again. 'Come back! Barney!'

Her hand had become an automaton, repeatedly moving backwards and forwards to slap him. She had no control over it. Her only thought was that she had to bring him back to life.

Her arm was swinging back when a hand closed round her wrist. Cassie screamed. Gin barked.

'Bloody hell,' Barney said. 'Will you stop hitting me? Are you mad?'

Mad? Too right she was mad. In fact, she was furious. What had he been sitting there for, letting her think he was dead? Cassie hit him with the hand he wasn't restraining.

'I thought you were dead,' she shrieked, recoiling as the final word came out wrapped in a sob.

'So did I, for a moment,' he said, and his voice held a gravelly vulnerability she hadn't heard before. 'So what were the slaps for? Do you have a fetish for dead bodies?'

How could he joke at a time like this? Cassie felt like hitting him again. He was still gripping her arm, as if his fingers had locked in place. The roof groaned, and increasingly heavy drops of rain fell on Cassie's face.

'We need to get out of here,' Cassie said. 'Are you hurt? Can you walk?'

'Probably, but I can't move.'

Picking up the torch, Cassie shone it on Barney and saw what he meant. Part of a roof beam had fallen on him. A chair had broken its fall and held the beam suspended precariously above his legs, but he was trapped against the wall. If he tried to wriggle out, there was every chance that the beam would dislodge and land on his legs. If she tried to move the beam, there was still every chance it might land on his legs, but the alternative was leaving him there in the certainty that the roof would fall on his head. There was no choice.

She put down the torch so it cast some light in the right direction. The beam was about as thick as a telegraph pole. She wrapped her arms round it, and tried to lift it but nothing happened. She braced her feet, took a huge breath, and tried again, but it didn't shift.

'Leave it, it's too heavy for you.'

'No, it isn't.'

Another blast of wind, and the tree dropped another foot. Cassie yelped as a twig scratched her cheek.

'Cassie, take Gin and get out of here. That wall isn't going to hold much longer.'

'I can do it.'

'Leave it!' Barney bellowed. 'Get out now.'

Cassie wasn't going anywhere. She hadn't slapped him back to life only to let him be crushed to death.

'We'll have to try together,' she said. 'But there'll only be one chance. When I shout "go", I'll pull, you push, and draw back your legs. Ready?'

They stared at each other, oblivious to the storm blowing around them. If they couldn't do it … if Barney couldn't move in time… In that moment of silence, they were both well aware of how those sentences might end.

'Ready.' Barney's voice was quiet, but Cassie was so wholly focussed on him that she was sure she could hear the brush of his eyelashes against his cheeks as he blinked.

She wiped her hands on her trousers, and hooked her arms underneath the beam.

'Three, two, one … go!'

Cassie pulled, her muscles burning along her arms, across her shoulders and behind her neck. Eyes closed, teeth clenched, she pulled with every grain of strength she had. She felt an answering pressure from Barney's side, and for a second the whole weight of the beam seemed to hang in her arms, before they gave way under the strain and the beam crashed to the floor.

Cassie looked up. Barney was standing in front of her, alive and legs intact. They had done it – although they weren't safe yet. She bent down and grabbed Gin's collar.

'Come on,' she shouted. 'Let's go.'

Barney didn't move. He gazed at the tree, hanging through the ceiling, apparently transfixed. Cassie wondered if he'd banged his head, and was concussed, or worse. With her free hand she got his sleeve and pulled him, not stopping until they emerged through the doors of the village hall.

The rain, the wind and the villagers attacked them as soon as they set foot outside.

'Barney!' Akram reached them first, and gave Barney a hug. 'I thought you were a goner, mate. When that tree crashed down...'

His words were drowned out as the tree finally won its battle with the wall, crushing the side of the hall as it collapsed. The reality of what might have happened hit Cassie and her knees buckled. She sank down to the pavement, and put her head between her knees. Her head was swirling as if she had the worst hangover, but she was vaguely aware of male conversation around her, and Barney's voice more distinct than the others. She felt a warm tongue lick her cheek, and Gin nudged up next to her and began to bark

'Cassie? What's the matter? Are you hurt?' Barney spoke close to her ear. Cassie shook her head, but that made the spinning worse.

'She's like a drowned rat.' Akram's words drifted over Cassie. 'Come on, Smiler. Let's get you somewhere dry.'

Akram looped his arm in hers and pulled her up, but the bones in her legs had vanished and she dropped back down, dangling off Akram like an oversized handbag. Before she could sink to the ground again, Barney scooped her off her feet, and staring silently ahead, marched towards the pub. Cassie was too exhausted to raise a protest.

The pub door opened as Barney approached, and Mel peered out, eyes wide.

'What happened? What was that noise?' She looked at Cassie. 'What have you done to Cassie?'

101

'Nothing!'

'I'm fine.' Cassie wriggled and Barney put her down. She leant against the wall, feeling far from fine. Her heart was having a funny turn, galloping in a way she hoped would stop now she was on the ground and not in Barney's arms.

'She's in shock,' Barney said. 'The tree has fallen onto the village hall. One wall and the roof have been destroyed.'

'Destroyed?' Mel's face was a slide show of emotion as it went through disbelief to horror and freeze-framed on fear. 'Akram? Where is he?'

She tried to rush past Barney, but he held her back.

'He's OK. He's on his way.'

The door opened and Akram sauntered in, followed by the other men who had been helping out. Mel flung herself on Akram, despite the water dripping off him, and gave him the sort of kiss that was barely decent in public. Their raw passion made Cassie's heart flip. She shuffled along the wall, heading towards the fire.

'I think I'm on a promise tonight, lads,' Akram said, when Mel detached herself from his lips.

'Any night,' she agreed, taking his hand. 'When we heard that crash...' She shuddered. 'I thought you were sure to be in the thick of it.'

'Nay, you needn't have worried about me.' Akram patted his stomach. 'The tree would probably have bounced off me. It's these two you should have been worrying about.' He waved a hand from Barney to Cassie, who had now reached the hearth. 'We almost lost the pair of them. It's a toss up which one is the daftest. Him

102

for going in the hall in the first place, or her for dashing to his rescue.'

'Not *his* rescue,' one of the other men said. 'It was the dog she was calling for.'

Everyone turned to Cassie, including her in their laughter, and the warmth radiating off them was as strong as any heat coming from the fire behind her. She had forgotten the pleasure of belonging, of sharing laughter rather than being the subject of it. She wanted more of this. She needed it.

'There's your proof she's not daft,' Barney said. 'She knew which one of us was worth rescuing.' And he smiled at Cassie. Even across the pub she could see the crinkles around his eyes and knew this smile was real. A bubble of hope floated into her head. Perhaps she could stay here, and belong, and be content.

'Come off it,' Mel said to Barney. 'There'll be a queue of women lining up to thank her when this news gets out. The Yeti look is amazingly popular.'

'Are you and Ethel at the head of the queue?'

'In your dreams.'

'I told you about that dream in confidence. You weren't meant to blurt it out in the pub.'

Mel snorted, and hugged him.

'You daft bugger,' she said. 'Don't ever do anything like that again. You know I'm keeping you in reserve as my next husband in case I wear out Akram.'

Barney laughed, while Mel wandered away to fetch towels and Akram handed out glasses of whisky. Cassie refused hers, but watched as Barney downed his in one. She wondered if he'd been hit on the head before she had gone into the village hall. There was *something* wrong with him. Where had this flirty Barney come from? He was laughing, smiling and joking, a totally different man. Perhaps the true character of a person was only revealed under the most extreme circumstances. And his true character... Well, it wasn't what she had expected.

'You'd have been better with the whisky to warm you up,' Mel said, as she gave Cassie the orange juice she'd asked for. 'You've not stopped shivering since you came back. Get that wet coat off and you'll feel more benefit from the fire.'

Cassie took off her coat, peeling the soaking sleeves from her arms. Her thin top was more wet than dry, and clung to her skin. She plucked it away from her chest, shivering as air crept below the fabric.

'Here, have this.' Barney walked towards Cassie, taking off his coat. Cassie thought he was giving her that, but he threw it on the table and continued to strip off the jumper he was wearing underneath. He tugged it over his head, lifting his T-shirt with it, and revealing a taut stomach, divided by a strip of dark hair like the shaft of an arrow, pointing below his belt.

A coil of lust twisted inside Cassie, rising up from her toes. She hadn't expected it. She didn't like him, and she would rather saw off her limbs with a blunt knife than become involved with a man again, but she couldn't deny what she felt.

It was wonderful. Mike had been wrong. She wasn't broken, or faulty goods, or frigid, or any of the other horrid things he had delighted in calling her. It was as if a match had been struck

104

in the darkness of her heart and mind – if Mike had been wrong about that, how much else that he'd said was a lie too? She looked again at Barney, catching another glimpse of skin before the T-shirt fell back down.

Barney held out his jumper, and Cassie pulled it on. The wool was so soft that she wanted to hug herself to feel more of it, and Barney's warmth clung to it. The jumper smelt of outdoors, and log smoke, and something else uniquely male. Lust writhed again. Cassie took a deep breath, savouring every tingle of desire that proved she was normal.

'What shall we do about the village hall?' Mel asked, when everyone had a towel. 'Do we need to report it?'

'I'll ring the Colonel in the morning,' Barney said. 'He'll need to inform the insurers, and see if there's any chance of them paying out.'

'And if they won't? Do we double our fundraising efforts? How bad is it?'

'We won't be sure until the storm is over, and we see it in daylight, but I think we could fundraise for the next ten years and not make enough for the repairs. It's too far gone. And don't forget we can't use the hall now. We've nowhere to hold the events, even if there was any point.'

'I hadn't thought about that.' Mel slumped into a chair. 'What will we do? So many groups use the hall. It's the life of the village.'

Barney shrugged.

'I know, but making it safe is the first concern.' He turned to Akram. 'Did you ring the fire service?'

'Yes, but they have a lot on their plate tonight. It might be hours before they get here.'

'At least they *can* get here,' Mel said. 'Without Cassie, they wouldn't be able to reach the village.' She smiled at Cassie. 'You really are the heroine of the night. Thank God Barney brought you with him.'

'What else have you been up to, Smiler?' Akram asked. 'Was saving a man from certain death not enough excitement for one night?'

'Mel's exaggerating my usefulness,' Cassie said, shrinking into Barney's jumper as all eyes in the pub focused on her.

'You can't be modest after what you've done tonight.' Mel turned to the men. 'While you lot were working on the tree, the bus shelter fell down and blocked the road.'

Amid the groans, Akram laughed.

'I hope there weren't any courting couples in it at the time. It's a popular place once it gets dark.' He gave Barney a nudge. 'I bet you could tell a tale or two about what you got up to in there in your heyday.'

'Never mind in my heyday. Now I'll have to rethink my date for tomorrow night.'

Laughter lingered over his face as he turned to Cassie.

'What were you doing in the bus shelter? You were safe in the truck when I left you.'

'Not very safe,' Cassie said. 'It was rocking, and it was dark.'

'Why would you leave her in the truck?' Mel asked. 'She's a woman, not an animal, as I'm sure you must have noticed.'

Barney ignored this, and, picked up his coat.

'Is the road completely blocked? We'd better go back out and clear it.'

'No!' Mel flapped her hand at him. 'Will you listen? That's what I've been trying to tell you. Cassie cleared the road.'

'By herself?' Akram laughed. 'Are you wearing a Wonder Woman outfit under that jumper?'

'I wouldn't mind finding out...' It was probably meant to be a whisper, but the group of men at the bar had taken control of the whisky bottle, and lost control over their voices. Cassie folded her arms over herself, hating the attention.

'How did you do it?' Barney asked.

'In the tractor.'

'Tractor? What tractor? We saw Joe out in his tractor. There wasn't another one.'

'You're being remarkably dim, Barney. Look at Joe. He's been like this for the last hour.' Mel gestured at Joe, who was slumped in his chair, snoring. 'It was Cassie driving the tractor.'

'It was just like the war!' Ethel added, removing her lips from her sherry glass for long enough to speak. 'Girl power!'

'What do you know about driving a tractor?' Barney asked Cassie.

'I grew up on a farm. My dad taught me.'

'But Joe's old Bertha? She's like a tank. I've struggled to drive her.'

'It had to be done. The road needed clearing.'

'Well, good for you, Smiler.' Akram leant down and kissed Cassie's cheek. 'You're one of us now, a true Ribblemiller. Welcome to the gang.'

A few whistles and a feeble round of applause

drifted over from the bar. Barney put on his coat and picked up Cassie's.

'You must be shattered. I'd better take you home.' He held out her coat, so Cassie could slip it back on. 'You should soak in the bath and then get to bed.'

'Oh aye? Planning on searching for that Wonder Woman costume yourself, are you?' Akram winked at Barney.

'Certainly not. I don't want her to catch a cold and pass it onto Frances.'

The wind was as strong as ever, but the rain held off as Cassie followed Barney out of the pub, and he drove back to Ramblings. He pulled up close to the front entrance, the engine still running, and switched on the interior light. Cassie blinked, partly at the sudden brightness, and partly at the full on Barney stare that fixed on her. But it was different from normal: less hostile, more curious.

'You're not what you seem,' he said.

'What?' Cassie felt colder than she had all night. What did he know?

'Frances told me you were tougher than you look. I didn't believe her until tonight.'

Frances and Barney had discussed her? She wondered what they had said, and whether Barney was still trying to persuade Frances to sack her. Surely she had done enough, tonight, to earn a reprieve? He had called Ramblings her home, and that was how she saw it, even after so short a time. The thought of leaving made her feel sick. She opened the truck door and turned to get out.

'Cassie.' Barney made to stop her, but as she swivelled in her seat, he missed her arm, and his hand caught hold of hers. She could feel the imprint of each warm finger against her skin. She stared down at his hand, noticing the gash across the back of it. He wasn't applying any pressure, but she couldn't move her hand away. 'Thanks for what you did tonight.'

'It was nothing.'

'Nothing to you, maybe, but saving my life means a lot to me. I owe you.'

'Anybody would have done the same thing.'

'No. It takes someone pretty remarkable to do what you did.'

He didn't smile; in fact, he appeared as surprised to be saying the words as Cassie was to hear them. His manner couldn't be more different from that in the pub. He wasn't flirting or trying to compliment her, but the atmosphere in the truck seemed charged. Their hands pulled apart simultaneously.

'I'd better check on Frances,' Cassie said, and she slid out of the truck and ran into the house. She closed the front door, and fastened the bolts, and only then she heard the clatter of gravel as Barney drove away.

CHAPTER TEN

Cassie drew back her curtains and peered out through the leaded panes of the window at the devastation the storm had wreaked in the garden. Twigs and branches were scattered over the lawns, as if the flowerbeds had been ransacked, and thousands of leaves had arrived overnight to give the appearance of autumn rather than spring. She wondered how the house had fared, thinking that all the chimneys and ornate stonework must surely be vulnerable, and she opened the window so she could lean further out and see if there was any evidence of fallen masonry on the ground.

A figure pelted round the corner of the house as if the devil was snapping at his heels. Sweat darkened his grey vest top, making it cling to a trim torso normally hidden under a woolly jumper. Cassie stepped back, but Barney didn't look up, and continued to run past at a furious pace.

Ruth was tidying up the kitchen when Cassie went down for breakfast.

'What are you doing up?' Ruth asked, as Cassie wandered in. 'I was sure you'd need a lie in after what you got up to last night.'

She made it sound as if Cassie had engaged in a night of passion. Remembering some of the thoughts of the previous evening, a blush crept across Cassie's face.

'It was a team effort,' Cassie said. 'The men were out for ages trying to tether the tree.'

'Shame they didn't manage it.' Ruth hugged Cassie. 'Thank the Lord you were there. Barney may be a grumpy bugger at times, but none of us would want to be without him.'

'Did he tell you what happened?' Cassie found it hard to believe that he was broadcasting tales of his rescue.

'Not a word. Ethel opened up the shop early in case anyone needed emergency supplies. The whole village will have heard the story by now.' Ruth poured out two cups of tea. 'How are you feeling? It's a wonder you haven't caught pneumonia going out in that weather.'

'My arms ache, but that's all.'

Every movement led to twinges of pain in muscles that had been underused until last night.

'Lucky the doctor paid a visit this morning, then.' Ruth handed a slim box over to Cassie. 'Barney thought you might be sore, and said you should apply this deep heat cream twice a day. I said the least he could do was to offer to rub it on himself, but you'd think I'd asked him to rub it on me he ran away so fast!'

Ruth laughed, and carried the mugs of tea over to the kitchen table. Cassie followed with a plate of toast.

'How are things in the village?' she asked. 'Is there much damage?'

'Not as much as I'd expected. I've never heard wind like it. I thought my house was going to blow away and I'd end up in Oz. Have you seen the news this morning? Half the country is flooded. We've got off lightly, except for the village hall. But aside from loss of life, that's about the worst thing that could have happened to us.'

'I didn't stop to look at it last night. How bad is it?'

'So bad that I'd be amazed if it could be repaired, rather than knocked down and rebuilt from scratch. It will be out of action for months. This will kill the village. People love living here because they get the country life and an active community. It will be the end for a lot of the groups that use the hall.' Ruth took a long slurp of tea. 'Our Becca's devastated.'

'Did she run an activity in the hall?'

'She helped with the Brownies, but I meant because of the party.'

'The party? Oh, her engagement party. The ceilidh.' Cassie had forgotten about it. Despite Ruth's invitation, she had never intended to go. 'When is it? Can't she find a new venue?'

Ruth shook her head.

'It's a week on Saturday. It's Easter Saturday, too, so the chances of finding somewhere free at this short notice are slim, even if she could afford to book a fancy venue. She wanted the hall, so that it would be a proper village knees up. She feels like it's put a jinx on the whole marriage.'

Ruth's words niggled at Cassie for the rest of the morning. She had met Becca twice, and had liked her, even though she had tried to entice Cassie to visit her shop to buy new clothes. Becca had shimmered with excitement about her engagement. Cassie might have lost her faith in romance and happy endings, but she didn't like to see anyone else crushed. But what could she do? Surely if there was another possible venue in the village, Ruth would have known about it?

Frances interrupted her thoughts. 'Cassie! You have read that paragraph twice. Do you need a break? Barney said I should give you the day off, but I assumed he was fussing as usual.'

Cassie put down the book. Usually Elizabeth Taylor held her enthralled, but she couldn't concentrate today. She stood up. 'Sorry. I don't

112

need a day off. Shall I make us some tea?'

'It is a little soon after lunch,' Frances replied, checking her watch. 'What is that awful smell? Something quite revolting wafted this way when you moved.'

'It's muscle rub.' Cassie sat down again, trying to disturb the air as little as possible. 'Barney brought it over. I can stop using it...'

'No, if he thinks you need it, you must use it. He might fuss, but there is no one I would trust more about health issues. He will find out if you stop applying it. He always does.' Frances spoke with resignation, but there was a surprising wobble in her voice. 'Perhaps I should have said before, Cassie, on behalf of the family, how very grateful we are...'

'There's no need,' Cassie said, squirming in her chair. All this attention was enough to make her wish she'd left Barney to the mercy of the tree.

'Yes there is. He is everything to his parents, and I could not manage without him. I suppose it did not cross his mind to thank you himself.'

'He did.'

'He was not always so grumpy,' Frances continued, as if Cassie hadn't spoken. 'He has had a difficult couple of years. It is hard to adjust when the dreams one has cherished for a lifetime are shattered in such a brutal way.'

The context of Frances' words suggested she was speaking of Barney, but the expression on her face revealed a personal angle and Cassie felt as if Frances had lifted the lid on her heart too. But she knew better than to ask questions. She couldn't risk questions being asked of her in return.

'Are there any large barns or outbuildings on the estate that are watertight?' Cassie asked. Frances' comment had again reminded her about Becca's problem, and more potentially shattered dreams.

'You would have to ask Barney,' Frances replied. 'He is in charge of the estate and grounds. I should have mentioned that he has arranged extra shifts for the gardeners to tidy up, and for a tree surgeon to check all the trees are safe, so do not be alarmed if you see strange men wandering around.' Cassie crossed her legs, and flicked an imaginary piece of fluff off her trousers, and wondered how Frances could know her so well. 'Why do you want a barn?'

'Ruth's daughter Becca was supposed to be holding a ceilidh for her engagement party in the village hall. It's a week on Saturday, and she won't be able to find another venue at short notice. I wondered if there might be an empty barn that they could use.'

'A ceilidh?' Frances leaned forward. 'What a marvellous idea. I had such fun at a ceilidh when I was a girl, before...' She broke off, and sat back in her chair. 'Well, it was a long time ago. Of course we must help Ruth's daughter. Ruth is an invaluable member of staff. I see no reason why the ceilidh cannot be held here.'

'Here? You mean in the house?' It had crossed Cassie's mind already, but she had let it ride straight out. As far as she could tell, the villagers didn't come to Ramblings, and Frances didn't go to the village. She had never imagined that Frances would entertain the idea. 'It could work in the hall,' she suggested. 'It's only slightly smaller than the village hall, and the rugs could be moved out.'

'No, that will not do at all.' Cassie felt Frances' blunt response like a wet sponge thrown in her face. 'Why should we use the hall when there is a perfectly good ballroom?'

Of course there was a ballroom. Cassie shouldn't have been so surprised. It sometimes felt that this house was magical, shrinking and growing to accommodate the needs of those living there. When she went exploring later, and saw the ballroom, she was sure she had found the centre of the magic. It was magnificent, there was no other word for it, and it dwarfed all the other rooms that she had seen so far. It must have stretched thirty metres long, with two grand fireplaces along the interior wall, and a row of graceful arched windows along the exterior one. The sun rushed in through the windows, picking out the warmth in the rich wooden floor, and highlighting scratches marked by dancing heels so vividly that Cassie imagined she could feel the draught of giddy couples waltzing past. Glass chandeliers hung down from a vaulted ceiling painted blue but decorated with hundreds of silver stars that would glisten when the bulbs were lit. Cassie wanted to move her bed in and never leave.

Ruth was stunned into an uncharacteristic silence when Cassie told her that Frances had offered the ballroom for Becca's party. She returned to Ramblings the next day to make plans while Becca was at work.

'Fetch the pen and paper, Cassie,' Frances instructed, as the three of them gathered over coffee in the morning room. 'We need to make a list.'

Rarely a day went by without making a list about one thing or another, so Cassie was already prepared.

'Write down cleaning first. It is a while since we used the room. How many people do we need? You two, plus Becca, and put down Melanie and her daughter. I will telephone her later and ask her to come over. What about food?'

'We were having a cold buffet, so there's no problem with that. And the No Name are providing the bar.'

Cassie hesitated, doodling on her pad, and looked up.

'I don't think you can sell alcohol here. You need to be licensed, don't you?'

'We can't have a sober ceilidh,' Ruth said. 'People are travelling down from Scotland. They'll expect a drink.'

'Could you ask people to bring their own?' Cassie suggested. 'I'm sure they won't mind, in the circumstances.'

'I think Mel will mind. She's bought in a shipping order of whisky. She'll never shift it all in the pub.'

'We cannot have the No Name out of profit,' Frances said. 'Ribblemill cannot afford to lose its pub as well as its village hall. I will pay for all the drinks. Consider it my engagement present.'

Ruth made a half-hearted protest, and Cassie a more forceful one, but Frances was determined and ploughed on with the list, ignoring them both. As the paper filled, Cassie marvelled at how Frances had thought of everything, even though the idea had only been suggested the day before. Cassie had never seen her so animated. She loved having a project to keep her mind engaged, and Cassie wondered, when the party was over, what else she could find to fill the days. She was racking her brains when she realised that Frances was calling her name.

'She's being a dilly-daydream,' she heard Ruth say. 'It will be all the wedding talk. She's probably wondering when her own big day will come.'

It would be hard to think of a subject further from Cassie's mind, or one she was less willing to discuss.

'Do you have another point for the list?' She turned over the page. It already seemed impossible that all this could be done in just over a week.

'I forgot about the chimneys,' Frances said. 'We will need to light the fires, and the chimneys will need sweeping first. Barney has the number for the chimney sweep.'

'Do I have to go and ask him?' Cassie couldn't disguise her reluctance. The night of the storm had been too strange, and had shaken her in too many ways. She had hoped to avoid Barney from now on. She had already snuck into his office this morning before he arrived, to return his jumper.

'Ha! Fancy a trip to Malta, do you?' Ruth laughed. 'I don't blame you. It's probably twice as hot over there. I wouldn't have minded going with him.'

'Malta?' Cassie repeated. 'Who's in Malta?'

'Barney. Didn't he tell you he was going?'

'No.' But why should he? They'd hardly ever had a normal conversation. 'Did he go today?'

'Yesterday. Isn't that right, Mrs S?'

'He flew out yesterday afternoon.' So had he been joking when he'd mentioned a date, Cassie wondered? It was none of her business. But it seemed an odd time for him to take a holiday, when the estate needed clearing after the storm, and the village was in crisis. She felt strangely disappointed in him.

'He wanted to cancel his plans, but I refused to allow him,' Frances continued, making Cassie look up from her notepad again. 'His mother would have been terribly disappointed if he missed her birthday. He always goes over for that. Such family loyalty is too rare nowadays.'

It made sense to have the chimneys swept before they cleaned the room, so Cassie went to Barney's office with Ruth to find the telephone number for the sweep. Barney's jumper was still hanging over the back of the chair where she'd left it.

'How long is he away for?' she asked. If it was a long time, she might borrow that jumper again. The central heating worked brilliantly in parts of the house, but in other parts it was switched off. You could open one door and step from the Bahamas to the Arctic.

'Until after the Easter weekend.' Ruth was shamelessly inspecting the room. 'I think I'll clean up in here while he's gone. There are crumbs everywhere.'

'Surely he'll have the chimney sweep's number on his phone? I can't see what we'll find here.'

'Chocolate!' Ruth laughed, and pointed at the desk drawer, which she had opened. Cassie joined her behind the desk. The drawer was stashed full of chocolate bars. Mars Bars appeared to be a particular favourite. They had once been Cassie's favourite too, and her mouth watered at the memory of the sticky caramel layer nestling under the chocolate coat.

'What's this?' Ruth had rooted past the chocolate and pulled out a worn red book, bulging with loose papers. She flicked it open. 'Oh, it's only his diary. I was hoping for something more juicy.'

Page after page was filled with appointments and 'to-do' lists, scrawled in the same black writing that slithered across Ruth's shopping list.

'Does he actually do all that?'

'All that and more. There were two or three people running this place in the olden days. Now there's Barney. What did you think he did down here?'

'I don't know.' She did her best not to think of him at all. 'But Guy said...'

Ruth made a noise that could have come straight from the Barney school of huffs. She didn't approve, that was clear.

'Guy Smallwood? I didn't know you'd been hanging round with him. Don't tell me you were dilly-daydreaming about him? Well, there's nowt so queer as folk...'

CHAPTER ELEVEN

The cleaning team met up on Sunday, after the chimney sweep had proved the power of money by visiting Ramblings on the day that Cassie had called him. Mel surprised everyone by turning up with Gin instead of her daughter Lydia.

'At least Gin won't keep stopping to check her phone,' Mel said, as she deposited piles of dog equipment in the hall. Gin barked at the sound of her name. 'We'll probably get more conversation out of her too.'

'Does she need all this for one day?' Cassie asked, pointing at the basket, bowls and tins of food. 'Anyone would think she was moving in.'

'Funny you should say that.' Mel ran her hand through her hair, making it stick up in a way that would never help advertise her hairdressing business. 'To cut a long and bitter story short, Lydia's pillock of a father – I'm using a stronger word in my head – has whisked her off to Tenerife for the Easter holidays.'

'Akram?'

'Akram's not Lydia's dad!' Mel laughed. 'Hadn't you spotted the obvious difference between them? Lydia is the only good thing I got out of marriage number one.' Mel regarded Cassie, who was fondling Gin's ears. 'You'll take her, won't you?'

'Take who?' The significance of the pile of dog equipment sank in. 'Gin?'

'Lydia was looking after her for Barney, but two weeks in the sun proved more attractive than dog-sitting in Ribblemill. Would you believe it? She's a lovely dog, but she's getting in the way in the pub, and I don't have time to take her out for walks every day. I thought it made sense for her to come here and you can look after her.'

It didn't make sense to Cassie. She couldn't believe that Barney would be any happier about her looking after his dog than about her looking after his aunt. But before she could think of a suitable excuse, Frances appeared from a doorway.

'Of course you will take her, Cassie. I have no idea why Barney did not ask you in the first place. You can take her for walks instead of reading to me this week. You are still too pale. The fresh air will do you good.'

'And here are his keys,' Mel said, handing over a heavy bunch. The key ring was a hammered copper heart with the letter B engraved on it, undoubtedly a woman's choice.

'Why do I need his keys?'

'To check his house. You only need to go every other day. I've been this morning.'

She had to go to his house? This was getting worse by the second.

'I don't know where he lives,' Cassie said, knowing as she spoke that it was never going to be a winning argument.

'The pair of you spend so much time in the same house without talking, you might as well be married!' Ruth replied. 'He lives down at Ramblings Farm. Take the track behind the house and you can't miss it.'

Cassie followed the others to the ballroom to start the cleaning, wondering why Barney hadn't mentioned that he lived on a farm when she had told him where she had been brought up. Unless his wasn't a real farm: perhaps it only retained the name, and had been chintzed up into the romantic vision of a farmhouse, with none of the purpose it would have once had. But two days later, when she took Gin for a walk, she saw Ramblings Farm for the first time, and her heart was lost.

It wasn't simply the house that hooked her – though it was gorgeous, built of huge dark stones broken up by mullioned windows, with a substantial porch set square in the centre. It was the whole scene that filled her with a pleasure as if she'd just come home and sat down in her favourite chair with her slippers on. There was the proper farmyard, cobbled with moss and bits of hay between the stones; the barn with the corrugated metal roof; the mound beside the barn, covered with plastic sheeting weighted down by old tyres; the sweet smell of damp hay that burned through the nose. All the signs were there that this was a working farm, albeit on a smaller scale than Cassie had been used to. It was instantly her favourite place in Ribblemill. It was a shame that her least favourite person in Ribblemill occupied it.

Gin recognised her home, tugged Cassie over to the front door and barked to be let in. The farmhouse was equally perfect inside. It hadn't been prettified at all: everything was plain, useful and well worn. Cassie collected the post from behind the door and added it to the pile on the refectory table, running her hand over the wood and feeling the rough grooves of old knife cuts scratch her fingers. The kitchen led straight through to the living room, also stone flagged and dominated by a massive open fire. A leather wing chair had been placed to one side of the fire, and on the table beside it lay an open copy of *A Tale of Two Cities*. Cassie couldn't bear to see the spine under strain, and closed the book, marking the page with a scrap of paper.

She checked the whole of the ground floor but drew the line at going upstairs, even though she longed to have a look. There were no personal items at all downstairs, so it didn't feel too much of an intrusion: the bedrooms were sure to be another matter. She had known from the moment he had shouted at her on the day she arrived, that she would not set foot in Barney Smallwood's bedroom if it was the last place on earth to shelter from a nuclear attack.

It had been an exhausting week, but by Saturday the ballroom was transformed and looked as if it belonged in a Scottish castle rather than a Lancashire country house. The whole village had rallied round, and throughout the week there had been steady deliveries of tables and chairs, which were now spread round the edge of the room, leaving the centre clear for dancing. White tablecloths with tartan runners hid the fact that nothing matched, and the soft light from the chandeliers would make it perfect on the night.

Balloons and tartan bunting hung along the walls, but when Frances had inspected this morning, she had declared that the Scottish theme was well represented, but the engagement aspect had been lost. She had sent Cassie down into the cellars, where among piles of boxes labelled 'Christmas' and 'Birthday', there had been a couple marked 'Weddings'. Rummaging through these, at Frances' direction, Cassie had pulled out a glossy banner, three foot high, reading 'Congratulations', which was now suspended over the makeshift bar at the far end of the room. One of the boxes had been carefully packed with beautiful glass tealight holders, decorated with the word 'love' in fine metal filigree. Cassie placed one on each table, along with a sprinkling of silver confetti, then stood back and admired the effect. It was certainly a step up from sausage rolls and crisps in the village hall. Becca had been banned from visiting all week, as Ruth wanted it to be a surprise, but she couldn't fail to love it.

'Well done, Cassie,' Frances said, rising from her chair at the back of the room, from where she had been supervising the finishing touches. 'That looks much more the thing.'

'Hello, what's going on here?'

Cassie spun round and saw Guy sauntering into the room. He wasn't expected, as far as she knew; although it wouldn't surprise her if Frances had known and not told her. She had a definite secretive streak.

'I've searched the entire house for you, and this is the last place I've looked. It's lucky I'm not a burglar.'

His smile was bland enough to mask any real feelings, so Cassie had no idea if this was intended as a criticism. She cursed herself for not having locked the door after Ruth left. Thank goodness it hadn't been Barney who found the house unlocked. She could imagine how clear his feelings would have been.

'Guy! You didn't tell us you were coming!' Frances looked delighted. 'Are you staying?'

'Just for tonight.' He bent down and kissed Frances' cheek, and in a seamless movement turned and kissed Cassie's too. Cassie caught a trail of vanilla as he wafted past her. She clenched her hands together, fighting the instinct to scrub her face. 'Am I interrupting something? It must be five years since this room was last used. Is someone getting married?'

'Ruth's daughter, Becca, is holding her engagement party here tonight. Isn't it marvellous to see Ramblings come to life again?'

'Are you sure about this, Mum? We've never encouraged people to come to the house.'

'Your father never encouraged people to come,' Frances corrected him. 'He cut off all ties with the villagers when they opposed that shameful scheme to develop the west fields. I went along with him, to my regret. I think it is high time I made my own decisions.'

'And what does Barney make of what you've done in here?'

'Barney is away visiting his parents.'

'I thought he must be.' Guy laughed. 'So can I gatecrash this party? Kilts aren't compulsory, are they?'

'Not for the English guests.' Frances turned and looked Cassie up and down, in a way that Cassie suspected could mean nothing good.

125

'Cassie, could you meet me in Rome, in an hour? Perhaps in the meantime you could make Guy a sandwich. It will be an excellent opportunity for you two to get to know each other better.'

An hour later Cassie escaped to Rome in relief. Guy wasn't bad company, and she was sure that many women would have been glad to be showered with smiles by one of the heirs to Ramblings. But not her. He had been witty and charming, and so totally inscrutable that she found herself unexpectedly longing for the plain-speaking Barney.

Cassie hadn't been in Rome before, and it turned out to be a strange room filled with wardrobes. A cloud of dust motes enveloped her as she walked in.

'Come in, Cassie, and stop loitering by the door,' Frances said. 'We need to discuss your clothes. I have not seen you wear anything but black since you arrived here. Do you not have anything more colourful?'

'I have a blue cardigan.'

It was the one frivolous item she had allowed herself to bring: a beautiful cropped cashmere cardigan, the colour of the forget-me-nots which grew under the trees at the bottom of the garden where she and Vicky had played as children. Vicky had given it to her for Christmas the year before last. It stayed in the drawer beside Cassie's bed, and sometimes she took it out, and stroked it, and remembered.

'A cardigan?' Frances repeated. 'I suppose that is something. Do you not own a dress, or a skirt?'

'I don't have any with me. I don't need them.'

'Of course you do. You can hardly turn up to the party dressed like that. You will cast a gloom over the celebrations.'

Cassie thought she could manage that even wearing a dress.

'I'm not attending the party,' she said. 'I'll hover in the background in case anything needs doing.'

The look Frances bestowed on Cassie would have repelled an invading battalion.

'Need I remind, you, Cassie, that I am paying you to be my companion. As I am attending the party, so are you. And I will not have you accompany me dressed like that.'

'I'll have to go out and buy something, then.' It was the last thing she wanted to do. How much of her precious savings would she have to waste on a dress for one evening, that she was unlikely to ever wear again? What were the chances of finding something in a charity shop that was her size and could be worn without washing it first?

'There is no need to go shopping. Look!' Frances opened the door of the nearest wardrobe. The rail inside was strung with a display of colourful dresses that would have made a sweet shop look dull. She stroked the skirt of a sapphire-coloured satin dress, and Cassie had a sudden vision of how she must have done that in the past, but with a hand free of wrinkles, without enlarged joints and liver spots.

'These are beautiful,' Cassie said, joining Frances by the wardrobe. The dresses were all 1950s evening dresses, with nipped in waists and full skirts. 'I can't borrow one of these. They

127

must hold so many memories for you. Besides, I think they would be too formal for a ceilidh.'

'They are full of happy memories,' Frances replied. 'These are all dresses I wore before I married. But perhaps they are too much for to-night. I forget that parties today are not what they used to be.' She closed the wardrobe door, and moved on to the next one. 'These are my day dresses. You might find something suitable here.'

'I'm not sure...'

'Cassie.' Frances' eyes were huge behind her glasses, and her expression softer than ever before. 'I have spent years living here on my own, seeing no one. I am a burden and an irrelevance to my children, have no friends, and know nothing of my neighbours. I am discovering, too late, that this is not what I wanted my life to be. Let me be useful. Allowing Becca to hold her party here has given me more pleasure than I could have expected. Lending you a dress, simple though it seems, will give me some more. It is one dress, for one night. Such a tiny thing to you, and such an important one to me. Let me lend you a dress. Go to the party. Have fun. Believe me, when you reach my age you will wish you had taken every opportunity for fun that you were offered.'

Cassie couldn't say no. Not because she was bothered about the party – she would much rather stay in the background – but because Frances wanted to help, and she couldn't turn her down. Feeling useful, making a positive difference to someone's life, was a basic human need, right up there with water, air, and a door that you could close on the rest of the world. She knew too well how damaging each rebuff could be, pushing you down until you no longer believed you had anything worth offering. So she walked over to the wardrobe, and started looking through the rail.

'What about this one?' Frances pulled out a dress, protected by a clear plastic cover. It was simple, but beautiful in summer-sky blue, covered in flowers, sleeveless, with a high neckline, tiny waist and floaty skirt. 'It might go with your cardigan.'

'It's lovely. But it looks brand new.'

'It is. I had it made when we were invited to a garden party at Buckingham Palace.'

'Did you decide to wear something else instead?' Cassie took the bag from Frances and couldn't resist holding it up against herself. The hem skimmed her knee. It looked a perfect fit.

'We did not go. My husband would not allow it, and there was no question of me attending alone.'

Cassie looked up from the dress. Frances' voice dripped with a cocktail of emotion: two measures of bitterness, one of resignation, with a dash of anger and a garnish of sadness. Cassie knew the taste well.

'There are some men,' Frances continued, holding Cassie's gaze, 'who must always have their way, by any means, are there not?'

'Yes.' The plastic bag felt hot and sticky in Cassie's hand. What did Frances know? How could she know anything, when Cassie went to such lengths to reveal nothing? But as they looked at each other, Cassie saw the understanding in Frances' faded blue eyes, and she realised that sometimes words were unnecessary. Sometimes people were so marked by their past that whatever they did to conceal it, the truth was there in every breath, every blink. It was as visible as the hair on their heads to anyone who knew what to look for.

'Go and try it on,' Frances suggested. 'I think it is time this dress came out of hiding and took its turn at a party. We can make our entrance together.'

Becca took one look at the ballroom and burst into tears. Little more than a week ago she'd seen her plans for an engagement party crushed by an enormous tree, and now all her family and friends were gathered in a place that looked magical, with the chandeliers and tea lights bathing everything in a soft glow. Cassie observed it, from her place at Frances' side, and even her withered heart fluttered and sighed at how romantic it all was.

Her plan to lurk in the background had been scuppered by Frances' meddling. The dress was bad enough: it fitted like cling film over her bust, and the clever tailoring made her waist look a fraction of the size it really was. Her legs were exposed to fresh air for the first time in months. But that hadn't satisfied Frances. She had asked Mel to come early and apply Cassie's make up, and arrange her hair so that tousled waves cascaded over her shoulders. Cassie might not have recognised herself in the mirror, were it not for the anxious eyes gazing back at her; nothing in Mel's bag of tricks could change them.

'Chin up, Smiler,' Akram said, sneaking up behind Cassie and whispering in her ear. 'You look like you're queuing to see the dentist, not at a party.'

'I'd take the dentist over this any day.'

Akram grinned. 'Wait till we get you dancing. You'll enjoy yourself then. How do you fancy joining me in the Gay Gordons later?'

'I'm not dancing!'

'How can you turn this down?' Akram shimmied, and his stomach wobbled like a dish of jelly. He peered at Cassie. 'Come on, that deserves a smile, doesn't it?' He leaned closer. 'Help me out here. I've got a bet on with Mel. If you crack a smile tonight, she has to get up for the next early delivery.'

'What makes you think I'd support you over Mel?'

'Charm, good looks, and as much naan as you can eat next time you dine in the pub.'

He might have won his bet, but Frances turned round and inclined her head at him in an impressively regal greeting.

'Akram, would you mind bringing a small glass of sherry over to my table? Melanie should have brought a bottle. What will you have, Cassie?'

'A glass of water, thanks. I'll go and get them. It's looking busy at the bar.'

By the time she had collected the drinks, the Colonel had joined Frances. Cassie watched as Frances' initial stiffness gradually eased, until they were deep in conversation, and scarcely noticed she was there. It suited Cassie perfectly. She relaxed in the shadows, enjoying the music and the guests' attempts to carry out Scottish reels and English country dances. Despite expectations, and though she was a spectator, not a participant, she was having a good time. Or she was, until Guy approached.

'I can't see you sitting here like a wallflower any longer,' he said, waving his whisky glass in Cassie's direction. She recoiled as the hateful fumes invaded her nostrils. 'You're missing all the fun. Come and join me for the next dance.'

'I'm not dancing. I need to stay here with Frances.'

'No, you don't.' Guy smiled, and interrupted Frances with a touch on her arm. 'Mum, you can spare your lovely companion for a while, can't you? I've asked her to dance, but she won't leave you.'

'Of course you must dance, Cassie.' It was hard to tell if Frances was giving permission or an order. 'I never expected you to spend the evening at my side. You young people should be having fun. The Colonel will keep me company. It will be a pleasure to watch you both dancing.'

Cassie followed Guy to the centre of the room, fully expecting that Frances would be the only one experiencing any pleasure over the next few minutes. But then the music started, and it was infectious: the caller shouted out the moves, and they skipped and spun, swapped partners, turned the right way, turned the wrong way, moved in, moved out, and all at once Cassie forgot anything but the dance, and the unexpected joy she felt. She linked arms with Guy, twirled round and round, and she couldn't help it – she laughed, at the sheer silliness of what they were doing. She felt lighter than she had in months.

As she laughed, delighting in a remembered

sense of happiness, a man walked into the ball-room. He had a well-fitted shirt, conker brown hair, a strong chin lightly dusted with stubble, and cheekbones so perfectly sculpted that Rodin would have been proud to copy them. He looked at Cassie, with a long, unblinking stare, and she realised that this man who had stolen her breath and made her internal organs spin faster than the dance, wasn't the stranger she had assumed him to be. The man her eyes were refusing to leave was none other than Barney Smallwood.

CHAPTER TWELVE

'Now there'll be trouble,' Guy said, swinging Cassie back into the dance. 'Look who's walked in. Another unexpected guest.'

'Trouble?' Cassie repeated, as her heart fluttered like an injured bird trying to fly. 'Why should there be trouble?'

'I assume Barney didn't know about any of this?'

Cassie shook her head, and as the dance moves separated her from Guy, watched as Barney remained in the doorway, studying the room.

'Why would he have to know?' she asked, as she caught up with Guy again. 'It isn't his house. You didn't mind the party taking place.'

'True. But I might have done if my wedding reception had been the last event to take place in here, and my decorations were being used again. I think that banner is hanging in exactly the same

133

place.' Guy grinned. 'It must have been quite a blast of déjà vu to walk in here, even with the tartan.'

Cassie pulled Guy out of the dance, a dew of foreboding settling over her skin.

'Is he still married?'

'No, they barely lasted three years. Nessa always was too good for him, and she finally saw sense when he screwed up being a doctor.'

So Barney had arrived home tonight, expecting to pay a quiet call on Frances, and instead had been taunted with a reminder of what must have been the unhappiest time of his life. Cassie's stomach churned. Why had Frances not mentioned where the decorations had come from? Even without the connection to Barney, Cassie wouldn't have used them if she'd known. It was hardly appropriate to celebrate an engagement with decorations left over from a marriage that had failed. As Cassie glanced round the room, those pretty tealights seemed to dim and darker shadows crept into the corners of the room, chasing away the romance.

She caught sight of Barney, stomping through the dancers, heading for the bar. He was repeatedly stopped by people trying to drag him into the dance, and by comments on his clean-shaven chin, judging by the smiles and the number of times he was stroked on the cheek – something the ladies were unable to resist. He smiled and laughed in return, but his movements were stiff and his shoulders tense. She rubbed the base of her thumb, wondering how cross he was, and what she ought to do. If he was cross, it was her fault; if he was upset, it was her fault. She had to apologise. It was the only thing she could do. Sorry wasn't a hard word to say when she'd had years of practice.

Cassie hurried over to the bar, arriving just behind Barney. She reached out and tapped his shoulder, too focused on what she needed to say to acknowledge the firm muscle under her hand.

'I'm sorry,' she said, launching into her speech before he had fully turned round. 'I had no idea you'd held your wedding reception in here, or that the decorations were yours. I would never have used them if I'd known. I can't take the banner down, but I can move the tealights if that would help. I found the box with wedding decorations, because Frances wanted it to be more romantic, but the box didn't have your name on, and Frances didn't mention where they'd come from...'

Cassie dried up when Barney did nothing but stare at her. Then he reached out and pulled her hands apart.

'It doesn't matter,' he said.

Even after a week, Cassie had forgotten how deep his voice was, rich with emotion on the blandest of remarks.

'It was a shock, that's all. It's not a day I want to remember.' He looked up at the banner, which hung down over his head. 'It's amazing that the decorations have survived unscathed. Nothing else did.'

Cassie was wrong-footed. She had made a mistake, and had expected him to be annoyed: it was what she was used to. She studied his face, searching for the tell-tale embryonic signs of anger that

135

she had learned to spot on a different man: the tightening lips, the pulsing in the cheeks as the jaws clenched, the disapproving eyes. None of them were there. In fact, Barney's eyes didn't meet hers at all, and this was so unusual that it told her everything she needed to know. He might sound indifferent about the end of his marriage, but he didn't fool her. He was as messed up inside as she was.

'I'm guessing this is Becca's engagement party.' His eyes were still swooping everywhere but in Cassie's direction. Two faint but distinct frown lines were beginning to deepen. 'Why is it taking place here?'

Cassie thought the answer was fairly obvious – unless he had forgotten the whole tree falling on the village hall incident – but she was spared having to answer by the arrival of Akram and Mel.

'Well, look who it isn't!' Akram said, booming with laughter and slapping Barney's cheeks. 'Were you over your weight allowance on the plane, and had to shed the hair?'

'You're a mean bugger, Barney Smallwood,' Mel said, stretching up to kiss his cheek. 'Hmm, that was a less prickly experience than usual. You know I've wanted to get my hands on you for ages. I suppose it's not a bad job,' she added grudgingly, turning his head from side to side. 'What made you smarten up at last? It's got to be a woman, hasn't it?'

'You're right.' Barney smiled. It was a lopsided smile, fractionally higher on the right than the left. Cassie hadn't noticed that behind the beard. She hadn't noticed, either, how full his lips were, and how well they sat together to form a perfectly shaped mouth. 'My mum insisted that the hair had to go. It was top of her list of birthday wishes.'

'Aye, you have to listen to your mam,' agreed Akram. 'Did you get here in time to witness the other transformation of the night? Smiler here has just been seen laughing.'

'I noticed.'

'I'm easily bought,' Cassie said, and she tested out a smile. It was easier now that the laughter had warmed up muscles unused for so long. 'It was a done deal as soon as you told me about the naan bread.'

'I would never have made the bet if I'd known Guy was going to be here,' Mel protested. 'It's a rare woman who can resist him.'

'You've always said the same about Barney.' Akram slapped Barney on the back. 'No offence, mate, but until now I thought she was joking. You're not a bad-looking lad, now you've scrubbed up. What do you say, Cassie? Does this face make you smile too?'

If only curving her lips was the only effect that face had. She could live with smiling. It was safe, and manageable, and couldn't lead to harm. She couldn't say the same about the merry-go-round that sent her internal organs on a wild spin every time she looked at Barney now. The burst of lust on the night of the storm had been a lovely reminder that her body still worked. She didn't need further proof. Cassie feigned interest in something behind Akram, and pretended she hadn't heard the question.

She sensed Barney shift, and look in the same

direction as her, as if to see what she was finding so absorbing. She focused, and realised she had been inadvertently staring at Guy. He smiled and raised his hand.

'What's Guy doing here?' Barney asked. 'Was he invited? I didn't know Becca knew him.'

'I don't think she does,' Mel said. 'But it is his home. And he's certainly brightened up the evening for more than one woman. You know what he's like.'

'All too well.'

Cassie felt Barney's glance flick over her.

'He's here to visit Frances,' she said. 'He turned up this morning.'

'Again?' The word throbbed with suspicion. 'There must be more to it than that. It's usually months between visits, not days.'

His gaze landed on Cassie again. She adjusted her cardigan, trying to create a draught, as heat slid across her body, making her appear guilty even though he hadn't made any accusation.

'Where is Frances?'

'She's in the corner, talking to the Colonel.' Except the table Cassie pointed at was empty. Neither Frances nor the Colonel was there. 'She was there a moment ago.'

'How long ago?'

'When I started dancing.' She wasn't surprised when Barney responded with a huff. Now Cassie thought about it, she had no idea how long she'd spent dancing. She spotted the Colonel across the room, and headed over to him, Barney close on her heels.

'Colonel, do you know where Frances is?'

'Ah yes, Mrs Smallwood asked me to give you a message. She has retired to bed, but said you were to carry on enjoying yourself and she will see you in the morning.'

'Was she not feeling well?' Barney asked, pushing forward. 'I'd better go and see her.'

'I'll go,' Cassie said. 'She won't be expecting you.'

'I'll be more use if she's not well.'

'I don't think she wants either of you,' the Colonel said. 'She was tired, and went to bed. I'm heading off myself. These late nights are for you young people. Why don't the pair of you go and dance?'

Without needing to confer, Cassie and Barney set off in opposite directions across the room.

Cassie was teased awake by the caress of warm breath on her cheek, and the tender stroke of fingers on her neck. She looked up into eyes the colour of autumn leaves. They were beautiful eyes. She smiled. Then she woke up enough to notice whose eyes they were, and she pulled away, wincing as her neck objected to having been held in an awkward position for too long.

'What's the matter?' Barney drew back, and sat down on the floor in front of her, cross-legged.

'You were touching me!'

'Don't get excited. I was only checking your pulse, to make sure you weren't dead. I couldn't see you breathing.'

'Sorry to disappoint you. You can't get rid of me that easily.'

'So I've noticed.' He smiled, and though it

139

wasn't the slightest bit funny, Cassie felt her lips copying his. 'What are you doing down here?'

The smile fell from Cassie's lips.

'I'm sorry. I shouldn't be here.'

She was in Barney's office. She had only popped down to check on Gin, and had sat down for a few minutes beside her basket. She must have fallen asleep.

'I came to make sure Gin wasn't disturbed by all the noise from the party.'

'Why do you apologise for everything?'

'I don't.'

The Barney stare felt even more potent without the beard, with the intensity of his thoughts etched on every angle of his face. Cassie bent and stroked Gin. The dog had stretched out of her basket, so her head rested on Barney's thigh, her body lay across Cassie's shin, and her tail wagged in contentment.

'I believe I owe you thanks again.' Barney rubbed behind Gin's ears. 'Mel told me that you've been looking after Gin this week. I hope it wasn't too much trouble.'

'None at all. I've enjoyed it.'

More than enjoyed it. She had used her spare time away from Frances and the party planning to take long walks around the estate and the surrounding countryside, Gin at her side. Every mile she walked had been another giant leap away from the past. The peace, and the solitude and the freedom had begun to wipe away the virus that had infected her for so long, and restore her to the person she had once been.

'Come and borrow her whenever you want.'

'Really?' Perhaps Cassie had been too eager. Barney's hand stilled over Gin's ear, and his attention honed back on Cassie.

'Really. She needs as much exercise as she can get. Do you miss having a dog?'

'I miss everything.' His gaze was like a leech, sucking the truth out of her.

'You look pale. Did you catch a cold on the night of the storm?'

'No.' Cassie pushed Gin gently off her leg, and scrambled to her feet. 'I'm not ill. There's nothing wrong with me.'

'OK.' Barney unfolded his legs – long legs, which Cassie had tried not to notice as he sat opposite her, denim straining over his thighs – and stood up.

'Is the party still going on?' She had no idea how long she'd been down here.

'Yes, but only the hard-core Scottish contingent is left. Most of the Ribblemill guests have returned to their beds. I thought you'd left with...' He stopped, and shoved his hands in his pockets.

'I'd better go back. I'll need to lock up when they've gone.'

'I'll do it if you like.'

Cassie only hesitated a moment before nodding to accept his offer. Despite the nap, she was exhausted, and wanted nothing more than to collapse into bed. She opened the door.

'Cassie?'

She turned. Her hand tightened round the door handle as she faced that smile again.

'Do you think I could have my jumper back at some point?'

Cassie glanced down. She had put on Barney's jumper when she came down to the office as it was so cold after the ballroom. She'd forgotten she was wearing it. Stifling a groan of embarrassment, she nodded and walked out.

The next day Cassie headed to one of her favourite places on the estate, where a broad river cut through the trees, and a row of ancient stepping stones led across to a path towards the village. She sat down on a rock overlooking the water and rang Vicky.

'Cassie? Is that you? What's the matter?'

'Nothing. I wanted to hear your voice and wish you a Happy Easter.'

She had thought of little else all through lunch. It had been an awkward family gathering – the hostility between Guy and Barney was so dominant that she may as well have set a fifth place for it. But eating the roast dinner, and feeling Gin settle on her feet under the table, had made her so homesick for the farm that nothing could have prevented her making this call.

'Happy Easter!' Vicky's voice shouted down the phone, bright and chirpy. 'It's manic here. The boys have eaten too much chocolate, and I'm including Stu in that. Stanley!' Vicky bellowed even louder. 'Come and say thank you to Auntie Cassie.'

'No, Vicky, I...'

But it was too late. Cassie heard whispers, and then her nephew's squeaky voice floated down the line.

'Thank you for our Easter eggs, Auntie Cassie.'

'You're very welcome,' Cassie said, mentally thanking Vicky for providing eggs from her. 'Have you done the Easter egg hunt?'

'Yes! I found eighteen tiny eggs and two medium ones, but Alfie only found sixteen tiny ones, because he dropped some on the way back to the house, and they don't count, do they? So that makes me the winner. When are you coming to see us, Auntie Cassie? You're normally here at Easter.'

'I know, and I wish I was with you this year, but I'm busy working.' Cassie dug her nails into her palms, willing herself not to cry or let him hear how wretched she felt about not being there. 'Did you remember to check for eggs in the hollow of the apple tree at the bottom of the garden? There always...'

Stanley didn't wait to hear the rest.

'We've not looked!' he said, and Cassie heard a clunk as the phone was dropped onto the kitchen worktop, and then a squeal of 'Alfie!' that faded away. She could picture the pair of them racing into the garden as clearly as if she were there, and her heart squeezed so tightly that it pushed the lurking tears from her eyes.

'You reminded him about the apple tree, didn't you?' Vicky's grumble was watered down with affection. 'Thanks for that. As if they weren't hyper enough without another burst of sugar... Cass? Are you crying?'

'No,' Cassie lied, as a tear plopped onto the phone. 'Maybe. I miss you all. Tell me what's been going on.'

So Vicky told Cassie how the lambing was going, and what the boys had done at school, and

143

Cassie knew she was making it all sound as funny as she could, to cheer her up, but it worked, because Cassie began to laugh, and once she had started it became so addictive, that she couldn't stop. She thought she must look completely mad, sitting by herself on a rock by the river, laughing, but with each burst of laughter she felt lighter until she thought that with one more gust she might float away, and fly through the air all the way to Devon. But when she tried, she was still by the river, and the coldness of the rock continued to penetrate her trousers.

'I haven't heard you laugh for months,' Vicky said. 'You must be feeling better. Are you happy, wherever you are?'

Happy? Cassie didn't expect to be happy, not any more. But as the river murmured soothing words to her, and as she looked across the water at the fields speckled with lambs, with the roofs of the village in the distance, and the scent of spring in the air, she knew this was as close to happiness as she had come in all the years since leaving the farm. It was better to be in the right place with no one than in the wrong place with someone – especially the wrong someone.

'I love it here,' Cassie replied, and she was surprised how easily the word came off her tongue.

'I'm so glad,' Vicky said, but before Cassie could wonder if there had been almost too much relief in her sister's voice, Vicky ploughed on. 'You weren't too badly hit by the storms last week, were you? They largely passed us by down here.'

'We had a bad night. A couple of trees blew down, one of them on top of the village hall.'

Cassie thought back to that night: the exhilaration of driving the tractor; the crash as the tree plunged through the roof; Barney carrying her back to the pub; the desire that had grabbed her as he had removed his jumper. She decided not to share all that with Vicky.

'That's awful. The main thing is to get everything back to normal as soon as possible. Do you remember when we were children, and our village hall flooded and was out of action for a couple of months? Dad rigged up heat and light in the barn, so all the activities could take place there instead. It was brilliant.'

Cassie had forgotten, but Vicky's words stirred a memory of hiding behind a hay bale and watching the boys from school at their Cubs meeting, wishing she could join them instead of Brownies. An idea crawled into Cassie's head, so obvious that she wondered why no one had suggested it already.

'We held an engagement party in the ballroom last night, instead of in the village hall,' she said. 'It was amazing how everyone pulled together to make it happen.'

'The ballroom?' Vicky laughed, and Cassie remembered that she hadn't told her anything about Ramblings. 'Where exactly are you living? Buckingham Palace? Do you spend your days riding around in carriages and attending garden parties?'

Another idea raced into Cassie's head, leaping and bounding and ringing bells, like a mental Morris dancer.

'Vicky, you're a genius,' she said. 'I miss you so much.'

'We miss you too.'

Vicky fell silent, and goosebumps crept over Cassie's skin, which had nothing to do with the April weather. This was the moment when Vicky usually urged her to go to the farm. They never had a conversation without her saying it. There could only be one reason why she hadn't said it this time.

'Mike's been in touch, hasn't he?'

'Yes.' Vicky sounded as if the word had been dragged out of her under torture. 'He phoned on Friday.'

'What for?'

'To see if you were here. You usually come for Easter.'

'And what did he say?'

'That it was all a misunderstanding. That he'll do anything to get you back.'

Cassie gazed out at the river, and the soothing murmur of the water turned into a vicious, mocking chant. Mike would do anything to get her back. It wasn't a promise. It was a threat.

'I can't come back to you yet.'

'No.' Cassie heard the sob bound up in Vicky's reply. 'You need to stay away. Just for a little while longer, until he gives up, or you're strong enough to resist him. You're getting there. You're sounding so much better today. This is the longest conversation we've had for months. Cassie, you're fantastic. We all love you to bits. Don't let him drag you back down.'

But it was too late. The happiness that had seemed close enough to touch had blown away on the breeze. Cassie walked back to the house by the

146

longest route she could, to give her time to compose herself before seeing Frances. She caught sight of Guy, taking photographs of the fields and Barney's farm, and swept past so he didn't see her. She reached the house and stood on the gravel drive, looking up at the elaborate stonework, all the eccentricities of the architecture that she had come to love. But at that moment she didn't see home, only the grandest form of prison.

CHAPTER THIRTEEN

Cassie waited until Guy had gone home, and Barney was nowhere to be seen or heard, before broaching her idea with Frances. She carried the tea to the morning room – proper china cups and saucers, and a warmed teapot, just as Frances liked it – and put the tray down on the table. Frances' eyes were closed, but she opened them as soon as she heard the tea being poured. She looked tired, Cassie thought, studying her properly for the first time that day. The skin seemed to cling more tightly to her face, and each breath was slow and audible.

'Are you feeling OK?' Cassie asked. 'It was a long day for you yesterday.'

'My day was the same length as yours, I assume,' Frances replied. 'I want none of that nonsense from you. One Barney is bad enough, without you turning into him as well.'

That was enough to make Cassie change the

subject, and she asked about Guy instead, knowing that Frances had enjoyed his visit.

'I saw him outside earlier, taking photographs,' Cassie added. 'He was up near Barney's farm.'

'Yes, he took some around the house too. He has always loved this place. And that reminds me, Hugh telephoned earlier to say that a friend of his will be coming up on Friday to have a look at the house. Would you mind showing him round?'

'Not at all. Is Hugh not coming too?'

'No, he has to work. Apparently his friend is a great admirer of Victorian Gothic architecture, and would like to inspect the whole house. You can show him everywhere except my rooms up-stairs. You can please yourself whether you allow him in your room.'

That was easily answered. Cassie had no in-tention of letting a man into her bedroom ever again, even if he was only interested in the room's aesthetic features.

'Will he want to know the history of the house?' Cassie asked. 'Is there a book in the library about it?'

'No, and I have always thought it a great shame. There have been some marvellously eccentric Smallwoods over the years, and more than their fair share of scandal. The Smallwood who built this house made his fortune in biscuits. You will have heard of the Woods brand? He added the prefix when he moved here, to disguise his con-nection to trade. Small was his wife's maiden name. It was an unfortunate decision, as she ran off with the butler less than a year after the house was finished. He then married Amelia, whose portrait is over the fireplace. He fell in love with her on sight, and rescued her from an unhappy engagement that her father had forced upon her. He gave her the bracelet she is wearing in the portrait, as a symbol that she was his forever wife, not just his second wife. By all accounts they were inseparable, and died within hours of each other.'

Cassie looked at the portrait, studying the beautiful bracelet and the smile of radiant contentment on Amelia's face, and wondered how it must feel to be loved like that. Cassie waited until Frances drank some tea, and her breathing had returned to a settled pattern.

'You should write these stories down,' she said. 'Everyone can see the beauty of the house, but it's only half the tale. Ramblings would be a museum, not a home, without people inside it.'

Frances stared at her for so long that Cassie though she must have offended her.

'It has taken you weeks to work out what I have only lately realised after thirty years. This house is dying. There is no one left to keep it alive with adventures and stories. It needs people.'

Cassie put down her cup and leaned towards Frances. There would never be a better opening for the idea that had taken shape while she sat by the river. Now she had to convince Frances that this would work. Her back-up had gone. She had no future beyond Ramblings, and she needed her time here to be a success. She needed to become indispensable.

'There is a way to let more people in,' she began. 'I was thinking about it earlier. I know that letting Becca hold her party here was a favour to

Ruth, but it showed how brilliantly the ballroom could work as a substitute for the village hall. Mel told me that some of the groups who use the hall have disbanded, because they have nowhere suitable to meet. Would you allow the village to use the ballroom for all the meetings?'

Frances said nothing.

'It will probably only be a temporary arrangement,' Cassie rattled on, her heart thumping, wondering if she had blown everything. 'Only until the hall can be repaired or rebuilt.' If that was possible. She hadn't asked. She might be making a promise that was impossible to keep. 'No one would come into the part of the house you use. And if you like, you could choose which groups could meet here, or do a test run with a couple of them and see how it goes. I can make all the arrangements. It needn't trouble you at all.'

'No,' Frances said, and Cassie wilted. 'I want to be involved. I will not sit in seclusion in my own quarters listening to life go on elsewhere. I have spent long enough doing that. There will be no selection of groups. Everyone who met at the hall must now come here. Ramblings was once the centre of this village, and it is time it took its place again. I believe the Colonel is in charge of the village hall. Ring him up, Cassie, and tell him to come for tea. We have much to do.'

The Colonel came round for afternoon tea on Thursday, and Cassie outlined the plan to him.

'That's a generous offer, Mrs Smallwood,' he said, picking up a crustless cucumber sandwich with a faint frown of bewilderment. Frances had been most particular about the menu. 'But perhaps before you commit to anything, I should explain the nature of some of the groups who used the hall.'

'The nature?' repeated Frances, and her look of horror was so acute that Cassie had to hide a smile behind her teacup. 'Whatever do you mean, Colonel? Surely none of the activities are illegal?'

'Goodness, no, that's not what I meant at all,' the Colonel said. 'I was thinking more of the young people. The mums and toddlers meet on Wednesday morning, the Cubs, Scouts, Brownies and Guides through the week, and the Youth Club on Friday night. They can sometimes be messy and boisterous. You may not appreciate the noise.'

'I will have abundant silence when I am in my grave, Colonel. Children are exactly what we need around the house. As the weather improves perhaps they can use the gardens too.'

'I'll need to check the insurance – public liability and so on – but if that's not a problem we'll be delighted to accept. I should warn you that it's going to be months before the village hall is back up and running, maybe as long as a year. You'll have to put up with us for quite some time.'

'That does not worry me at all, Colonel.'

There was a brittleness in Frances' voice at odds with her words, and her mouth opened and closed a few times as if she were deliberating whether to say more.

'Why will it take so long?' Cassie asked, when Frances stayed silent. 'Will it not be covered by insurance?'

'Storm damage is covered in principle, but

they've got wind of the fact that the roof was in a bad way. That needs to be resolved before we can even think of rebuilding.' The Colonel helped himself to a biscuit. 'I've put Barney in charge of dealing with the insurers. He knows how to talk to people.'

Or shout at them, as Cassie assumed the Colonel meant. Although to be fair, she reflected, guilt poking at her conscience, he hadn't shouted at her for a few weeks now. Perhaps he was becoming resigned to her presence. She hoped so. If they could maintain a state of mutual tolerance while largely avoiding each other, it would make life at Ramblings much less complicated.

'You must telephone Cassie and let her have a list of all the clubs, so we can be prepared. Is there anything else we need to ask for now, Cassie?'

'I don't think so. But I did have another idea.' Cassie took Frances' tilt of the head as permission to speak. 'I wondered if we could set up a community library, perhaps on Saturday morning if nothing else happens then.'

'Good idea,' the Colonel said. 'But I don't think Mrs Smallwood will thank you for lending out her books. We've no money to buy new ones.'

'I wasn't thinking of using the books from Ramblings. We could ask for donations. If everyone in the village gave one or two used books we'd have a decent collection to start off with.'

'It could work,' the Colonel said to Frances. Cassie felt as if she were waiting for permission from her parents.

'I think it is a marvellous idea. Perhaps we can supply tea and coffee, for a small donation. But

152

how will we keep track of the books?'

'I could borrow Mel's computer and set up a spreadsheet,' Cassie suggested. She couldn't believe how well this idea had gone down. Frances was as animated as when they had been planning Becca's party.

'Do you know how to do that?'

'Yes.' Cassie hesitated. 'I used to be a PA.'

Confessing that much of the past, even in passing, sent a wave of nausea rolling over her. Frances turned towards the Colonel in enquiry.

'I believe it's the modern-day term for a secretary,' he explained.

'Now I understand your proficiency with lists,' Frances said, but the intense look she gave Cassie suggested she understood much more than that.

It was late afternoon when the Colonel left. Cassie was bolting the front door behind him when she heard the heavy, purposeful tread of footsteps that could only mean Barney.

'Was that the Colonel?' he asked. He was wearing the jumper she had returned to him, though it wasn't a cold day.

'Yes.'

'Was he here to see me?'

'No.' Barney's gaze expected elaboration, and Cassie gave in. 'He was visiting Frances.'

'Frances? Since when has Frances received visitors?'

'She met him at the party and invited him for afternoon tea.'

Barney appeared too surprised to speak – something that Cassie thought was worth bearing in mind for future reference. But how sad it was, that he should he so surprised. Had Frances really never had a visitor before, who wasn't family, or paid to be there? What sort of life was that?

'And that's all there was to it? Tea and a chat about the good old days?'

'There were biscuits and cucumber sandwiches too.'

It wasn't the detail he was looking for, and he acknowledged that with a flash of uneven smile. But Cassie was reluctant to tell him the real reason for the Colonel's visit. He was going to find out sooner or later – it was becoming increasingly apparent that he was a vital part of the village, and no one sniffed without consulting him – but she would prefer it to be later, and preferably from someone else. She had an uneasy feeling that there would be trouble when he found out; and life at Ramblings was so much better when he smiled than when he frowned.

CHAPTER FOURTEEN

The next couple of weeks rushed by as preparations got underway to transform the ballroom into a makeshift village hall. Cassie rolled into bed exhausted each night, wondering how her simple job as a companion had morphed into that of village dogsbody; but she wasn't complaining – she loved it. She was being useful and making a difference. Frances and the Colonel had said that they couldn't have managed without her. She had sucked in that compliment and nurtured it until she had felt little shoots of self-confidence rise up, fragile but undeniably there.

The idea for the community library had gone down well. Mel's daughter, Lydia, had designed a poster asking for book donations to be brought to the pub. The response had been so overwhelming that today, for the second time in a week, Cassie had used her break – now a somewhat theoretical concept – to go down to the No Name to collect them. She was carrying a box towards the ball-room when she walked into Barney. Barney swore.

'Sorry,' Cassie said, holding the box in front of her like a shield. 'Are you hurt?'

'Probably a few broken ribs and a punctured lung, but I expect I'll live.'

He was clearly joking, unusual though it seemed.

'Sorry. I wasn't looking where I was going.'

'I noticed.'

Barney rubbed his chest. His shirt was a snug fit. Cassie looked back to his face.

'You seem happy. What's in the box?' he asked.

'Books for the library.'

'The library?' Barney laughed. 'You could take away a hundred books and no one would notice. Has Frances ordered more?'

'No, they're for the community library,' Cassie said, and then cursed herself, because she hadn't intended to be the one to tell him. It was clear from his frown that he hadn't known until now.

'I saw a poster about that in the pub. Why are the books coming here?' He worked out the answer before Cassie could reply. 'The library is going to be here? At Ramblings? Does Frances know?'

'Of course she does.'

'But she doesn't invite people to the house. I thought Becca's party was a one-off. Is she sure about this?'

Cassie nodded. Judging from the question, Barney didn't yet know about the other plans for the ballroom. If she kept her mouth shut, surely he wouldn't be able to draw it out of her with that penetrating stare of his.

'You will make sure she doesn't overdo it, won't you? I know what she's like when she gets an idea in her head. She forgets her limitations.'

He spoke affectionately, but Cassie still felt a prickle of irritation on Frances' behalf. So she was old – it didn't make her incapable. Frances' children might think she was, but she had expected better from Barney. He paused for a response, and she nodded again.

'It's a great idea. I've some books at home I can donate. Shall I bring them in?'

Cassie nodded for the third time, and set off down the corridor towards the ballroom, certain that Barney's suspicious stare was following her all the way.

Judging by the crowd and the noise, the whole village had turned out to support the opening of the library. Children played in one corner of the ballroom, people stood and chatted over tea and coffee, and the books flew off the shelves. Frances was in her element. She sat in a grand chair – rather throne-like, Cassie had thought, but Frances had insisted – and shared a word with everyone who passed, with a reserved but undoubtedly genuine pleasure. She caught Cassie's eye and smiled, and gave a tiny bow of her head. Cassie understood. This had been a success, and there was every reason to think that the meetings of the village groups, starting next week, would be too. Ramblings had come alive.

Fifteen minutes before noon, when the library was due to close, the happy atmosphere was shattered by a cantankerous cry.

'Mother! Mother!' Diana's voice reverberated down the corridor long before she arrived in the entrance to the ballroom, resplendent in pristine jodhpurs, knee-high riding boots and a quilted Musto gilet. The outfit didn't show her figure to any advantage

She marched over to Frances' throne, the thud of her boots echoing around the now silent room.

'What's going on, Mother? I've just been welcomed to my home by a stranger.'

'I expect that was the Colonel,' Frances replied. 'He is a charming man, Diana, and not at all strange.'

'But what's he doing here? And why are all these people in the ballroom?'

'It is not the ballroom today. It is the village library.' Frances looked at her watch. 'You still have ten minutes to select a book if you would like to borrow one. Take it to Cassie and she will check it out for you. I think we can allow you to be an honorary villager.'

Cassie focused on her computer screen, as she typed an entry into her spreadsheet, but the vibes of Diana's displeasure were hard to ignore.

'Why are you holding a library here? Do Hugh

and Guy know about this? I thought there was a community centre in the village?'

'There was, but it was destroyed in those terrible storms a few weeks ago.'

'Really? One of our fence panels blew over and splintered. It was incredibly inconvenient to have it replaced.'

She was deadly serious. Cassie had to glance over to check. Diana really was comparing the damage to one piece of her fence to the village losing the hall. Ethel slapped a Maeve Binchy down on the desk.

'Awful woman,' she said to Cassie, leaning over the computer, in a whisper that could surely have been heard by the Colonel in the hall. 'She was an awful child too. Used to kick up such a stink if I didn't let her jump the queue in the shop!'

Cassie smiled, and her eyes flicked back to Diana in time to catch a glare so full of daggers it was a wonder her eyeballs weren't bleeding.

'Did you have to do this today, Mother? You knew I was coming.'

'I don't believe I did know that.' Frances denied it, but Cassie heard the subtle undercurrent of doubt in her voice. 'When did you tell me?'

'I left a message.'

'With Cassie?' Frances looked over at Cassie, who shook her head.

'On the machine, Mother. You have an answering machine attached to the telephone. I left you a message to say that we were going to come over today and ride the estate.'

'Has Grace come with you?' Frances peered past Diana, her face radiating pleasure as she looked for her granddaughter.

'No, it's Grace's day to help at the stables.' Diana put her hands in the pockets of her gilet, and threw back her shoulders. 'I've brought a friend.'

There was something odd about the way Diana said this, and she was blinking far more than Cassie thought normal.

'Where's Barney? I need to check where it's safe to ride. I don't suppose the bridleways have been used for years, and there may have been damage in the storms.'

'I presume he is in the office, or at the farm. Cassie, did he tell you what his plans were for the rest of the day? You spoke to him this morning.'

'He didn't say.'

Cassie joined in the conversation reluctantly. Diana's strident voice had driven away the last few lingering visitors, and only Ruth remained, clattering cups and saucers on the other side of the room, and trying to pretend she wasn't listening.

'He only brought a couple of books,' she added.

They had barely spoken. He had asked if the books would be of any use, and she had confirmed they would. He had said the library was looking great, and had smiled. Cassie couldn't remember if there had been any further words after that.

Diana checked the office and tried telephoning Barney but without success.

'You'll have to go and find him,' she said, pointing her phone at Cassie as if it were a remote control that could force Cassie to do what she wanted.

'Me?' Cassie couldn't see how she was involved in this. 'I'm tidying the library.'

'That can wait.' Diana waved the phone at

Cassie. 'It won't take long to walk up to the farm and collect him. If you've been sitting at the desk all morning, the exercise will do you good.'

The exercise would have done Diana even better, and Cassie could tell from the ponderous silence that she wasn't the only one thinking that. Frances cleared her throat.

'You do seem wan, Cassie, after being cooped up in here,' she said. 'Would you mind going to see if Barney is available, please? I am sure you will enjoy a walk in the sunshine.'

Cassie would enjoy a walk, if she could choose her own route, one that took her in the opposite direction to Barney's farm. It was the one part of the estate she tried to avoid, and not only because of him. It made her more homesick than any other place, but she couldn't refuse Frances, so she set out towards the farm, along the track which led north from Ramblings, and which provided the only vehicle access to Ramblings Farm.

Cassie had barely travelled twenty metres from the house when she was confronted by a man leading a huge chestnut horse. She stepped to the side to let them pass. This must be Diana's mysterious friend, she presumed, as he was wearing an almost identical outfit – hat, boots and jodhpurs. While the clothes emphasised all the wrong bulges in Diana's figure, it highlighted all the right ones on him. Cassie watched him go, objectively aware that he was an attractive man, and equally aware that she wasn't feeling the slightest flicker of desire. So that must be it: back to normal after a last brief rally of lust. And it was a relief, in the main, not to be bothered with feelings that were unwanted, and were destined never to be acted upon. She had done with the highs and lows. If her emotions could flatline for the rest of her days, that would be good.

She trudged along the path, relishing the warmth of the sun sinking into her skin. As the track turned, Cassie saw the farmhouse ahead, sunshine washing over the stone and making the windows sparkle. And then she spotted Barney.

He was knocking a wooden post into the ground, and a row of other posts lay behind him, ready to form a fence around a field. He was wholly absorbed in the job, muscles flexing as he moved in a perfect rhythm that was mesmerising. A patch of sweat darkened his T-shirt where it clung between his shoulder blades. There was no flatlining now. Cassie was shaken by a jolt of lust well off any scale she had known before.

She didn't think she'd made a sound – she desperately hoped she hadn't – but Barney turned round and saw her. He dropped his mallet and wiped his face on the arm of his T-shirt.

'Hello.' He smiled. It did nothing to help Cassie control the lust. 'What are you doing here?'

'I was sent to find you.'

'What's wrong?' He took a step forward. 'Is it Frances? Why didn't you ring?'

'You didn't answer your phone.'

Barney patted his pockets, but Cassie could have told him his phone wasn't there.

'I must have left it in the house. What's the matter? Isn't she feeling well?'

'Frances is fine. Diana wants you.'

'Diana? Diana's here? Is she ill?'

'No one's ill,' Cassie snapped. He really was infuriating. They could have been halfway back to Ramblings by now if he'd stop all the questions. 'Diana has come to ride round the estate, and wants you to tell her where it's safe to go.'

'She's brought her horse all this way? It would have made more sense to ring before she came.'

Cassie had thought the same thing, but it wasn't her place to say it. She turned to walk away, having delivered her message, but Barney called after her.

'Do I have to come now? I was hoping to finish this side of the field today.'

'Are you getting some animals?' Cassie wandered back. She might prefer to avoid him, but farm talk was irresistible.

'Eventually. A small flock of sheep to start off with. Joe is teaching me all he knows.'

'What breed? The Lonk is native here, isn't it?'

'Yes. How have you heard of that? I'm going to have Herdwick, but I want to specialise in rare breeds when I know more.'

'How much land belongs to the farm?' Cassie looked across the field, to where a fence had already been constructed around the far perimeter. A scrubby piece of land lay on the other side, and an extensive field beyond that. 'Does it end at the fence?'

'Yes, for now. The fields on the other side are part of Joe's farm, which I'll take over when he retires. This strip of land in the middle is a problem.' He scratched his chin, seeming to forget the beard was no longer there. 'The original owner of Ramblings Farm fell out with the first Smallwood and kept hold of that strip when he sold the land to build the house. It means that the only access to the farm is past Ramblings. Apparently he took great delight in parading his animals up and down, especially when the Smallwoods had visitors. If I owned that land I could make a more direct route out to the road, as well as linking the fields together.'

'Can you buy it?'

'Possibly.' Barney pulled his sticky T-shirt away from his body, giving Cassie an unexpected and unwelcome flash of his chest. 'The owner died a while ago, and I've heard it may come up for auction soon. I can't think who else would want to buy it.'

Cassie leant on the post that Barney had so recently hammered in, and considered the lie of the land.

'Have you thought about pigs?' she asked. 'There are some fantastic rare breeds you could consider. My brother-in-law has Berkshire pigs. If you fenced off over there' – she pointed past the farm – 'they could wander through the wood as well.'

'That's a good point.'

Barney had moved next to her, and was looking where Cassie was pointing. She had never been so aware of someone. Her body seemed tuned to his, picking up every breath, every blink, every twitch.

'Do you think...' He turned, and as he looked at her his words died away. He took a step back and folded his arms across his chest. 'Sorry,' he said. 'I forgot I wasn't talking to Joe.'

'Thanks.'

163

So he'd confused her with a wizened old man? At least he was honest about it. And at least it confirmed that he didn't reciprocate her feelings of lust. That would have been a disastrous complication.

He grinned. 'I didn't mean...'

'It doesn't matter.'

Cassie knew he was gazing at her. She could have sworn she felt the sweep of his eyes over her face.

'Why are you here?'

'I told you. Diana...'

'No,' he interrupted. 'Why are you in Ribblemill? Why aren't you managing your own farm, or living as a farmer's wife with a brood of apple-cheeked children at your feet? What drove you to this half-life, when it's clearly so far-removed from what you want?'

He genuinely wanted to know, she could see that, and his forehead bore faint creases of frustration that he couldn't work it out. She wondered what he would do if she told him the truth. Whose side would he be on? Would he believe her? It sounded far-fetched even to her, and she had lived through it. The temptation to tell him suddenly and inexplicably burned in her brain. She forced herself to walk away without answering.

Frances was all for an immediate invasion of village activities in the ballroom, but the Colonel and Cassie persuaded her that introducing them gradually might be best. They would start with a few low-key meetings – the WI, the OAP's bingo club, and the knit and natter group – and build up only if Frances was sure she was happy and not inconvenienced. Within a week Frances had torn up their careful plans. She wanted to hear children's voices echoing around the house again. Ruth and Cassie had spent the last hour making an army of gingerbread men for the first meeting of the mums and toddlers group, at Frances' insistence, and were waiting for the last batch to bake, when the kitchen door crashed open.

Cassie hadn't seen Barney so angry since the early days of her stay at Ramblings. It was interesting to see how well he could bristle even without the beard. It was just a shame he was bristling at her.

'What's going on?' he demanded. 'I found Frances trying to carry a box of books into the ballroom. I thought you were in charge of the library.'

'Books?' Cassie repeated. 'There aren't any more books for the library.' She groaned, and spoke to Ruth. 'She did mention that there were some children's books in the cellar. I told her the mums and toddlers would bring everything they need. She must have gone down to get them while we were here.'

'There's no stopping her when she's got an idea in her head,' Ruth said. 'She's as stubborn as a mule. But if I make it to her age, I'm not going to do what I'm told either. Why should I?'

'It's your job to make sure she does what she's told,' Barney said, glaring at Cassie.

'I don't think it is...'

'And what's all this about mums and toddlers?' he interrupted, not waiting to hear Cassie out. 'Why are they coming here?'

165

'They always meet on Wednesday morning.'

'Not here.'

'They do now the village hall is out of use.'

Cassie shrivelled under Barney's glare.

'Are you telling me that the ballroom is now being used as a makeshift village hall for every group that wants it? Every day of the week?'

She wasn't telling him anything. She had been very careful never to add 'tell Barney what we're doing' to any of the lists she had drawn up. She'd had so many things to do. Surely it wasn't too much to have expected someone else to do that one tiny, terrifying thing?

'Didn't you know, love?' Ruth asked, giving a masterful performance of stating the obvious. 'I thought someone would have mentioned it to you by now. It's a great idea, isn't it?'

'Someone should have mentioned it to me.' He hadn't moved his gaze from Cassie. There could be no doubt which someone he had in mind. 'Could we have a word please? In my office.'

The kitchen door banged. Ruth nudged Cassie.

'I think he means you. Grumpy today, isn't he? Here, take him some gingerbread.' She thrust a gingerbread man on a napkin into Cassie's hands. The red iced smile seemed entirely inappropriate. 'It might sweeten him up. Perhaps he hasn't had his sugar fix this morning.'

Cassie shuffled down the corridor to Barney's office with all the reluctance of a school child summoned to the headmaster's office. She hovered outside, hoping he might be on the telephone so she had an excuse to slip away, but all was quiet. Clinging to a feeble hope that he

166

might not be there, she knocked, and walked in. Barney was standing by the window, hands in his pockets. He turned when Cassie entered.

'This won't take long. You didn't need to bring a snack.'

'Ruth sent it for you.' Cassie put the biscuit down on the desk, in the one clear space she could find among the shower of paper. She decided not to repeat the 'sweeten him up' comment. He didn't look in the mood to find it amusing.

'Tell me what's happening in the ballroom.'

'The mothers and toddlers are meeting there.'

He waited.

Cassie crumbled. 'Frances has agreed that all the organisations that used to meet in the village hall can use the ballroom instead. It's only until the hall can be rebuilt,' she added. That detail didn't soften his face.

'That won't be for months. Has she any idea, how many groups there are?'

'Yes. We've drawn up a timetable.'

'And does she know what they all are? Does she really want horny teenagers lurking in dark corners of the house, getting up to God knows what? What made her think this was a good idea?'

It might have been a rhetorical question, but Cassie's face answered it, and for once her flush of guilt was entirely justified.

'You? You put her up to this?'

'I didn't put her up to anything. I might have made the suggestion, but she was happy to do it.'

'What the hell were you thinking? This is too much for her. She's...' He hesitated. 'She's an old lady.'

'You're as bad as her children. She's old, not senile. She's perfectly capable of deciding what she wants to do in her own home. I thought *you* might have been able to see that.'

'I see a lot more than you do. You have no idea what's going on here. You're paid to look after her and keep her out of any harm. You're putting her at risk. You have to stop this.'

Did she? It seemed to Cassie that here was another man thinking her useless, looking at her with eyes full of disappointment and reproach, and telling her what to do. Cassie didn't see Barney in front of her: she saw a bully – another one. Suddenly she couldn't take it any more: not here, not now, and not from him. She took a deep breath. She had to fight back, for herself and for Frances.

'I'm not stopping anything. Frances wants to do this and I'm going to help her. How can you think I'd put her at risk? Haven't you spoken to her over the last couple of weeks? She's happy, and bright, and alert, and loving being useful. She's meeting new people. She's fulfilled, which is more than she was when I arrived. What were you thinking, letting her moulder away here on her own?'

'I was thinking about what was best for her. I'm more interested in her being well than entertained.'

'You're pulling rank because you were a doctor? But you're not now, are you? You're no more a doctor than I am. And, as I heard that you killed your last patient, I don't know why anyone would take advice from you about keeping well.'

Cassie regretted the words long before she witnessed desolation steal over Barney's face, taking

168

away all colour and animation. A crushed expression that she recognised too well hung over him. She knew how those emotions worked. She stepped forward at the same moment that he stepped back, their movements co-ordinated as if they were dancing.

'Let me guess,' he said, in a flat voice. 'That nugget of information came from Guy, didn't it?'

Cassie nodded, all bravado gone. What had she done? Her words had flown out without thought and she had hurt him. She had more reason than most to know how devastating words could be, and now she had discovered that causing pain was a thousand times worse than receiving it. She would gladly hear hours of abuse from Mike to be able to rewind the last few minutes. How could anyone set out deliberately to hurt someone like this and take pleasure from it? She saw the truth at last. No normal person could. Only a cruel, unnatural human being could take satisfaction from seeing another brought down. Nothing that had happened to her had been her fault. She wasn't the abnormal one. She had thought she was, but she wasn't. Accepting that made Cassie's earth spin a fraction, twisting her away from the darkness and back towards the light.

CHAPTER FIFTEEN

'Am I not paying you enough, Cassie? You must let me know if I am not.'

'Sorry?' Cassie had begun to write this down, before realising that it was a question and not part of the history of Ramblings that they had now started to record. 'You do pay me enough. I haven't complained.'

'I know. You never complain about anything. But your clothes...' Frances glanced at Cassie and shook her head. 'This constant black makes me think you are preparing for my funeral. You are wearing the same things now that you did in February. Surely you are too warm. Look at the weather! The sky is flawless.' She sighed. 'It is the sort of day that makes one wish to feel the sea breeze and smell the sea air one last time.'

'Does it?' Cassie put down her pen and swivelled round in her chair. 'Do you want to go to the seaside? How far from the coast are we? I could drive you there.'

'My travelling days are over. I have not ventured further than the church in ten years.'

'That doesn't mean you can't.'

Cassie thought it was more likely that no one ever asked if Frances wanted to go anywhere else. It was convenient for her family to have her safely ensconced in Ramblings, out of harm, as Barney would say, but out of the way of any pleasure too.

'We can make a day of it. You know we won't be travelling very fast in the Volvo, and we could stop whenever you wanted. You wouldn't even need to get out of the car if you didn't want to. We could take a flask and have a cup of tea over-looking the sea.'

'Would you like to go, Cassie?' Frances smiled. 'You rarely leave the house or garden even on your day off. You should go out more. You can borrow the Volvo whenever you like.'

'Me? No, I was only thinking of what you might like.' Although that was a lie. As soon as Frances had mentioned the sea breeze, Cassie had imagined she could feel the north Devon wind rushing through her hair, and had longed to be able to walk along the headland again.

Frances studied Cassie.

'You do make it sound tempting,' she said, and Cassie smiled. 'But I could not bear to have a day out with you dressed like that. You would cast such a gloom over the occasion. Perhaps if you could buy something brighter?'

'I can't use my wages on clothes,' Cassie said.

Money was far too precious to fritter away. And after years spent dressing to please someone else, the freedom to please only herself was even more precious.

'Of course you can. It makes no odds to me what you do with it.' Frances looked at Cassie shrewdly. 'Or do you mean you won't use it for that? Are you saving for something particular? If I can help, you need only ask.'

Did she mean it? Cassie's fingers curled round the spindles on the back of her chair, and she held

171

on tight, as if to prevent herself from holding out her hands and begging. Would Frances really lend her the money she needed? It was tempting – but she could never ask. She needed too much; and besides, she could never take advantage of Frances.

'Cassie?'

'One day,' Cassie replied, picking the one part of the truth that she felt she could reveal, 'I'd like to have a house of my own. Or a flat. Anywhere,' she admitted, 'as long as I can lock the door, with me on one side and the world on the other.'

'Oh Cassie,' Frances said. 'I understand that feeling better than you know. What do you think I have been doing all these years? But when you have a place of your own, let it be a retreat and not a prison. Or one day you will find your face looks like mine, the lock on your door has grown stiff, and your useless hands can no longer open it. The world isn't all bad. There will be someone you can trust with a key to your door. You must keep on looking for them.'

Cassie turned back to the desk, and doodled on her notepad. Sometimes Frances read her mind so well it was scary, but she couldn't have been further off the mark this time. Cassie wasn't looking for anyone, and had no intention of ever looking again. She heard a chink as Frances placed her cup back on the saucer.

'I have a proposal. If you agree to borrow some more of my old clothes – the ones that are not too dated – I will allow you to drive me to the seaside.'

'Are you trying to bribe me?'

'I would never be so vulgar.' Frances smiled,

and Cassie laughed. She picked up her pen again.

'Are you ready to carry on?'

They had been doing this for a week now. Cassie had suggested that Frances might like to make a record of her knowledge of the Smallwood family and Frances had wanted to start at once. As all she had to do was sit in her chair and talk, drinking occasional cups of tea, Cassie didn't think that anyone could object that she was overtaxing Frances.

'Why are you writing by hand today? I thought Melanie had lent you her computer?'

'She did, but she needed it back as she's working on the accounts. I don't mind writing.'

'But you are a remarkably fast typist. Why not ask Barney if you can borrow his computer?'

'There's no need for that.'

'Nonsense. Call him now, and he can bring it straight up.'

'He'll be using it. We don't need to trouble him.' Cassie hoped that Frances had been convinced to let the subject drop. She was met by a shrewd look.

'Barney has been particularly sore-headed recently. Have the pair of you had words?'

The guilt was too raw for Cassie to deny it. Frances had summed the situation up perfectly. They had had words, mainly unpleasant ones, and mainly from Cassie.

'Yes. He wanted me to stop the activities going on in the ballroom.'

'He asked you to stop it? On my account, I presume.'

'Yes.'

'And you refused.'

Cassie nodded. It was impossible to read Frances' thoughts, and to know whether she had done the right thing or not, but she couldn't lie.

'Thank you,' Frances said. 'I appreciate your support very much. If I cannot be allowed to choose my own course now...' She drifted off, and didn't finish her sentence. 'Try not to be too hard on Barney. He never speaks of it, but this is a particularly difficult time of year for him.'

'Is it? You mean on the farm?' Cassie wondered how he would cope when he had animals, if he was finding it tough now.

'I know nothing about the farm. That is entirely Barney's business. I meant that it was around this time of year when the trouble developed at the hospital.'

'When his patient died?' The words fell from Cassie's lips before she could think better of it.

'It was not his patient. You should not believe everything you see in the newspaper. I would not trust the journalists who came here to report the date of Christmas accurately.'

Frances' lips were pressed together so tightly they had almost disappeared.

'It was all so unfair. If only they had seen him as a boy! He was the most delightful child. We all doted on him. All he ever wanted was to be a doctor and to look after people. He received a plastic doctor's case one Christmas and after that we never saw him without a stethoscope round his neck and a bandage in his hand.' Frances smiled. 'He would run about the village, asking if anyone needed help from Doctor Barney. It meant everything to him.' The smile withered. 'I will never forgive that woman for letting him give it up.'

Cassie didn't understand most of what Frances was saying. There were a thousand questions she wanted to ask, but Frances had closed her eyes, and was shaking with dry coughs. Cassie put down her pen and crossed the room.

'Frances?' she said, reaching out for Frances' hand. It was cool, and the soft wrinkled skin slid over the bones as Cassie grasped it. 'Do you want to stop for today? Would you like to go upstairs to rest?'

'I think I will.'

The words were faint. The usual vitality and strength of character that transformed Frances were gone, and a tired old body sat in her chair.

'There is no need for you to help, Cassie. Perhaps you could bring me some tea in a couple of hours. You should have a rest yourself. You look too pale again. I hope you are not sickening for something.'

It wasn't illness that was making Cassie's cheeks pale, and keeping her awake at night: it was guilt. She had never regretted anything in her life as much as accusing Barney of killing a patient – and in a life so full of regret, that was quite something. The tantalising conversation with Frances had made it worse. The picture of the cute little boy with his plastic stethoscope was so strong in her head that she couldn't stop wondering how he had turned into the man who stormed and huffed his way through life. What had happened to bring about such a transformation? She had to find out.

175

Two nights later, having settled Frances for the evening with the remote controls for the television and the radio, Cassie claimed a night off and drove down to the No Name. She slipped in through the kitchen door and met Mel.

'I've left the laptop in the living room,' Mel said. 'Top of the stairs, second on the left. You can bring it down here if you want. The snug's quiet.'

'No, I'll be fine upstairs.' Cassie had been caught in the snug before. She definitely didn't want it to happen again.

Mel grinned. 'Need privacy, do you? That sounds fun. Just make sure you clear the search history, OK?' She laughed. 'Lydia sometimes uses the laptop if hers isn't working, and I wouldn't want her to see anything she shouldn't.'

'It's nothing like that!' Cassie protested. 'I only need to Google something.'

'That makes it even more intriguing. If you're looking up how to order a hot Russian husband, make sure you bookmark the site. You never know...'

Laughing, Cassie ran upstairs while Mel returned to the bar. She turned on the laptop, opened the Google search page, and typed in 'Barney Smallwood'. She glanced over her shoulder to make sure the door was closed, and then hesitated, her breath fast, before pressing down on the 'enter' key.

Less than a second later, Cassie was faced with a page full of links to articles that were undoubtedly about the Barney Smallwood she knew, and with the promise that there were thousands more available. She clicked on the first one – 'Dishy

Doctor Death' ran the headline – and jolted back in her chair as a large head and shoulders photograph of Barney filled the screen in front of her. At least, it was recognisably Barney, but it was a smooth, polished version of him, all wide smile, laughing eyes, neat hair, with none of the roughened edges that marked him now.

The basic story, from what she could understand, was that Barney had been the most senior doctor on duty one night when a patient had died from a pulmonary embolism. It was reported, briefly, that the patient hadn't been given sufficient medication to thin her blood over the preceding fortnight, but the focus was on the night she had died, and why she hadn't been treated more quickly. The family of the dead woman had complained, and had gone to the press. It was abundantly clear to Cassie that during a lull in real news, the tabloids had taken one look at Barney and decided to run with the story. Every article was covered in photos of him, some dating back to his university days: 'Doctor Drunk' was the caption on one, due to the glass of wine in his hand.

The early articles were bad enough. Barney was made to sound like the sort of Lothario doctor who scoured the wards for buxom nurses in the old *Carry On* films with little interest in his patients. But then the story had taken a twist. Someone had discovered that there had been two Dr Smallwoods on duty that fatal night – and the other had been Barney's wife. Now there were photos of the two of them together, a glamorous, good-looking couple who appeared to have everything. Cassie peered at a photo from their wedding, taken on the lawn at Ramblings. Barney's wife, Nessa, was looking at the camera, a cool smile on her lips. Barney was beside her, one arm round her waist, the other holding her hand. He was looking at his new wife, and the adoration and happiness in his face tugged at Cassie's heart. No one had ever looked at her that way.

The thrust of the allegations, as the story developed, was that the Drs Smallwood had been satisfying their own needs while their patient gasped her last breath. Some newspapers had been much more graphic. The NHS Trust had denied it. Staff shortages and broken equipment had been mentioned. Compensation had been paid to the family, and Dr Barney Smallwood had resigned from his post for personal reasons. And that was it: apart from a grainy photograph of a bearded man who may or may not have been Barney, in a feature on what had happened to those who made the news the year before. He had been destroyed, and then forgotten.

Cassie cleared the search history and shut down the computer, her hands shaking. She wished she had browsed for hot Russian husbands after all. Reading for the facts and through the lurid speculation, one thing was clear: Barney had been blamed for his good looks, his country-house background and his privileged life as much as for anything he had done or not done. Little Doctor Barney had not deserved to grow up to this. Cassie's heart ached for that boy, losing everything he had dreamed of – and for the man, trying to cobble together a life from what little he had left. She knew exactly how that felt.

Cassie was pushing open the door to Frances' sitting room, a tray of tea in her hands, when she heard a familiar laugh: familiar enough to cause a jump in her breath and a cramp in her stomach, though she had heard it so infrequently. She walked in and saw Barney sitting in her chair opposite Frances. He was sprawled out, relaxed, long legs crossed at the ankle, feet almost poking into the fireplace.

He stiffened when Cassie entered, drawing back his legs and sitting up straight. Cassie hated to see it. She hadn't said a word, hadn't yet moved into his line of sight, and she had chased away his peace. Her very existence made him uncomfortable – unhappy, even. How was she supposed to bear that? Ramblings had been a refuge for him long before it had been one for her.

The teacups rattled on their saucers. Cassie put down the tray on the table between the chairs.

'I'm sorry, I didn't realise you were here,' she said to Barney. 'I'll go and get another cup.'

She glanced up at him, ready to smile, but he was staring at the fireplace. Cassie hadn't properly seen him since she had read the newspaper reports online, and seen those photos of the old Barney. The contrast was striking. He was handsome, that hadn't changed, but the hope and enthusiasm that had lit up his younger face were gone. Weary resignation dulled his eyes and left lines across his forehead. Had she contributed to that? Were the lines worse than before she had made her accusation? She thought they were. It was excruciating to see.

Barney jumped up.

'Don't trouble yourself. I need to get back to work'

He edged round Cassie, excessively cautious to avoid her, and hovered by the window. This was exactly how he had been since the day they had rowed. He spoke to her when he needed to. He sometimes glanced at her if she spoke. He had made her a CD of an audiobook when she had asked, and left it in the kitchen for her to pick up. He was never impolite. He kept his distance in every way. It should have been what she wanted. So why did she miss the huffs, and the stares, and all the other quirks that made him uniquely himself?

'Sit down, Cassie. You know I do not like it when you lurk.'

Frances was still uniquely Frances, and Cassie obeyed, sitting down in the chair Barney had vacated. It was still warm. 'I forgot to tell you. I am giving you the day off on Thursday.'

'Are you?' It made no odds to Cassie which day she had off. She had nowhere to go, although now the weather was better, she had thought she might explore more of the local countryside. 'I don't mind changing my days.'

'You misunderstand. I am giving you an extra day off. Guy telephoned earlier. He is coming over on Thursday.'

Cassie sensed Barney shift by the window. He was watching Frances, and it was evident from his expression that he hadn't known about this.

'No problem,' she said. 'I'll keep out of the way.'

Frances laughed.

'You misunderstand again. I am not asking you to avoid Guy. You are going out with him.'

A heavy breath – almost a huff – wafted over from the direction of the window. Cassie was tempted to huff herself.

'Going where?' she asked, trying to stay calm until she knew the facts. It might be unfortunate phrasing on Frances' part, although she was usually careful with her words.

'A stately home. I think he said it was on the border with Cumbria. He wanted to show me how the house operates as a family home and makes money from tourism, but it would be too much for me. I thought you might enjoy the excursion, as you show such interest in old houses.'

Cassie might have enjoyed it on her own. She couldn't see how she would enjoy it with Guy. She flicked a glance over to Barney and caught his eyes moving off her.

'Thursday wouldn't be a good day,' Barney said, leaning against the window frame. 'The knit and natter group will be here in the morning, and I need to be out at an auction. You'd be on your own.'

'Is that the auction for the land next to your farm?' Cassie asked.

Barney looked at her for almost a full second and nodded.

'Good luck. I hope you get it.' She was ready to smile at him again, but he turned away.

'Ruth will be about the house,' Frances pointed out. She paused to drink some tea. 'And perhaps we could ask the Colonel to come over. He is a very interesting man.'

181

Cassie was watching Barney as a smile spread over his face. He looked at her, and she smiled back, sharing his warm amusement, everything else forgotten. Frances and the Colonel! The idea of the potential romance made even Cassie's heart soften.

'We could invite the Colonel,' Barney replied, unable to repress his smile despite the stern look Frances was giving him. 'But does Guy know? Why would he want to take Cassie out?'

'Why would he not? If you lifted your head from your work sometimes, Barney, you might have noticed that Cassie is quite enchanting.'

Cassie closed her eyes in embarrassment, not before witnessing Barney's smile fade.

'She's certainly enchanted you,' he murmured.

'She needs to go out more, and who else is going to take her?' Frances asked. 'I have considered the men who come here for the clubs and societies, and I have seen no one remotely suitable. Are there no eligible young men left in this village?'

Cassie opened her eyes in time to see Barney's lips twist with wry humour.

'One or two.' He seemed to be making extraordinary effort not to look in Cassie's direction. 'But I wouldn't include Guy in that category. And Cassie is hardly his type.'

That may have been an insult or a compliment, but Cassie was too relieved to hear it to care.

'Guy is as susceptible to a pretty face as any other man,' Frances replied, while Cassie wished her chair would swallow her whole. 'You know how dearly I wish to see him settle down.'

Something in the silence that followed Frances'

words made Cassie look up, and she felt, as she had before, that there was a layer to the conversation beyond her understanding. Barney strode over and stood behind Frances' chair.

'I know,' he said, and he rested a gentle hand on her shoulder.

Thursday didn't start well. Frances paged Cassie well before she was usually out of bed. Cassie ran down the corridor to her bedroom, dreading what might be wrong. She found Frances sitting on her bed, looking curiously fragile in her embroidered dressing gown, and with a dress bag beside her.

'Is something the matter?' Cassie asked, gasping for breath, and torn between relief at seeing Frances well, and dismay at the sight of the bag.

'Good morning, Cassie,' Frances replied, smiling. 'The only thing the matter is your clothes. I suspected you would not be suitably dressed for a day out, so I have selected something for you to wear.'

'I've put on a T-shirt,' Cassie protested. She couldn't see what was unsuitable about that, when the weather outside was warm and sunny. OK, it was a black T-shirt, but her arms and face were pale enough to brighten the outfit.

'This is a beautiful dress.' Frances ignored Cassie, and gestured at the bag. 'It is fortunate that you are the same size I used to be. Diana has always been large-boned. I could never have the satisfaction of seeing her wear my clothes.' She played her trump card. 'It will make me very happy to see you in this.'

So Cassie had no choice but to wear the dress;

and Frances was right, it was beautiful. The skirt swished against her legs as Cassie ran down the stairs to the hall when she heard Guy's voice. He held out his hand to lead her down the last few steps: it was an unexpectedly old-fashioned gesture, and Cassie accepted the hand, not knowing what else to do. He pulled her towards him and kissed both cheeks.

'I believe Mum's lending me her companion for the day,' he said. 'I can't pretend to mind.' He smiled at Cassie and winked. 'Even the weather has been kind to us. You look like the most charming posy of spring flowers in that dress.'

Cassie was too embarrassed to respond to this nonsense with anything more than a brief smile.

'You don't have to take me,' she said. 'I know Frances suggested it, but I don't mind if you'd rather not. Perhaps you could take Frances out somewhere closer to home one day. You must have better things to do.'

'What could be better than a day out in the sunshine with a beautiful woman? Is Mum in her room? I'd better go and see her before we leave.'

He jogged up the stairs. Cassie jumped as Barney materialised in front of her.

'You scared me,' she said. She clutched her throat, and could feel the pulse in her neck throbbing.

'You're dolled up.'

Briefly, the intense Barney stare made a re-appearance as his eyes swept over her from head to toe. She didn't mind; she preferred his blunt-ness to Guy's meaningless compliments.

She smiled. 'Blame Frances.'

'Oh, I do.' He began to walk away, then, as if he couldn't help himself, sighed and turned his head back. 'Be careful.'

The stately home they were visiting turned out to be a red brick manor house, slightly larger than Ramblings, but more subtle: like a plain older sister who could be relied on to stick around when the showy younger child went off gallivanting. The car park was almost full when Guy pulled in.

'It's busy for a Thursday morning, isn't it?' Cassie said, as they followed the other visitors in the direction of the ticket office.

'It's the first day of the season,' Guy replied. 'The house only opens to the public for ten weeks of the year – from Thursday to Saturday. There are special events and weddings on top of that, but the rest of the time it's a family home. It's not a bad compromise.' Guy paid for their tickets. 'Mum seems more willing than she used to be to let people in our house. The library was surprising enough, but now I hear that the whole village has the run of the place.'

'It isn't quite like that,' Cassie said. She glanced at Guy: he was smiling, but that meant nothing. Criticism could come wrapped in a smile as well as a frown. 'Frances is enjoying seeing the house used.'

'That's why I thought she might like to see what happens here. There's a balance between openness and privacy, with the added bonus of making some money. But you'll tell her all about it, won't you?'

'Yes, if she's interested.'

185

'I'm sure she will be.' Guy stepped back to let Cassie into the house first. 'She was very keen this morning to hear how we would be spending the day.'

Cassie was glad that the sudden coolness of the entrance hall provided a good excuse for her shiver of discomfort. Guy's tone was light, amused, quite the opposite of how she was feeling. And what did he mean about spending the day? She had assumed when they set off early that they would be back at Ramblings by lunchtime: she had banked on it. She felt the early warning of a headache push against her forehead.

'She certainly sounds happier now you're here,' Guy continued, as they followed the marked route from the hall into a sitting room where an enormous fireplace dominated one wall. 'Perhaps we should have thought of it before, because none of us can get over as much as we like. Have you seen much of Hugh or Diana recently?'

'Diana came over a few weeks ago.' Cassie fell silent as an uninvited vision of Barney hammering at a fence post flew into her head.

'Really?' Guy sounded suspicious and Cassie hoped he couldn't tell what she was thinking. 'What did she want?'

'She'd brought her horse. They rode round the estate.'

'They?' Guy halted and looked down at Cassie. 'James doesn't ride.'

'She wasn't with James. She had another man with her.'

'Did she? And what about Hugh? Has he been up again?'

'No, but a friend of his came for a tour of the house. He was a fan of Gothic architecture.'

'How convenient.' Guy smiled. 'I wonder what those two are up to?'

Conversation lapsed as they wandered upstairs and into a picture gallery that ran almost the length of the house. Guy had picked up speed, and was racing round with little interest. Perhaps it was nothing special for someone who had been brought up at Ramblings. Cassie caught up with him as he gazed out of the window.

'Look how many people are here! We'd be able to try something like this at Ramblings if it weren't for Barney.' Guy banged on the glass with the back of his hand. 'It was bad enough when Mum rented the farm to him and let him hang about the place. She told me this morning that he's actually going to have animals. Who's going to want to hold a wedding at Ramblings when there might be stinking sheep and cows parading past the house at any moment ruining the photos?'

Cassie would, but she didn't think it would help to point that out. He was surprisingly annoyed, but he didn't need to be. She could sort this out, and spare Barney another row with Guy. It was the least she could do for him.

'The animals shouldn't be going past Ramblings. Barney has gone to an auction today to buy a piece of land so he has better access to the farm.'

'What land? Gilver's field?' Guy swung away from the window. Cassie stepped back.

'I've no idea. It's the field between his farm and Joe's.'

'I didn't know that was for sale.' Guy smiled.

187

'That changes things. It's a good job you told me.'

Cassie relaxed. It was only a minor thing, and Barney would never know, but it made her feel fractionally better to have helped him.

'There's rumoured to be an early portrait by George Stubbs here, before he turned his hand to animals,' Guy said, looking up and down the vast gallery. 'Why don't you take one side and I'll take the other, and we wave if we find it?'

Cassie headed down her side of the room, fascinated by the portraits and the brief biographical details beside each one. She forgot all about Guy, until she heard a mobile phone ring, and saw him on the far side of the gallery, his iPhone to his ear. She looked again when she reached the end of the gallery, and he was hunched over his iPhone again, so engrossed in tapping in his message that Cassie heard an old lady complaining about him causing an obstruction. She checked her watch. Although they had started off quickly, the gallery had slowed their progress. They would have to hurry to make it back to Ramblings for lunch. She was about to chivvy Guy along when he put away his phone and headed across.

'I'm sorry about this,' he said, flashing a smile that was superficially charming but which left Cassie unmoved. 'I can't escape the office even for one day.' He rolled his eyes. 'Shall we go on?'

Cassie nodded, and let Guy usher her out of the gallery. The Stubbs seemed to have been forgotten and they zipped through the rest of the house at a pace that might have challenged a professional athlete. There was no time to notice more than the purpose of each room – bedroom, bathroom, music room – before they were on to the next one. Cassie was exhausted and irritated in equal measure by the time they left the house.

Guy looked at his watch. 'You're not interested in gardens, are you? If we leave now, we could stop for lunch on the way back if you like.'

'There's no need for that. Ramblings is only about twenty minutes away, isn't it?'

Guy laughed. 'Not even in *my* car. It took us an hour to get here. But that's fine, we'll go back. You can make sure Mum eats something. She looks like she's lost some weight.'

Did she? Cassie was temporarily distracted. She hadn't noticed any change. Perhaps she was too close to notice anything about Frances' appearance: she was simply Frances. But surely Barney would have said something if she didn't look well? All the same, Cassie vowed to pay more attention. She glanced at her watch. She hadn't realised they were so far from home. She wasn't sure she could wait so long to eat. There had hardly been time for breakfast by the time Frances had finished dressing her, and the headache she had noticed earlier was getting worse.

'Perhaps food would be a good idea.' She ignored Guy's surprise at her change of heart, and looked around until she saw the sign she had hoped for. 'There's a café here. We have time for a quick snack, don't we? I'm starving.'

'If that's what you want.'

Cassie started moving before he had finished. The café was on the other side of the house, and she headed that way, aware of Guy hurrying behind her along the gravel path. She climbed up

189

three steps to the next level, and stumbled on the last one. Guy immediately put his hand on her waist to steady her.

'Careful,' he said, laughing. 'If I take you back injured, Mum will never forgive me.'

Cassie was about to reply when a movement over Guy's shoulder caught her attention. Another couple emerged from the garden, also heading in the direction of the café: middle-aged, camera-toting tourists, enjoying a day out at a stately home. But they were no ordinary tourists. Cassie couldn't breathe, and without thinking, put her hand on Guy's arm to stop him moving.

Brendan and Gail. Mike's closest friends, but too fond of his ex-wife to ever be friends to Cassie. She had never expected to see them again – had hoped not to. What were they doing here? She dismissed that question at once. It didn't matter. There were only two questions that counted. Had they seen her? And if they had, would they tell Mike? That last one needed no thought. Of course they would. The headache tightened around Cassie's skull.

'Cassie?' Guy's voice brought reality crashing back in. 'Are we going for lunch or not?'

Cassie hesitated. She should eat, but the risk of being seen by Brendan and Gail outweighed all others.

'No,' she said, resisting the light pressure of Guy's hand that was trying to propel her forward. 'You're right. I should get back to Frances, make sure she has her lunch.'

'I thought you were starving?' Guy smiled, but his voice was laced with irritation that was all too familiar. Cassie recoiled, and the decision was made. She couldn't go back to that. She needed to return to Ramblings and hide again.

She turned and walked to the car, and Guy drove home at a speed that suggested he was keen to get rid of her. But it wasn't fast enough. Hunger clawed at Cassie's stomach, and her head began to spin as if she were drunk. She opened her handbag, her sweaty hands sliding off the clasp, and realised that it wasn't her handbag: Frances had lent her a more ladylike one, but Cassie had forgotten to fill it with her things. She yanked open the glovebox, and started throwing the contents into the footwell, but this wasn't Barney's truck: there was no food there.

'What are you doing?' Guy looked bewildered.

'Looking for food.'

'I don't have any. You said you could wait.'

'I can't. Is there somewhere we can stop?'

'No! We're only ten minutes away. I'm sure you can survive.'

Cassie closed her eyes to try to ease the dizziness, and started counting seconds in her head. It was just over eight minutes, by her one elephant, two elephant counting, when she felt the car stop. She opened her eyes, and saw Ramblings. It had never looked so beautiful.

'There, I've delivered you back in record time,' Guy said. 'I won't come in. Give my love to Mum. Don't forget to tell her how impressive the house was this morning.'

'Thanks.' Cassie was already half out of the car. 'Sorry, I have to run.'

And she did run, across the drive and in

through the door, nearly colliding with a man on his way out. She stumbled into a chair in the hall, swore and kicked it in frustration, then aimed for the corridor to the kitchen, but banged into a cabinet, making the contents rattle. She rubbed her eyes, trying to clear her vision. Mel and Barney were in front of her, staring.

'Hello!' Mel laughed. 'We weren't expecting you for hours. What's wrong? You look terrible.'

'I need food.' Cassie tried to squeeze past them, but crashed into Mel, who grabbed hold of her.

'Didn't he buy you lunch? The mean bugger.' Mel sniffed, and her eyes widened. 'Have you been drinking? That's not very sporting. If you were going to fall off the wagon, you could at least have given the profit to the No Name.'

'I'm not drunk. I need food. I'm di—' She couldn't finish the sentence.

'You're not dying, you're hammered!'

Cassie heard Mel laugh, was dimly aware of Barney speaking, and then there was nothing.

CHAPTER SIXTEEN

Cassie woke up in bed, the duvet pulled high under her chin. She heard a chair creak, and turning her head saw that Barney was sitting at her side. He was watching her, the trademark stare in place. Cassie lifted the duvet quickly and looked down. She was missing her shoes, but was otherwise fully dressed. She glanced back at

Barney. He smiled.

'You've only been out a couple of minutes. I didn't have time to strip and molest you. How are you feeling?'

'Exhausted. As if a car has just driven backwards and forwards over me.'

Cassie tried to sit up, but a hand restrained her – a female hand, on her other side.

'Don't get up,' Mel said. 'You still look very pale. Sorry for thinking you were drunk. You gave us quite a fright.'

'She gave *you* a fright,' Barney corrected. 'I'm surprised the whole village hasn't shown up, you screamed so loudly.'

'Because I thought she was dead! Anyone would have done the same. Except you,' Mel added, and she nudged Cassie's arm. 'He was amazing. He knew what was wrong straight away. He carried you up here, and found that injection thing in your bedside drawer. If I wasn't half in love with him already, I am now.' She laughed towards Barney. 'If you ever fancy an older woman, ask me first, won't you?'

'I'll bear it in mind.'

Cassie closed her eyes, but the darkness couldn't hide the mortifying thought of Barney lifting her dress and injecting her thigh.

'Mel, why don't you make yourself useful. Could you go to the kitchen and bring Cassie a glass of fruit juice and some cheese and crackers?'

Cassie felt the duvet shift as Mel got off the bed, and then heard the door close behind her. She tried to keep her eyes shut, but it felt too vulnerable, lying there exposed to Barney's scrutiny, and she opened them again.

'How long have you had diabetes?'

'Four years.'

'Type 1?' Cassie nodded. 'That's quite late.'

Cassie nodded again. It was exactly what Mike had said. Except from Mike it had been an accusation: he had never believed that it had come out of the blue, instead assuming that she had known about it for months and deliberately kept it from him. His complete misunderstanding of her character had been almost as devastating as the news the doctor had given her.

'How often do you have hypos?'

'Not often. I can usually control it. I haven't had a serious low for months.' She turned her head on the pillow, and squeezed her eyes tightly shut, but still felt a tear escape, tickling as it rolled across her cheek. She brushed it away with her knuckles. She was not going to think about the last time. She had spent months trying to erase that memory.

'The Jelly Babies,' she heard Barney murmur. 'Of course. No alcohol, no chocolate ... I should have worked it out. I would have done, if...' He sighed, and the chair creaked as he shifted. 'Why the secrecy? Why didn't you tell us?'

It was the first question she had expected him to ask. Was he furious? She needed to look at him to know how bad this was: to see how low his eyebrows had sunk, and how deep his frown was. She leaned on her elbow and shuffled into a sitting position. Barney was on his feet, propping up the pillow behind her before she was even halfway through the move. He pulled the duvet

194

up under her armpits before he sat down.

He looked at her, waiting for the answer to his question. Cassie explored every detail of his face, but there was no hint of anger, or annoyance, or any negative emotion at all. If she read anything in his face, it was concern. But why would he be concerned about her? He didn't like her; and after what she had said to him about his past, he had every right to hate her.

'I didn't mention it, because...' Her voice sank. 'It's embarrassing.'

'Embarrassing?' He leaned forward, as if doubting what he had heard. 'Why should you be embarrassed? It isn't your fault.'

Cassie didn't correct him. She hadn't meant that it embarrassed her. But how could she explain? He was a kind, decent man, as far as her judgement counted for anything. He probably wouldn't even believe her, let alone understand.

'You should have told us,' he carried on, when Cassie made no answer. 'What if I hadn't been here? You must know that you need to notify your employers. The car insurance has probably been invalid for months. But the main thing is, we need to make sure Frances is safe.'

He was going to sack her. It was what she had expected since the moment she opened her eyes. And the worst thing was, she couldn't blame him or argue that it was unfair. She cared too much for Frances. What if she had been out with Frances when she collapsed? What if she had been driving? Oh, she could tell herself that the circumstances were exceptional: that she never normally skipped a meal, and on any other day

195

she would have had a snack in her bag. But she couldn't give the sort of cast-iron guarantee that Frances deserved, and that she would demand if she were Frances' family. Barney had no option but to sack her. Knowing it was fair didn't make it any easier to accept. The tears rolled again.

'What's happened?' Mel came in, took one look at Cassie, and put her tray down on the floor. 'Is she worse? Does she need another injection? There was only one.'

'I don't know what happened.' Barney stood up. 'Cassie? What's wrong?'

'You're going to sack me.' Cassie took a huge breath, and tried to get the crying under control. 'I can't lose this job. I have nowhere else to go.'

Mel thumped him on the shoulder. 'Barney! You can't sack Cassie because of this. I take back everything I said about being half in love with you. The offer to be your cougar is withdrawn.'

'There's a relief.'

Barney sat down on the bed. Cassie could feel his buttocks pressing up against her thigh, and even though the thickness of the duvet separated them, and despite the drama of the day, an untimely warmth spread from that point of contact. He plucked a tissue from the box beside the bed and handed it to Cassie.

'I never mentioned sacking you. Even if it were legal to sack someone for having diabetes, I doubt that Frances would let me. We just need to make sure it's well managed. I assume you've registered with a doctor and a diabetes clinic?'

Cassie nodded. She didn't trust her voice, not after that 'we'. She had spent four years dealing with this on her own, with no support at all. The idea of having someone look out for her, care for her, was too much; the satisfaction of a craving that she didn't know she had. Then she realised how stupid she was being, and disappointment overwhelmed her. Barney was thinking in terms of a doctor managing a patient, nothing more. What was she doing, imagining it might be anything else? It was the unexpected weakness, the vulnerability, making her fanciful. It would pass. She clutched the cover of the duvet tightly.

'Cassie?' Barney's hand was over hers. It really didn't help. 'Are you in pain?'

'No. I need to get up.' She threw back the duvet. Her dress was rucked up around her knickers, exposing all her legs. Before Cassie could react, Barney had pushed the duvet back over her, and jumped off the bed. His nails scratched the absent beard.

Cassie looked at Mel. She was staring at Barney, her mouth slightly open. She caught Cassie's eye and smiled.

'I think perhaps you need to speak to Frances,' Mel said to Barney. 'She saw me downstairs with the tray, and heard the screaming. She might be worrying.'

'Of course. I should have gone before.' Barney turned back to Cassie. 'Test your blood now and every hour. And if there's any more talk of getting out of bed today, or if you don't eat all that food, I might have to rethink getting rid of you.'

He was almost out of the door when Cassie spoke.

'Barney. Thanks for what you did.'

197

'You're welcome. But let's make sure it doesn't happen again, OK?' He hesitated. 'I'm glad it's out now. I knew you were hiding something, and to be honest, I imagined much worse.'

Then he smiled – the huge, dazzling smile that she had seen him give to other people, never to her – and Cassie had to close her eyes as her head started spinning more wildly than it had done before.

Mel wouldn't go away. Cassie had pretended to sleep, but that made things worse. Mel prodded at her, wondering out loud whether she had lost consciousness again and whether Barney needed to come back, which was enough to make Cassie's eyes snap open again.

'Don't you need to get back to the pub?' Cassie asked at last. 'You can't leave Akram on his own.'

'He can manage. He's a big boy.' Mel accompanied this comment with a wink that Cassie really wished she hadn't seen. 'I sent him a text so he knows what's going on. I'll read you his reply.' She tapped at her phone. '"Give my love to Smiler,"' she read, doing a terrible impression of Akram's Yorkshire accent. '"Tell her to follow the doctor's orders. She's in the best hands there."' Mel looked up and smiled. 'I wouldn't say the best, but they're not bad hands to be in, are they?'

'Not when a glucogen injection is needed, no.'

'I didn't mean that, and you know it. Don't tell me you didn't see him get a good eyeful when you flashed your knickers at him.'

Before Cassie could begin challenging that sentence, the door opened and Frances walked in. She hadn't visited Cassie's room before, and it was as surprising as if the Queen had called into the royal laundry. Cassie fought to untangle herself from the duvet and get up.

'Stay where you are,' Frances said, waving a hand at Cassie. 'I have not come to disturb you. If Barney should ask, I have not come at all. If he had his way, none of us would ever leave our beds.' Frances looked over at Mel. 'What are you doing here, Melanie? You finished my hair hours ago. Surely your family must need you by now.'

'Barney asked me not to leave Cassie on her own.'

Mel flashed an apologetic smile at Cassie.

'I am here now, so I think you can safely be on your way.'

'Cassie?'

'Of course you should go. I've been trying to tell you that all afternoon. I thought you were being suspiciously stubborn.'

'Barney was very insistent you were looked after.'

'He's a good doctor.'

'He's a good man.' Mel kissed Cassie's cheek, and left.

'I'm sorry about this,' Cassie said, gesturing at the bed. 'I should get up. It must be time for your afternoon tea.'

'Barney took care of that.' Frances sat down in the chair Mel had vacated. 'Not very well, mind you. He brought me a mug of tea. I drank some of it as I suppose he was trying to be kind.'

'I'm sorry,' Cassie said again, but she couldn't help smiling, knowing that the disgusted expression on Frances' face was nothing compared to the one that would have been levelled at Barney. 'I really am feeling much better. Normal service will resume tomorrow, with tea in china cups as it should be.'

'Take as long as you need,' Frances said. 'While I would not have wished ill health on you, it has its advantages. He has not fussed over me once this afternoon. I am quite old news now.'

Cassie laughed, and Frances shuffled forwards in her chair, and reached out so that her hand lay over Cassie's. The thick wedding band felt heavy against Cassie's knuckles.

'I wish you had told me, Cassie. When I think of all the work I have given you, cleaning this house, running round after me, organising the use of the ballroom... From now on, you will be taking it much easier.'

'Is this another of Barney's rules?' Cassie's earlier pleasure in being looked after was rapidly disintegrating. How could Frances have put up with him for so long? 'Because I don't need to take it easy. This is the easiest job I've ever had.'

Perhaps she shouldn't have admitted that: she still thought she was overpaid for what little she did, especially when she enjoyed it so much; but Frances smiled.

'You are happy here?'

'Happier than I have been for years.'

'So am I.' Frances squeezed Cassie's hand, and sat back in her chair. 'I thought you would be out all day with Guy. Did something go wrong?'

The warmth of the duvet couldn't prevent the chill spreading along Cassie's skin. She had forgotten. After all the trouble since returning to Ramblings, the reason she had rushed home had slipped from her mind. How was that possible? It could be devastating. Mike might find out where she was. So what should she do? Cassie looked across at Frances, saw the tiredness, the anxiety and the affection in every line on her face, and knew in that moment what she would do. She would do nothing. She wasn't going to run again. She was in the place she was meant to be, she could feel that in every cell of her being. She would stay, and take her chances. Oddly, having made that decision, she felt the perpetual worry ease and contentment sweep down to her toes.

'Nothing went wrong,' she said to Frances. 'I began to feel ill. Guy may have thought I was behaving oddly. I'll have to apologise next time he rings.'

'He has never been good with illness. Needles always made him faint. I think he may not be the man for you, Cassie, however much the idea pleased me.' Frances stood up. 'I will have to ask Barney again.'

'He's definitely not the man for me!'

'Barney?' Frances laughed. 'What an idea! That woman he married did not leave a great deal of him for anyone else. I meant that I would have to ask Barney about the village men.'

'Please don't. I'm not interested in a relationship with a man from the village or anywhere else.' Frances was almost out of the door when another memory from earlier in the day flashed into Cassie's head. 'Frances? Did you have a visitor this afternoon? I saw a man leaving when I came back.'

'That would have been my doctor, I expect.'

'Your doctor? I thought Barney...'

She remembered, with a pang of guilt, that Barney was no longer a registered doctor – as she had pointed out herself, not so long ago. She sat up, and looked more carefully at Frances. Was she leaning more heavily on her stick than usual? Her cheeks were pale, but Cassie had attributed this to concern about her own ill health. Was Barney right to suggest that Frances was overdoing it?

'Why did you call the doctor out?'

'It was a routine check up. They are sadly necessary when you reach my age. I have better things to do than sit in a surgery waiting to be seen.' It was such a typical Frances remark that Cassie decided she was imagining the odd note in Frances' voice. 'Shall we reach an agreement? I will not make a fuss about your health, if you do not make a fuss about mine. I think we are both old enough to know what is best for ourselves.'

'That suits me,' Cassie agreed.

'Good.' Frances smiled. 'It is interesting that you should have noticed the doctor. He is an attractive man. I will make enquiries about whether he is married.'

Cassie had worried that Barney would be a nuisance, so it was a surprise – and in some ways, a stupid, irrational, disappointment – when the next day he made no fuss at all. He popped into the kitchen when she was having breakfast to ask how she was and what her sugar levels were, but that was it. She didn't see him during the rest of the day, or at all on the following day.

Sunday came, and Cassie was searching the

hall for the keys to the Volvo, so she could drive Frances to church, when Barney walked in. Cassie assumed he was heading for his office until she noticed his shoes: proper shoes, not the walking boots or hiking socks he usually padded round in when he was working.

'Do you know where the keys to the Volvo are?' Cassie asked. 'They're not on the hook in the kitchen. I thought I might have left them round here.'

'I've got them.' Barney took the keys from his pocket and held them up. Cassie stepped forward, her hand out to take them, but he clutched them in his palm.

'Can I have them?'

'No.'

Cassie sighed. He was being deliberately difficult, and she had no choice but to play along. 'Please?'

'No. What do you want them for?'

'I need to take Frances to church.'

'That's why I'm here. I'll drive you both.'

Cassie looked beyond the shoes, and noticed that the rest of Barney was also smarter than normal. He was freshly shaven – those cheekbones stood out above a chin uncluttered with stubble – and, she sniffed, he was wearing a subtle fruity aftershave.

'Have you got a cold?'

'No.' Cassie checked her watch, though it was a pointless gesture when she was standing next to a grandfather clock. Barney was so irritating. How could anyone bear to live with him? He missed nothing. 'I feel absolutely fine.' She let her eyes

203

return to his face, and found that he was smiling. Perhaps that was why someone could bear to live with him. 'I'm sure I can manage to drive a couple of miles.'

'Your insurance is invalid. You can't drive until I notify them that you have diabetes.'

'Can't you ring them?'

'I will, when I'm sure that you have it under control. I won't let Frances be at risk.'

Cassie sighed. Frances was lucky to have someone who cared about her so much. Cassie had Vicky, but there was only so much caring possible from several hundred miles away. It wasn't the same as having someone around, actively thinking day by day how to make you happy and keep you safe.

'So I'm confined to the house?'

'You can walk wherever you want, or get a bus or a taxi. But don't go out without a snack again, will you? And make sure you have my number programmed in your phone.'

'I can't get a taxi to the diabetes clinic. It will cost a fortune.'

'Let me know when you're going and I'll take you.'

'But...'

Whatever objection Cassie was about to make dried on her tongue. A seductive image filled her mind, of what it would be like not to have to do this alone: to have company, someone holding her hand, even if only metaphorically. She'd faced every appointment so far on her own, even the one at which she'd been given the diagnosis, and the explanation of what her life would be from now on. What must it be like to be one of those normal people, who turned up to appointments in pairs?

'Why would you do that?'

'Because it might help.' He made it sound so simple; no, he made it sound odd that she even had to ask the question.

'I've always gone on my own.'

'That's because you kept it secret. You didn't have anyone to go with you. You do now.'

Barney took Frances' arm and tried to steer her back to the car after the church service.

'Stop yanking me, Barney. You are going the wrong way,' Frances objected. 'The vicarage is over there.'

'What do you want to go to the vicarage for?'

'Tea and biscuits, of course.'

Barney turned to Cassie for interpretation. She smiled at his bewildered expression.

'The vicar's wife serves tea after the service,' she explained.

'And Frances goes? Since when?'

'Since Cassie offered to take me,' Frances replied. 'You may have noticed that she did not huff her way through the service either. Sunday morning has been transformed.'

Cassie laughed, though she didn't want to dwell on today's service. Barney had sat between her and Frances, and if he had huffed, she didn't hear it. She had heard his rich baritone singing the hymns; had felt the warmth of his body radiate across the inch of pew between them; and had been plagued with thoughts that ought not to have dared entered her head in church. Sometimes it was hard to think of him as Barney, and not as an attractive man.

They were the last to reach the vicarage, but the armchair under the window had been left for Frances as usual. The living room was ringed with an assortment of chairs foraged from the rest of the house, but there wasn't enough for everyone, and as one of the youngest present, Cassie normally stood up. Not today. Ethel thumped her husband on the arm as soon as Cassie walked in.

'Get up!' she said to him. 'Let Cassie have that chair.' He put down his teacup and stood up, moving away from the chair.

'I don't need to sit down,' Cassie said, stepping back. 'I'm happy to stand.'

'Of course you can't stand up,' Ethel said. She glanced round the room, and with one nod set off a Mexican wave of pensioners rising from their chairs, until only Frances remained seated. Cassie looked round, mortified that guests twice her age were wobbling on their sticks, offering her their chairs.

'Sit down,' Barney murmured in her ear. His breath ruffled through her hair. His lips were so close that to her starved mind it felt as intimate as a kiss. 'No one else will until you do.'

Cassie sat down, and everyone followed suit. With a little judicial shuffling from Barney, seats were found for everyone who wanted one. Ethel moved her chair closer to Cassie.

'You'll be all right,' she said, nudging Cassie's arm. She opened her handbag, and showed the contents to Cassie. 'I've brought some Jelly Babies, just in case. And I've ordered extra bags for the shop, so we don't run out. Let me know if there's anything else we can stock for you. You're lucky to have Barney, aren't you?'

'It's not an area I've ever specialised in,' Barney said. He was still hovering, and seemed to have no qualms about eavesdropping whatever conversation took his fancy. 'But I went to see an old university friend yesterday, who is an endocrinologist, and he brought me up to date.'

'You talked about me?'

'Of course not. He works in Birmingham, not round here. I asked about developments since I trained. It's what any responsible employer would do.'

Was it? Cassie wondered if she should object: it was her health, her body, and her business, surely? Then she realised what he had said. Had he spent his Saturday travelling to Birmingham to learn more about diabetes for her benefit? Who would do that, for little better than a stranger? She looked up. The kindness in his eyes answered her question. Barney would do that.

'I've separated the biscuits,' the vicar's wife said, leaning over to put a plate of biscuits down on the coffee table in front of Cassie. 'Anything with chocolate on is at the other end of the table. I had a look on the Internet and I saw you might be able to eat Rich Tea and plain digestives, so I got in some of those. Or there's fruit if you prefer.' She added a fruit bowl to the table. It was about the size of a punch bowl, and was overflowing with fruit.

'I have cheese and crackers, too, or could make you a slice of toast, white or wholemeal,' the vicar's wife continued. Cassie realised that she might go through her entire kitchen cupboards unless she ate something, and so reached out and took a bunch of grapes. She saw Barney's amused smile as he wandered over to the other end of the room – there was no chance he was going to make do with the non-chocolate biscuits – but he wasn't the only one smiling. It seemed as if the whole room had stopped to watch whether she ate or not, and now the other guests relaxed, exchanging satisfied looks.

Belatedly, two things occurred to Cassie. The first was that everyone here already knew about the diabetes; and the second was that they were concerned about her. She didn't know what she'd done to deserve it, but the people of Ribblemill, such a close-knit circle, had opened their chain of hands and let her in. Cassie ate her grapes and thought she had never tasted anything so delicious.

The Colonel had taken his regular place on the other side of Frances, and Cassie heard him mention the village hall.

'Will the repair work be starting soon?' she asked. There had been no visible progress since the storm as far as she could see.

'I was just explaining to Mrs Smallwood that there's a delay with the insurance. They won't pay out in full because the roof was in need of repair anyway. The figures are still being discussed. Barney is helping sort it out, so I'm confident we'll make progress soon.'

Cassie's gaze flickered across to Barney. He was perched on the arm of a sofa, next to Ada, the oldest resident of Ribblemill. He was holding her hand, and leaning towards her to catch every word, even though Cassie knew he must have heard her memories often enough to know them by heart.

'So we'll still need to raise funds?' Cassie asked, trying to concentrate on the Colonel.

'Not as much as we feared, but some, yes. Barney thinks we should be able to negotiate a deal, so that the money from our usual events will be enough. Not that your auction wasn't a good idea, and it may be something we pick up another year.'

'Oh, I don't mind,' Cassie said. She'd forgotten having ever made the suggestion. So much had happened since the night of the village meeting; her opinion of everyone involved had changed so much. 'So what is the next event? The summer barbecue? Where do you hold that?'

'Ah well, there is an issue over that,' the Colonel admitted, running his finger over his moustache. 'We hold it in the field behind the village hall. We still can, but it will have to be scaled down, because there'll be no power, and no contingency for if it rains.'

Cassie looked from the Colonel to Frances. Surely the answer was obvious to more than her? So why wasn't Frances suggesting it? She had previously been so keen for Ramblings to be used in place of the village hall, for any and every activity. She wouldn't draw the line here, would she, when it was for such an important cause?

'Frances,' Cassie began, but Frances lifted her hand to stop her.

'No, I do not think so, Cassie.'

Cassie flopped back in her chair. Frances didn't meet her eye. The Colonel coughed and reached for a biscuit. Cassie glanced round the room, wondering how many people had witnessed her rebuff, and as she did, Barney looked her way and smiled. Something about that smile prodded her to try again. Perhaps Frances had the idea that Ramblings would be polluted with the stench of hot dogs and onions. Cassie had something much better than that in mind.

'Frances?' she began again, and this time she ignored the raised hand. She was getting this idea out if it killed her. 'Do you remember what you told me about being invited to the royal garden party?' The hand lowered. Cassie took that as permission to continue. 'What if, rather than a summer barbecue, we hold a garden party at Ramblings? We could do it properly: afternoon tea, and games for children on the lawn, if the Colonel thinks that would work.'

'It sounds just the job,' the Colonel said. 'If Mrs Smallwood doesn't mind having people trample on her lawns.'

Cassie wished he hadn't used the word 'trample': it was hardly encouraging, especially when Frances was being so uncharacteristically quiet.

'I have spent years looking out at my perfect lawns without deriving any pleasure from them,' Frances said. Cassie leaned forward hopefully. 'But while I can see great merit in the idea the answer must still be no.'

'Why?' Cassie couldn't help herself. 'I know

you would enjoy it. I'd organise everything. All you would need to do is turn up. You'd be the Queen for the day.'

Frances smiled, and took hold of Cassie's hand.

'I know you would organise everything, Cassie. That is precisely why I will not allow it. Not after last week.'

'No fuss, remember?' Cassie said in a low voice, squeezing Frances' fingers. 'We agreed.'

'And she won't be organising everything,' Ethel chipped in. 'You can bet Mel will want to be in on this, and we'll all help, won't we?'

The group of pensioners nearest to Cassie nodded. She hadn't realised that anyone else was listening, but the numbers appeared to reassure Frances.

'Very well,' Frances said, 'we shall have a garden party at Ramblings... Oh!' She gasped, and Cassie at once forgot all about their agreement.

'What's the matter?' she asked. 'Are you in pain? Shall I call Barney?'

She searched the room to see where Barney was. While they had been discussing the garden party, three more people had arrived: a couple in their early thirties, with a toddler girl. Barney was with them, and as Cassie watched, he took the child in his arms. The girl reached out a chubby little hand and poked his chin. Barney grasped her hand, and pretended to gobble it up, all the way to her elbow, making her giggle. Cassie stared, unable to wrench her eyes away, because it was impossible to believe this was the same man she'd known for four months. The frowns and the weariness were chased away by happiness.

'Look what he could have been!' Frances whispered, and it was as if she had read the line direct from Cassie's head.

'Who is it?'

'The vicar's daughter, his childhood sweetheart until he met that woman he married. She lives in Wales. I have not seen them together in years.'

If Frances said more, Cassie didn't hear it. Her attention was entirely on Barney. He was talking to the couple, laughing, jiggling their baby, and Cassie realised that she wasn't seeing the man he could have been: this was the man he was. His delight was selfless. He was happy that someone he must once have cared about was happy. There was no taint of regret, or bitterness that his life had taken a less fortunate path. Cassie would never forget this moment: the scent of lavender from the plug-in behind the sofa; the crackle of conversation punctuated with a child's laugh; the discomfort of the ladderback chair digging into her spine; and the disobedience of her heart, in falling in love with Barney Smallwood.

CHAPTER SEVENTEEN

Cassie was sure of one thing above all else: love wasn't good, or desirable, or something that could make her happy. She hadn't asked for it to descend on her, and would do everything she could to keep it at bay. It was easy enough to avoid Barney at first. He was a creature of habit, wandering round to the kitchen for a drink or snack at the same time every day. Cassie made sure she was at the opposite end of the house when he did. She could tell his tread from anyone else's, was more sensitive to his voice than any other, and turned away whenever she detected his approach. She could have kept this up for weeks, months, if Frances hadn't reminded her of the proposed trip to the seaside. She couldn't go ahead without a car, and for a car she had to see Barney.

Cassie went down to the office in the middle of the morning. He should have had his tea break, she calculated, and be busy enough not to want a prolonged interruption. Short and sweet was the best approach: dash in, ask the question, and escape with the car keys. How hard could it be?

The door was propped open with a log, and Gin spotted her at once, thumped her tail, and wandered out to rub against Cassie's legs. Cassie crouched down to stroke her.

'You're going to have to be quieter than that if you're trying to steal my dog.'

Cassie looked up, her eyes sliding along ancient jeans, a well-fitting T-shirt, and up to Barney's smiling face. She stood up, but closer proximity to the smile didn't help. Now she could see the light behind his eyes, too, and her heart made a few erratic pumps that she worried his medical training might detect. She stared instead at some biscuit crumbs caught on the folds of his T-shirt. She focused on the crumbs, but then imagined how it would feel to wipe them away – how muscular his chest would be – and that didn't help her heart rate either.

'Have you come to take her for a walk? That would be great. I'm stuck inside waiting for a phone call. What do you say, Gin? Would you like a walk with Cassie?' He bent and patted the dog's side, and was rewarded with an enthusiastic wag of her tail. He smiled back at Cassie. 'I think that's a yes. She's missed you. She's had to put up with only my company recently.'

'Sorry. I've been busy...' Busy reading to Frances, listening to the radio with Frances, continuing with the Ramblings history, and thinking what to do about the garden party. It must sound pathetic to a man who had been used to saving lives and now ran a huge estate single-handedly. It was hardly surprising that a frown should creep on to his face.

'You are finding time to exercise, aren't you? I told Frances that you needed a break in the morning and the afternoon, especially when the weather's good, so you can go for a walk if you want. That reminds me, I have something for you.' He walked back into the office, and Cassie and Gin followed. He picked up a booklet from the shelf behind his desk. 'It's a guide to twenty circular walks starting from the village. None are more than six miles long. This booklet was put together a few years ago to raise money for the village hall, but I've been through it and made a note if any of the landmarks have changed since then.' He held the booklet out, but Cassie didn't take it. He scratched his chin with his free hand. 'You don't need to use it if you'd rather stick to the gardens. I thought you might appreciate some variety.'

'I would.' Cassie took the booklet. 'It's just...' But what could she say? She wasn't used to people being kind to her, or thinking about what she might like? That it wouldn't help her deal with being in love with him if he did things like this? 'Thanks.'

'Ask if you need any more ideas. I must have tramped round every public footpath within a ten-mile radius thousands of times over the years.'

Cassie could imagine Barney as a teenager, striding through the countryside to use up an excess of energy and hormones and as a hard-working doctor revisiting his favourite places to relieve the stress of work. She wondered who he had tramped the footpaths with – the vicar's daughter, or his wife, or both? What would it be like to explore the fields and paths with Barney at her side, showing her things that only a local could know, smiling at her, the way he was doing now? But he hadn't offered to accompany her, and she was certainly not going to ask.

Short and sweet, she reminded herself. She had been distracted from her purpose, but he had given her the perfect opening.

'I could have even more exercise, with greater variety, if I could leave the village. Can I use the Volvo again now?'

Barney laughed, and the crumbs fell off his T-shirt.

'I wondered when you were going to ask about that. I thought it might be a test to see how many sermons and vicarage teas I could sit through before I cracked.'

'It would never be enough to make you anything but a huffing heathen.'

'Is that right?' He laughed again. 'And I suppose Frances thinks of you as her ministering angel?'

'How did you know? Do you creep round the house, spying through doors?'

'Only if I might hear or see something interesting.'

The smile flashed up, and something about it struck Cassie as so flirtatious that she had to put her hand out to the desk to remind herself what reality felt like. This was impossible, she thought. One smile made her delusional. She had to try harder to control this. She took a couple of steps back.

'Is that a yes? Can I have the keys?'

'How have you felt? Is it back under control?'

'Yes. I've not had any problems.' Not with the diabetes. At this moment, *he* was the greatest risk to her well-being.

'OK, I'll ring the insurance company later and see what they say. Where are you so desperate to go?'

Cassie hesitated. She suspected he wouldn't approve – but that would be good, wouldn't it? If he reverted to the grumpy bear he had been when she first arrived, she would forget all this nonsense about being in love with him.

'I've promised to take Frances to the seaside.'

It worked better than Cassie could have hoped. The switch from the smile to the frown was instant.

'Was this your idea?'

It was tempting to say yes, to make him crosser, but it was as difficult as ever to lie under the power of that searching stare.

'Frances mentioned that she'd like to go, and I didn't see any reason why not. Don't tell me she's too old to go to the seaside.'

'It's not her age that's the problem.' He sighed, and brushed aside some papers on his desk. 'Where were you planning to go?'

'Southport.'

'Have you ever been to Southport?' Cassie shook her head. 'It's not what you're probably expecting.'

'I don't expect anywhere to compare to the Devon coastline.'

That was the wrong thing to say. The Barney smile returned.

'And Frances was keen on the idea? It's a long drive, especially on a hot day. There's no air-conditioning in the Volvo.'

'Frances was very keen. She thought it might be the last time she sees the sea, but if it goes well, we could go more often. I suppose we could choose a cooler day, or even wait until September when the children go back to school.'

'Don't wait,' Barney said. He flicked through the diary on his desk. 'Can you make it the end of the month? I'll drive you.'

'You can't do that!'

'Of course I can. Frances can hardly complain about me taking a day off when I'm with her.'

That hadn't been the reason for Cassie's objection. It was the prospect of a whole day with Barney. How she would bear that bothered her more than the assumption that she wasn't fit to drive beyond the village.

'You don't need to make such a fuss. I told you

217

I've been fine. I'll take snacks. I can drive.'

'Do you even know where Southport is?'

'Yes. On the coast. How hard can it be? Keep going until the land runs out.'

'If that's how you plan to find it, I'm definitely driving. I'm not making a fuss over you. I want to keep an eye on Frances.'

'Fine. You win. Drive us if you want.'

'It's not a question of winning. We're not at war.'

She nodded, and turned towards the door.

'Cassie? Have you forgotten Gin?'

She had. It took too much effort to repress any reaction to his smile to think of anything else. Cassie called for Gin, who padded over and thrust her nose into Cassie's hand. She tried to leave again.

'Cassie?'

What now? So much for short and sweet. This was like the worst slow torture: death by Barney.

'Do you think you could look after Gin on Friday night? I could ask Lydia, but I'd hate to interrupt whatever teenagers get up to at the weekend.'

'Of course. I'd love to.' She wondered what Barney got up to on a Friday night. Did he have a date? He was smiling at the thought of it. Before she could stop it, her mouth opened. 'Will it be for the whole night? Are you going on a date?'

He laughed as if she'd said something bizarre, when really, the only bizarre thing was that he wasn't on a date every night.

'I'm meeting some old friends from med school. Is that OK? You really have become part of this village. You sound exactly like Mel. Don't worry. If I ever decide to start dating again, you'll be the first to know.'

It was inevitable that Frances would insist on Cassie wearing a dress, especially as the day Barney had chosen for their excursion turned out to be dry and sunny.

'You look beautiful, Cassie,' Frances said, when Cassie entered her bedroom wearing the red polka-dot dress that Frances had chosen, and some wedge-heeled sandals borrowed from Becca.

'Not too overdressed?' Cassie smiled, knowing full well what the answer would be. Frances had one rule when it came to fashion.

'You can never be too overdressed.'

Frances was living up to her own rule today, wearing a tweed suit, silk blouse, pearls and a hat. The paisley fur-trimmed slippers were an incongruous final touch.

'Are your shoes downstairs?'

'I think I will wear these today.' Frances indicated a pair of brown brogues, with laces and an inch-high block heel – quite different from her usual rubber soled slip-on shoes. 'I will put them on downstairs.'

When they met in the hall a short time later, waiting for Barney to arrive, it was clear that there was no way that Frances could bend over to tie the laces, even from a chair. It was equally clear that she had no intention of asking Cassie to help. There was a tacit boundary to Cassie's duties, and assisting Frances with personal care was beyond it. This was the first time that Cassie had noticed.

'I think perhaps the normal shoes might be more sensible,' Frances said, trying to pull her feet back out of the shoes she had spent several minutes putting on. Cassie couldn't bear to hear the proud attempt to cover her disappointment.

'Certainly not. You've got me in this dress, and I'm getting you in those shoes. Deal?'

Frances gave a gracious nod, and Cassie bent down to tie the laces. When she stood up, the front door was open and Barney was standing there, the sun streaming in around him, sculpting his body into a tantalising silhouette. Cassie gripped the back of Frances' chair.

'The car's ready.' Barney stepped forward, and the silhouette became solid. He smiled. 'You're looking smart, Frances. Should I have made more effort?'

'Yes, you should have, but it is too late now.'

Barney was wearing jeans and a checked shirt that brought out the colour of his eyes. Cassie couldn't imagine any other woman finding fault.

'You see I even persuaded Cassie into a dress. Doesn't it make her look beautiful?'

Cassie picked up the picnic basket, desperate not to hear his inevitable denial. Ruth had found the traditional willow basket, complete with cups, plates and cutlery. Now it was stuffed with food, it weighed a tonne. She staggered under the load and grimaced as the corner of the basket bumped her leg. Instantly it was whisked out of her hands.

'Legs that are black and blue would totally ruin the look,' Barney said, and he strode towards the door.

Barney drove to Southport at a sedate pace, as if they were taking part in a royal procession. At last they turned onto a bumpy coastal road, and

220

Cassie saw her first glimpse of sand. She sat up, her forehead pressed against the window, waiting to see the sea ... and she waited and waited. There was sand stretching out for miles – Barney even drove down a ramp and parked on the beach – but still there was no water. Cassie got out of the car and held up her hand to shade her eyes, squinting into the distance. She heard Barney laughing and turned round.

'It is out there, if you look hard enough.'

'I would have brought binoculars if I'd known. Is the tide out, or has it evaporated in the sun?'

'It goes out a long way because the land is so flat. I did warn you it might not be what you were expecting.'

That was some understatement. Cassie had hoped for cliffs, wild waves and salty breezes tangling her hair – a taste of home. There was sand, and seagulls soared overhead but the memories she'd longed to bring to life remained pale two-dimensional images in her head.

'I thought you were a country girl?'

'I am, but our farm is only three miles from the sea. We used to walk there whenever we could spare the time.'

'Come on.' Barney brushed his hand along her arm. 'Let's go to the end of the pier and get you a bit nearer the sea. I can't bear those woebegone eyes.'

Barney walked round to the other side of the car, while Cassie looked down at her arm, amazed that it looked the same when it felt a million times hotter than the rest of her body.

'Frances? Are you happy to go to the end of the

pier? We can catch the tram.'

'The tram?'

Cassie wished she could have taken a picture to capture Frances' disgust. It could hardly have been greater if Barney had suggested they travel in a dustcart.

'I have never taken the tram along this pier in my life, and I have no intention of starting now.'

'Frances...'

'If you are going to fuss, Barney, you can wait in the car and Cassie and I will go.'

Frances and Barney looked at Cassie. They both expected her support, but there was no hesitation over which way she would go. A smile from Frances was infinitely safer than a smile from Barney. So Cassie skirted round Barney and joined Frances.

'It will be good to stretch our legs after the journey,' she said. Did she imagine that Barney's eyes flicked across her legs as she said that? 'We'll stop for a rest if it gets too much, OK?'

Cassie had expected a small huff, at the very least, but Barney looked at her with an amused expression hovering too close to a smile for comfort. He didn't say a word as he followed Frances and Cassie along the pier. But even though Cassie maintained a sedate pace, and stopped to admire the donkeys and the view of Blackpool Tower, and for numerous other spurious reasons, Frances became visibly tired before they were even halfway along. They would never make it to the end. The bigger concern was how they would make it back to the start.

'Wait there,' Barney said, though she hadn't

asked for his help. 'I'll be back in a few minutes.'

He jogged away. Ten minutes later he re-appeared, pushing an empty wheelchair. Cassie felt Frances stiffen beside her.

'Where's that come from?' Cassie asked. 'Have you mugged someone?'

'I brought it.'

'I told you not to,' Frances said. 'I am not an invalid.'

Cassie swivelled back to her, wondering when this discussion had taken place. She knew nothing about it.

'No one said you were. You've gone further than I thought you would. But we can't keep up this leisurely pace. Cassie will need to have her lunch soon.'

He made her sound like a baby – or worse, as much of an invalid as Frances. With an expression of great suffering, Frances sat down in the chair.

'I don't know why you didn't bring a double wheelchair, and push us both along,' Cassie grumbled. She wasn't sure what annoyed her more: Barney acting as if she were a feeble, sickly creature, or him having the foresight to bring the wheelchair. What would she have done if he hadn't come with them? She should have thought more about Frances, and less about irritating him so he wouldn't smile. Then, as if he were deliberately trying to provoke her, he brought out one of his biggest smiles.

'Who said I was going to push?'

He walked away, his shoulders rippling as he laughed.

It was a glorious, relaxing, uplifting day. They made it to the end of the pier, still some distance from the sea, and Frances got out of the wheelchair to walk the last part. They picnicked on the beach, and Barney took them out on the boating lake in a motorboat, expertly steering them under the pier and round the ducks, while Frances sat regally at the back.

They were back on the beach, Frances sitting on a deckchair, and Barney and Cassie spread out on a picnic rug, the remains of afternoon tea between them. Cassie shuffled to the edge of the rug, kicked off her shoes and dug her toes into the sand. It was cold beneath the top layer, and when she clenched her toes the sand clumped together rather than running between them. She dug her heels-in and pushed her legs out, creating two trenches, and then did it again, enjoying the scratch of the gritty sand against her skin.

'If you're looking for buried treasure you'll be disappointed. This coast isn't known for smugglers and pirates.'

Cassie smiled but didn't turn until she heard movement behind her. Barney had stood up, and was rummaging in the picnic basket. Frances had fallen asleep.

'Does she normally sleep in the day?' Barney asked.

'She has done recently, for about an hour.'

'Will you tell me if there are any other changes?'

Cassie nodded. She couldn't be churlish; he had saved the day with the wheelchair. He sat down, and stretched his long legs out across the rug behind Cassie. He had a bar of chocolate in his hand, an expensive-looking one in a dark wrapper.

'That's a step up from your usual junk chocolate. Have you won the lottery?'

'Sadly not.' He ripped open the foil wrapper. 'It's 85% cocoa. If you want to eat chocolate, this is a good one to try.'

'Who told you that?'

'Philip, the endocrinologist I mentioned.'

'So you bought this for me?'

'I'd love to say yes, but no. That would suggest I could hand this over and not eat any. But I did buy this thinking you might like to try it.' He held out the bar. 'Tempted?'

Oh she was tempted, more tempted than he must ever know. But not by the chocolate, delicious though it was, with its dark, glossy finish and bitter aroma tantalising her senses. She was tempted by the hand holding the chocolate, blue veins raised in the heat; by the long fingers gripping the bar, skilful fingers that had once saved lives – and what other skills might they have? She was tempted by the tanned forearm, scattered with dark hairs, exposed when he had rolled his sleeves up. Tempted, in fact, by every bit of the man reclining on the rug beside her, especially the good heart that had thought about what she might like. How could she not be in love with him when he was like this?

'I can't,' she said, answering her own question and his.

'That's a shame.' Barney drew back the chocolate, broke off a chunk and put it in his mouth. Cassie watched as he closed his eyes, imagining how the chocolate would be melting over his tongue, the sharpness pricking his taste buds. She dug her toes deep into the sand, searching for that cool relief.

'That's incredibly good.' Barney's eyes snapped open, catching her staring at him. He smiled. 'So are you – more than some of the diabetics I used to come across. Did you cut out everything when you were diagnosed?'

The reminder of her condition was an effective cold shower. It was how he defined her now, just as Mike had. Barney at least viewed her with sympathy, as he had probably been trained to do. Whereas Mike... She shuddered. She wouldn't let thoughts of him spoil this day.

'When you realise something is bad for you, sometimes the only answer is to cut it out completely,' Cassie said, gazing out across the sand. She felt a tug on the rug as Barney sat up, bringing him nearer to her.

'Is this about more than chocolate?'

'No.'

'Cassie...'

Cassie jumped up, pulled a blanket out of her bag, and tucked it round Frances' legs. She spent a couple of minutes shaking and arranging it, while she tried to do the same with her feelings.

'Thanks for bringing us today,' she said, steering the conversation back onto safe ground. She sat down on the rug, in the small gap left by Barney, who was lying on his side, his head resting on his hand. 'I'm sure you must have had better things to do. I'm sorry you've had to drive us round because I'm...' She could have finished that sentence in a thousand different ways, but she hadn't shaken Mike out of her head as well as she'd thought. 'Defective,' she ended, and reached out to brush some sand off her leg.

'Defective? Why would you call yourself that?' Cassie looked across at Barney, and saw pity soften his eyes. It wasn't an expression you ever wanted to see on the face of the man you were in love with. 'The diabetes is not your fault, and is nothing to be ashamed of. I can show you what a real defect is.'

He sat up, and lifted his shirt over his right side. At first she saw nothing but taut flesh, golden brown as if he had been working outside without a top on; and then the shirt went higher, and Cassie saw a pale, jagged scar, running a couple of inches diagonally across his lower ribs. It was old, as healed as it was ever going to be, a shiny pink worm crawling across his skin. She couldn't see it as a defect. It was part of him, as much as the perfect almond-shaped eyes, the uneven smile and the unblinking stare; and it was impossible to think of any part of him as less than beautiful. She leant back, resting on her hands, making sure they couldn't obey the instinct to reach out and touch him.

'How did it happen?'

'I was stabbed by a drunk during one of my first shifts in A&E, in the days when I thought being a hero was a good idea. It turned out that the white coat wasn't the invincible shield I'd always believed it to be.'

He let the shirt fall back down. It was a relief – and a huge disappointment. He lay back down, watching a seagull circle over their heads.

227

'Do you miss it?'

He closed his eyes. 'Yes. In the sense that I believe I was good at it – at dealing with the patients. I could have done so much more.' He rubbed his chin. 'But also no, I don't. Animals and land are much simpler to deal with than people. I like doing my own thing. I like doing a good job, whatever job that is. Sometimes contentment creeps up on you again when you thought your turn was over.'

It was exactly how Cassie felt about her time at Ramblings. It was the house of lost contentment: the people there all seemed to have been knocked off the course they had expected to follow. But somehow it was a house that restored contentment too.

'I'm sorry about what I said that time,' Cassie said, 'about you not being a proper doctor.'

Barney opened his eyes.

'I thought we'd cured you of this constant apologising.'

'Only the unnecessary ones.'

'So you don't think I'm a murderer?'

Cassie flinched at the word. 'Of course not.'

'What changed your mind?'

What answer could she give to that? That she'd fallen in love with him? She curled her legs up underneath her. The truth was embarrassing, but better than that.

'I Googled you.'

'Ah.' Barney sat up, and picked up the chocolate. He broke off a chunk. 'So you saw...'

Cassie nodded.

'Doctor Death. I saw it all.'

He was munching chocolate, but Cassie thought his shoulders sank at the name.

'And you really didn't know before then? When you first arrived, I thought...'

'What?'

'That you might have been a journalist.' He shrugged. 'There's one tabloid which keeps trying to revive the story, find a fresh angle on it. I don't know why.'

If he looked in the mirror, it would be obvious. His face would sell plenty of newspapers, but Cassie didn't point this out. Instead she tried to make him smile.

'Is that why you had the beard? As a cunning disguise?'

'Can't I claim it was a fashion statement?'

'No. You were lucky there were no reports of escaped bears in Lancashire. You might have been shot.'

Barney laughed. The sound knocked against Cassie's heart, tumbling her further into love. A couple of children tore past them shrieking, racing each other to the sea. He turned to Cassie and smiled. She was hooked – totally, hopelessly hooked. There was no escape.

'Why didn't you believe what it said in the papers? It was damning stuff.'

'It was. But you're not the person they described.'

'You don't know me.'

She didn't know everything about him, that was true, but she didn't need to. It wasn't necessary to know every detail of a person to understand the essence of them. And the essence of him was ... the

229

same as the essence of her. If only she had met him years ago! But there was no point thinking that way. It was too late, far too late. She had to break this strange, intense atmosphere hovering around them. So she forced herself to laugh.

'Perhaps you're right. Vicky has always said I'm a better judge of sheep than men.'

'Vicky?' Barney leaned forward. 'Is that your sister? The one in Devon?'

'Yes.' The single word came out more wistfully than she'd intended.

'Don't you want to visit her? I can speak to Frances, get you some time off.'

'I can't go there at the moment.'

'Why not?'

She might have told him – the truth might have been drawn out of her by the power of that stare – if Frances hadn't woken up.

'What?' Frances looked round, and then down at Cassie and Barney. 'Who is going where?'

'We were just saying it's probably time to be going home.'

Cassie stood up, brushed the sand from her feet, and put her shoes back on.

'What is this doing here?' Frances lifted the blanket that Cassie had wrapped around her knees. 'I hope that neither of you think you can get away with making a fuss, just because I am asleep.'

Cassie smiled, they packed up the picnic things, and Barney drove them back to Ramblings. Frances went inside while Cassie and Barney unloaded the car. Barney lifted the folded wheelchair out of the boot.

'Thanks for bringing that,' Cassie said. 'I would

never have thought of it. You were right, I need to remember that Frances can't do as much as she thinks she can.'

'But you were right too. She's happier than she's been for ages. It was great to see her having fun today. You've done that for her.' Barney smiled, and held out his hand. 'Ceasefire?'

Cassie nodded, and they shook hands. Before she could take her hand away, Barney pulled it towards him, and ran the pad of his thumb over the bony knuckle at the base of hers. It had healed: she hadn't rubbed it for weeks.

'Looks like she's not the only one who's happier,' he said, and for a heart-stopping moment Cassie imagined she felt his hand squeeze hers, before he dropped it and walked into the house.

CHAPTER EIGHTEEN

'This is going to be amazing,' Mel said, smiling round the table at Cassie, Ethel and the Colonel, who had gathered in the No Name to discuss arrangements for the garden party. 'You are such a star to have talked Frances into this, Cassie.'

'No one talks Frances into doing anything she doesn't want to do,' Cassie replied. 'The Colonel has had the greatest influence. She trusts him to keep us giddy young things in check.'

'So as long as we don't show him the secret list, containing the plans for the twenty-four hour rave, we're OK?' Mel laughed as the Colonel choked on his coffee. 'Don't worry, Colonel, we wouldn't do that to you. Nothing will jeopardise the sweetest romance this village has seen for years.'

'Romance? Don't be ridiculous. Mrs Smallwood is a neighbour.'

'Shall we get back to the invitations?' Cassie said, as Mel opened her mouth no doubt to tease the Colonel some more. 'Everyone in the village is automatically invited, but what about people living further away?'

'I still have forwarding addresses for Ribblemillers who have moved away,' Ethel said. 'I can get invitations out to them. There'll be a good turnout. No one will want to miss the chance to look round Ramblings gardens, even for a small charge. What about the Smallwood children? Can't they bring some of their rich friends?'

'I don't know whether any of them will come,' Cassie said. 'None of them were very interested when I told them we were raising funds for the village hall.' She had mentioned the garden party to all of Frances' children when they had telephoned, and the reaction had ranged from indifference to indignation.

'Guy Smallwood doesn't normally turn his nose up at a party,' Ethel said. 'He's been at Ramblings more often than usual these last few months. What's the sudden attraction?'

Guy had visited twice more after the disastrous day out with Cassie. She had tried to apologise for her weird behaviour, but he had laughed it off, and been as charming as ever. Cassie looked up from doodling on her notepad to find Mel and Ethel exchanging smiles and nodding in her direction.

'What?' She shook her head as the meaning of the gesturing sank in. 'It's not me! Guy isn't interested in me.'

She was about to point out that she wasn't interested in him either – really, that should have come first – but it was too late. Mel was looking over her shoulder, and with a sinking sense of inevitability, Cassie turned round and saw Barney.

Gin ambled over and stuck her nose into Cassie's hand. Cassie bent and ruffled her fur, while her heart steadied. At least her secret was safe, she reflected. If Mel and Ethel were speculating about her relationship with Guy, Cassie must be doing an excellent job of disguising her true feelings. But when she looked up from showering affection on Gin, Mel was regarding her with an expression too curious for comfort.

'Drinking in the afternoon, Barney?' Ethel said. 'Are things so bad?'

'Yes.' He smiled, and with a click of his fingers reclaimed his dog. 'I have a mountain of admin to get through. I can't put it off any longer. I need fortifying first.'

'You need someone to help you with the paperwork,' Mel said. She smiled at Cassie, whose stomach sank for the second time with the sure knowledge of what was coming next. 'You should ask Cassie. She reorganised our office space in return for borrowing the laptop. Now we have everything in files and folders and trays, all properly labelled. Even Akram can't go wrong with this system.'

'Can you type?' Barney moved round the table, so he was in Cassie's view.

233

'Of course she can,' Mel said. 'Cassie, what's your typing speed?'

'Seventy words a minute,' Cassie mumbled.

'Slightly faster than my two-fingered approach. Where did you learn to do that? It's an unusual skill for a farmer.'

'She's a qualified PA!' said Mel.

Apparently not qualified enough to speak for herself.

'Seriously, have you two ever had a conversation? Do you know he used to be a doctor?' she went on.

'Yes. I know all about that.'

She glanced at Barney, and they smiled at each other. Mel regarded her with even greater curiosity.

'That's settled. Cassie can help with your admin. You'll still have that drink, won't you? I don't want to have talked myself out of a sale. And you can't have her yet. We haven't finished here.'

'What are you lot up to?' Barney peered over the table at Cassie's notepad. 'Flower design?'

She pulled the pad away from his prying eyes, relieved that flowers were all she had doodled. She had decorated one of Frances' to-do lists with hearts the other day, quite unconsciously.

'Plans for the garden party. Care to join us?' The Colonel sounded delighted at the prospect of male support. 'We will need to consult you at some point about which part of the grounds we can use.'

'I'll think about it and let you know. Let's get the midnight ramble out of the way first. I need to make sure all the paths are clear ready for that.'

Everyone nodded. Cassie had no idea what they were talking about.

'What midnight ramble?' she asked. 'Is this another fundraising event?'

'No, love, it's been going on long before there was a village hall,' Ethel explained. 'There are records referring to it happening back into the sixteen hundreds. Every July, the Ribblemillers walk the village boundary at midnight, shining lanterns and ringing bells. It's said to ward off evil spirits and protect the village for another year.'

'Does it work?' Cassie asked.

'It's superstitious nonsense,' Barney replied. 'But no one dares stop now, just in case.'

'Can anyone join in? Can I do it?'

'Only the villagers take part, not outsiders.'

Cassie dug the nib of her pen into her pad, stung by Barney's dismissal. An outsider? Is that how he thought of her? Was this his definition of a ceasefire? He avoided her gaze, and wandered over to the bar.

'I don't think there's any rule about who can take part, is there?' Mel asked Ethel.

'Not that I know of. I'm sure people have brought along guests before. The more noise we can make, the better. Besides, Cassie lives in the village. She has every right to come.'

Cassie pushed back her chair and followed Barney to the bar. A fresh pint and a newspaper lay on the counter in front of him.

'Why have you never mentioned the midnight ramble before?' she asked.

He sighed. 'Because I knew you'd want to come.'

That was frank – and more hurtful than Cassie had expected.

'But why shouldn't I? Ethel said there's no rule

235

against outsiders. And I'm not an outsider because I live in the village.'

'For now.' Barney reached for his pint and pulled it nearer, spinning the glass round in circles. Cassie's thoughts were following suit. What did he mean by that?

'You said you weren't going to sack me!'

'We're not.' He looked at Cassie with a smile on his lips and concern in his eyes. 'But you know this job can't last forever. The more tightly you bind yourself to Ribblemill, the harder it will be when you have to leave.'

Leave? She couldn't think about leaving, not when she was close enough to smell the sunshine on his skin.

'Frances isn't so old. I could be here for another ten years, at least.'

Barney silently drank his beer.

'And when the job ends...' She faltered, not wanting to contemplate how it must end. 'When it's over, I don't want to move away. I should have saved up enough to rent or buy somewhere, and I can work as a PA again...'

'You want to stay?' Barney stared at her. It was intoxicating at close range. 'Why?'

'Because I love...' Gin brushed against her leg, and lay down on Cassie's foot. It distracted her for long enough to make sense return. What had she been about to say? 'I love it here,' she said, bending down to give Gin a grateful stroke.

'More than Devon?'

'Some things, yes.' She dared to look at Barney again. He was twirling his pint, staring into the glass, and it was impossible to tell what he was thinking. 'Does that make a difference? Will you not mind if I join the ramble?'

'I don't know.' He looked up, frowning, as if she had asked him to solve one of life's greatest mysteries. 'I've given up trying to understand what I think about you.'

It was three days before Barney asked for Cassie's help: she'd assumed he must have forgotten Mel's suggestion. But then one afternoon when the Colonel was visiting, and Cassie was pretending to be busy and feeling like an old-fashioned chaperone, he poked his head round the morning room door.

'Frances, do you mind if I borrow Cassie? She volunteered to help with some of the paperwork in the office.'

That wasn't exactly how Cassie remembered it, but as Frances thought it a marvellous idea, and declared that Cassie had nothing else to do, she wasn't left with any choice.

'Brace yourself,' Barney said, smiling as they reached the office door. 'Now that I know that you're a qualified PA, with a fondness for files, folders and trays, I realise this may be your idea of hell.'

He wasn't exaggerating. Cassie saw that the desk was strewn with piles of paper, with some sheets flirting between two piles. More stacks lay on the windowsill and spread over the floor.

'You're not going to pass out at the state of it, are you?' Barney asked, when Cassie looked round but said nothing.

'I'll try not to. At least you know how to give

the kiss of life if I do.'

Cassie burned hot and cold in quick succession. What had she said that for? If she was going to be cooped in this small room with Barney for hours – days, judging by the amount of paper – there must be no thought of kissing. She walked over to the desk and flicked through a few of the papers. Some dated back several months.

'I dug out everything,' Barney said. 'In case you need to set up a system.'

Cassie ignored the smile that he seemed to think excused the chaos.

'How could you have been a doctor? Surely you had to do paperwork?'

'Too much paperwork. It's not my strength. I prefer the hands-on stuff.'

This wasn't going to work. Cassie was hearing a different conversation in her imagination: a layer of flirtatiousness that wasn't really there.

'Why don't you leave me to it?' she suggested. 'You must have your own work to do.'

'I do. I'll have this corner.' He pointed to the edge of the desk where his laptop was. 'You can have all the rest. I've brought you a chair.'

The chair was also covered in paper. He must have been hoarding for months. Cassie picked up the pile on the chair so she could sit down, asked a few quick questions about how he wanted things sorted, then set to work. Soon the task engrossed her, the simple pleasure of forming order from chaos. Even if she couldn't forget Barney's presence, she was able to concentrate despite it.

She was kneeling on the floor, arranging documents in ordered piles, when she felt a hand lightly graze her back. All thoughts of filing instantly vanished. Cassie sat up – her muscles twinging after too long bent over – and stared at Barney. He was laughing.

'You were miles away. I've spoken to you three times.'

That was good news: it meant her efforts to ignore him were working. 'Have you? What did you want?'

'I thought it was time for a break. You've been at it for over an hour.'

'Really? I should check on Frances.' Cassie stood up, but her legs had gone numb from kneeling on them, and she stumbled. Barney grasped her elbow.

'I'll pop round while I'm making the drinks.'

He disappeared and Cassie stretched. She had spent too long on the floor, but it had been worth it: once she had become familiar with the types of document, it had been quick work to divide them. She prowled round the office, exercising her stiff limbs, and stopped to look at an old map, framed and hanging on the wall. It showed Ribblemill and the surrounding area in 1934 and, as far as Cassie could see, it had hardly changed.

'Fascinating, isn't it?' Barney stood next to her, and handed over a mug of tea. 'Most of the other villages have developed but not Ribblemill.'

'Why hasn't it?'

'Because most of the land is owned by Ramblings, and the Smallwoods have always prevented new building. Frances' husband had plans to build a housing estate on these fields, but the villagers opposed it so strenuously that he had to back down. That's when the relationship between Ramblings and Ribblemill broke down. Until you came, and persuaded Frances to restore it.' He smiled at Cassie.

'So there's your farm,' she said, turning back to the map. 'And that must be old Joe's farm.' She pointed to another small building, which was officially called Beech Farm. 'I see now why you needed that strip of land between the two.' It all made sense now Cassie could see it spread out on the map. 'It's like someone has stolen a slice out of a cake.'

'The vital slice with the birthday candles on.' Barney picked up a packet of chocolate digestives and pulled one out. 'Someone has stolen it again.'

'What? I thought you went to the auction to buy it?'

'I did. I was beaten by a telephone bidder.'

'But who else would want it?'

'I've no idea. I've not been able to find out. Either someone causing mischief, or someone who will try to make a profit by selling it back at an inflated price. But I can't afford more than I bid. It's a disaster. I'm going to have to rethink all the plans for the farm.'

He looked and sounded so downhearted that it took a huge effort not to hug him. Instead Cassie distracted herself by studying the map again.

'Can you show me where the midnight ramble goes?'

'It starts at the No Name and goes all round here.' He traced the route with his finger. 'Then back to the No Name for a celebratory mug of hot punch. It's over four miles round. You don't

240

have to do it.'

'I can walk four miles!' Cassie put her empty cup down on the windowsill. How helpless did he think she was? Ethel and the Colonel and a considerable number of other pensioners were joining the ramble. 'I go walking everyday.'

'But this will be in the dark.' He rubbed his chin. 'Even on a dry, clear night it will be almost black going through the woods. You won't like it.'

He was remembering the night of the storm, Cassie realised. But he hadn't listened to what she'd said.

'I told you I wasn't scared of the dark.'

'I know, but...'

'I'm scared of not being able to see.'

It took him a few seconds, but Cassie saw his face change when he understood what she was saying.

'You're worried about going blind, because of the diabetes?'

'Wouldn't you be?'

'It's not going to get to that stage.' He reached out and ran his hand along her arm, in a gesture so fleeting that afterwards Cassie wondered if she had imagined it. 'We're not going to let that happen.'

The Colonel paid an unscheduled visit the next day. Within ten minutes of his arrival, Barney appeared to collect Cassie.

'Did you arrange this?' Cassie asked, as they wandered across the hall and through the servants' door to the wing where Barney had his office.

241

He smiled. 'It was your idea. You convinced me that Frances should be enjoying herself more. She enjoys the Colonel's visits, so I asked him to come again. Do you mind?'

Mind? Another couple of hours confined with Barney, acutely conscious of his every twitch, and of breathing in air that may have already travelled through his body? Of course she minded. But it was too delicious a torture to resist.

'As long as Frances is happy, I suppose I can endure it,' she said, and savoured the laugh that followed.

They had probably been working in easy silence for half an hour when a mobile phone rang out. Cassie waited for Barney to answer it, and looked up when he didn't.

'It's not me, it's you,' he said, smiling.

'It can't...' she began, but as she pulled the phone from her pocket, she realised that it was hers that was ringing, and her lungs refused to take another breath. Only one person had this number. It would only be used in an emergency. Cassie jumped up, spilling one of her carefully arranged bundles of paper, squeezed past Barney, and ran down the corridor until she reached an open door. She dashed into the flower room, leant against the ceramic sink and answered the call.

'Vicky? What is it? What's wrong?'

'Nothing!' Vicky's voice was full of warmth and smiles, and utterly heartbreaking to hear. 'Sorry, is this a bad time? You sound out of breath. Please tell me I'm interrupting something exciting.' Vicky laughed.

'I've been doing paperwork.' Which didn't sound

exciting – but Cassie had the advantage of Barney's image in her head, with his sleeves rolled up to his elbows, his shirt collar open to reveal a delectable hint of chest, and the smile that Cassie occasionally interrupted for no reason that she could fathom. She filed the image away. 'We agreed you wouldn't call unless there was an emergency.'

'This is an emergency. It's your birthday in less than a week, and I don't know where to send your present.'

Her birthday! Cassie had lost track of time. It was the day before the midnight ramble. She hadn't given it any thought.

'You don't need to send a present. It will be another working day, not worth marking. It's not as if I have much to celebrate this year, is it?'

'Your freedom? Come on, Cass. Mike hasn't been in touch for a while now.'

Cassie didn't answer. It felt too soon to be sure of that. Mike wasn't an impulsive character: he would plot and plan, and let things slowly brew to achieve maximum impact. Silence meant worry, not safety, in her experience.

'And the boys have made you a special card, which you're going to love.'

'Don't tell me. Cottonwool sheep eating a birthday cake?' It was the same every year: Alfie had designed it once, and when Cassie had loved it, he had insisted on making the same one for every subsequent year.

'Actually, Stanley has made it this year.'

It was said so casually that only someone who knew Vicky as well as Cassie would have noticed

243

anything amiss. It was too casual, too quick, too artificially bright. All Cassie's fears rushed back in.

'What's the matter with Alfie?'

'Don't panic, OK?'

Cassie did, at once, and her hand gripped the cold sink.

'Alfie had an accident at the weekend. He fell out of a tree, but he's fine. He had concussion and he's broken his arm.'

Cassie bent forward to try to get the blood back into her head. Not Alfie – the favourite she could never admit to having. She had nursed him as a baby, when Vicky had been too ill to look after him; she had cared for him as a toddler when Vicky had struggled after Stanley's birth. Cassie adored them both, as much as if they were her own, but Alfie was her special boy. And now she was stuck here, hundreds of miles away, not able to see that cheeky grin to be sure that he really was fine.

'Do you promise he's OK? You're not just telling me that?'

'Promise.' Vicky laughed. 'You know what he's like. He's thrilled with the attention, and that we're all running round after him. It was a clean break. The doctor said it will be as good as new in a few weeks.'

'Why didn't you ring me?'

'Oh Cass, you can't believe how much I wanted to. But there was no point upsetting you until we knew how bad things were.'

'Of course there was a point. I could have helped. I could have done something.'

'Not from wherever you are. And I didn't want you to feel forced into coming back. You have to put yourself first.'

But Cassie didn't want to. It had never been her way, and she hated that it had to be now. How was this freedom if she couldn't be there for her family when they needed her? Cassie walked back to the study, her heart churning with anxiety about Alfie, frustration at being so far away, and an overwhelming yearning to be with her family again.

Barney was in the doorway waiting for her. 'What's wrong? Cassie? What is it?'

'It's Alfie ... my nephew ... he's had an accident.' The words spattered out. 'He's broken his arm...'

It was too much. An image of Alfie, lying senseless on the ground, was caught in her head. Horror over what had happened to him was all jumbled up with relief that it hadn't been worse. Her throat tightened and she couldn't say another word.

Barney pulled her into his arms, wrapping himself round her, shielding her from any harm. It felt incredible; she had been born to be here. She rested her head against his shoulder – he was the perfect fit – and sobbed, while his hand slid up and down her back with slow, comforting strokes.

But as the sobs subsided, what had felt so safe began to feel dangerous. Cassie became conscious of the heat of Barney's body where it joined hers: of the smell of him, Imperial Leather soap and floral laundry powder; of the light pressure of his head, resting against hers. His hand had moved from stroking her back, and was tangled in her hair. His heart quickened and his breaths deepened – or perhaps it was hers – they were pressed

245

so close it was hard to tell.

Cassie was content down to the centre of her bones. So she pulled away, because whatever this was, she couldn't allow it to happen.

'Sorry,' she said, and she rubbed at her cheeks to wipe away the tracks left by her tears.

Barney came and perched on the desk beside her. Cassie glanced down at the small gap between their hands.

'What for? Someone you love is hurt. How could you not be upset?'

That wasn't why she had apologised, or wasn't the only reason. She was sorry because she wasn't in his arms any more; and because when she had been in his arms, she had forgotten all about Alfie. She was sorry, more sorry than she could ever explain, because for one amazing moment she had imagined that her feelings weren't entirely one-sided. Doing the right thing was excruciating when there was a glimmer of hope that the wrong thing might be possible. The gap between their hands was so small. It may as well have been a million miles.

'You need to go home,' Barney said. 'Whatever it is that's stopping you going back to Devon, you can beat it.'

'I know. I'll go after the garden party.' She had already made the decision, during the brief walk from the flower room to the office. She had to see her family. The ache to be with them had become too great to ignore, for any reason. If she stayed away because of Mike, he had won and she hadn't really escaped. As long as she restricted her life through fear of him, he still had control.

It was time for her to take back control, whatever the consequences – and however much the idea terrified her.

'I'll take you,' Barney said. Cassie looked up at his face.

'Why would you do that?'

'It's a long drive.' He smiled. 'And I've heard such great things about Devon that I'd like to see it for myself. In the meantime, why don't you Skype?'

'I don't have a computer.'

'Use this one.' Barney gestured to the desk behind him. 'Let's set it up now. You can be admiring Alfie's plastercast within the next few minutes.'

She could have cried again. He was the most incredible, kind man she had ever met. Instead she looked back down at their hands and watched as, quite of its own accord, her little finger stretched out until it rested against his.

The kitchen door swung open to let in Ruth, Barney and Frances. Barney was carrying his laptop, which was switched on, with the screen facing away from him. Something was moving on the screen, and a high-pitched chirruping noise was coming from it.

Barney walked towards Cassie, and lifted the laptop so that it was level with her face. The chirruping stopped, and as Cassie smiled at what she was seeing on the screen, her nephews launched into an exuberant rendition of 'Happy Birthday'. It was followed by a barrage of rude noises, face-pulling and monkey impressions which Alfie and Stanley found hysterical, until Vicky appeared to wish Cassie a happy birthday and whisk her children off to school. Barney put the laptop down on the table.

'Happy birthday,' he said, with a smile so hot it dried the tears hovering on Cassie's eyelashes.

'Thanks.'

It felt an inadequate response, but she didn't dare do more when her heart had already swollen to twice its size, and was pounding so loudly she was amazed no one had noticed.

'How did you do that?'

'I abused your privacy in a good cause, and contacted Vicky. Do I need to apologise?'

She laughed, and shook her head. She would have forgiven him anything for arranging that for her.

'How did you know it was my birthday? I didn't tell anyone.'

'You told me your date of birth months ago, when you first arrived and I had to sort out the car insurance.'

He had remembered it since then? There wasn't time to dwell on that. Ruth gave her a hug.

'Happy birthday, my love. It's a good job he remembered. What were you planning to do, let the day go by without a word?'

Cassie smiled. It was exactly what she had been planning – but she wouldn't have missed this for the world.

'Many happy returns, Cassie,' Frances said. She had taken a seat at the kitchen table. It was the first time Cassie had seen her in the kitchen for weeks. 'You are lucky to be young enough for birthdays to be so disposable. When you reach my age, you will want everyone to know that you have made it through to the next one.' Barney rested his hand on Frances' shoulder. 'Birthdays are the one exception to my no fuss rule. Here, come and take your present.'

Cassie took the parcel from Frances, and unwrapped it. Inside lay a beautiful dress, cream silk with tiny flowers on it.

'It is for the garden party,' Frances explained, blinking rapidly as Cassie held the dress against herself in delight. 'I wanted you to have a new dress, not a borrowed one. Becca chose it from her shop, but I am sure she can exchange it if you would rather have something else.'

'I wouldn't. I love it.' Cassie laid the dress carefully over the back of a chair and kissed Frances. She tried to hug her, but was waved away with a waft of lavender and a warning that she didn't condone unlimited fuss even on birthdays.

'Here's something to go with it,' Ruth said, passing over another parcel. This one contained a pair of sandals, strappy and sparkly, with higher heels than Cassie had worn for months. She put one on, and rolled her ankle from side to side, admiring it. Barney watched, smiling.

'You're all too kind,' Cassie said, putting the shoe back in the box. 'I don't deserve it, but thank you.'

'Nonsense,' Frances replied. 'You have not been treated as kindly as you deserve for a long time. I may not have said this as much as I should have done, but the months you have spent here have been the happiest I have known for many years, and happier than I ever expected them to be.'

This time Cassie refused to be batted away, and managed to get one arm round Frances. When she pulled back, Barney was waiting, holding out another gift.

'It's not much,' he said, hovering nearby with his hands in his pockets, while Cassie pulled off the paper with fingers that were trembling too much to work properly. She tore off the last piece, and found a black frame, about A4 size, which contained a black and white engraved print of Ramblings, dated 1889. The precise dark lines showed off perfectly the quirky architecture of the building. 'I thought it might remind you of your time here. But perhaps it's not as exciting as a dress and sparkly shoes.'

'It is. It's beautiful. Thank you.' This time words definitely were inadequate. Cassie stepped forward and kissed his cheek briefly. The scent of soap lingering on his skin brought back deliciously vivid memories of being held in his arms a few days ago. His eyes met hers as she pulled away.

'Right, I'll make your breakfast now,' Ruth said. 'Don't argue,' she continued, when Cassie opened her mouth to protest. 'You're being spoilt today. Besides, you need to be fresh-faced and rested for tonight.'

'Why? What's happening tonight?'

'Drinks in the pub. Mel insisted, and it's not as if you do much else with your evenings, is it? Unless you have a fella lined up to take you out as a birthday treat!' Ruth laughed. Cassie shook her head, and her eyes met Barney's again. He smiled.

'I'll pick you up at eight,' he said.

It was actually five minutes to eight when he

turned up, wearing dark jeans and a pale shirt, which made his hair look richer brown as it curled over the collar. Frances had coerced Cassie into a dress.

'You are keen,' Frances said, as he walked over to kiss her cheek. Cassie's stomach fluttered as she caught a waft of his aftershave. 'I do hope you are not planning to get drunk and show yourself up.'

'No, because I'm not sixteen any more.' He smiled. 'I'm driving, so if I show myself up it won't be down to alcohol.'

'It's silly for you to drive,' Cassie protested. 'Let's go in the Volvo. I can drive, and you can have a drink.'

'You're the perfect date,' Barney said, and then his smile locked, and he stroked along his jaw. 'I didn't mean that the way it sounded. You'd only be perfect because you would always drive.'

An awkward silence hovered. Barney rubbed his neck.

'I didn't mean that the way it sounded either. Of course you have qualities that would make you a perfect date, other than the fact you don't drink.'

At last his tongue was so tied he stopped talking.

'Really, Barney. One wonders whether you gained any benefit from your education, if you are so incapable of making yourself clear,' Frances said. 'Surely you do not intend to take Cassie to her birthday party in a truck? Look at her! She is dressed for a Rolls Royce at least. Unless you have arranged one of those, the Volvo will have to do.'

Cassie took pity on him.

'The Volvo is fine. You drive me there, and I'll drive you back.'

They were still arguing over it – in a friendly, trying to forget the earlier awkwardness way – when they walked into the No Name. It was busy: half the village seemed to be there. There was a thick crowd round the bar, making a lot of noise. Cassie had never seen the place so lively.

'Are you ready for this?' Barney asked, bending his head until his mouth was against her ear. She nodded, and tilted her head, so his eyes were only a few centimetres from hers. He had the most beautiful eyes: one minute deep enough to wallow in, the next twinkling with amusement. Now they revealed an extra dimension, a special glow that sizzled along Cassie's limbs. 'Whatever Mel has planned has nothing to do with me.'

He smiled and Cassie sucked in a breath, which rushed straight out again when Barney's hand rested on her back to steer her towards the bar. Every nerve-ending gathered in that one spot where the heat of his hand penetrated the flimsy fabric of her dress. She was vaguely aware of moving forward, of receiving birthday wishes, but all she could think was how that hand would feel if it strayed from her back, roamed over every part of her... She had never felt so wholly conscious of another person, so alive, so obsessed. She looked into Barney's face; his smile grew, and his thumb swept a sure stroke across her spine.

And then she heard Mel say, 'Here she is,' and Cassie was wrenched away from Barney, and she was thrust around like a pass the parcel, kissed by Mel, by Akram, by Ethel, by old Joe... The Colonel was there, Becca and her fiancé, Ruth and everyone that Cassie had met over the last few months, all here, it seemed, to show their affection and celebrate her birthday. Cassie laughed, and glanced over her shoulder to check that Barney was still there, still real, still smiling, then she turned back and her friends had shifted so that she could see the bar. And there, leaning one arm casually along the oak counter, stood Mike.

It was as if Cassie had been anaesthetised in every limb and organ. She had no idea if she breathed, or moved, or what her face was doing. Eyes wide, she stared at the man she hadn't seen for almost a year, in a place he should never have been.

'Sorry Cassie,' she heard Mel say from close beside her. She saw that Mel's hand was on her arm. She couldn't feel it. 'Let me introduce you. This is Mike Barrett. He's staying in one of our rooms for a few nights, and I invited him to join the party so he's not on his own. You don't mind, do you? He's a good laugh.' Mel walked over to Mike. 'This is Cassie, the birthday girl I was telling you about.'

Cassie watched as Mike put down his whisky glass with slow precision, eased up from the counter and walked towards her with heavy, deliberate steps.

'Hello Cassie,' he said. The sound of his voice restored her feeling, as revulsion, fear and despair crawled over her. 'You didn't think I'd miss your birthday, did you?'

253

He put one of his thick arms round her neck, pulled her towards him and kissed her, shoving his tongue deep into her mouth. Her taste buds recoiled at the lingering Glenmorangie.

'Cassie?' Mel's voice was too loud; or perhaps the pub had fallen silent. 'Do you know Mike?'

Mike laughed, the jolly boom he used in company. His arm remained round Cassie's shoulders, pinning her to his side. She stared at a crack in the flagstone floor, tracking it with her eyes, trying to convince herself that this wasn't happening.

'Of course she knows me.' One fat finger oozed along Cassie's collarbone. 'Although I can't blame her if she hasn't mentioned me. We had a ridiculous argument, and I behaved like an insensitive oaf. She ran away before I could make it up to her. I never imagined she would stay away so long. But I've learnt my lesson. From now on, darling, I promise I'll be the husband you deserve.'

There was a gasp – Cassie thought it came from Ethel, but it was hard to tell, because while she had been gazing at the floor, the occupants of the pub had gathered round like an audience at a play, or a lynch mob. All except the one person Cassie looked for now. Barney was alone, at the back, staring at her. His lips were flat, as if they had never known a smile. She forced herself to look away as Mike's finger dipped below the neckline of her dress.

'You can't believe how much I've missed you,' Mike said. His finger rubbed across the top of her breast. Bile churned in Cassie's stomach. 'Life without you has been intolerable. And not just for me. I can't wait to tell the children that

254

you're safe.'

The pub door crashed shut and Cassie knew, without needing to look, that Barney had gone.

CHAPTER NINETEEN

'Oh Cassie. You left your husband and kiddies? How could you?'

The disappointment in Ethel's voice tore at Cassie's heart. It was mirrored on every face she could see. The weight of disapproval in the room crushed her. She shrank back against Mike, as all the old thoughts resurfaced, ready to suck her back in. She was worthless. Mike was the only person who cared about her. She was lucky to have him. How could she have thought she deserved more?

'Cassie?' Even Mel was regarding her with sad incomprehension. 'Is this true?'

'Yes.' Her voice sounded strange: flat and robotic. 'Mike is my husband.'

'Don't be too hard on her,' Mike said. 'I'm as much to blame as she is. I thought we'd had a trivial row about the number of dresses she'd bought, but it obviously meant more to Cassie than I realised, we men aren't programmed to understand the importance of shopping.'

He laughed, his large body vibrating against Cassie's. 'And of course, she's been under a great deal of pressure with her illness.'

There were nods and smiles around the pub. It

was Mike's way. He was 'good old Mike'. People were always on his side. There was no point correcting his lies.

He could twist concrete if it stood in the way of what he wanted.

'But the children?' Mel persisted. 'How could you be away from them for so long? And never mention them? I thought we were friends.'

'They're not my children.' The appeal to friendship sparked a flicker of life back into Cassie. 'They're Mike's. They live with their mum.'

'Cassie's been marvellous with them,' Mike said. 'She's always treated them as her own. They adore her.'

'They don't.'

'Oh darling, you are funny.' Mike kissed the top of her head. 'Teenagers never mean what they say. Of course they don't really hate you.' He smiled round at everyone. 'I think, if you good people don't mind, that I'd like to take my beautiful wife upstairs and convince her how much she's been missed.'

'No.'

The cloud that had been swirling round Cassie, numbing her senses and dulling her brain, lifted at Mike's words – at the intentions they made clear to her. She might be married to this man, but she was in love with another. Even though nothing could come of those feelings, she couldn't bear to have Mike paw her when her nerve-endings still tingled with the memory of Barney's touch. Sex with her husband would be adultery to her heart. She ducked and escaped Mike's arm.

'I'm not going upstairs.'

256

'I suppose you're determined to have your party. What can I say? You know I can't deny you anything.' Mike smiled. Cassie wondered if anyone else could see how false it was.

'Let's do it in style. Mel, can we have drinks all round? Put it on my bill.'

There was an immediate dash for the bar.

'I'm sure I can wait a little longer. We have all night.'

'No.' It was no easier to say the second time. Sweat prickled under Cassie's arms. 'I'm not staying here tonight.'

'Then I'll come to you.' Mike's smile dropped, now attention was focussed on the bar. 'You have a lot of making up to do.'

'You can't come. My employer wouldn't allow it.'

'I am your employer.' He leaned forward, so close that she could count the broken veins that had appeared around his nose. 'Or have you forgotten your job as well as your marriage?'

'I haven't forgotten anything.'

She had scars on her heart that were never going to heal. She looked round, and saw Mel carrying a tray of drinks over to the other side of the pub.

'Mel, could you explain to Mike that I need to stay with Frances tonight?'

'Do you? I'm sure...' Mel stopped, as Cassie stared at her, willing her to help. 'I'm sure she would worry if you were away. Perhaps tomorrow night, after you've had chance to talk to her? Barney would surely offer to stay with her, in the circumstances.'

Cassie wished she was still numb, so the sound of Barney's name didn't hurt so much.

'Do you two want to use the snug? It will be a bit more private, and I'll make sure no one else comes in.'

Cassie nodded, and led Mike through the doorway into the snug. It was colder in here, and quieter, and Cassie pulled the edges of her cardigan across her chest.

'What was all that about, you stupid bitch?' Mike's voice rammed into her ear. 'Are you trying to humiliate me? Or are you still as frigid as when you left?' Cassie sank down onto the nearest chair, as tremors attacked her legs. 'Perhaps someone else shares your bed now, is that it? Who is it? One of the men in here?'

'There's no one else. These are my friends.'

'Friends? Do you think so? They didn't look friendly when they found out you'd lied to them.'

Mike yanked out a chair and sat down opposite Cassie. He reached across the table and grabbed her hand.

'I didn't mean to shout. You don't understand what it did to me when you left. Don't you realise that I'm the only friend you need? No one else would have spent the best part of a year trying to find you. No one will ever love you like I do, even the way you are now.'

'What's wrong with me?'

Mike scoured her with his eyes.

'You've put on weight. You'll have to get that off again.'

Cassie looked down at herself. Was she fat? She had put on weight since she arrived at Ramblings. She'd thought that was a good thing.

'And your hair needs cutting. You know I don't like it to go past your shoulders and cover your breasts.' He leaned forward and flicked her hair back over her shoulders. 'That's better. I'll book you in at the salon for a make over. They'll soon get you back to normal.'

Normal? Is that what she had been before? If life with Mike had been normal, what had her time at Ramblings been about? The power of Mike was sucking her back in, scattering rational thought. She was obese, wild haired, unkempt, but he still loved her. She heard the babble of voices drifting in from the bar, and the odd burst of laughter, and imagined it was about her. She thought she had made friends here, but perhaps Mike was right – perhaps they would all condemn her. Had running away been a mistake? Was Mike the only person who truly cared about her?

'You don't look very pleased to see me, Cassie.'

'I'm sorry.' It was odd how quickly that phrase had re-established itself on her tongue. She tried to smile, but the fog had settled back over her brain, and messages didn't seem to be getting through from there to her body.

Mike stood up and walked round the table. He stood behind Cassie and bent over her, one arm hanging over each shoulder, one large hand covering each breast. His breath scorched her ear.

'Look happy,' he said, 'or do I need to go back in there and find out which man is putting a smile on your face now?'

'Sorry, Cassie, I ... oh!' Mel dashed in, took one look at Cassie and turned her head away. 'I didn't mean to interrupt. Barney dropped these off for you.'

Mel put the Volvo keys on the nearest table and hurried out. Cassie stared at them, while Mike slobbered kisses down her neck. Barney had come back, and brought the keys. Despite what he must think of her, he cared enough about her to make sure she could get back to Ramblings. Mike was wrong. She did still have a friend, and not just any friend. Barney. A decent, kind man, so different from the man who even now was prising her dress off her shoulder. Cassie's heart started beating again, shocked into life by her love for Barney.

Revulsion crawled over her skin as Mike's tongue licked the hollow behind her collarbone. She lifted her arms and fought him off, and while he was still reeling in surprise, she grabbed the car keys and ran.

Frances dispensed with the usual greetings when Cassie joined her in the morning room the next day.

'Gracious, Cassie, I know it was your birthday yesterday, but you look ten years older this morning. Were you in the pub all night?'

'No.'

'Did you enjoy yourself?'

'Yes. Thank you.' Cassie went over to the desk and pulled out her notebook. 'Shall we carry on with the history today?' She needed to immerse herself in other people's lives, and forget about her own.

'Perhaps later, when you look more awake. I cannot have you mixing up your Ralphs and your

Richards, even if a certain Celia Smallwood acted as if they were interchangeable.'

Frances smiled, but Cassie's lips refused to respond. 'You are terribly pale, Cassie. Would a walk to the village do you good?'

'No!' Frances' teacup rattled on the saucer at Cassie's emphatic response. 'I do feel tired. I'll stay in today.'

'Should we call Barney, to check you over?'

'No! I didn't sleep well, that's all.'

She'd seen every hour go past, and every minute in between. Her head had whirled with questions: how had this happened? What should she do? Must she spend the rest of her life running? The alarm had gone off before she had worked out the answer to any of them.

'Is there not a meeting about the garden party this morning? You must go to that.'

'I'm sure they can manage without me today.'

Frances put her cup down on the side table, clasped her hands together and looked at Cassie.

'Why are you acting so oddly? Did something happen last night that I ought to be aware of?'

'No. Everything is fine.'

'Cassie, to date you have been one of the few people not to treat me like a senile old fool. Please do not start now.'

Cassie plucked at the cover of her notebook. If Frances didn't already know Cassie's secret, she didn't want to be the one to tell her. She couldn't bear to see disapproval in Frances' eyes too, but she couldn't bear to lie to her either.

'Has anyone told you about last night?' she asked.

'I have not heard a thing. I never listen to gossip.'

'You haven't seen Barney?'

'No. I hope he has not disgraced himself after I warned him to behave.'

'It's nothing to do with Barney. There's a man staying in the pub...'

'A paying guest?' Frances interrupted. 'How marvellous for Melanie. I told her she was wasting her money decorating those rooms. I am glad to be proved wrong. How is the man relevant?'

Another question that had bothered Cassie all night. She gave Frances the simple answer.

'He's my husband.'

She watched Frances closely, waiting for the flash of surprise, for her face to sag with disappointment or harden with disapproval. It didn't happen.

'What is he doing here?' Frances asked. She took hold of her stick, levered herself up and walked over to Cassie. 'Did he harm you last night?'

Frances' face was creased with worry, not disapproval. She patently wasn't surprised by Cassie's admission. Cassie didn't understand.

'You knew I was married?' Cassie asked. 'How?'

She was sure she hadn't let it slip in any way. There was no tell-tale mark on her finger where her ring had once been.

'I recognised the look in your eyes on our first meeting.' Frances touched her hand to Cassie's shoulder. 'Being mistreated by the person you should be able to trust implicitly leaves an unmistakeable mark.'

'You?'

Cassie couldn't believe it, and yet, why not? Money and a grand house were no protection from evil.

'Your husband?'

Frances nodded. 'He was an unhappy man, and was at pains to quash signs of happiness in those around him. There were beasts among men before either of us existed, and will continue to be long after we are gone.'

'But you stayed with him?'

'I did. For the children – and for myself. Where else would I have gone? Women did not walk out of marriages lightly in those days. He was very careful. Nothing ever showed, except the one time.'

It suddenly all became clear.

'The Buckingham Palace garden party?'

'Yes. I had been looking forward to it so much.'

Frances pressed her lips together and Cassie vowed to herself that whatever happened with Mike, she was staying here, and giving Frances the best garden party she possibly could.

'Were you hurt last night?' Frances asked.

'Not physically. Mike uses words, not fists.'

Frances surprised her again. 'It is all the same, and all inexcusable. What will you do?'

'I don't know.'

'Then I will tell you. You will not let him trap you in this house, or stop you from doing what you want to do. I will not watch you make my mistake. So this morning, you will go to the village, and attend the meeting.'

The meeting was in the No Name. The idea of going back there formed a ball of anxiety in

Cassie's throat restricting her breathing.

'I don't think I can...' she began.

'I know you can,' Frances replied. 'And you must. I have a list of items I need you to collect from the shop. Write them down, and then you can go.'

Cassie walked across the fields to the village, pausing at her favourite spot, where the stepping stones led the way across the river. She took out her phone, and turned it in her hands, wondering whether to ring Vicky. She wanted to – she was desperate to hear a friendly voice, and for someone to tell her what to do, but she put the phone away without dialling. Vicky had enough to worry about, without Cassie sharing her burden. She had to deal with this herself. She had spent the last year hiding from Mike, fearing that if he found her, he would snare her again. Last night he almost had. Somehow, if she wanted the hiding to end, she had to find the strength to resist him.

She reached the village green and saw Mike sitting on a bench facing the No Name. Cassie lurked behind the gable end of a cottage, her heart fluttering, and studied the man who was technically her husband. He had put on weight. She hadn't noticed that last night. Always a large man – larger than life was his signature style, and what had initially attracted her – he was now on the perimeter of being overweight. Thin strands of hair blew in the breeze over his shiny scalp. He was fourteen years older than Cassie, and looked every day of it.

Keeping a close eye on his back, Cassie walked

briskly round the other two sides of the triangle, making it to the shop without him noticing. A queue snaked round the Post Office counter, but the shop area was empty, apart from Ethel, waiting to serve at the till. Cassie grabbed a basket and scoured the shelves for the random items Frances had requested, including tinned mandarins... When had she ever shown interest in eating those?

Ethel smiled when she reached the till, but to Cassie it felt like the polite gesture of the shopkeeper, rather than the warmth of a friend.

'Are you feeling better now?' Ethel asked, as she delved into the basket.

'Better?'

'Mike explained that you were taken poorly last night. What a shame, on your birthday, and spoiling your reunion like that. You should have known better than to have that whisky.'

Cassie managed a tight smile as Ethel rang a tube of toothpaste through the till. So that was the story Mike had given: that she had made herself ill with drinking. It was her fault, of course. It always was. But how had no one doubted it? She hadn't touched a drop of alcohol since she arrived in Ribblemill. It was the power of Mike. He could convince Eskimos that they were living in the middle of a burning hot desert.

'Poor Mike was ever so upset,' Ethel went on. 'After he'd waited so long to see you, as well. Still, he put on a brave face, and was the life and soul of the party. We've not had a night like it in the No Name for years. I don't know how you could have abandoned him, Cassie. Surely he can't have done anything so bad? He's devoted to you, we could all see that. You young people want marriage to be easy and perfect. You need to put in a bit more effort.'

'I put in a lot of effort,' Cassie said, handing over her money, but she knew before Ethel shook her head that she was wasting her breath. Mike had snared Ethel, and presumably the whole village. No words from Cassie could undo that. Ethel looked at her watch.

'Time for the committee meeting,' she said, and bellowed for her assistant to mind the shop. 'Shall we walk over?'

Mike was still sitting on the bench when they stepped outside.

'There's Mike!' Ethel cried, as excited as a child seeing Father Christmas. 'Bless him; he must be waiting for you. I think I mentioned last night that we had a meeting this morning. Coo-ee!'

Her screech could probably have been heard at Ramblings. There was no chance that Mike would miss it, however much Cassie hoped. He stood up and lumbered towards them.

'If it isn't my two favourite ladies! I hope there are no ill effects this morning, Ethel, after all those sherries.' Ethel simpered and giggled like a teenager. 'And my lovely Cassie, aren't I lucky to catch you this morning? And looking so irresistible.'

He swooped down and pushed a kiss onto Cassie's lips. She stepped back, and wiped her mouth, but not quickly enough. Barney's truck was driving past. Gin's head poked out of the passenger window, and beyond Gin, Barney's head was turning back to face the front. He must have seen them.

'We have to go to our meeting,' she said.

'Ethel, you wouldn't mind if I delay Cassie for a few minutes, would you?'

Ethel shook her head.

'Don't worry, I won't let her run away.'

Ethel laughed, and crossed the road to the No Name.

Mike waited until she disappeared through the front door.

'Where did you disappear to last night?' The contrast between the public face and the private voice was stark. 'Why must you always show me up? What do you think the people in the pub thought when you ran out?'

Cassie shrank back, her lips refusing to open.

'Well?' he pressed.

'I don't know.'

'They thought you were being ridiculous. This is what happens when you're away from me. You behave irrationally. You can't manage on your own.'

He reached out and pushed her hair back over her shoulders.

'Look at you. You're a mess. I hate seeing you like this. You've fallen to pieces without me.'

'I haven't. I have a job...'

'I've heard all about that.' Mike laughed. 'Wiping the arse of some rich old biddy? If there was anything in it for you, it might be worth-while, but why bother when she has children?'

'Frances is my friend.'

'No, she's not.' He spoke slowly, as if she were stupid. 'She pays you to stay with her. I've ex-plained this to you before. You think people are your friend when they're not. How many times have I had to save you from false friendships? Don't look so glum.' He stroked her cheek, and his finger felt like sandpaper grazing her skin. 'You'll always have me.'

That was exactly what Cassie was afraid of – that she would never truly be free of him. And worse, that she would be sucked in again, and not want to be free. Part of her – smaller than it used to be, but still there – was responding to him, grateful that he cared. She had to squash it.

'I need to go,' she said, seeing the Colonel heading into the pub. 'The meeting is about to start.'

'I'll walk with you.' He strolled along at her side, with every appearance of being a devoted husband. Cassie knew he wanted to check whom she was meeting. Even in the days when she had been allowed out without him, he had always insisted on taking her and collecting her. He followed her into the pub, and smiled when he saw Mel, Ethel and the Colonel gathered round a table, with one spare place left for Cassie.

'This is a very select meeting, isn't it? As there are so few of you, I think it's safe to give Cassie her present. Mel, is it still behind the bar?'

'Yes, I'll get it.'

Mel brought over a thin rectangular parcel, immaculately wrapped in red foil. Mike took it and put it on the table in front of Cassie.

'A small part of what I wanted to give you last night,' he said, resting his hand on Cassie's shoulder. 'Aren't you going to open it?'

She picked it up. It was light and rattled. She knew at once what it was, and sure enough, she picked off the paper to reveal an expensive box of chocolates.

'Ooh, Hotel Chocolat, they're posh,' Ethel said, peering across the table. 'Aren't you lucky!'

'They're your favourites, aren't they?' Mike squeezed her shoulder. Cassie nodded.

'Yes. Thank you.' They had been her favourites, when they had first met, in the days when Cassie still ate chocolate. He knew she wouldn't touch them now. That was the point of the gift: to make him look good and her feel bad. It was a double whammy. A confused frown hovered over Mel's face as she looked between Cassie, the chocolates and Mike.

'I'll save your other presents for tonight,' Mike said. 'We may need more privacy for those.'

'I'm busy tonight.'

'Doing what?' Cassie squirmed as Mike's fingers stroked her throat.

'A midnight walk. It's for villagers.'

'Oh, don't worry about that,' Ethel said, beaming at Mike. 'You count as an honorary villager as you're Cassie's husband. You'll join us, won't you? We can find a spare torch and bells if you haven't got any with you.'

'It sounds like an event not to be missed.' Mike laughed. 'As long as I'm with Cassie, I don't mind what I do.' He kissed her neck. 'I'll see you later.'

The Colonel and Ethel hurried off after the meeting. Cassie loitered, packing up her notes and pens as slowly as she could, dreading going outside in case Mike was waiting for her.

Mel carried the coffee cups over to the bar.

'Is everything OK?' she asked, sitting back down next to Cassie. 'There were a couple of times during that meeting when I had to look twice to check you were still awake.'

'I didn't sleep well.'

'Because Mike's here? He must have gone to a lot of trouble to track you down.' Mel paused. Cassie didn't respond. 'You don't seem happy to see him.'

'I'm not. He wasn't meant to find me. I left him.'

'If I had a pound for every time I'd threatened to leave my husbands over the most trivial things...' Mel laughed. 'Let's just say the labels in my clothes wouldn't say George at ASDA.'

'It wasn't over something trivial.'

Cassie twisted a pen in her hand. She had to tell someone. She had to hear the words out loud, because as long as she stayed silent it was as if the truth didn't exist.

'I left him because of some fundamental things, things I wish someone had warned me about before. Such as never assume a man who has children wants more. Never assume that a man who wants to marry you enjoys your company as well as your body. And,' she stumbled over the words, 'never assume that the man who says he loves you will be kind to you.'

She looked up, straight into Barney's eyes. He was standing behind Mel, and Cassie had no idea how long he'd been there, or what he might have heard. Despite everything going on, her heart shifted at the sight of him. He was crumpled and stubbly, tousle-haired and tired, and beyond doubt the loveliest man she had ever seen. But how could she let that thought linger in her head when her husband's touch was so freshly imprinted on her skin?

'Sorry,' Barney said, and he dropped his gaze to the table. Cassie hid her hands in her lap. 'I saw the Colonel outside and assumed the meeting was over, or else...'

He didn't finish, and didn't need to. Or else he wouldn't have come in and risked seeing Cassie: that was what he would have said. It hurt whether he spoke the words or not.

'You've treated yourself with these, haven't you, Mel?'

The box of chocolates from Mike lay open on the table. There were a few left after the meeting. Barney reached down and took one, popping it whole into his mouth.

'Delicious, aren't they?' Mel said. Barney nodded. 'Mike bought them for Cassie.'

Barney swallowed. 'Sorry, I didn't think they were yours. You said you didn't eat chocolate.'

He rubbed his hand against his mouth, as if to wipe away any trace of it. Cassie felt as if he were wiping away any connection to her.

'You're pale. Have you checked your blood sugar?'

'No, because I haven't eaten any of the damn things!' Cassie shoved the box across the table so hard that a couple of chocolates fell out. 'You can have them. Why does everything have to be so medical with you? Can't I just be a normal person, with problems that don't all relate to my health?'

There was a moment of silence, and then Barney came nearer and grabbed her trembling

271

hand. 'Why have you done this?'

Cassie tried to pull away, but he was holding on too tightly. The red raw patch on her skin was in front of him, evidence of a long night of anxious rubbing.

'What do you have to be worried about? Wasn't it the perfect birthday, being reunited with your husband?'

The faint tone of sarcasm was infuriating. Cassie snatched her hand back.

'It was perfect until we walked into the pub.' She pushed back her chair and stood up. 'We're not reunited and we never will be.'

She gathered up her bag, and took a few steps towards the door.

'Cassie says she's left Mike,' she heard Mel whisper to Barney.

'Has she?' Barney made no effort to lower his voice. 'Women give up on marriage at the slightest provocation. I know that only too well.'

Cassie turned back. The frantic beats of her heart thudded in her ears. She looked at Barney and he met her gaze with his long, unblinking stare.

'Do you want to know why I left him?'

She wrapped her arms round herself, wondering if she was really going to do this. Not even Vicky knew what had finally made her snap. She hadn't wanted to acknowledge it to herself, let alone anyone else. But this wasn't just anyone else – this was Barney – and she couldn't live with him thinking badly of her.

'I didn't leave him because of any slight provocation. I didn't even leave him when he locked me in the house on my own one night, and took the fuse out so the lights wouldn't work.'

She closed her eyes and braced herself to say it.

'I stayed with him through everything, until the day when he took away my insulin, and refused to let me have it back until I had sex with him. So I did, and then I left him.'

'Mike?' Mel had stood up, and her palm was pressed against her forehead, as if it were hurting to take this in. 'He did that? But he seems such a great guy, and so devoted to you...'

The adrenalin rushed out, leaving Cassie flat. It shouldn't be so disappointing. It was the reaction she had always anticipated, if she tried to tell the truth. Mike won over everyone. It was hard for the watching world to distinguish between the appearance of devotion and the reality of control. It had been hard enough for her to understand the difference. She looked at Barney. His hands were gripping the back of the chair in front of him, his knuckles shining white.

'I saw it often enough in A&E,' he said. His eyes bored into Cassie's, from a face paler than she had ever seen. 'Too often. And the ones that seemed most devoted were the worst. But you...' He took a step towards Cassie. 'How can anyone have done that to you?'

Did he believe her? Could she have some support at last? Hope flared, and then faltered. Her judgement was unreliable. She didn't need Mike to tell her that; her involvement with him was proof enough. So when the pub door opened and a group of walkers surged in, she used the diversion to escape back to Ramblings.

CHAPTER TWENTY

It was the perfect night for a ramble. The sky had deepened to the colour of squid ink and the full moon played out with the stars. Cassie drove to the No Name, deliberately going at the last minute to avoid conversation, and found a huge crowd gathered, ready to walk. There must have been a hundred people there, of all ages, from pensioners balancing on walking sticks to children running round, and even a couple of babies strapped on to their parents.

It was an extravaganza of light and noise. Everyone had a torch or lantern, so it looked as if a swarm of giant fireflies had huddled together for a party. Beams of white light duelled with yellow and bizarrely, one disco light flashing neon pink and green. Everyone had a bell of some description too, and the night air jingled and echoed with lively sleigh bells and solemn hand bells.

Cassie had taken a torch from Ramblings, and would have managed without bells, but Frances had other ideas. She made Cassie spend a dusty half hour in the cellar, searching for a box labelled 'midnight ramble'. It contained a couple of broken torches which looked old enough to be prototypes, an old-fashioned gas lantern and numerous cuffs with small bells sewn on. Most of these were too big for Cassie's slim wrists, but at the bottom of the box Frances discovered two elastic bracelets with sleigh bells sewn on. They had clearly been made for children, but as the elastic had deteriorated over the years, they now easily stretched to fit Cassie. So to Frances' delight, Cassie now joined the other ramblers with bells adorning her wrists, tinkling with every move she made.

She lurked at the back of the crowd, peering over shoulders as well as she could to see who she recognised. Mel and Akram were at the front, easily visible in their matching hats with flashing lights left over from Christmas. Cassie smiled to see Lydia hanging about with a couple of friends, pretending that Mel didn't exist. Ethel was also easy to see, because she was wearing a fluorescent yellow jacket and head torch, as if she might be heading down a mine rather than round the village. There was no sign of Barney, or of Mike. A spark of hope lifted Cassie. Might he have changed his mind about coming?

Cassie jumped as a gong sounded. The jingling and the chattering stopped, and the crowd turned to face the No Name car park. The Colonel was standing on a crate so everyone could see him.

'Ribblemillers, friends and guests, welcome to our midnight ramble,' he boomed though a megaphone. His greeting was returned with a cheer and a ringing of bells. He raised his hand for silence. 'Every year we gather and walk the boundaries of our village, in a ceremony that has taken place for centuries. We unite and ring our bells to warn any evil spirits that there is no home for them in Ribblemill.' Another loud cheer rose up. 'So on behalf of Ribblemillers gone before, Ribblemillers here now, and Ribblemillers yet to come...' A few wolf-whistles broke out. 'Let the chant begin. Evil spirits be gone! Evil spirits be gone!'

The crowd took up the chant, and rang their bells and stamped their feet to accompany the words. The noise, and the energy, and the camaraderie between the villagers were incredible. Cassie was transfixed. She wanted to be part of this; she wanted to be a true Ribblemiller, chanting and rambling with family and friends – not hiding at the back, worrying about who might see her. She would have been a part of this, if Mike hadn't turned up and spoilt everything. And as she was swept along in a cacophony of sound and warmth, determination stiffened her bones. Mike had taken so much from her. He wasn't taking this away too.

With a cry of 'Let's away!' the Colonel led a procession from the No Name, past the boarded up ruins of the village hall, and over a stile into a field. The villagers formed a solid snake of light at first, as they chanted and jingled along, but as the walk went on, groups broke off and the chants largely died away, replaced by chatter and laughter. Cassie was alone, but there was something wonderfully invigorating about walking out at this time, feeling the night air tousling her hair, seeing only one torch beam ahead, and with the pervasive silence of the countryside almost drowning out the sound of human life.

The path continued through a small wood, and as Cassie stepped into the trees to let a family of fast walkers go by, a hand clamped round her wrist. Mike yanked her further into the trees, and turned on her. His breath was laboured and panting, and every exhalation carried the pungent stench of cheese and whisky. Cassie held her breath for as long as she could, until her chest quivered and she had to gasp for air.

'Where have you been all day?'

His anger was a relief, in a way: better that than the usual possessive pawing.

'At work.'

'Until this time? I expected you hours ago, after you'd spoon-fed the old dear.'

'Frances can feed herself.'

'Then you should have left her to it.' His hand tightened, and the sleigh bells on Cassie's wrist jingled. 'I'm starting to get the idea that you're not as pleased to see me as you should be. We could have been in bed, not out on this ridiculous walk. We could have been at home. I've spent a lot of time and trouble trying to find you. You need to be showing considerably more gratitude.'

Cassie raised her torch and pointed it in his face. His nose shone Rudolph red; sweat pooled in the lines on his forehead and trickled down the sides of his face. It was hard to believe she had ever loved him, but she supposed she must have done. When he had smiled, and laughed with her, not at her; when she had still believed that the look and words of love were true, not just bait for the trap, so he could possess her. She had never felt the love that she now knew was possible; and whatever there had been was long gone.

'I'm not pleased to see you,' she said, keeping her voice low as another group rambled past. 'You're wrong if you think I'll be returning to Bristol with you. I'm staying here.'

Mike dragged her closer, until she was pressed

against him, and with his free hand he snatched her torch and threw it on the ground. The light went out. He switched off his own torch, so the darkness of the night crept round them.

'You silly bitch, what are you going to do in this dump? Do you think anyone cares whether you're here or not? No one gives a toss about you. I can't see any of your new friends rushing to walk with you, can you? You're nothing.'

His fingers crushed her wrist. His voice rose with every word.

'Do you think you're going to find someone better than me? Don't count on it. No man would be interested in a defective freak like you. You don't drink, you're full of puncture marks, you make the most godawful fuss over what you eat, and frankly you're as exciting as a stiff old doll in bed. You don't have any other options. I'm all you've got. You're coming home with me.'

'Never!' Cassie shouted, and instantly, as if it had been a code word, a semi-circle of light surrounded them. Cassie squinted against the brightness, unable to see the figures behind the lights.

'Let her go, you brute,' Mel said.

Cassie thought she had never heard a sweeter sound. Then she did.

'You're wrong. We all care.'

Barney's voice was loud and crisp, and one light moved forwards, breaking rank with the others. Cassie knew it was him, even before the torch beams lit him up from behind. He strode towards them, until he stared down on Mike, who at last dropped Cassie's arm.

'Don't you dare speak to her like that. And for

278

the record,' he added, quiet enough that Cassie could hear but not the others, 'no decent man would be bothered about any of those things.'

Before Cassie could process that speech everyone moved at once. The circle of light closed round them, and Cassie made out Akram as well as Mel, and Ethel and her husband, and various other people she had met at the Saturday library or knew from the meetings held at Ramblings. Mel pulled her back, and suddenly everyone was patting her shoulder, or rubbing her arm, and asking how she was, and showing that what Barney had said was true. They cared. Cassie's throat burned with tears that she wouldn't allow to fall, because she was never going to let Mike have the satisfaction of thinking he had upset her again.

'Walk's over for you, mate,' Akram said, and he and another man took hold of Mike by the arms. 'We're taking you back to the pub.'

'You can stay for the rest of the night,' Mel added, 'since you've paid. But I want you gone first thing in the morning. And you won't be getting breakfast!'

Akram dragged Mike round to lead him away. Ethel darted in front of him.

'Evil spirits be gone!' she shrieked, and waved a stick of bells in his face. 'That told him,' she said, as Mike was finally escorted off. 'Good riddance to bad rubbish. No offence, Cassie love.'

'None taken.' She bent down and picked up her torch. She shook and thumped it, but it wouldn't switch on. 'What are you all doing here?'

'Looking for you,' Mel said. 'We were worried. Barney told us that we hadn't to leave you on your own tonight, but we all thought you were walking with someone else.'

She put her arm round Cassie, and gave her a big squeeze.

'I'm sorry. We really cocked it up. You shouldn't have had to go through that.'

'I'm glad it happened.'

Mel looked doubtful, and Cassie rushed to explain.

'He's told me for years that no one cares about me apart from him. You've all proved him wrong. I can't begin to tell you how much that means.' Cassie's voice wobbled.

Mel brushed her hand across her eyes. 'I wish you'd told me before. I would never have let him within a mile of the No Name.'

She gave Cassie another hug.

'We'd better get a move on. Ruth should have the punch well underway, but she'll never serve this crowd by herself. We must have a record turnout this year. Are you coming, Barney?'

'In a minute. We'll catch you up.' He took the torch from Cassie's hand. 'I'll see if I can fix Cassie's torch.'

'OK.' It was too dark to see Mel's expression, but the amused curiosity in her voice needed no illumination. 'Come on, everyone, let's get going.'

Mel led her gang though the trees and back to the main path, and their lights faded out of sight. Barney handed his torch to Cassie, while he un-screwed the top of hers, and poked around inside it. It didn't work when he put it back together.

'I think it must be knackered,' he said. 'How are you feeling?' He rummaged in his pocket and pulled out a familiar yellow bag. 'I brought Jelly Babies.'

'I don't need them.'

The words came out more sharply than Cassie had planned, but really, why did he always have to see her as a patient? She had never felt better. She had resisted Mike, not been dragged down by his words. She was exhilarated, not ill.

'Thanks,' she added, a little too late.

A couple went by on the path. A low male voice floated through the gloom, answered by a feminine giggle. It made Cassie acutely aware that she was alone in the dark with Barney, standing so close that his warm breath blew across the top of her head, and if their arms weren't quite brushing, it would take only a twitch on one side or the other to close the gap. Cassie eased back, and the bells on her wrists tinkled.

Barney reached out for her hand and lifted it for a closer look. Cassie's breathing went wild, as she seemed to take in too many breaths and not let enough out. She wondered if it was too late to change her mind about the Jelly Babies.

'Where did you find these?' he asked, plucking at the elastic band round her wrist. The bells jingled at his touch. 'We used to wear these when we were young.'

'Frances.' It was as much as Cassie could say, with Barney's finger tantalising the inside of her wrist.

'You know...' His thumb drew a faint circle on her skin.

'Yes?' The word rushed out on a gasp.

'Sexual problems can be a common issue with

diabetes. You should mention it at clinic. There are various things that might help.'

It wasn't what she had been expecting – hoping – he would say. Disappointment punched her with such a forceful right hook that her head spun and any chance of making a sensible reply vanished.

'Will you stop being a doctor for once? The diabetes isn't the problem,' she snapped. 'I didn't want him. I didn't find him attractive any more. Is that plain enough for you? It doesn't mean that I have no desire.'

And then, without stopping to think whether it was a good idea – because she would surely have concluded that it wasn't – she curled her arm round his neck, pulled him nearer, and with the accompanying jingle of sleigh bells, she kissed him. It was meant to be an angry kiss, to prove her point, and she kept her eyes wide open; but it was too dark to see much, and the limited vision en-hanced every other sense. His lips were warm against her cold ones. The hair at the nape of his neck threaded softly between her fingers. She heard his breathing change, the breaths becoming deeper, and then – unexpectedly – he kissed her back.

The torches fell to the floor. Barney pulled her into his arms. She felt every flex of his muscles as his hands explored, awakening delicious sen-sations across skin that hadn't felt a tender touch in too long. And she realised, in her last few moments of lucidity, that this was the only time she was ever going to kiss Barney Smallwood – ever going to kiss the man she loved more than anyone she had ever known – so she threw herself in to it, unable to conceal her feelings. And then there was no more thought.

'Cassie?'

Cassie hardly registered the sound, until Barney's back stiffened beneath her hands and his lips stilled. A beam of light flashed across them. It was as good as a bucket of cold water. Cassie stumbled back, shivering as the night air replaced Barney's embrace.

'I think I've proved my point,' she said.

'I think you have.' Barney's voice sounded as unsteady as hers.

But if she had been proving a point – and Cassie's thoughts were still whirling too much to think this through – what had he been doing? She hadn't imagined what had just happened. He had kissed her, as much as she had kissed him. He had been as consumed as her. Her chest burned at the memory of it. She lifted a foot, as if to take a step forward again.

'There you are!' Mel was back, shining a torch at Cassie. 'We met someone with a spare torch, so you can have this one. We were worried when you didn't follow, even if you were in Barney's safe hands.'

Safe? There was nothing safe about Barney's hands. Mel linked her arm in Cassie's.

'Shall we get going? Barney, you're faster than us. Would you mind running on ahead to the No Name and giving Ruth a hand with the drinks?'

'But...'

'Thanks! You're a star.'

Mel lifted her lantern so the light spilled onto Barney's chest and sent a soft glow over his face.

His hair was sticking out at the side. He looked shell-shocked.

'Off you go then!'

He picked up his torch and jogged away. Mel squeezed Cassie's arm and they set off on the ramble again, Mel keeping up a constant stream of chatter. Cassie knew what Mel was doing: she was trying to distract her from thoughts of Mike, and what he had said. But it wasn't Mike she needed distracting from. What had she been thinking of, kissing Barney? More interestingly, what had he been thinking of, kissing her? Had it been real, or a pity kiss, to make her feel better? Wasn't it exactly the sort of kind thing he would do, after hearing Mike's cruel words? How could she face him again in that case?

'I won't come in for a drink,' Cassie said, pulling her arm free from Mel's as they arrived at the pub car park.

'I don't think he'll show his face downstairs, but I don't blame you,' Mel said. 'You've had quite an evening.'

There was no arguing with that. Rejecting her husband and forcing herself on another man seconds later... It certainly made a change from her usual night, watching *News 24* with Frances. Cassie headed over to the Volvo, but her steps slowed when she saw Barney leaning against the side of the car. He met her in the middle of the car park. Cassie stared at the floor. It was impossible to look at him without a bullet train of desire racing from one extreme to the other. She knew what those lips tasted like. She knew what those hands could do. She knew what that body felt like, welded against hers. How could she unknow those things, so she could behave normally again?

'Cassie.'

Even his voice saying her name made her yearn to reach out for him. He came close, but didn't touch her. She focussed on his walking boots.

'What you said this morning ... about him withholding your insulin...' He stumbled over the words. 'Did you report it? You could probably get an injunction to keep him away. You know what that was, don't you?'

'Yes. Bullying.'

'I can think of a much worse name for it than that.'

'Don't!' Cassie looked up. Under the lights of the car park, Barney's eyes glittered. 'Don't say it. Don't make me think of it that way.'

'Cassie...' His hand stretched out, but stopped short of touching her. He let it fall back down. 'What can I do?'

'Nothing. There are some things not even you can cure.'

He remained in the car park, watching her, as she drove away.

Despite the late night, the library was open in the ballroom as usual the next morning. The Colonel was at the head of a queue of villagers waiting outside when Cassie unlocked the door.

'Good morning, Cassie.' The Colonel nodded at her. 'Beautiful day.'

Cassie peered past him at the dull grey sky, which looked as if it had been lightly shaded in with a pencil. It wasn't raining, so she supposed for Lancashire it did qualify as a good day. The Colonel walked in and gave her an awkward pat on the arm before taking up his habitual post on a chair near the door. The other villagers offered similar gestures of support. It was hard to keep smiling when every act of kindness confirmed how far the news of her humiliation had spread.

The library had been running for half an hour, when the sound of raised voices drifted down the corridor, and Mike burst into the room, a panting Colonel close behind.

'There was no stopping him,' the Colonel said.

Mike stomped across the room to where Cassie was sitting behind the desk. He looked terrible. His bloodshot eyes suggested a late night with the whisky bottle, and he wore yesterday's clothes, crumpled down one side as if he had slept in them. But these things were only temporary distractions from his face. His nose was bulbous and red, dried blood crusted round his nostrils, and his top lip was swollen and cut. Cassie jumped up.

'What's happened to you?'

Had he been mugged? He would be furious, especially as he was only here because of her. How could it have happened in Ribblemill? She hadn't heard of a single crime since she'd lived here.

Mike took a step closer, and loomed over the desk.

'Your lover happened.' He gestured at his face. 'Did you put him up to this?'

Cassie moved behind her chair.

'What lover?'

'How many have you got, you fucking whore?'

The words bounced round the vast expanse of

the ballroom, straight into the ears of everyone there. No one moved. Cassie closed her eyes, and drew her elbows into her side, trying to shrink into herself, and become invisible. And then she heard Frances' voice

'Cassie dear, who is this appalling man?'

Cassie opened her eyes. Frances had risen from her chair, and was leaning on her stick, gazing across at her.

'It's Mike,' she said. 'He's...' She couldn't bring herself to say it.

'I'm her husband,' Mike finished. 'A fact she seems determined to forget.'

'I think we should adjourn to the Green Salon.' Frances turned to Mike. 'You may follow. Colonel, would you mind keeping an eye on the library? We will be down the corridor if there are any problems.'

Frances led the way to a gloomy, north-facing room, with dark wood panelling along the walls and soft furnishings in an unpleasant shade of bottle green. She patted an upright chair, making dust billow out, and sat down. Mike stared at her.

'We don't need an audience. I want to speak to my wife alone.'

There was a sarcastic inflection on the word 'wife'. Cassie shuffled towards the fireplace, and leant against the wall.

'I do not know where you were brought up,' Frances said, 'but here in Lancashire, it is the custom for a house owner to dismiss a visitor, not the other way round.'

The expression on her face as she looked Mike up and down would have made Cassie laugh if

287

the last few days hadn't chased away her sense of humour.

'I would not trust you alone with one of the stuffed birds in the gallery, never mind with Cassie.'

She sat up straight, her stick in her hand. 'Say your piece.'

His piece proved short. 'Pack your bags. You're coming home.'

'No. I told you last night. I'm not going anywhere with you. This is my home.'

'Are four bedrooms not enough for you now? You grasping bitch. I gave you everything. Designer clothes, five-star holidays, hair done at the best salon in town. What more could you have wanted?'

'Kindness? Love? Children? Those other things were for you, not me.'

Cassie was betrayed by a wobble in her voice, and Mike changed tack at once.

'Children? Fine. I'll make you pregnant, if that's what it takes.' He bent towards Cassie, and lowered his voice. 'But don't think I'll have anything to do with it, if it turns out defective like you.'

Frances rapped her stick on the floor, and Mike stepped back. He was smiling – although the burst lip turned it into a grimace. He thought he had won, that he had offered the one thing that Cassie couldn't resist. She could see it in the confident way he was standing, hands in pockets, chest forward, chin jutting out, challenging her to turn this down. And somewhere low in her stomach, she felt a dormant part of her ache. This was what she had wanted, from the moment she had married him – a little Alfie of her own. But that was before she had come to know the real Mike. She had killed her dreams years ago. She would never risk him treating a child the way he treated her.

'I don't want your baby,' she said.

'Are you so confident you're going to find someone else?' Mike laughed. 'Your prospects aren't good, are they? Those big eyes aren't going to be so attractive when you're blind. Your voice won't sound sexy when you're constantly asking for things to be done for you. It's me or nothing.'

'Then I choose nothing.' Cassie clenched her hands behind her back, her thumb rubbing away at already raw skin. 'It would be better to live alone for the rest of my life than spend another night with you. I would rather never have children than make you a father again.'

'She's not going to last much longer, is she?' Mike jerked his head towards Frances. 'You won't have a home when she dies. You'll come running back to me then.'

'Young man, I intend dying at my own convenience, not yours.'

Frances spoke in a voice that could have quelled a Roman army. Mike turned towards her, and took a stride forward.

'You senile old bat, I could kick that chair away and finish you now.'

'Don't you dare go near her!'

Cassie grabbed the nearest item off the mantelpiece, and marched up to Mike. She stopped in front of him, fury not fear causing her breath to pump out in rapid puffs.

'What are you planning to do with that?' Mike sneered.

Cassie glanced at her hand. She was holding an ivory monkey, its hands clamped over its mouth. It wasn't the ideal weapon. He didn't think she had the guts to do it Laughing, he took a step nearer Frances. Cassie swung back her arm, and whacked him on the chin with the monkey.

It didn't do much damage – his head was thick enough to withstand more force than Cassie could offer – but the exhilaration that surged through her was like nothing she'd ever known. She pulled her arm back to have another go, but he grabbed her wrist, snatched the monkey and threw it to the floor. Pieces of ivory scuttled across the room.

'Get out,' Cassie said. 'Go home, and don't ever come back here.'

'You don't mean that.'

He reached out, as if he was going to stroke her cheek, but Cassie moved back.

'It's the illness, making you irrational. I understand that. You can't abandon our marriage, or your home. All your things are still exactly where you left them, waiting. You'll have to come back eventually.'

The smugness in his voice was infuriating, but his words still found their mark. Cassie's eyes stung as she thought of what she had been forced to leave behind: her books; family photographs; a box of love letters exchanged by her parents; the old sewing machine on which her mother had run up so many of their childhood clothes. She had been devastated to go without them, but they were only possessions. She could sacrifice the lot to be free of Mike. She walked over to the door and held it open.

'Leave this house, or I'll go and fetch all the villagers from the library and we'll throw you out together. And don't tell me they don't care,' she said, as Mike opened his mouth to hurt her again, 'because I know they do. I don't believe you any more, and I don't love you. You've lost your power.'

Cassie leant against the door, her grip tight on the handle. This was harder than she had expected.

'We're finished. I deserve better than this.'

Mike walked over to Cassie. He didn't take his eyes off her. Her hand ached with the effort of clinging on to the handle, and though she longed to stretch her fingers, she couldn't prise them away. This time when he reached out there was nowhere for Cassie to go. She pressed her back against the panels of the door while he ran his hand down the side of her face, her neck, and on to her breast.

'You're mine.' He leaned down so that his face was close to hers, and she pushed her head back as far as she could, feeling the ridges in the door through her hair. 'You love me. You'll be home soon enough, and I'll be waiting.'

'Don't.'

Cassie glanced over at Frances: she was watching, but was far enough way not to hear. She turned her attention back to Mike, and brought her head closer to his so she could speak quietly.

'I did love you, more than you ever deserved. But that was before I understood what love could really feel like, and before I met a man who shows more kindness and decency in one hour than I expect you to show in your whole life. And though I might not have a future with him, he and everyone else in this village has reminded me what normal life is like, and it's not what I had with you. There is nothing you can say or do to make me go back to you. This is over.'

She met his gaze, defiant in a way she had never been before, and stared him down until she saw his expression harden as he realised that she was serious.

'You cheating tart,' he snarled at her, backing away as if she were contagious. 'I'll never agree to a divorce. You and your thug of a lover won't get a penny from me.'

He stomped out, and Cassie closed the door behind him. It was over, at last.

CHAPTER TWENTY-ONE

'Where's Cassie?'

The door of the Green Salon crashed open and Barney burst in.

'Cassie?' He strode over to where she was kneeling at the side of Frances' chair. 'Are you OK? Ruth phoned. She said he was here. I came as soon as I could.'

Straight from his bed, by the looks of it. His hair was scruffy, his chin unshaven, and his shirt buttons were fastened out of order. He was a glorious sight.

'Why?' It was all Cassie could manage.

'Because...' Barney was no more eloquent. His frown suggested he hardly knew the answer himself.

'Cassie saw him off. She was quite magnificent.'

Barney looked at Frances as if he'd noticed her for the first time. His eyes swept over Frances' knees, where Cassie was holding her hands.

'Frances? What's the matter?'

'Nothing at all. Cassie is making a fuss. Take no notice of her.'

Frances tried to free her hands from Cassie's grasp, but Cassie wouldn't let her.

'Could you just...' She nodded towards Frances. Barney understood at once. Ignoring the protests, he checked Frances' pulse and chest.

'Take it easy for the rest of the day, OK?' He looked down as something crunched under his foot. 'What happened? What's all this on the floor?'

'It's ivory.' Cassie stood up. 'I'm so sorry about the monkey. I'll pay you back, or you could stop paying me until we're even.'

'Certainly not. It was hidden in here for a reason. It was a hideous item. I was glad to see you put it to good use. Cassie hit that man with it,' Frances explained to Barney.

'You're bleeding.'

Barney gestured at Cassie's leg. Blood was dripping down from her knee.

'It's nothing. I must have knelt on a piece of ivory.'

'I'll clean it up.'

He was gone before Cassie could object, bringing warm water and a First-Aid kit back with him. Cassie sat down, and he crouched at her feet, wiping away the blood with damp cottonwool. His touch was gentle, quite different from last night, but no less potent. She closed her eyes, wondering which was worse: the sting of water against the cut, or the sting in her heart from knowing how hopeless this was. She had loved this man for weeks, in secret, and had to keep on doing so. One kiss, however wonderful, made no difference. She was just as married as she had been before: to a man who hadn't scrupled to advertise all her shortcomings. Why would Barney want her now?

She thought she had squeezed her eyes tightly shut, but a rogue tear leaked out. The touch on her leg stilled.

She looked down into eyes that were fathoms deep, pulling her in. 'Is it hurting?' She shook her head. 'Does it hurt anywhere else?'

'No.' Not anywhere he could heal, unless he had a special tube of cream he could rub into her heart. He knelt up and brushed away the tear with the backs of his fingers.

'Barney?' His hand dropped down when Frances spoke. 'Have you injured your hand?'

The gap before he replied stretched out. He tidied away the First-Aid kit. His right hand, Cassie noticed, was slightly swollen.

'I hit a wall,' he said at last. He scooped up the First-Aid kit and bowl of water and carried them over to a table near the door.

'Well done,' Frances said, smiling. 'Some walls deserve to be hit.'

294

He shook his head once, but said nothing. Cassie stared at him, but he wandered over to the window and looked out, purposely ignoring her gaze, or so it seemed. What had he done? The wall story was nonsense, of course. So what had he hit? Mike? She couldn't imagine him doing it, but Mike had a battered face, and Barney had a battered hand. It fit, but if it was true, why had he done it? She carried on watching him, hoping the truth would somehow spill out of him, but she had never seen him so still.

'What did he come here for?'

It was a surprise when Barney eventually spoke.

'To take me back,' Cassie said.

He spun round. 'Are you going?'

'Of course not.'

'What did he do to you, to make you hit him?'

'He called her the most appalling names,' Frances said. 'That man has a filthy tongue.'

Barney didn't take his eyes off Cassie. She shrugged.

'It was nothing worse than normal.'

'Normal!' The word sounded more like a growl. 'There's nothing normal about it.'

'I cannot bear to think that you lived with that man. You are such a gentle soul, and he is...'

Frances shook her head. Her hands were trembling again. Cassie crossed the room and sat next to her.

'And yet they can be so very convincing. It is like that rhyme about the little girl with the curl. When they are good, they are so very, very good. But when they are bad...'

Frances shuddered, and Cassie gently squeezed

her hand. She had never seen Frances so shaken, though she was trying to hide it. This was Mike's fault, and that, above everything else, was unforgivable.

'But you say he never touched you,' Frances continued. 'I am glad of that.'

'He wasn't violent,' Cassie said. She was conscious of Barney prowling round the edge of the room. 'That wasn't his style. I had to look just so, the way he wanted me to look. He would never have marked me. He couldn't stand the daily injections and blood tests. He saw them as vandalism of what was his.'

Another inhuman noise escaped Barney. 'Why did you stay?'

'Because you loved him, I suppose?' Frances answered for Cassie. 'You cannot understand how it is, Barney.'

'No, I can't.'

'It was that,' Cassie said, 'but also because I thought he loved me. It was a shock when I was diagnosed with diabetes. I didn't take it well. I was scared and upset, so when Mike began to treat me as if I was damaged, I was only too ready to believe it.'

She saw Barney sit down, his head in his hands. He might not want to hear it, but she had to carry on. Frances understood. It was cathartic to explain it to someone who knew what it was like.

'At the same time, he kept telling me he loved me, and that he was the only one who did. It was a masterpiece of manipulation. It was like living in one of those vacuum bags for storing spare bedding. At first you feel safe, looked after. The air is sucked out so slowly that you don't even notice. Until one day you find it's all gone, and you can't move. You're completely in the power of someone else. You have no thoughts and opinions that aren't his. He can say what he likes, call you any name he wants, and you take it, because he is all you have, and all you think you deserve.'

'But your friends, your family – they must have noticed what was going on. How could they let this happen to you?'

'I wasn't allowed my own friends. We worked together, and went out together.'

Barney's face was creased in an effort to understand, but Cassie knew he never would, not really. How could a good man get inside the head of a bad one? She didn't want him to. He wouldn't be the man she loved if he could understand it.

'Visits to Devon were limited, and he was very careful how he behaved. He always was, in public. No one would have believed me if I'd told the truth. And I didn't see how destructive it was, until...'

She stopped. Barney jerked out of his seat, and stomped over to the window, and then the fireplace, and then the door, wearing out the floor in an agitated circuit.

'Will you stop pacing, Barney,' Frances called to him. 'I am trying to think.'

'I can't.'

Frances put her hand over Cassie's. 'I am sorry I have been an interfering old woman and tried to matchmake you,' she said. 'I will not do it again. Now I understand why you said you would never want another relationship.'

The pacing stopped. Cassie tried to resist, but it was no good. She looked over at Barney. He was staring at her. She thought she knew everything about his face, from the way his long eyelashes curled as black and as glossy as a raven's feathers, to the slight lack of symmetry where the right side of his lips curved up fractionally more than on the left. But she didn't recognise the expression on his face now. It wasn't disappointment, however hard she might look for it, and however much she might wish it. It wasn't indifference either. Something was making him stand so motionless that his chest barely rippled as he breathed. And Cassie longed to know what it was, and opened her mouth to say something, though she hadn't worked out what, but as she did, Barney seemed to regain focus, and he took a few steps back and scratched his nails across the stubble on his chin.

Cassie knew that gesture. He was embarrassed – and was it because of her? Did he think she had opened her mouth to contradict Frances – perhaps even to claim a relationship with him, because of last night's kiss? Cassie stared at the floor, humiliation burning her cheeks. She had to put him straight, and it was easily done.

'I can't imagine ever changing my mind,' she said, hoping that she was the only one who could hear the treacherous quaver in her voice. 'I never want to be in a situation like that again.'

'What will you do?' Frances asked. 'Can you divorce him if he refuses to agree?'

'I looked into it when I left,' she said. 'I could argue unreasonable behaviour, but I don't know if it would work. It would be my word against his.'

'Not any more,' Barney said. 'You have a dozen witnesses of what he did last night. We can ask the family solicitor for advice if you like.'

Cassie nodded.

'And as a last resort, if we live apart for five years, I can divorce him and he can't object.' Cassie smiled at Frances. 'I hope you can put up with me for a while longer.'

'Oh Cassie, there is nothing I would like more. I would take the whole five years if I could.' And then, to Cassie's horror, Frances pulled a hand-kerchief from up her sleeve and dabbed her eyes with the corner. Cassie leaned forward.

'It can be for as long as you want,' she said. 'I love it here. I don't want to go.' She turned to Barney, bewildered by Frances' reaction, but he was staring out of the window, hands stuffed in his pockets, shoulders hunched to his ears. 'I'm going to stick with you so long, you'll end up begging me to leave.'

Frances didn't smile as Cassie had hoped. She stood up, leaning heavily on her stick.

'It has certainly been a dramatic morning,' Frances said.

It was exactly the sort of thing she would say, but the tone was off, the weariness thinly dis-guised.

'I think I will lie down for a while before lunch. No,' she added, as Cassie reached for her arm, and Barney took three quick strides across the room. 'I do not need either of you to make a fuss. I will be right as rain by lunchtime.'

'I'm sorry,' Cassie said, as soon as the door closed behind Frances. 'This is all my fault.'

'How do you work that out?'

'Because if I hadn't come here, Mike would never have followed, and he wouldn't have upset Frances and made her ill. I've never seen her so frail.'

'He hasn't made Frances ill. There's nothing unusual about an elderly person needing a rest.'

Cassie knew that. She also knew that his thick eyebrows were drawn closer together than normal, and that whatever he might say, he was more concerned than he was letting on. He must have read the doubt in her face, because he smiled.

'Don't start blaming yourself for everything again.' He put his hand on her shoulder. 'You're free of that now.'

The warmth of his hand spread through her T-shirt. His hand had rested there last night, too, and then trailed lower, sweeping gently and not so gently as far as it had been able to reach. Cassie felt as if she was about to combust. Was it going to happen again? Her heart was jumping about so wildly that he could probably feel the vibrations against his own chest. But then he patted her shoulder, in an awkward, brotherly sort of way, and walked out.

Frances was brighter at lunchtime and well enough to argue when Cassie mentioned that she would be staying in rather than going for a walk during her break.

'There will be time enough for you to sit around when you reach my age. You need your exercise. The Colonel is on his way. I think we are a little old to need a chaperone.'

Thus dismissed, Cassie set off towards the stepping stones, intending to walk to Ribblemill, for no other reason than that it lay in the opposite direction to Barney's farm. Her phone rang as she approached the village green. Cassie had tried to ring Vicky earlier, to let her know what had gone on over the last few days, and it was a relief now to sit down on a bench and pour everything out.

'I'm so sorry, Cass,' Vicky said when she had finished. 'I feel terrible for not taking this seriously enough. I know you were worried, but I never really believed he would try to find you, other than the few calls he made here. Why would he go to such lengths?'

'A bully is nothing without a victim,' Cassie said. 'I suppose he needed me to feel good about himself.'

'Don't you dare make excuses for him! He's a nasty, evil brute. What did he do to you? How bad was it? You've never said.'

'It could have been a lot worse,' Cassie replied, thinking of Frances. 'He didn't hit me.'

'Oh Cass.' Cassie heard the sob in Vicky's voice. 'Is that the best thing you can say about your marriage? I'm not sure I can bear to hear the rest.'

She wouldn't be able to bear it, Cassie knew that very well. There were things she could never tell Vicky, top of the list being what had happened to make her finally leave. Vicky's assessment of that would be sure to match Barney's. It wouldn't do Vicky any good to know.

'How could we not have seen it?' Vicky asked, when Cassie said nothing. 'He was so convincing. He seemed so devoted to you, obsessed even.

301

Perhaps it was too much, the way he never stopped touching you, but I was thrilled that you had the perfect marriage you always wanted. I should have looked more closely. How will you ever forgive us?'

'There's nothing to forgive.' Cassie wiped tears off her cheeks with the back of her hand. 'He didn't fool anyone as much as me. But it's finished now. I don't need to hide any more.'

'Come home then. Come back and live with us, while you decide what to do next. Or stay for good, if you want. It's your house as much as mine, and you know Stu would love to have you helping him out on the farm. There's nothing to keep you away.'

Cassie gazed round the village green, at the No Name and the Post Office, the butchers and the hardware shop, and returned the wave of a villager. There was nothing to keep her away from Devon, but there was a great deal to keep her here. She was part of this community, and she had become part of it on her own merit, not because she was her parents' daughter, or Mike's wife. There were people here she wasn't ready to leave. She belonged here, for now, and now was all that mattered.

'I'll come for a visit,' she said, 'but it will have to be in September. We're holding a garden party on the August Bank Holiday weekend, and I'll be busy with the arrangements before then.'

'We want you for at least a week. Two would be even better.' Vicky laughed. 'Would your reluctance to come home have anything to do with that delicious face that filled our computer screen when it was your birthday?'

'What face?' As if Cassie couldn't guess. There was only one person who sprang to mind at the reference to a delicious face – and he hadn't been far from her mind to start off with.

'Barney,' Vicky confirmed.

'What do you know about Barney?'

'He made a Skype call the day before your birthday to arrange for the boys to sing to you. It was quite a surprise,' Vicky added pointedly, 'as you'd never mentioned that you knew any men, never mind a man like that. What's going on there?'

'Nothing!' Cassie said – because of course, she hadn't told Vicky *everything* about last night. A few vital Barney-shaped minutes had been missing from her account.

'Is that a real nothing or a 'not wanting to talk about it' nothing?'

'Somewhere between the two?'

They both laughed, and it reminded Cassie of the carefree hours they had spent as teenagers, winding each other up over the local boys. It was a relief to know that she could still be that person; that Mike had only crushed, not destroyed her. She ended the call with Vicky, and gazed across at the No Name.

'It's OK, he's gone.' Mel came up behind Cassie, making her jump. 'He left a couple of hours ago, after making his scene at Ramblings.' She squeezed Cassie's arm. 'Sorry about that. We didn't know he'd escaped.'

'Escaped? You make it sound like you'd locked him up!'

'Of course we didn't.' Mel pushed her fringe to

303

one side, and gazed round the village green in a shifty way that didn't convince Cassie to trust her answer.

'Mike's face was a mess,' Cassie said. She watched Mel carefully, but apart from some fast blinks, there was no obvious reaction. 'Do you know what happened to him?'

'No idea.'

Mel grinned brightly. She was almost convincing.

'He probably fell over. I've never known a man put away so much whisky. I hope he doesn't try to sue us.' Her smile relaxed, and she nudged Cassie. 'The more interesting question is what happened to you last night.'

'Me? I went back to Ramblings, you know that.'

'I meant earlier on in the woods, when you were alone with Barney. It must have been ten minutes before I came back. It can't have taken more than thirty seconds to realise the torch wasn't working. What were you doing in the other nine and a half minutes?'

'We were talking...' Cassie stopped. The talking had probably taken another thirty seconds. Surely she hadn't kissed Barney for nine minutes? Sex with Mike had rarely taken that long, from start to finish. She opened a bottle of water and glugged it down so quickly that it made her feel sick.

'Really? Is that all? Because at first when I flashed my torch your way, I thought there was only one person there. You must have been standing very close together.' Mel laughed. Cassie fiddled with the lid of her water bottle. 'So close that if it didn't seem so unlikely, I'd have sworn you were kissing.'

'Why is it so unlikely?'

Cassie realised her mistake as soon as she saw Mel's eyes bulge.

'So you were!' Mel laughed. 'How was it? I can't believe he'd disappoint.'

'I'm not admitting anything.'

But Cassie couldn't help laughing too.

'You can't deny it! You don't get cheeks that pink from remembering nothing. Wow, you and Barney. Now I understand...' She broke off, and her smile dimmed. 'You will be careful, won't you? I mean, I love him to bits, but I wouldn't want you to get your hopes up about a future with him. There's no harm in having some fun, and Lord knows you deserve it after what you've been through. But I don't think he'll ever get over Nessa.'

She put her arm round Cassie's shoulders and gave her a half hug.

'As long as you don't start getting serious about him, you'll be fine.'

CHAPTER TWENTY-TWO

The remaining weeks until the garden party rushed away. Every time Cassie thought they were ready, Frances came up with a new idea, and the closer it came to the date, the harder it was to fulfil her wishes. The cost of the project was careering out of control, and though Frances told her not to worry about the expense, Cassie couldn't help it, especially as the party had been her idea. They were charging a small admission fee, but every penny of that was going to the village hall fund. Frances was paying for everything else herself. As Cassie added 'brass band' to her list – in addition to the string quartet already booked – she knew she had no choice but to discuss her concerns with Barney. He managed the estate; if there were no funds for any of this, she needed to know while there was still time to rein it in. So she wandered down to his office, and braced herself to go in.

She had avoided coming down here since Mike's visit to Ribblemill. It didn't do her any good to remember the companionable times they had spent working side by side, or the way Barney had held her when she had learned of Alfie's accident. She'd intended to avoid him entirely at first, knowing that she couldn't look at him without remembering their kiss, and fearing that her feelings might be cartwheeling all over her face. But it was inevitable that they would run into each other, and as Barney's behaviour continued to be friendly – brotherly – and nothing more, Cassie relaxed and began to believe that she could get away with it. She had to. She had promised Frances that she would stay. Heartache was an inconsequential price to pay to make Frances happy.

The door opened while she was still psyching herself up to knock, and Barney stood in front of her. Bare feet poked out of the bottom of his jeans, and Cassie stared at them to distract her from the welcoming smile that had flashed up.

'You can't hide outside a room that Gin's in,' he

said. 'She sniffed you out at once.'

Gin rubbed against Cassie's legs, and Cassie bent to fondle her head.

'I wasn't hiding, I was...' She couldn't think of any excuse for loitering outside his door, and gave up. 'I need to talk to you about the garden party.'

'Is there a problem?' Barney stepped back to let Cassie in to the office. The spare chair – her chair – was still in the room, but had been moved into the corner. Cassie sat down on it, and Barney perched against the desk.

'I'm worried about how much it's all costing,' she said. 'Frances decided today that she wanted a brass band to open the party, because apparently that's what they do at Buckingham Palace. Yesterday she ordered us to buy giant garden games so the children have things to do. That was a compromise after I talked her out of the mini funfair...' Barney laughed.

Cassie swivelled the seat of her chair from side to side. 'We're now having three marquees, because she thought two might be a squash, as well as the beer tent which has to be hidden behind the trees.' Cassie smiled as Barney continued to laugh. 'Even the portaloos have been upgraded to executive ones with floral wallpaper.'

'Would you rather have had a different pattern on the wallpaper? Don't mention it to Frances. She'll probably have one specially commissioned.'

Cassie laughed. Barney was impossible to resist when he was in this sort of mood.

'Doesn't it bother you?' she asked, trying to steer the conversation back to safer ground.

'Not particularly. She's loving planning this

307

garden party. Let her have what she wants, if it makes her happy.'

'But she's spending a fortune!'

Barney cleared the desk behind him and sat on it properly. His thighs filled his jeans without a millimetre to spare. Cassie gripped the seat of her chair, swivelling more quickly.

'Why are you so worried about her spending money?' he asked.

'Well obviously, she's an elderly lady, and she has no income...'

Barney laughed and shook his head, so that his hair shimmied around his face. 'You really are one of a kind, aren't you?'

Barney smiled, but Cassie wasn't convinced it was a compliment.

'Did you honestly think that Frances runs this place on the state pension?'

'I never thought about it.'

But now she did think about it, she realised how stupid she was being. The house was massive, but somehow she no longer noticed that. It was home. She'd stopped thinking about it in any other terms.

'The Woods biscuit business is one of the country's biggest brands,' Barney said. 'The company includes a few other well-known names. Frances doesn't need to queue up at the Post Office to collect her pension.'

'You mean she owns the company?'

'She's the major shareholder. She inherited when my uncle died. So you really don't need to worry. She can afford to hire every brass band in the country if she wants to.'

His smile died, and he looked at Cassie with a peculiar intensity, as if his eyes were passing on a message independently from his mouth.

'Indulge her in whatever she wants. Make it a day she'll never forget.'

Cassie nodded, and stood up. She had raised her concern, and Barney had reassured her. There was no reason for her to linger. She wandered over to the door, but before she had got further than reaching for the handle, Barney spoke again.

'Cassie?'

She turned, and he jumped down from the desk.

'You had a letter from the hospital yesterday. Was it about your next clinic appointment?'

'Yes, it was a reminder.'

She cringed at the knowledge he had seen her addressed as Cassie Barrett, her married name. She had been able to hide under a different identity for most purposes, but not with the NHS. Over the past few months she had learnt the postman's routine, and been able to intercept the post everyday, just in case. She had been caught out yesterday by a temporary postman delivering several hours too soon.

'When is it?'

'Next Wednesday.'

Barney picked up his diary off the desk, and flicked over the pages.

'What time?'

'Eleven.' Cassie watched him write it down. 'What are you doing?'

'Writing it down.' Barney looked at her. 'I said I'd take you.'

'You don't have to.'

'I'd like to. I told you that before.'

He had – but that had been before such a lot. Before he knew she was married, before he knew that she had lied about her entire history prior to coming to Ramblings, and before they had shared somewhere in the region of nine minutes of delicious, disastrous madness. But he wasn't thinking about that, was he? Her health was the only thing on his mind. Still, she would much rather go with him than on her own. So Cassie agreed, and wondered, as he flashed her a delighted smile and her heart leapt in response, how she was ever going to pass her check up, when only a few minutes with Barney made her feel so out of sorts. After a morning spent with him, she'd be lucky not to be admitted.

Cassie left the consulting room light-headed with relief that all was well, and ready to share the good news with Barney, but someone else was occupying his seat in the waiting room. Turning a corner, she found him deep in conversation with a pretty, blonde nurse. She was about to walk away when Barney saw her. He pointed at her, kissed his nurse on the cheek – Cassie's lips tingled with the memory of what his felt like – and hurried over.

'Sorry,' he said. 'I didn't expect to see Faye here. We used to work together in Birmingham. How did it go?'

'She's very pretty,' Cassie said, looking past him to where Faye was still standing, watching them curiously. She dragged her gaze back in time to see Barney smile.

'She's also very married.'

He said it with absolute finality, and it put Cassie in her place. Married women were clearly on the wrong side of a moral line that he wasn't prepared to cross. He wouldn't be Barney if he thought any differently. It was as well to be reminded about that, before she let his smiles breathe oxygen on the embers of hope that wouldn't quite die down.

'So how did the tests go?' he asked. 'What did the doctor say?'

'Everything's fine. I'm managing it well.'

'That's fantastic.' He took a step nearer and gave her a hug – a brief, platonic hug, no kiss on the cheek for her. 'We'll have to go out for lunch to celebrate.'

He ignored Cassie's half-hearted objection, and grilled her on every word the doctor had said while he drove them out to a beautiful village, where stone cottages clustered along the banks of a stream that ran parallel to the main road. A three-storey coaching inn stood opposite a village garden, where wooden benches nestled among abundant roses.

'It's idyllic here,' Cassie said, as Barney parked the truck and led her to an empty table on the cobbled courtyard in front of the pub.

'I know. It's one of my favourite places. Don't tell Mel we came here, will you?'

He smiled and went inside to collect drinks and menus. Cassie spent ages working out what she should eat. Mike would have been fidgeting within seconds, making rude remarks, but Barney sat back in his chair, savouring the sun and his pint, with complete unconcern. The food, when it

311

came, was delicious, and as Barney tucked into his steak and ale pie, he told her stories about growing up in Ribblemill and about his medical career with such humour and enthusiasm that she could have listened to him all afternoon.

'It's good to see you laughing again,' Barney said, pushing his plate aside.

That dried up Cassie's amusement. She had laughed a lot over lunch; she felt empty across her chest, as if every anxiety had been laughed away. Now they crept back. Had she enjoyed herself too much? Had she given herself away?

'It's a relief not to have to worry about hiding any more,' she admitted. 'In fact, I thought that I might be able to take a break, and go to stay with Vicky for a few days. There's nothing to stop me, unless you think Frances would object.'

'Of course she won't. She will miss you, though. When are you thinking of going?'

'Not until after the garden party. Perhaps a couple of days later, so I can spend some time with the boys before they go back to school.'

Barney frowned and swirled the last centimetre of beer around his glass.

'What's the matter? Don't you think I should go?'

'You deserve a break. I just didn't realise you would want to go then. It's my dad's birthday on the Tuesday, and I've booked to fly out to Malta first thing. I would normally have gone over the weekend, but I put it back because of the garden party.'

'So you're away all week?'

'Ten days. I was going to ask if you'd look after

Gin, as she seems to think she's as much your dog as mine. I could sort something else out for her, but I don't really want to leave Frances without either of us for so long.'

'No, that's fine. I'll have Gin, it's no problem.'

Cassie twitched her lips in the semblance of a smile. It was hard to distinguish what devastated her most: the delay in visiting her family, or the prospect of ten days knowing there would be no fleeting glances at Barney, no chance of hearing his voice or his laugh drifting round the house. She sighed, and sipped her water.

'Oh God, Cassie, don't look so heartbroken.' Barney's hand shot out and covered hers. 'I'll cancel my flight. You go to Devon.'

'You can't do that.'

Cassie looked down at the table, where her hand was barely visible under Barney's. Her brain sent a signal to her hand to move, but it wouldn't obey.

'I'd give anything to spend another birthday with my dad. I won't let you miss it. I can visit Vicky when you get back.'

The waitress arrived to clear the table, and Barney withdrew his hand. Cassie slid hers over to her side of the table, and traced the back of it with her finger, where Barney's touch had been. Her veins stood out, blue worms twisting across her pale skin. Cassie fanned herself with the dessert menu, trying to cool down.

Barney had ordered chocolate brownie for pudding. It came in three rectangular pieces stacked on a plate, glistening dark and rich. Cassie stared at it, her mouth watering as the intense chocolate aroma wafted in her direction.

'Sorry, was this an insensitive choice?' Barney's spoon hovered over his plate. 'Should I take it back?'

'No, go ahead. It must be a few hours since you had chocolate. You must be desperate by now.' Barney smiled, and cut off a corner of brownie. 'Brownies were always my favourite, but I can cope.'

'Have some.' He held out the spoon, laden with the first mouthful of brownie.

'I can't. I wouldn't be able to stop at one bite.'

Barney didn't push her, and ate his pudding with obvious pleasure, while Cassie distracted herself by watching the stream rolling over its rocky bed, and the birds feasting on nuts from a bird feeder in the garden across the road. Barney scooped up the last mouthful of brownie and held out the spoon again.

'Have it. There's no risk now of you not being able to stop.'

'I don't know...'

'You don't need to worry. I won't let anything bad happen to you.'

She looked between the brownie and Barney. She was tempted, so tempted, in more ways than he could ever know. She had never experienced desire like it. It was beyond desire. It was need, which had her hooked on a line that ran straight from him, and which she couldn't escape. Faced with these two temptations, she gave in to the only one she could. She leaned forward and wrapped her lips round his spoon, pulling off the piece of brownie. She closed her eyes as the sweetness and the bitterness, the crunch of chocolate and the gooiness of the cake teased her tongue. It was bliss. It was the second most delicious thing she had tasted in years.

She opened her eyes to fall straight into Barney's gaze. Neither spoke. Then he blinked, long black lashes wiping away whatever expression had lurked in his eyes.

'Good?' His voice held a husky edge. Cassie nodded. 'You see, you don't have to deny yourself everything. Sometimes you can have what you want, in moderation.'

Could she? Could she really have what she wanted without coming to any harm? Cassie watched him go into the pub to pay, and wondered if he would still say the same if she told him that what she wanted most was him.

None of Frances' children had confirmed whether they would be attending the garden party, though each had rung the house several times and tried to worm out of Cassie whether the others would be present. With less than a week to go until the big day, it was frustrating not to know whether extra bedrooms needed to be prepared on top of all the other last-minute details.

'Have you heard anything yet about who will be staying this weekend?' Cassie asked Frances, when she brought in the tea tray on the Tuesday before the party.

'No one is staying,' Frances said quickly, pointing to where Cassie should put the tray. 'Whatever made you think there was?'

'I thought your children might have come. It's a big day for Ramblings.'

'Oh yes, they will all be here. I have asked them to present their ideas for what they would do with the house on Sunday afternoon, so they will stay over that evening and leave after the party. Would you mind adding it to your list to get their usual rooms ready?'

Cassie didn't mind, but it did worry her that Frances appeared to have forgotten that they were expecting visitors. She decided to mention it to Barney when she next saw him, but he didn't appear at the house over the next couple of days. Ruth said that he had popped in for breakfast, but that he was spending a few days working on the farm while the weather was good. No Barney meant no laptop and so no Skype calls to Vicky. If she hadn't desperately wanted the ground to be dry for the party, Cassie would have prayed for rain to bring him back to Ramblings.

Frances wasn't herself on Thursday either, and Cassie grew increasingly concerned that she might not be well enough for the party. She was on edge all day, checked her watch repeatedly, and insisted that she couldn't be left when Cassie tried to take her break after lunch.

'That's it, I'm ringing Barney,' Cassie said, striding over to the phone. 'You're normally kicking me out of the house to go for some exercise. There must be something wrong for you to want me to stay.'

'Nonsense, I merely think it would be a good idea for us to go over the list again.'

'Nothing has changed since we looked at it this morning.' Cassie picked up the handset. 'Barney won't mind coming to check you over.'

'Stop being difficult, Cassie. Put down that telephone and–' A long note from a car horn sounded outside. Frances sagged in her chair. 'Thank goodness for that. Would you mind going out and seeing what that racket is all about?'

So now she was being sent away after all! Vowing to make sure Barney examined Frances later, Cassie went along to the hall, opened the door and stepped outside into dazzling sunshine. A battered old Saab was parked on the drive – a very familiar old Saab.

'Auntie Cassie! Auntie Cassie!'

The back door of the car opened and two over-excited little boys spilled out and hurtled across the gravel, crashing into Cassie's embrace.

'Alfie! Stanley! How...? What...?' Cassie gave up and smothered them with kisses and a fair share of tears too. She looked over their heads and saw Vicky and Stu. Giving the boys a final squeeze, Cassie ran over to Vicky, and received what felt like a year's worth of hugs in one.

'What are you all doing here?' she asked, when at last Vicky released her enough to breathe again.

'We were invited to a party,' Vicky said, laughing and shedding as many tears as Cassie. 'We couldn't say no to that. I even have a new dress.'

'A party? You mean the garden party? But I didn't invite you to that.'

'No, but luckily someone else did.' Vicky nodded her head towards the house. Cassie turned, and there he was: Barney was standing in the shadows, smiling. And suddenly it all became clear. Who else could have organised this? Who else would think of doing something so kind? The whole scheme had Barney's name running right through it.

'I'll be back in a second,' she promised Vicky, and ran across the drive.

'Thank you,' she said, and threw her arms round Barney's neck. 'This is amazing.'

His arms flew round her, holding her tightly. Her breathing fell in to line with his as if they were moulded together. She hid her face in his chest, knowing it would betray her, and let the soft cotton of his T-shirt soak up her tears.

'Are these happy tears?' he murmured against the top of her head.

She nodded, and after a final deep breath of him, she pulled back. There was a momentary resistance, and then his arms let her go.

'Very happy.' She wiped her cheeks with the backs of her hands. 'I can't believe you've done this.'

'I couldn't bear to make you wait.' He smiled. 'Go and be with them. Everything is arranged. Ruth has prepared the bedrooms, Mel is taking charge of the garden party and the Colonel is coming to spend time with Frances over the next few days. All you need to do is enjoy yourself.'

He had thought of everything. He was an incredible man, and he wanted her to enjoy herself. How could she refuse, after all his efforts? So she reached up, pressed a kiss on tender, unresisting lips, and went back to her family.

CHAPTER TWENTY-THREE

'Right, I've given you two days, but I can't stand it any longer,' Vicky said, turning on her sun-lounger to face Cassie. It was a brave move – the loungers were ancient and fragile, the fabric so stretched that their bottoms hung only centi-metres above the ground. 'I want to know every-thing, and if you don't tell me I'll set the boys on you. They'll soon tickle the truth out of you.'

'Not the tickle torture!' Cassie laughed. 'I've told you everything. You know I went to London and worked as a cleaner, and you know I came here after that. There's nothing more.'

'Yes, there is. Don't think I haven't noticed that you've talked about everyone in this village except one.'

In case Cassie was in doubt about who that one might be, Vicky pointed across the lawn.

Cassie looked out over the grass. Barney, Stu, Alfie and Stanley were playing two-a-side football on the lawn behind the house. The boys had taken their T-shirts off to help mark out goals. Sadly Barney hadn't done the same. He had stayed away since Vicky's arrival, but after lunch today he had wandered in with a box full of old sports equipment and offered it to Alfie and Stanley. Vicky had insisted he play, and so far they had tried cricket, tennis and football. They were all getting on brilliantly. Regular squeals from the boys and laughter from the men drifted across the garden to where Cassie and Vicky were sitting, enjoying the sun. It was hard to imagine a more perfect afternoon. At least, it had been perfect, until Vicky started her interrogation.

'I know we weren't able to speak much on the phone, but how come you didn't mention Barney even once?' Vicky pressed on, when Cassie said nothing.

'I'm sure I must have done.'

'No,' Vicky interrupted. 'I think I'd remember you telling me about a man who looks like that.'

'Like what?' Cassie glanced over at Barney. He was running over to high five Alfie, who had scored a goal against Stu. He hadn't stopped smiling all afternoon.

'He's gorgeous. Look at those cheekbones – if you can tear your eyes from lower down. Don't pretend you haven't noticed.'

'I won't. He is gorgeous. And clever, and thoughtful and kind. I'm not blind yet.'

Vicky stretched across and squeezed Cassie's hand.

'So what's the problem? Do you not fancy him?'

'Of course I do. Who wouldn't?'

She laughed at Vicky's surprised expression. Vicky clearly hadn't expected her to tell the truth.

'But it's complicated. Fancying him is easy. Contemplating another relationship is much harder. Besides, I can't divorce Mike, and Barney has made it quite plain that he isn't interested in married women. I don't think he sees me in that way, anyway. He treats me like a doctor would a patient.'

Vicky roared with laughter.

'If that's how doctors treat patients up here, I'm moving. Seriously, Cass, how can you not see it? Barney watches you as if he can't understand why you aren't in his bed, and has no intention of letting you out of his sight until you are.'

'He doesn't!'

Cassie laughed, but all the same, lust forged through her veins. Barney didn't look at her like that – did he? She couldn't have missed that, not when she was so aware of everything about him.

'I wish he did. I'd be there like a shot at the slightest hint that's what he wanted.'

'Isn't the fact that we're here a big enough hint for you? What more are you waiting for? For him to stand here naked, with a sign dangling off his willy reading, "This way please"?'

'Wouldn't that be something? Can you imagine...?'

Cassie closed her eyes, lay back on the lounger, and let her thoughts feast on that image for a few moments. She opened her eyes when she heard Vicky clear her throat. Barney was standing by the side of her lounger – fully clothed and with no signs dangling off him, she was disappointed to see. Her eyes flicked over to Vicky, who winked, and they both set off laughing again.

'What are you two cackling about?' Stu asked.

'Cassie?' Vicky grinned.

Cassie shook her head, but she couldn't stop the smile that seemed imprinted on her face. She hoped that Barney hadn't overheard any of their conversation. She glanced up at him. He was watching her, head tilted slightly, open curiosity on his face. Cassie flapped her hand in front of her face to try to cool down.

'We're going to walk down to the farm,' Barney said. 'Stu might be able to give me some advice.'

'Can we come?' Vicky hauled herself up off the lounger.

'You live on a farm,' Cassie said. 'Why do you want to see another?'

'Because it's where Barney lives.'

'Won't you come?' Barney asked, holding out his hand to Cassie. 'It's ages since you've been down. I'd like to know what you think of the changes.'

Cassie took Barney's hand and let him pull her up. He pulled a little too vigorously so she almost crashed into him, and his other hand landed on her waist to steady her.

'Are you OK?' he asked, not moving either hand. 'You're looking flushed.'

Laughter played across his face. He had heard the conversation with Vicky, he must have done: either that, or he could see inside her head. She wouldn't put anything past him. It was impossible to think rationally when he was looking at her like that and when his hands, though neither was moving, were sending tremors of desire all over her body. She squirmed out of his grasp and went over to stand with Vicky.

'Well done for throwing yourself at him,' Vicky murmured. 'If you want to be left alone just say the word...'

'Shut up.'

They walked down the track leading from Ramblings to the farm, Stu and Barney in the lead, each carrying a child on their shoulders, and Vicky and Cassie following behind. Cassie noticed the changes at once. The fields were all ready, the fences complete, waiting for the animals to arrive. The farmyard had been tidied, so it still looked like a working farm, and well kept. Even the house had been spruced up: the window frames and front door gleamed with fresh paint, and flower-beds bloomed below the windows, softening the exterior.

'What do you think?' Barney said.

'It's lovely,' she replied, and was rewarded with a warm smile.

'How much land do you have?' Stu asked.

'Only fifteen hectares. Most of the original farmland was used to build Ramblings and its grounds.'

'It's a huge estate,' Stu said. 'We walked round some of it yesterday. Surely developers must be queuing up to build on these fields?'

'We've been approached a few times, but it's never going to happen. It would ruin the character of the village to have an estate of new houses built here. The family promised the village council that they would never allow it to happen, and no Smallwood would betray that.'

Alfie wandered over and prodded Barney to get his attention.

'Why haven't you got any animals? This isn't a proper farm.'

'It isn't a proper one yet, is it?' Barney laughed. 'Now I've repaired all the fences, my next job is to buy the animals.' He looked over at Stu. 'I wish you could stay longer. You could have given me some advice.'

'Take Cassie,' Stu replied. 'She knows as much, if not more, than I do.'

'No, I don't.'

'She does,' Vicky said. 'Where most teenage girls had posters of pop stars on their bedroom wall, Cassie had a poster of native sheep breeds.'

'Is that right?' Barney asked.

Cassie nodded.

'So would you come with me?' Barney moved closer.

'If you want me.'

'I do.' A smile blazed across his face, melting Cassie's bones, and for the first time she wondered, hoped, wished that Vicky might be right.

Frances' children arrived the next day, and immediately did their best to dampen the happy atmosphere around the house. Diana walked round looking as if she was sucking an everlasting boiled sweet when she discovered that Cassie's family were guests in the house, and Hugh was only too ready to join in her complaints.

'You're a miracle worker,' Barney whispered in Cassie's ear. 'I've rarely seen them so quick to agree on anything.'

The grumbles didn't bother Cassie until Hugh questioned Frances' health.

'Are you quite well, Mother?' he asked, peering down at her in a way that would have alarmed even the most robust old lady. 'You don't look yourself.'

'Whom exactly do I look like?' Frances asked. 'The Mona Lisa? The Archbishop of Canterbury? The...'

'I meant you don't look in good health. You've lost weight.'

Hugh turned to Cassie and glared at her in accusation. 'Isn't she eating?'

'Yes, of course she is.'

'You're clearly not giving her enough. Her face has drawn in since I was last here.'

Had it? Cassie studied Frances. Her face did look thin, the skin clinging to the outline of her skull – but was that different from before? It was hard to notice a change when you saw someone every day, but she was paid to notice any change in Frances. Had she missed a problem? She looked over at Barney for reassurance. He smiled at her.

'Cassie has been nothing but good for Frances since she came here,' he said to Hugh. 'You should be glad that Frances has someone who is willing to spend so much time with her.'

'It's what she's paid for,' Hugh snapped.

'It goes well beyond that. You'd have seen for yourself if you were ever here.'

'At least I live in the same country as my parent. I have a job to do, which happens to be in London. I can't spend my days hanging around here.'

'Quite right, Hugh,' Frances interrupted. 'No one expects or wants you to be here. The three of us are perfectly happy as we are. We need no one else.'

Later that night, when Cassie went to Frances' bedroom to wish her goodnight and lay out her clothes for tomorrow, she found Frances sitting up in bed, a velvet bedjacket round her shoulders, waiting to talk. Stripped of her jewellery and

325

daytime clothes, she looked unexpectedly fragile and tired – or perhaps, following Hugh's words, Cassie was more inclined to notice it.

'I think you should go straight to sleep,' Cassie said, seeing that Frances had a remote control in her hand, ready to listen to an audiobook. 'It's a big day tomorrow.'

'Yes it is, and perhaps the last of its kind that I shall see here.'

'Don't say that. It's not like you to be maudlin,' Cassie said.

She sat down on the bed and took hold of Frances' hand. She could feel every bone and joint, as if it were a skeleton not a human hand. She cradled it protectively between hers.

'We can hold the garden party every year. All the plans we've made this year will carry over. The garden party can become one of the highlights of the Ramblings year.'

'There will be no Ramblings if my children have their way.'

'You mean they want to knock it down? Surely none of them are planning to do that?'

'No, or at least they did not suggest it in my presence.' Frances sighed, and shrank further into her pillows. 'Hugh wants to divide it into luxury flats. They would keep one each, and sell the rest for what he called a decent profit. I see nothing decent about the scheme.'

Nor did Cassie, and though it had nothing to do with her, she fumed at the idea that this unique building could be broken up and ruined just to make money for people who already had more than they needed. And what would happen to the land – to the farm – to Barney?

'And what about Diana?' she asked. 'Does she agree?'

'Not at all.' Cassie felt her first flicker of warmth towards Diana. 'She has plans to turn the house and grounds into the country's leading equestrian hotel, modelled on a place in Ireland. My morning room would become a conference room for something she described as corporate bondage.'

'Bonding,' Cassie corrected – but who knew, with Diana?

'What about Guy? What was his idea?'

'Nothing. He wants the house to stay as it is, but to open to the public for a summer season each year, like the place he took you to visit.'

'That could work, couldn't it?'

Cassie didn't want to be reminded of that day, or all the trouble that had followed as a result, but she needed to be positive. She had never seen Frances so downhearted.

'It was the perfect compromise to allow the family and the public to enjoy the house.'

'Guy has too much of his father in him. Compromise is not a word that has ever found a place in his vocabulary. I fear there may be more to his plan – and if he will not say it, it can only be because I will not like it.' Frances' hand twitched beneath Cassie's. 'The house has come alive over the last few months, and been at the heart of the village. I want that to continue. None of them have understood that.'

'They will do tomorrow, when they see the garden party. And if that doesn't convince them, we'll think of something else. We've got years to persuade them to change their minds, haven't we?'

Frances was silent for so long that Cassie thought she was never going to reply.

'You are right,' she said at last, removing her hand from Cassie's. 'We should both get some sleep. Tomorrow is going to be an important day for both of us.'

CHAPTER TWENTY-FOUR

Cassie ticked the last item off the last list, and finally the Ramblings garden party was ready to start. There had been no eleventh-hour emergencies: everything and everyone had turned up just as planned. Even the sun blazed down from a sky that entertained only the occasional wisp of white cloud amidst the unrelenting blue.

At precisely two o'clock, Cassie led Frances out through the French doors in the drawing room, and onto the terrace overlooking the garden. Her eyes were on Frances, and it was only when she saw her smile, and felt her grip tighten on Cassie's arm, that Cassie relaxed and allowed herself to survey the garden. Her breath caught. It was everything she had hoped it would be. No, it was more. It was magnificent.

Three pristine white marquees stood at right angles to each other on the lawn, the sides billowing gently in the breeze. Inside the tents, long trestle tables covered in thick linen cloths groaned under the weight of the afternoon tea: delicate sandwiches, miniature pies and pasties and exquisite cakes that had tested Cassie's will power to the limit when she had inspected the food earlier. A discreet sign pinned to a tree pointed to the beer tent, which was partially hidden behind a bed of rhododendron bushes. In the centre of the lawn, between the marquees, a Punch & Judy tent waited to entertain the children. It had been another last-minute whim of Frances', along with the donkey rides that were taking place on a side lawn, where the giant games had also been placed. Frances had been determined that no one who came would be disappointed. Cassie had fulfilled every wish, equally determined that Frances wouldn't be disappointed.

The gates had opened for guests at one thirty, and as Cassie looked down over the gardens, she didn't think there could be a single person left in the village. The grass swarmed with spots of colour like a living Dulux paint catalogue. Hats jostled with fascinators, ties with bow ties and even a cravat. There had been no official dress code, but Cassie was thrilled to see that the Ribblemillers understood the significance of the event, and had dug out their finery.

At a signal from Cassie, the brass band played a fanfare, and all eyes turned to Frances and Cassie as they descended the stone steps down into the garden. Her skin was warm with embarrassment at being the centre of so much attention; but when the crowd launched into spontaneous applause, and Frances whispered an emotional 'thank you', Cassie felt like dragging her back up the steps and doing it all over again.

Barney met them at the bottom of the steps. He had exchanged the morning's jeans and T-shirt for linen trousers and a pale blue shirt, and his chin looked so freshly shaven that Cassie longed to reach out and let her fingers slide along the smooth skin, and up to the lips that had curved into a smile that she could have basked in all day.

'That was quite some entrance,' he said. 'I'm not sure you needed the fanfare. No one could fail to notice you. You are far and away the most beautiful women here.'

He looked only at Frances as he spoke, and leaned forward to kiss her cheek.

'I assume we have the beer tent to thank for that nonsense,' Frances said, but Cassie was sure the colour in her cheeks wasn't entirely artificial. 'I will allow that you might have a point where Cassie is concerned. I am thinking of asking Becca to send her over a whole new wardrobe. She clearly understands what suits Cassie better than Cassie does herself. That dress could have been tailored to fit.'

Cassie was wearing the cream silk dress and sparkly sandals that she had been given on her birthday. There had been no choice: Frances had made her write on one of the ubiquitous lists, 'wear the birthday dress'. In comparison to Frances' demure dress and matching primrose coat and hat, she felt as if she had far too much flesh on display – flesh that Barney was now studying.

'You're right, it really is an excellent fit.'

Cassie caught his laughing gaze before she turned her head away. She hoped Frances wasn't going to invite all the men here to ogle her. She had promised not to matchmake any more, but perhaps in Frances' mind a respite of a few weeks was long enough.

'This is fantastic, isn't it?' Barney continued. 'Ramblings was made for days like this. We should have done it years ago.'

'We did not have Cassie years ago. It would never have happened without her.'

'I was only a small part of it,' Cassie protested. 'There was a whole team involved.'

'With you at the helm.' Frances wasn't going to be dissuaded. 'Today is the perfect proof of what I have known for some time. Everyone should have a Cassie in their lives.'

'We need to start circulating,' Cassie said, desperate to put an end to this embarrassing praise. She began to steer Frances away, but Barney caught hold of her free hand.

'Cassie?' She turned her head. 'Can we talk later? When you're not so busy?'

She was about to ask him what he wanted to talk about, but something about the expression on his face – the way his smile was tinged with an unmistakeable trace of anxiety – stopped her. She nodded, and led Frances on.

'What does Barney want with you?' Frances asked, as they headed across the grass towards the first marquee.

'I don't know. He probably wants to give me some instructions about looking after Gin. He goes away tomorrow, doesn't he?'

'That would be just like Barney, making a fuss as usual,' Frances replied. 'You have organised this whole day, and he still does not trust you to feed and water a dog.'

They neared the marquee, Frances nodding regally at the villagers as they passed, and Cassie thought that was the end of it. But at the entrance to the marquee, Frances paused and faced Cassie.

'Of course, it might have nothing to do with the dog,' she said, patting Cassie's arm, 'and everything to do with how delightful you look in that dress. Would that not make a much more interesting conversation?'

Cassie didn't need Hugh to point out that Frances grew visibly tired as the afternoon wore on. Her pace slowed and she leaned more heavily on Cassie's arm, but she was determined to speak to as many guests as possible, and refused to even consider Cassie's suggestion that she should have a lie down.

'I have waited a long time to attend a garden party,' she said firmly. 'I will not be leaving early.'

'Will you at least sit down for a rest? It must be time for another cup of tea.'

'I could manage some tea, and perhaps another of those lemon cakes if you can find one. But you are not to stay with me. Find the Colonel and send him this way. I am sure you must want to spend some time with your family before they leave tomorrow. And remember that Barney is waiting to speak to you.'

As if she could have forgotten! She'd barely thought about anything else all afternoon. It was bound to be something mundane he wanted to talk about: arrangements for when he was away, to do with Gin, or Frances, or his house. But why couldn't he have mentioned that in front of Frances? Why ask to speak to her, as if he wanted her alone? Her hopes were already floating away, higher than the balloons released by the children, despite every attempt to anchor them down with commonsense. Because if Barney wanted her alone for the reasons why she longed for him to want her alone, why wait until now? Why give no sign of it before – or no sign that had been visible to Cassie. It had to be about something dull, hadn't it?

It was unbearable. She was driving herself demented, imagining that Barney's hand had squeezed hers, and that there had been some significance in the way he had looked at her when he had asked to talk. Even while she was playing a giant game of Snakes & Ladders with Alfie and Stanley, Barney was all she could think about. She headed towards the steps up to the house, hoping to gain a height advantage to find him in the crowd, but Ethel accosted her before she could make it.

'It's going well, isn't it?' Ethel said, planting herself in Cassie's path. 'This is a step up from the field behind the village hall. Do you think Mrs Smallwood will agree to host this every year?'

'I've suggested it, but it would be hugely expensive for her.'

'She can afford it.' Ethel flapped her hand, swatting away Cassie's objection. 'Ribblemillers eat thousands of packets of Woods' biscuits. Have you visited the Portaloo yet? Make sure you try it out. It's posher than my bathroom at home.' Suddenly she reached out and clutched Cassie's arm. 'I don't believe it. I've seen some brass necks in my time, but none as thick as that.'

'What? What's the matter?' It was hard to tell where Ethel was looking; her face was largely hidden beneath a hat so wide it could have sheltered a family if it rained.

'There!' Ethel pointed, and Cassie turned to see an elderly couple strolling at the edge of the garden, away from the crowd. A tall blonde woman sauntered behind them. She looked vaguely familiar, though Cassie couldn't name her.

'Who are they?'

'The Hartleys!' Ethel said this as if it were obvious, and somehow significant. The name meant nothing to Cassie.

'Who are the Hartleys?'

'Who would have invited them?' Ethel went on, ignoring Cassie. 'An invitation must have slipped through. I can't believe they'd have come without one, not after...'

'Do they live in the village? I thought everyone in Ribblemill was invited.'

'Everyone except them. No one would have gone near their house, unless...' Ethel tipped her head far enough back to look at Cassie. It wasn't exactly an accusatory look, but it may as well have been. Guilt was already filling Cassie's arms with goosebumps.

'Where do they live?' she asked.

'The house on its own, half a mile past the pub.'

'The one with horses' heads on the gateposts?' Cassie knew she was right, even before Ethel's nod condemned her.

'It was me,' she said. 'I pushed the invitation

through. Who are they?'

The grim expression on Ethel's face made Cassie dread the answer. She braced herself for hearing that she had invited the local mafia at the very least. But it turned out that the truth was worse – much worse.

'They're the Hartleys,' Ethel repeated, in a tone that put them on a par with the Krays. 'Barney's in-laws. Ex-laws, I suppose I should say.'

Cassie stared across the grass. The elderly couple were dressed in their best, and could have passed for any of the other villagers enjoying a day out. Although, when she looked carefully, they were walking stiffly, heads bent down, as if they were ill at ease. Her gaze moved on to the figure trailing behind them.

'And the woman?' Her question hardly needed an answer. Ethel gave one anyway.

'That's Nessa Smallwood. Barney's ex-wife.'

There was only one thought in Cassie's head. She had to get rid of them, before Barney found out they were here, and that they were here because she had invited them. Or had he seen them already? Was that why he was missing? Cassie glanced round again, but none of the dark heads she could see were his. He had put in huge effort behind the scenes to make sure the grounds were perfect for today. He had appeared so happy earlier on. She couldn't let the day be ruined for him because of her mistake. So she ducked round Ethel and marched across the grass towards the Hartleys.

She aimed for the parents, who looked surprised to see her approach; Cassie guessed, if Ethel's reaction was anything to go by, that they hadn't received much of a welcome from the other Ribblemillers. They offered her a hesitant smile, and Cassie cringed at the thought of having to ask them to leave; but so what if she felt awkward? It was nothing to how Barney would feel if he ran into them. 'Mr and Mrs Hartley?'

It was awful to witness how pleased they appeared to be singled out. Cassie had to force herself to go on.

'I'm sorry, I don't know how to begin to explain this to you, but there's been a mistake...'

She stopped as Mrs Hartley dropped her smile, and sagged back against her husband.

'You don't have to explain,' she said, and the kindness in her eyes stabbed Cassie more effectively than anger would have done. 'We were surprised to be invited, but so pleased, after...' She stopped and straightened up. 'I'm glad we could see it. You've done a fantastic job organising this. But of course we'll leave now.'

'Leave? We're not going anywhere.' The blonde woman – Nessa – had crept up behind Cassie. 'What do you mean by kicking my parents out of the party? What harm are they doing?'

'None, no one suggested...'

'Then why should they leave? They were invited just as much as anyone else here. And who are you to be telling them what to do?'

'We told you, Nessa, Frances has a companion living with her. It's Cassie, isn't it?'

Cassie nodded, wondering how they could know about her, when until five minutes ago she hadn't been aware of their existence. Nessa swept her with a glance of such impressive indifference that Cassie felt lucky not to have ended up under the nearest carpet.

'I don't see how Frances' companion has any right to throw us out. We haven't even had a cup of tea.'

Nessa turned, as if to head towards the marquees. Cassie's reaction was automatic. She stretched out and grabbed Nessa's arm to stop her.

'Wait,' Cassie said, while Nessa stared at her in disbelief. 'I'm not trying to throw or kick anyone anywhere. But don't you think, for Barney...'

Nessa smiled. Cassie didn't like the smile. It made her feel stupid and irrelevant and worthless, all the feelings that she had hoped to have shaken off with Mike.

'Is that how it is?' Nessa said. 'You and Barney? Surely not.'

'No! I...' She wasn't allowed to finish. She was pulled back by a tug on her arm.

'Come on, Cassie,' Mel said. Cassie had no idea where she had appeared from. 'It's not good to be arguing with a pregnant woman.'

'Pregnant?'

The word distracted Cassie from the unfairness of Mel's accusation. She looked properly at Nessa for the first time. She was tall, blonde, elegant ... all things she had noticed before. But she hadn't noticed before that underneath the expensive shift dress, there was a small but unmistakeable bump. Cassie stared at it.

'Barney's going to be a father?'

'No, I'm not.'

Cassie wished people would stop sneaking up behind her. She turned, to find out how many more were waiting to surprise her, but there was only Barney, standing quite still, and looking past her at the guests she hadn't wanted him to see – the guests who shouldn't have been here, except for her mistake.

'I'm sorry,' she began, but Barney interrupted her.

'Hello Brian, hello Ann,' he said, and to Cassie's astonishment, he walked over to them, shook Brian's hand and kissed Ann's cheek. As he passed her, she felt a fleeting touch on her back, so light that she could almost have imagined it. But she knew she hadn't. Was Barney really, even at this moment, trying to comfort *her*?

She couldn't take her eyes off him. He smiled, and treated the Hartleys with perfect friendliness. It wasn't what Cassie had expected, after Ethel's reaction. Then he turned to Nessa, and his smile didn't change.

'Hello Nessa.' He didn't move near her. There was no handshake or kiss for her. His eyes dropped to the bump. 'Congratulations. How are you feeling? Are you keeping well?'

'Never better. I'm sixteen weeks, so over the worst for now.'

Nessa stroked her bump and smiled, and this time it was a real smile, making her face soften and glow, transforming her, Cassie presumed, into the woman Barney must have loved and married. Then his smile did change. It increased, in response to Nessa, and Cassie stepped back, feeling as if a jealous troll had woken up inside her and was scratching away with sharp talons, fighting to get out. Mel anchored her arm through Cassie's.

'It's great to see you again,' Nessa said.

'I didn't realise you were coming today.' Barney turned back to Nessa's parents. 'Have you only just arrived?'

'Actually, we were about to leave,' Ann said, flashing an embarrassed smile.

'Actually, your girlfriend was about to make them leave,' Nessa corrected. She raised her eyebrows at Barney in a gesture that came so naturally it could only be a relic of their relationship.

'There's no need for that. It's a party for the entire village. Your parents have every right to come.'

'But I don't?'

'You always hated Ribblemill. I doubt that's changed.'

Cassie had hardly breathed, watching the interplay between the two of them, but in the fractional pause that followed Barney's last comment, she mentally wound back and replayed the conversation. Nessa had mentioned Barney's girlfriend. Who was that? Did she mean Cassie? It wasn't true – so why hadn't he corrected her? Had he missed it? Or... She tried to move forward, to stand at his side, but Mel's arm held her back.

'Don't get involved,' Mel whispered.

It was probably good advice: Nessa had lost her smile, and was so focused on Barney that she might have chewed up and swallowed anyone who interfered.

'Of course that hasn't changed,' Nessa said. She waved her hand towards the lawn. 'I mean, look at this! All these people dressed up to the nines – in fascinators for God's sake! – as if it were a society event worthy of *Tatler*, not a tea tent and some sticky buns in the village that time forgot. How can you bear to bury yourself here again?'

She reached out and ran her hand down Barney's chest. Mel tightened her grip on Cassie's arm.

'You don't belong in a place like this. You could have so much more. You deserve more.'

Cassie had heard enough. Nessa didn't sound like a woman confronting the man she had divorced. She didn't sound like a woman who was carrying another man's child either. She sounded to Cassie – and it was her specialist subject, after all – like a woman who had loved Barney, and who was still in love with him. Cassie couldn't bear to stay and listen to any more, because if she heard any evidence that Barney returned Nessa's feelings, her heart would surely disintegrate into a pile of ashes that would never so much as spark again.

She nudged Mel and indicated with a flick of her head that they should go. With obvious reluctance, Mel nodded, but they had only taken two steps when Barney spoke again.

'I do belong here. There's nowhere I'd rather be, which is lucky, because there's nowhere else I can go.'

'Why not?' Nessa looked genuinely puzzled. 'You mean because of all that nonsense in the newspapers? No one remembers that any more.'

'I do. That nonsense cost me my career and my marriage.'

'Only because you let it. You could have survived.'

'Not after the press found out that you were involved, and splashed those photos of us across the papers.'

'That was a misunderstanding. I never meant...' Nessa stopped abruptly.

'Never meant what?'

There wasn't a hint of love in Barney's voice. If anything, it reminded Cassie of the way he had spoken to her in the early days at Ramblings: suspicion and distrust overpowering all else. Nessa must have recognised it too, because she backed towards her parents, one hand covering her bump.

'I only did it to show them what you were really like – that you were a kind and loving man, not the monster they were describing...'

Cassie heard Mel draw in a shocked breath. No one else moved. The sound of the string quartet floated towards them on the breeze – a piece of Bach, Cassie thought, concentrating on the notes, so lively and cheerful, and so inappropriate as a score to what was going on over here.

'Oh Nessa,' Ann Hartley said. 'You didn't!'

'I had to do something. I knew it wouldn't be long before Barney brought out his "knight in shining armour" act.'

'You talked to the press?' Barney spoke slowly, as if he was struggling to take it in. 'You gave them the photos? The one from university? The one of our wedding? The one of us kissing? All the ones that were used to ruin me?'

'I didn't know they would twist everything! I only spoke to one friendly journalist, but then the others got hold of it and it went out of control...'

'So you actually betrayed me twice.'

Barney stopped and glanced round. He faced Mel and Cassie, and dragged up a smile.

'Mel, would you mind taking Ann and Brian to the marquee for tea? I need to talk to Nessa.'

He spoke to Mel, but his eyes were locked with Cassie's, and then he turned away.

Cassie spent the next half hour making small talk, smiling until her cheeks ached, laughing at a Punch & Judy show with Alfie and Stanley, and thinking only of where Barney was and what he needed to talk to Nessa about. He had wanted to talk to Cassie at the start of the party. Had he chosen Nessa instead? Or was she imagining that there had ever been a choice? Perhaps it had always been Nessa, and Cassie was a convenient dogsitter and nothing more. Yet there had been something about the way he had looked at her – like a swimmer taking a desperate gulp of air before going underwater – that gave her hope; and while there was a twinkle of hope, she wasn't giving in.

'You do not need to be glued to my side,' Frances said, as Cassie brought her a fresh round of tea and sat down beside her. 'You must have more interesting things to do. Have you spoken to Barney?'

'No, he's...' Cassie stopped herself in time. Frances didn't need to know that Nessa was here. 'I've been busy,' she said.

'You are not busy now. If you have time to sit down for a drink, you have time to see Barney. He might want something important.'

Frances was smiling in a way that Cassie could only describe as suspicious.

'Do you already know what he wants?' Cassie demanded.

'Of course not. He never tells me anything interesting.' Frances patted Cassie's hand. 'But I am not so old that I cannot see it for myself. Be off with you. The Colonel is over there, and can walk with me when I have finished my tea.'

Cassie spent ten minutes checking all the marquees and the beer tent, but there was no sign of Barney, nor was he playing garden games or riding a donkey. Might he have gone home? She cut through the private area of the garden, intending to skirt round to the farmhouse, when it occurred to her that if he had gone home, he might not be alone. So she turned round, and fell over some feet poking out from beneath a giant weeping willow.

She pushed aside the branches and found Barney lying on the grass, his arms folded under the back of his head. He smiled.

'It's killing me not to make the obvious joke about you falling for me at last.'

Cassie looked at him, at that smile. What should she do? There was no conscious choice. She let the branches fall back behind her, closing them in.

'Are you on your own?' she asked, stepping forward.

'Not any more.'

'No Nessa?'

He shook his head.

'She's probably gone off to look for someone else to be a father to her child.'

'That's what she wanted?'

'It seems so. Only Nessa could refuse to have my baby and then come back and offer me someone else's.'

He was still smiling. There was no obvious sign that he was sorry that Nessa had gone. That was good, wasn't it? Cassie kicked off her sandals and sat down on the grass next to him. Then, when he carried on watching her but said nothing, she wriggled until she was lying down beside him. Sunlight filtered through the leaves above them, creating hot spots on her skin. All she could hear was Barney's steady breathing, and a riot of bird-song. She lay still and listened.

'It's beautiful here,' she said, gazing up at the tree, trying to catch a glimpse of the birds.

'Yes it is. It's always been my favourite place in the garden.'

'Do you come here often?'

Barney laughed and turned his head to the side to face Cassie.

'It's a great place to hide away,' he said.

'Does that mean you want me to leave?'

'No.' He rolled onto his side, propped up on his elbow, only a few centimetres between them. 'I like what Frances called you. You're a gentle soul, very soothing to have around.'

'Soothing? Like a throat lozenge? Must you always think of me in medical terms?'

'I'm not thinking of you in medical terms now.'

'Then how?'

'The way any man would think about a beautiful woman who lies down next to him.'

That stunned Cassie into silence. She watched, so wholly mesmerised that it was amazing she remembered to breathe, as Barney sat up. His gaze travelled leisurely from her face all the way down her body, leaving a trail of goosebumps in its wake.

'Although,' he continued, smiling, 'you do have a very shapely talus.'

Before Cassie could ask what that was, he leaned over and traced circles round her ankle. Her foot jerked in response, and he ran his finger along the sole and then over her toes, and up the inside of her leg to her knee. Every drop of his attention was focused on the progress of his finger. It ran across her knee.

'A perfect patella,' he murmured. His finger moved on, under the hem of her dress and on to the inside of her bare thigh. 'And well-formed quadriceps.'

His finger paused. Cassie couldn't move. She didn't want to move. She didn't want him to stop. His touch was creating hot spots more powerful than a thousand suns could manage. The anticipation of where it might land next was exquisite. It made the agony so much more acute when he removed his hand – until he lay down again, the length of his leg pressed against hers. He put his hand on her chest, between her breasts

'A good strong heartbeat.' He laughed. 'Though rather fast.'

Fast? What did he expect? He was lucky it

hadn't burst from Cassie's chest and exploded over him. At last his eyes fixed on hers again.

'Should I stop?'

'No.'

He stroked the side of her face, so gently that it was almost unbearable, then his finger ran over her lips, right to left, top to bottom.

'These lips,' he said, 'and the voice that comes out of them ... you can do magic with those. Say my name.'

'Barney,' Cassie said. 'Barney.' But she didn't think the voice sounded like hers: it was deeper, breathless, desperate. Barney smiled, and she wanted to reach out and grab his face, and hold it in the position it was in now, so that he never stopped looking like that and never stopped looking at *her* like that. The Barney stare had taken on a whole new dimension, so instead of the truth being sucked out of her, it felt like something was pouring in. And then he lowered his head and kissed her.

Their first kiss had been amazing. This one was magnificent. The bad memories that had tormented Cassie for so long were buried in an avalanche of happiness. When Barney rolled on top of her, and drizzled lingering kisses down her neck, she savoured the thrill of being desired, not possessed. She adjusted to his weight – so much lighter than she was used to; wrapped her arms round a body that was thinner but stronger than she had known before; and every difference that she noticed erased the unwanted images from her head and her body. He really did have a healing touch.

Cassie had lost track of time – of everything, other than the sensation of Barney's lips and hands – when she was distracted by the sound of a child's voice close by. Barney's lips stilled against hers, and he laughed and rolled off.

'That was a close call,' he said. 'I think we were almost caught. That would have been embarrassing.'

The happy bubble surrounding Cassie popped. A sharp leaf scratched her leg, bringing reality crashing back in. This wasn't what she wanted it to be. She sat up, straightened her dress, and brushed her hair with her fingers, trying to tidy it up.

'It's OK,' she said, unable to look at Barney. Her lips still stung in protest at being parted from his. 'I know what this is.'

'I should think so. I'm not being terribly subtle.'

'I don't mean that. I mean it's fine; you don't need to be embarrassed. I'm not expecting anything. I know that this is just a reaction to seeing Nessa again.'

'You think I'm proving a point? Like you were when you kissed me at the midnight ramble?'

'That was different.'

It had to be. She might have started the kiss at the midnight ramble to prove a point, but she had continued it because she loved him. This wasn't the same at all. Cassie stood up. Barney jumped up after her.

'It seems no different to me.' He smiled, and pulled a leaf out of her hair. 'Clearly I'm being too subtle. This isn't just some knee-jerk reaction that I'm going to regret tomorrow. I've wanted to do this for a long time. Seeing Nessa again only made me more certain.'

'You don't have to say that.'

'You are incredibly frustrating.' Barney laughed, and put his arm round Cassie's waist to pull her against him. 'In more ways than one. OK, let's do this properly, and I'll convince you. When I get back from Malta, I'm taking you out to dinner.'

Was this real? Was Barney Smallwood suggesting they go out on a date? A normal food and conversation and – she trembled at the thought of what else there might be – date? The desire in his eyes was real. The stroke of his hand along her side was deliciously real. Cassie smiled, and his arm tightened round her.

'Is this what you call doing it properly?' she said. 'In Devon it's the custom to ask if someone wants to go out to dinner, not tell them.'

'Asking would give you the opportunity to say no.'

'I'm not going to say no.'

That earned her another kiss. Barney drew his head back so his eyes looked down into Cassie's.

'Come to the farm.'

'Are you asking or telling?'

'Whatever it takes to get you there.'

'I can't. I can't abandon Frances.' Cassie glanced at her watch, to confirm what she already knew. She hesitated about saying it, but she had to test him; she had to be sure. 'And it's time for an injection.'

'We'd better get you back then.'

And that was it: no repulsion, no annoyance, no embarrassment. He had proved to her, if she needed proof, that the difference was more than physical. Not every man would treat her as Mike had done. Could she have hope again of an equal relationship, and of being accepted as she was? She had hardly dared believe it until now. Cassie leaned in towards Barney and he enclosed her in his arms, stroking her hair, while nerves that had been taut for too long relaxed in the unfamiliar feeling of safety. Then he took hold of her hand and led her back towards the house.

'What about tonight?' he asked. 'Will you come to the farm then?'

'I promised Alfie and Stanley that I'd camp out with them tonight if the weather was fine. Frances told them where to find a tent and sleeping bags.'

'Did she? I wish she hadn't.'

Cassie had to laugh at his frustrated expression.

He smiled. 'I think the tents hold four people. Perhaps I ought to bring my sleeping bag and join you.'

They reached the edge of the lawn. It was as busy as ever; there was no sign that people had started to go home yet. Barney was still holding her hand, even though anyone could see them. She expected him to let go; instead he gripped her more securely.

'You should go.'

'Yes.'

Neither of them moved. Cassie couldn't help worrying that as soon as she walked away, that might be it: the fantasy of the last hour might vanish as if it had never happened. But she had no choice. She prised her fingers out of Barney's grasp. She took two steps away and turned back.

'I forgot. You said you wanted to talk to me.'

Barney smiled.

'I lied.'

'Oh.' Cassie noticed a grass stain on the sleeve of his shirt, and the memory of how it got there clouded her head with a new fog of lust. 'So what did you want?'

'Do you still need to ask? I want you.'

And regardless of the crowd of friends, family and villagers swirling around them, Barney pulled her back into his arms and kissed her.

The day after the garden party, while the marquees were being dismantled and the garden tidied, Frances' thoughts turned to Christmas. Cassie was allowed five minutes to compose herself after saying an emotional goodbye to Vicky, before she was summonsed to Frances' bedroom to start a whole new series of lists.

'There may be a suitable tree in the garden,' Frances instructed. 'Barney will know, or if not, he will know where to find one. Cassie? Are you writing this down?'

'Yes.' She looked down at her paper. There was one word – Barney – in looping handwriting, underlined three times. She scribbled down 'tree' next to it.

'The tree must go in the hall, to the left of the stairs. Make sure it obscures the portrait of Reginald Smallwood. The Smallwoods have historically produced handsome men, but Reginald inherited a rogue gene from somewhere. Barney will know where the decorations are stored in the attic.'

Cassie wrote down 'Barney' again. How could she be missing him already? It was barely two hours since he had called in to deliver Gin and his door key, on his way to the airport. He had dragged Cassie away to his office for what he called 'last-minute instructions'. She had learnt a lot, not least that he had a ticklish spot behind his left ear that made him... Frances coughed and Cassie looked up.

'Would you like some more water?'

'Perhaps half a glass. All this talking is drying my throat.'

Cassie poured the water, and handed the glass to Frances. It was unusual for Frances to stay in bed so long, but she had said she was tired after the garden party. Cassie had tried to persuade her to have a nap, but Frances had refused with the crushing words that she was 'neither an infant nor feeble-minded'. She was adamant that she had to tell Cassie the Christmas arrangements, even though it was four months away.

'The villagers must be invited up on the last Sunday before Christmas,' Frances continued. 'There will be carols around the tree at 4 p.m. The children should sing "Away in a Manger". It has always been my favourite.' Frances paused, and Cassie glanced up in time to see her dab her eye with a tissue. She reached out to take Frances' hand, but Frances flapped her away. 'Ruth will need to make mince pies for everyone, and Mel can bring the special Ribblemill mulled punch. Each child must be given a gingerbread star to hang on their tree at home. Ask Barney if you are unsure about anything. He may remember what a Ramblings Christmas used to be. Really, Cassie, if you are going to smile in that way every time I

351

say his name, you might at least tell me what is going on!'

Cassie wondered how she had been smiling. She had drifted off to a memory of last night, when true to his word, Barney had appeared at Ramblings with his sleeping bag, ready to join the camping expedition. Vicky hadn't minded – in fact her enthusiasm had been equalled only by her smugness. The boys had zipped their sleeping bags together to keep warm, a cunning suggestion from Barney that he had swiftly copied with his and Cassie's sleeping bags. It wasn't how she had imagined spending a night with Barney, but cocooned chastely in his arms, conscious of his heart beating beside her all night, she had enjoyed her best sleep for months.

'Remember the advert you placed,' Cassie said, putting down her pen, and smiling at Frances in what she hoped was an affectionate way. 'It was the one thing you insisted on. "Must not chatter". It was underlined.'

'It was a foolish advert. Barney was quite right about that, although I doubt if he would dare to criticise me for it now. And how can I regret it, when it brought me you?' Frances matched Cassie's smile, and reached out to take Cassie's hand between her own. 'And now I insist that you chatter, and tell me exactly what Barney wanted to speak to you about yesterday.'

'He invited me out for dinner.'

'Did he? Well! I am not too old to be surprised.'

'Isn't it what you expected?'

Cassie had been sure yesterday that Frances was suspicious.

'I never expected him to make such a proper offer.'

Cassie laughed.

'I accepted. Do you approve?'

'Nothing could make me happier.' Frances patted Cassie's hand. 'Although my approval must have its limits. Technically you remain married. I will not condone adultery in my house.'

Frances freed her hands to drink some more water. Cassie picked up her pen and doodled a rose on the corner of her notebook, trying to chase away the idea of smuggling Barney into Vienna. Frances coughed.

'I am going to trust you with a secret, Cassie, that only Barney and I know.'

Cassie put down her pen. This sounded intriguing.

'Ramblings Farm is not part of the estate any more. I gave it to Barney on his twenty-fifth birthday, in case he ever needed a bolthole.'

'That was kind of you. He did need it, didn't he?' Cassie said, relieved that they were off the subject of adultery, even though the secret hadn't turned out to be that exciting. Frances tutted at her.

'Do not be so obtuse, Cassie. Listen to what I am telling you. Barney owns the farm. It is not my house. Whatever he – or anyone else – gets up to there is no concern of mine. I would make no fuss whatsoever. Now where are we up to with that list?'

CHAPTER TWENTY-FIVE

It was the silence that struck Cassie first. She pulled back her curtains and saw nothing but greyness, parallel lines of rain falling in vertical perfection, muffling all sound. There was no wind crying through the gaps in the windows or rattling in the chimney; no birdsong; no one working in the garden, or jogging past the house. Everywhere felt cold and still and lifeless.

She went down to the kitchen, diverting to Barney's office, but he wasn't in yet. She smiled when she saw the calendar hanging on the wall: he had returned from Malta two days ago, and had dragged her into the office to watch him draw a thick red circle round tomorrow's date, when he was taking her out for dinner. There was a new dress hanging in her wardrobe ready for the occasion, a gift from Frances that she hadn't been allowed to refuse. She left a note on his chair, and went to the kitchen to make a pot of tea for Frances.

The silence hit her again as she walked along the corridor to Frances' bedroom, tea tray in her hands. She normally had her first inklings about what sort of mood Frances was in when she heard either Radio 4 or Classic FM drifting down towards her. Today there was nothing: no music, no voices, no human sound at all. Cassie put down the tray and ran.

The curtains were still closed in Frances' room. Enough light filtered in for Cassie to see Frances lying in bed, her head turned to the side, her mouth slightly open. She could be asleep. She had been tired for a few days, ever since the garden party. But Cassie knew it wasn't true, even before she forced herself to move forward and touch Frances' cold hand. Frances wasn't ever going to wake up.

Cassie picked up the phone at the side of the bed and dialled. Barney answered at once, his voice rich with warmth and life.

'Frances,' Cassie said. No more words came out.

'I'll be straight over.'

He was there in less than ten minutes, time which Cassie spent arranging the room, so it looked the way Frances would want it to: slippers tucked neatly under the bed, dressing gown hung up, used tissues thrown away, bedside table tidied. It was the only thing left for her to do.

Barney came in and with only a quick glance at Cassie, went over to the bed and checked Frances – for a pulse, Cassie presumed, though he must have known by sight that he wouldn't find one. Then he leaned down and kissed Frances' forehead.

'Sleep well,' he said. He waited by the side of the bed for a few moments before joining Cassie.

'Are you OK?' he asked.

She nodded. How could she do anything else, when he had lost his aunt, and when a trail of tears shone on his face? He wrapped her in a hug, and she rested her head against his shoulder. She wasn't OK, not really. She was numb, unable to cry. This shouldn't have happened. Frances had been tired recently, but not ill. Her doctor had visited last week, and not raised any concerns with Cassie. Last night they had watched the news together, and Frances had been her usual strident self. So how had this happened? And the awful question, which hammered in Cassie's head: what should she have done to stop this happening? She was Frances' companion, paid to look after her. She had failed.

'I need to ring the doctor,' Barney said, pulling away.

'I'll stay with Frances.'

He nodded and left. Cassie sat down at the side of the bed and waited. She couldn't leave Frances now. This would be her last duty as companion. Her tears came tumbling down.

The doctor issued a death certificate and Frances left Ramblings for the last time. The house already felt wrong without her: a museum, not a home.

The news had spread to the village. Ruth came to Ramblings to make sure that there was food and drink for anyone who wanted it. A local florist delivered a couple of bouquets, which Cassie placed in the hall, even though she knew Frances would have dismissed them as 'showy'. The Colonel called round to pay his respects, which seemed to consist of shaking Barney's hand, patting Cassie's shoulder, and rubbing his moustache. The whole day felt unreal. Cassie kept waiting for Frances to come in and tell them all to stop making a fuss.

Diana and Guy arrived late afternoon; Hugh

was on holiday and Barney hadn't yet been able to contact him. Cassie bumped into them in the hall. Guy was carrying in a large suitcase for Diana. It looked as if she was going on holiday – either that or moving in.

'I'm very sorry about Frances,' Cassie said.

'I dare say you are,' Diana replied. There were no signs of tears on her cheeks, or evidence that any had been shed. 'You've lost a nice, easy job now, haven't you?'

'That's not–'

Cassie wasn't allowed to finish. Diana flapped her hand to silence her. Tears rushed to Cassie's eyes to see a gesture so physically reminiscent of Frances, carry so little of her spirit.

'It clearly wasn't a job you were any good at. We should have trusted our instincts when we first met you and insisted that you left. How have you let this happen? There wasn't anything wrong with Mother. She was in perfect health only two weeks ago when we were here for the garden party. You haven't looked after her!'

'I'm sorry.' Cassie wiped her eyes, but the tears wouldn't stop. She wanted to defend herself, but how could she? Diana was only saying what she had thought herself. There was no defence.

'Obviously your employment is terminated now,' Diana continued relentlessly. 'Could you make sure your bags are packed and the room cleaned in the next hour? I'll be staying in Vienna.'

'Of course. I'll move into one of the other rooms.'

'No. You'll move out of the house. You have no place here now.'

'Surely one more night can't do any harm, Diana,' Guy said. He offered his sister a decidedly chilly smile. 'We don't yet know whether you have any right to say who stays here.'

Diana's face flushed puce.

'It's fine,' Cassie said, desperate to avoid the inevitable argument. 'I'll go.'

But of course it wasn't fine, and where exactly was she supposed to go? All day she had thought only of Frances; now she thought about herself, and the reality of her new situation. Diana was right. Her job was over. She had no work, no income, no home – and no Frances. That was still the worst of it. She headed for the stairs, bubbling with grief and fury that Frances' children could be thinking of what they might gain, instead of what they had lost.

'Cassie?' Barney caught her at the bottom of the stairs, took one look at her face, and grabbed hold of her hand. 'What's going on?'

'Diana has asked me to leave. She wants her room back.'

'For God's sake, Diana. Does it matter where you sleep? Don't we all have other things to think about today?'

'We wouldn't be here today if she'd done her job properly. She hardly deserves our charity. She failed to look after Mother, so why should we look after her? And I can't understand how you missed what was happening, with all your medical qualifications.'

Diana looked at Barney's hand, still wrapped round Cassie's.

'Or has your attention been elsewhere recently?'

'Distracted by a woman while someone dies?' Guy said. 'Wouldn't be the first time, would it?'

Cassie gritted her teeth as Barney's hand clenched round hers tightly enough to hurt. She imagined it was nothing to the pain he must be feeling.

'Don't worry about it,' she said, shaking his arm.

She had to end this. How could they be behaving this way, when Frances had only left the house a few hours ago?

'Give me ten minutes to pack and I'll go.'

Barney dropped her hand and crossed over to Diana.

'You're wrong,' he said. 'This had nothing to do with Cassie. Frances has been seriously ill for some time. She was diagnosed with chronic heart failure last year. The doctors thought she had six months at most. She went well past that. Cassie gave her more time and more happiness than she ever expected.'

Cassie stared at him. Why was he saying this? Was he lying to protect her? How could he lie about something so serious? It made no sense.

'That can't be true,' Diana said, echoing Cassie's thoughts. 'She would have told us.'

'When? You never came to see her. You only started making an effort when you thought your inheritance was at risk. But if you don't believe me, check the death certificate. Speak to Frances' GP. He'll confirm it.'

It was true? Frances had been dying through all the time that Cassie had known her? This awful day ... the horrendous discovery of Frances' body

359

... had been lying in wait for her from the start? That was bad enough. But for Barney to have known, and said nothing... Cassie didn't know what to think, or feel. One of the things she most valued about Barney was his honesty. That he spoke the truth, with no ambiguity and no deception. Did she know him at all? She ran upstairs, letting the row go on without her.

She had taken her rucksack out of the wardrobe, and stuffed her underwear in, when Barney burst into the room.

'Don't do this,' he said, snatching the rucksack out of her hands. 'Diana is totally out of order. She can't throw you out. This is your home.'

'Not any more.'

Cassie picked up the framed engraving of Ramblings that Barney had given her on her birthday, and which had been so precious that it lived at the side of her bed.

'And was it ever? I thought it was home. You let me think it was. But this was only ever a temporary stay, wasn't it?'

'Yes.'

Barney sat down on the bed. Grief hung heavily on his shoulders, slumping him forwards. Cassie thought back over her time at Ramblings. So much made sense now that she had misunderstood or misinterpreted before: the secret exchanges between Frances and Barney, where more seemed to be said than she had heard in the words spoken aloud; Barney's repeated opposition, at least in the early days, to Frances employing her. Perhaps the truth had been there all along, but she hadn't seen it. She'd been given no preparation for the events of today, and how the life she thought she had built would melt away in an instant.

'You should have told me,' she said, yanking the rucksack back out of his hands. 'I've spent the whole day blaming myself, wondering what I might have done or not done to cause this. It seemed so sudden. I had no idea that Frances was ill.'

She flicked through her memories again, looking for signs of illness rather than old age. She couldn't think of any – or not, she suddenly realised, from Frances. She sank onto the bed.

'Oh God, it *was* my fault, wasn't it? All those events I persuaded her to hold in the hall – the trip to the seaside, the garden party. It was all too much, wasn't it? You warned me, and I thought I knew better. Why didn't you tell me the truth and make me stop? Why did you have to be so bloody secretive?'

'You were keeping plenty of secrets yourself.'

Cassie supposed she deserved that. What had happened to them, that she and Barney were sniping at each other in this way? Were they even a 'them'? Cassie was no longer sure. What had they ever had? Nothing more than a few delicious kisses. No promises had been made, no feelings exchanged. Barney sighed.

'Frances didn't want you to know. I told her it was unfair, but she was adamant. I had to do what she asked.' He looked up. 'What would you have done, if I'd told you?'

'I would have looked after her better. I'd have made her rest more. I wouldn't have exhausted her with writing a history of Ramblings, or mak-

361

ing constant lists, or discussing what we're going to do at Christmas...'

Cassie stopped. Now she understood why Frances had been so insistent on making the Christmas list. She had known she wouldn't be here, to arrange it herself. Cassie scrunched the bedspread in her hand, and tried not to cry.

'I think that proves her point. You wouldn't have made plans, you wouldn't have done anything with her, and you wouldn't have treated her as if she still had a long life ahead of her. Frances would have hated that. She would have hated you to fuss.'

'You fussed over her!'

'And you saw how much it annoyed her.' Barney gave a brief, sad smile. 'I didn't do it because she was ill. I made a fuss over her because I loved her.'

'So did I,' Cassie said. 'And if I'd known that this was going to happen, I would have told her. I would have let her know how much she has done for me. I could have said goodbye.'

'I think she already knew.'

Cassie could hear in his voice how deep his sadness reached, and the anger she had felt at him fizzled away. It wasn't her place to feel anything, was it? This was about Barney, and Frances' family, and she wasn't part of that. She didn't matter today. She leaned forward and hugged him.

'I'm sorry,' she said, not knowing what she was most sorry for: the loss of Frances; his obvious pain; the cruelty of his family; her helplessness in the face of his grief. And perhaps, despite her best intentions not to think about herself, she was sorry about what Frances' death must mean for them – for Cassie and Barney – because she couldn't see where they could go from here. So she hugged Barney, rubbed her cheek against the softness of his hair, and refused to dwell on whether she would ever do this again.

Conscious that her ten minutes to pack must have passed, she went over to empty the wardrobe. There was hardly anything in it: just the black clothes she had brought with her, the dress she had received for her birthday, and hanging by itself, in one half of the wardrobe, the dress Frances had given her to wear to dinner with Barney. She took it out carefully, and with her back to Barney, held it up against herself, feeling not the fabric swishing against her legs, but the soft draught of a dream rushing past and out of her grasp. Then she stuffed the dress in her rucksack with everything else.

'I cancelled the restaurant.'

Cassie turned. Barney was standing behind her. She nodded, but didn't meet his gaze. What was there to say? Of course they couldn't go out for dinner now.

'This doesn't change anything.'

He brushed the back of his hand down her arm with a touch so light it barely made contact with her skin. Cassie held her breath, fighting not to react, because everything had changed. She had worked that out in the couple of minutes before Barney had come to her room. She had no job, nowhere to live, and not enough money saved up to rent somewhere, even if there was a vacant place in Ribblemill. She couldn't stay here. She had no choice but to return to Devon. She could live there, work on the farm; and this thing with Barney would fizzle out before it had ever really started. He might want her now, while she was close and convenient, but he had given her no reason to think that her kisses meant more to him than anyone else's. She couldn't see how it could be any other way.

She fastened the backpack, and took a last look round the room. She had been happy here; however far away she was, she would remember that. On a whim, she pulled out her phone and took a photograph of the room, turning at the last moment so that she caught Barney's profile on the edge of the picture. She would remember him too.

'Come on,' Barney said, opening the door. 'Let's go to the farm.'

'The farm?' Cassie didn't move. 'Why there?'

'You're coming to stay with me.' Two tiny frown lines appeared between his eyebrows, visible over the marks of grief on his face. 'Aren't you?'

She hadn't expected that, and yet wasn't it exactly like Barney to offer? If she couldn't remain at Ramblings, there was nowhere else she would rather be. So she had to say no. At most she had another week here, until Frances' funeral. A week spent with Barney would only make it harder to leave.

'I think it would be better if I went to the No Name,' she said.

Barney didn't reply.

'Your parents are coming tomorrow. They'll want to spend time with you, not a stranger. And I think Diana expects me to leave the whole estate, not just the house.'

She sounded like she was making excuses, and she could tell from Barney's silent stare that he thought so too.

'If that's what you want.'

Cassie nodded, and they headed out to the drive. She hoisted the rucksack onto her shoulders.

'I'll take you to the village.'

'No, I'd better walk. I haven't had any exercise today.'

'I'll come and see you later.'

'Don't worry. I know you must have a lot to discuss with Diana and Guy.'

Before Cassie could move, and put an end to this unbearable awkwardness, Barney bent forward and pressed a gentle kiss to her lips. There was something tender and, to Cassie's mind, final about the gesture. She reached round and squeezed him, putting every drop of love she had into it, resting her head against his chest to hear his heart beat for one more time. Then she walked away.

CHAPTER TWENTY-SIX

Frances' funeral was to take place the following Wednesday, as soon as Hugh could return from his holiday. Now that her days in Ribblemill were officially numbered, and with nothing else to do with her time, Cassie spent her hours repeating favourite walks – avoiding the Ramblings estate – and taking photographs on her phone of the hills, the stone walls, the clouds, and anything else that would remind her of Lancashire when she had gone.

Two days after moving into the No Name, Cassie returned from her walk and sat down on the bench on the village green, loath to go inside when the September sun was so warm. She flicked through the photographs she had taken that morning, and then went back through the others on her phone, smiling as she came across Alfie and Stanley tucked up in their sleeping bag on the camping night. Going back further, she stopped at a picture of Frances taken at the garden party. Frances had been standing on the steps of the house, surveying the scene in front of her on the lawns, and the expression on her face was unmistakeable. She was happy; there was no doubting it. She had loved the whole day. Cassie refused to feel guilty about arranging that one event, at least.

'Cassie?'

She looked up and saw an attractive woman with a smooth silver bob, wearing jeans and a floral blouse. The woman smiled at Cassie in a kind, and oddly familiar way. Cassie hadn't seen her in Ribblemill before.

'Yes. How do you know that?'

'You're one of the few people I've seen who look genuinely upset.'

Cassie wiped the tears from her cheeks. The lady's smile deepened.

'And Barney's description was picture perfect. I'm Hazel Smallwood, Barney's mum.'

Cassie stood up and put out her hand awkwardly, but Hazel ignored it and grasping

Cassie's shoulders, kissed each of her cheeks.

'I don't think we need to be formal, do we?' Hazel said, laughing.

It was odd: Cassie hadn't heard anyone laugh since Frances died. Her surprise must have shown.

'Oh, don't think me heartless,' Hazel said. 'The last thing Frances would have wanted is for people to mope about with long faces, wearing black...' She stopped as she took in Cassie's outfit: she had returned to wearing the black clothes she had arrived with, as she could no longer borrow Frances' old clothes.

'You're right,' Cassie agreed, and for the first time since that terrible moment of finding Frances, she smiled. 'She never failed to tell me how much she hated these clothes.'

'She never mentioned them to me. She talked of you with great affection when we spoke.'

This was news to Cassie: she'd had no idea that Frances was in touch with Barney's mum.

'You shouldn't take anything Diana says to heart. Those children all have too much of their father in them. Everyone else knows what you did for Frances. You gave her a happy ending, and that's all any of us want, isn't it? And now Barney is going to be annoyed with me for making you cry.'

She pulled a tissue from her handbag and passed it to Cassie.

'I'd better get on before I make things worse. Ethel is treating me to lunch.' She rolled her eyes and smiled. 'On past form it will be a buffet of whatever is past its best from the shop. I'm so glad to have met you at last.'

She gave Cassie a quick squeeze and headed towards the Post Office.

'Hazel?' Cassie called after her. Hazel turned round. 'Frances has a favourite dress. It's blue wool, with embroidery round the collar and cuffs.'

Hazel understood at once.

'You think that's the one she'd like to wear?'

Cassie nodded.

'I'll find it.' Hazel hesitated, then spoke again. 'Why don't you join us for dinner at the farm tonight?'

'I don't know...'

'There'll be no Diana or Guy, I promise. We'll smuggle you in without them knowing.'

When Cassie still didn't accept, Hazel carried on.

'Barney will be happy to see you. He says you're never at the No Name when he calls. I know he was close to Frances, but he's more subdued than I expected. Do come. It won't be anything fancy – stir-fry at the kitchen table I expect – but you're more than welcome. Perhaps you can make him smile again.'

Every sensible cell in Cassie's body urged her to refuse. She ignored them. The chance of one last supper with Barney – of seeing the real him, at home and with his family round him – was too enticing to refuse. It was already going to be un-bearable leaving Ribblemill. How much harder could one meal make it? So she heard herself agree, and shut her ears to all the other voices in her head telling her what a bad idea it was.

Frances' funeral was a dignified, moving and uplifting occasion. Every detail had been planned
by Frances and enshrined in a long list given to
her solicitor, Hazel told Cassie with a smile.
Hugh, Guy and Barney carried the coffin in to
church, joined by Akram on behalf of the village
and two representatives from Woods biscuits.
Only Diana and the vicar wore black. Everyone
else took heed of the instructions spread around
by Hazel, that this was to be as colourful and as
joyful a day as possible, and many villagers gave
their garden-party outfits another airing. The
church was packed, a tribute to the affection
Frances had earned in recent months, after years
of living as a recluse. Cassie remembered her
photograph of Frances at the garden party, and
imagined her looking down on them now, with a
similar pleased expression. It was a stylish farewell, and exactly what Frances deserved.

The wake was held in the Ramblings ballroom,
with caterers chosen by Frances and drinks
ordered from the No Name. Cassie hadn't
planned to go, fearing a hostile reception from
Diana, but in the end she had no choice. Hazel
caught her as she was walking back to the pub,
and bundled her into Barney's pick-up without
saying a word, and Cassie was glad she did. She
hadn't told anyone that she was leaving for Devon
the next day, and she used the opportunity to
speak to all the friends she had made in Ribblemill, and to say her silent goodbyes. There was
only one person she avoided. She had no idea
how she was ever going to say goodbye to him.

She left while it was still busy, in the hope that no

one would notice her departure, but as she hesitated in the doorway, taking a last wistful look at the Ribblemillers, a suited man approached her.

'Mrs Barrett?'

Cassie had hoped never to be called that name again. She stared at the man, her heart lurching, wondering who he could possibly be, and how he had found her. His smile wobbled.

'Cassie Barrett?' he asked again. 'I was told that you were Cassie.'

'I am.' She wouldn't accept the rest of the name. The man looked relieved, and held out his hand.

'I'm Nigel Boot, Mrs Smallwood's solicitor. Would you be free tomorrow morning? I need to talk to you about Mrs Smallwood's will.'

'Her will? I don't know if she had one. I wouldn't know where to find it. Isn't it with you?'

Nigel smiled.

'Yes, it is with me. I wasn't asking you to find it. I need to discuss the contents with you. I'm sorry to be mysterious, but Mrs Smallwood gave very clear instructions that all her children had to be given a copy of her will first, and at the same time, and we've been held up by Hugh's absence. I'm meeting them here at nine o'clock tomorrow. Could you come up at ten?'

'I suppose so,' Cassie said. Her train wasn't until the afternoon; she should have time to come to Ramblings first.

'Good.' Nigel smiled. 'Don't look so worried. It's not bad news.'

Cassie turned up at Ramblings just before ten the next morning. Ruth let her in.

'I'm ten fifteen, after you,' she said, closing the door behind Cassie. 'It's like being at the doctor's, isn't it? And needless to say, he's running late. The family are still in with him.' Ruth leaned nearer and lowered her voice. 'There's trouble by the sounds of it. I happened to pass the library earlier, and there were definitely raised voices.'

'Perhaps I should wait here.'

'No, you go on, see what's happening.' Ruth prodded Cassie forward. 'Let me know if you hear anything juicy.'

Cassie didn't hear anything at all when she reached the library, so knocked and stuck her head round the door. The solicitor was sitting in a wing chair by the window, eyes closed, rubbing his temples. He opened his eyes when Cassie closed the door, and gave her a weary smile.

'Mrs Barrett, come and sit down.' He waved at a chair in front of him. 'I know it can never make up for the loss of a friend, but I'm pleased to tell you that Mrs Smallwood has named you as a beneficiary in her will.'

'Has she?' Cassie had thought about it over-night, and had realised that this could be the only reason why the solicitor would want to see her. It was still a mystery how Frances had been able to change her will without Cassie knowing. When had she seen the solicitor? She must have squeezed it in between the doctor's visits and the conversations with Hazel, and all the other things that Cassie had known nothing about.

'There are two bequests to you,' Nigel Boot continued.

He took a paper from a file on the table and

held it out to Cassie.

'The first is a selection of dresses, as listed.'

Cassie looked down the list. There were detailed descriptions of all the dresses that Cassie had worn during her time at Ramblings.

'Some of these are vintage items,' she said, giving back the list. 'They must have some value. Shouldn't Diana have them?'

'Mrs Smallwood was most insistent.' Nigel smiled. 'She said they would tide you over until you bought some suitable clothes of your own.'

Cassie smiled, though tears blurred her eyes. It was exactly what Frances would say; and it was exactly like Frances to disregard the fact that she couldn't afford to buy new clothes.

'The second bequest is more straightforward. Mrs Smallwood has left you the sum of twenty-five thousand pounds.'

Cassie stared. Twenty-five thousand pounds! Surely she hadn't heard that right?

'Are you sure?' she asked. 'Why would she do that?'

'I'm quite sure.' Nigel pulled an envelope out of his file. 'She asked me to give you this letter. Perhaps that will explain it. All she said to me was that she hoped you would see it as a freedom fund.'

Cassie took the envelope and saw her name on the front. The frail handwriting belonged to Frances, and Cassie knew what an effort it must have been for her even to write the single word. Blinking back tears, she thought about what the solicitor had said. This was a freedom fund, and already Cassie's heart raced as she considered the possibilities. This could change everything. What if she used it to pay for a deposit and a few months rent on a cottage, while she looked for work? What if she stayed in Ribblemill? She could have that date with Barney. They could see whether those precious kisses could be the foundation of something more. Perhaps he was the one who could finally persuade her to take a risk on another relationship.

'Thank you,' she said, springing from her seat. She needed to talk to Barney.

'There is one other thing,' Nigel said, before Cassie could get away.

She turned round, her hopes fluttering. Was there a catch, after all?

'I've just explained to Mrs Smallwood's family the position regarding the Ramblings estate.'

That would explain the raised voices that Ruth had heard, Cassie thought. She wondered which one of them had inherited.

'Mrs Smallwood set up a charitable trust for the benefit of the people of Ribblemill and some other causes. The house and estate have been left to the trust.'

Cassie wasn't sure what that meant. Had none of the children inherited?

'So does the village own the house?' she asked.

'No, the trust owns it, but one of the rules is that the house must be used to benefit the village. There are detailed instructions in the trust deed, and trustees will be appointed to ensure they are carried out. Mrs Smallwood requested that you be asked to be one of the trustees. It's an unpaid role,' Nigel added.

Cassie's head was reeling. It was too much to take in. This morning she had woken up with nothing, reluctant to open her eyes and start the day that would take her away from here. Now she had enough money to stay, and a reason to be here. More than that: she had the satisfaction of knowing that Frances had cared enough about her to give her this. Twenty-five million pounds couldn't have brought Cassie more pleasure.

'Do I–?' Her question was interrupted as the library door burst open and Guy marched in, a wad of paper in his hand.

'What's this about the shares?' he demanded.

He looked up from the papers and saw Cassie. His face hardened, the superficial attractiveness displaced by accusing eyes and tight lips.

'You didn't waste any time coming to claim your inheritance, did you?'

'Mrs Barrett came at my request, Guy,' Nigel said, 'the same as all the other beneficiaries I'm seeing this morning. Once that's done, I'll be happy to explain anything else to you.'

'All I want you to explain,' Guy replied, 'is how we can challenge this will and stop our family home from being given away to a bunch of half-wits for OAP lunches and bingo afternoons.'

He moved towards Cassie, followed by Hugh and Diana.

'This is your fault,' he said. 'You put all these stupid ideas into her head. You had to keep interfering, pushing her to do more, didn't you? Look what you've done! You've cost me a fortune.'

'Don't speak to her like that!'

Barney pushed past Hugh and came to stand

beside Cassie. He reached for her hand and squeezed it. She clung on to him.

'This has nothing to do with Cassie. Frances knew perfectly well what she was doing. She's left you a fortune that most people could only dream of, even without the house.'

'What do you know? You're no better at managing an estate than being a doctor. We could have made millions if you'd sold those fields for development instead of playing farm with them.'

Cassie could feel the anger vibrating through Barney.

'How could you have made anything?' she asked. 'Barney owns the farm.'

It seemed an innocuous comment, but it brought silence crashing down onto the room.

'Is that true?' Hugh asked. 'That's not in the will. Nigel?'

'Mrs Smallwood transferred the farm and several hectares of land to Barney a few years ago,' Nigel confirmed. 'It no longer forms part of the Ramblings estate.'

'How did you know?' Barney turned to Cassie, the makings of a frown hovering over his face.

'Frances told me.'

'Then why the hell couldn't you tell me, before I forked out for a bit of land to give me access to the building site?' Guy shouted at her. He turned to Barney. 'At least it clears up what she sees in you. She obviously had more modest ambitions than we feared.'

Barney's grip on Cassie's hand loosened.

'The land? Gilver's Field? *You* bought it at the auction?' Barney shook his head, and hair danced around his face. 'How did you know it was for sale?'

Guy smirked.

'Why don't you ask Cassie?'

'What?' Barney let go of Cassie's hand. He scratched his nails along the edge of his jaw. 'Cassie wouldn't have told you. She knew that land was vital to my plans for the farm. She knows how opposed the village would be to any development. She wouldn't betray me or Ribblemill.'

He stared at Cassie, waiting for her to deny it. She wished she could. Seconds passed as she wished and wished, desperate to contradict Guy. But she couldn't. It had been innocently done, but she had betrayed Barney. Doubt swirled in Barney's eyes like fine Lancashire mist.

'I'm sorry,' she said. It was automatic – and fatal. The mist thickened, obscuring any expression.

Guy laughed.

'What did you expect? Nessa's not the only one who talks when she shouldn't.' He grinned. 'Nessa just never stops, does she? Even when she's asleep...'

The silence in the room was so thick it was a wonder anyone was still breathing.

'It was you?' Barney's voice was as flat as his eyes. 'You and Nessa?'

'I can't believe it's taken you this long to work it out. Of course she turned to me. It was always between the two of us, wasn't it? And why should I have said no? You've always had everything: parents who doted on you, brilliant exam results, the great and noble career. It was my turn.'

'Then I hope it makes you happy to see me now

I have nothing.'

'Barney?'

Cassie took his hand, and ran her fingers over the back of it, rubbing his knuckles to try to ease the tension in them. He yanked his hand away and without looking at Cassie, walked out.

'Why did you say all that rubbish?' she shouted at Guy. 'Go and tell him it's not true.'

'He knows it is.'

'Are you saying you had an affair with Nessa?' Diana confronted Guy, arms folded across her chest.

'Not an affair.' He shrugged. 'It was a casual thing.'

'But not too casual to ruin Barney's marriage! How could you do that to him?'

'Why should he have it all? I've spent my whole life hearing how perfect he is, and what an unfortunate accident I was.'

Cassie had heard enough. She didn't care if Diana and Guy wanted to spend the rest of the day arguing. All she cared about was Barney, and she needed to find him before she ran out of time. She only had a couple of hours left to decide whether to catch her train to Devon. She tried his office first but it was empty; the calendar still hung on the wall, taunting her with its red circle round the day when they should have had dinner. She moved on to the kitchen, but Ruth was there on her own. Ruth suggested he might have gone back to the farm, but he wasn't there either. Nor was he answering his phone. And then Cassie kicked herself. She knew where he would be. Hadn't he told her where he went to hide away? He was

377

under the willow tree, she was sure of it.

She kicked off her shoes and ran across the garden, pausing before she reached the tree to wipe the perspiration from her face and steady her breathing. She parted the trailing branches and ducked in to the tree's centre, her heart thumping with the memory of last time she had been here. Barney wasn't there. She slumped to the floor, winded by disappointment. She had no idea where to look next.

She sat under the tree, fidgeting to find a less knobbly patch of trunk to lean against, and regarded the envelope in her hand. Frances' letter. Should she read it now? Her hands were already peeling carefully along the glue line on the flap. There was one sheet of paper inside, covered in a different handwriting from the envelope. It was a masculine hand, not Barney's: the Colonel, Cassie guessed. So Frances must have told him her secret. That hurt more than it should. She unfolded the paper and read the letter.

'My dear Cassie,

I have delayed writing this letter for as long as I could, but no amount of raging or fuss on my part can change what must be. By now you will know what a selfish old woman I am. I invited you to work for me, knowing that it would only be a temporary job, and knowing that in all likelihood one day you would find me dead. Forgive me.

Why did I do it? There is nothing like a death sentence to make one reassess life. I had lived alone for many years, but suddenly all I could think was that I did not want to die alone. So I advertised for a com-

panion: to keep me company while I died, not while I lived.

You were not what I was looking for. I am so glad of that. I knew from our first meeting, despite the appalling hair and clothes, that you were the right one, and that you were strong enough to deal with this. I could not have imagined how much more you would do. You were supposed to give me a better death, and instead you have given me a better life. You have restored Ramblings to where it should be, at the heart of the village. These last few months have been the best part of over twenty years. I cannot thank you enough.

It has given me enormous pleasure to see how you have changed in your time here, and perhaps in its turn, Ramblings has restored you to who you should be. You are a kind and generous woman, and it has been the greatest privilege to know you. The vicar assures me there is a heaven, and if he is proved right, I will look out for your parents and tell them how proud they should be of what you have become. Never let anyone make you doubt yourself again.

You will have heard that I have left you something in my will. It would have been more, if I had believed you would take it, and that my children would not contest it. The money is your freedom fund, to pay for your divorce, or a deposit on a house of your own, or whatever would make you happy. You have years of life stretching ahead of you. Use them well. Surround yourself with people you care about. Believe that there are people who care about you. Invite them in, and give them a key. Do not end up like me.

Friendship is not measured in years, but by what is in our hearts. Mine may be old and failing, but it could not hold greater affection for you, my dear Cassie. You have been a joy to know, and a companion beyond measure, and for that I am and will always be,

Your grateful friend,
Frances Smallwood

PostScript: Against the Colonel's advice, I must interfere for one last time. I long to see you happy, Cassie, not living your life alone. You deserve more than this. I think there is someone you could trust. You have already saved his life, and I believe he could be the one to save yours. Nothing would give me greater pleasure than to see you share a life together. Whoever you choose, take your time and be sure. Have faith that your forever one will come.'

Cassie read the letter a second and third time, holding the paper vertically in front of her so that her falling tears didn't smudge the ink. It was heartbreaking to have these final words from Frances: the goodbye that she wished she too could have had the chance to make. But at the same time, she wallowed in the words, and satisfaction jostled side by side with sadness. Frances had valued her. Cassie had made Frances' last months happy. She should feel proud, not guilty, of what she had done. This letter was a thousand times more precious than anything else Frances had given her.

Drying her cheeks on her sleeve, Cassie read the postscript again. Frances was clearly referring to Barney; the letter must have been written before the garden party. Frances must have died content, thinking that they were a couple. But what was the truth? Cassie loved him – she was sure of that. But she wasn't sure about his feelings, and the more she thought about it, the less sure she became. He desired her – she had no doubt about that, as her blood still steamed at the memory of what he had done to her in this very spot. He had said he wanted her. And what had Vicky said? That he looked at her as if wondering why she wasn't in his bed. But it was all physical, not emotional. He had never said he loved her, in those or any other words. How could he be her forever one if he felt nothing stronger than lust?

Cassie folded the letter and slipped it back into the envelope. Frances was right. She needed to be sure, and she wasn't. She had been running around, trying to find Barney, and for what? To apologise? She had done enough of that in the years with Mike. She could still go after him, tell him how she felt, but what would be the point? She had lived through a relationship with love on one side and lust on the other, and it hadn't worked. Frances was right about that too. Cassie deserved more. She wouldn't contemplate a relationship again unless there was equal love and commitment. And if that meant not having a future with Barney... She swallowed, feeling sick at the idea. She could do it. It was possible to live without the people you loved. She had done it after the deaths of her parents. She had done it over the last months, not seeing her family. She was strong enough to deal with it.

Cassie glanced at her watch. She knew what she had to do. She was going to catch her train, go home, and work out in her own time what she wanted her future to be. But first she had to put right the wrong she had done Barney. She ran back to the house, and peered into all the downstairs rooms until she found Guy. He was in the morning room with Hugh, enjoying an intimate acquaintance with the contents of a bottle of whisky.

'What do you want?' he asked, when Cassie burst in. 'Do you think you have the run of the house in your new role as trustee? Well we're both trustees too, and on a show of hands you're outnumbered. Get out.'

He was well on his way to being drunk. Cassie didn't care. He could drink himself to death as long as he agreed to what she wanted first.

'I want the land you bought at the auction.'

'Haven't you already got more than you deserve from our family? That's a valuable piece of land.' He studied Cassie and she waited, hoping that her instinct had been right. 'What are you going to give me for it?'

'Five thousand pounds,' she said, relieved that the prospect of money had prevented him refusing her outright.

'Five? No deal. You haven't a clue how much land is worth, have you?'

Cassie wasn't thinking about how much it was worth, only how much she could afford.

'OK, ten thousand,' she said. She'd worked it out on her way over. This would still leave her with her savings, and some of Frances' money. It was more than she had arrived with.

'I don't think so.' Guy picked up a wad of papers from the table beside him and waved it at Cassie. 'I know you have twenty-five thousand.'

He wanted all of it – the entire freedom fund;

382

everything that Frances had given her. Cassie looked at Hugh, but he was staring into his whisky glass. She would find no support there.

'Fine. Twenty-five thousand.'

She had no choice. Frances would understand. Frances had loved Barney too.

'I think you could go further,' Guy said, filling up his glass. 'You've worked here, what – six months? You must have been paid at least a grand a month. I'll knock off tax and expenses. Let's call it a round thirty thousand.'

'Thirty thousand?'

Panic tightened Cassie's throat, making the words sound faint. She coughed.

'The land isn't worth that.'

'It is to you. And it's priceless to Barney.'

He smiled, clearly knowing full well what Cassie was doing, and why.

She gazed round the room, letting her eyes rest on the empty chair where Frances used to sit. She didn't want to give Guy the money. She didn't want to give him the satisfaction of taking it off her. She would be left with nothing to show for her time in Ribblemill. But as she stared at the chair, remembering Frances, feeling her spirit, she realised that it wasn't true. She still had Frances' letter, rustling in her hand. She had her self-worth back. She had learned to love again, a depth of love she suspected Guy had never known. So he could have the money, every penny of it. In the things that mattered, she would still be far better off than him.

'Very well,' she said. 'I'll pay you thirty thousand pounds for the land.'

'There are the dresses too,' Guy replied. 'They must be worth something.'

'No. You're not having those.'

'Then perhaps you're not having the land.'

They stared at each other, at a stand off.

'For God's sake, Guy!' Hugh's bellow made Cassie jump. 'Don't push it. You've caused enough trouble today. Let her have the land if she wants it so badly. It's no use to you.'

'Fine.' Guy shrugged. 'It's yours.' He smirked. 'That's the easiest thirty grand I've ever made.'

'I want our agreement in writing, while the solicitor is still here.' Cassie didn't trust Guy, especially drunk. Surprisingly, he agreed without argument, and Nigel Boot drew up a document to record their deal until the formal paperwork transferring the land could be prepared.

There was only one thing left to do. Cassie took the agreement down to Barney's office. He wasn't there: she hadn't expected him to be, but all the same, she deflated at the sight of the empty room. She photocopied the agreement, and wrote a short note to Barney, promising to give the land to him as soon as it was officially hers. She signed her name, and put the note on his chair, ready for him to find. She stroked his keyboard, trying to grasp a connection from where his hands had been, and bent to smell the back of his chair, breathing deeply and searching for the scent of Barney. Then she left Ramblings for the last time, through the servants' door, and went to collect her bag to begin the journey to Devon.

CHAPTER TWENTY-SEVEN

'You're not going to stay, are you?'

'No.'

Vicky handed Cassie a dripping plate, and Cassie dried it and added it to the pile. They had done this hundreds of times before, and their roles never changed: Vicky made the soapy mess, and Cassie wiped it away. She had been in Devon for four days, and already they were settled in a routine. She was back in her old bedroom, complete with sheep poster on the wall. She helped Vicky with the housework and the boys, and went out with Stu when he asked for an extra pair of hands on the farm. They couldn't have made her more welcome. Perhaps that was the problem. She felt like a guest. It was no longer her home. No one really needed her here.

'Where will you go? Back to Ribblemill?'

'I don't know.' But if she thought about it, no one needed her there either. 'I'll try to find a PA job somewhere, perhaps in Exeter, or wherever there's work. I can always temp until something comes up.'

'And that's what you want to do?'

Bubbles cascaded to the floor as Vicky turned to give Cassie a sharp look.

'That's all you're planning to do with the rest of your life?'

'That's what I can do,' Cassie replied. 'And I

want to give you and Stu my share of the farm. It makes no sense for me to own half of it. Clinging on to it won't bring Mum and Dad back.'

'You can't do that. You love it here. It's your home.'

'No it's not. It's yours, and Stu's, and it's your inheritance for the boys. You shouldn't have to check with me every time you want to change something. Everyone should have the freedom to do what they want with their own home.'

'You know you're the best sister ever, don't you?' Vicky gave Cassie a very wet hug. 'I'll talk to Stu, but if he agrees, we'll buy your share, as long as you don't mind instalments.' Vicky relaxed the hug enough to draw back and look into Cassie's face. 'You won't go straightaway, will you? And not without telling us? Promise not to run away.'

'I promise. You're stuck with me for a few more days yet.'

It was like déjà vu, Cassie thought the next day, as she crossed the fields that would take her to the coastal path. She was doing the same now as she had done in her last few days at Ribblemill: exploring her favourite walks, revisiting her favourite places, and storing them in her memory for when she had to go. It wasn't a permanent farewell this time. She could come back and visit here as often as she wanted. It would never be the same again, though. She had pulled up the roots that tied her to this place. She sat down on the grass at the top of the cliff, gazed out at the sea stretching into apparent nothingness before her, and wondered if her future was equally empty.

Would the goodbyes ever end? Would she find somewhere to put down roots again?

An excited bark interrupted her thoughts, and seconds later, sharp claws dug into her leg and an enthusiastic tongue licked her hand. The tongue and claws belonged to a dog that looked remarkably like Gin. In fact – Cassie looked more closely – it *was* Gin. She threw her arms round Gin and buried her face in the dog's fur.

Cassie heard movement and the sound of someone sitting down beside her. A draught of air sent goosebumps chasing over her skin in a Mexican wave. Her heart was already racing in anticipation of who it was. She couldn't look up. She couldn't bear to be disappointed.

'Did I mention how frustrating you are?'

It was Barney, and Cassie's head shot up to match the face to the voice. It was him, and he was real, and he was in Devon, and he was smiling at her with his garden party smile. It was a lot to take in.

'What are you doing here?'

'Shouldn't I be asking you that?'

Cassie let go of Gin, who nestled in the small gap between her legs and Barney's. Barney laughed.

'I've heard so much about the delights of Devon that I thought I ought to see it myself. And I can't argue.' He nodded towards the view. 'This is better than Southport. You can see the sea, for a start.'

'You've come all this way to see the sea?'

'I've come all this way to see you.'

'How did you know I was here?'

'Vicky told me.'

'When did you speak to Vicky?'

'The day you left. You just vanished. No one in Ribblemill knew where you were. Of course I phoned Vicky. I needed to know you were safe.'

He *needed* to know? The words spread a tiny glow of warmth though Cassie. She stroked Gin, trying to stay calm, and not let herself be carried away.

'Vicky thought you needed some time on your own,' Barney continued, 'or else I would have driven straight here. But then she rang last night and said you were planning to leave. Where are you going?'

'I don't know. Perhaps Exeter. I can't hide away here. I need to get on with life.'

'What about Ribblemill?'

'There's nothing for me there.'

She glanced up to see him squeezing his eyes closed. He hadn't been fast enough. She had glimpsed the pain in them first. Before she could begin to process that, and work out what it meant, he stood up and walked to the edge of the cliff. He stood with one hand in his pocket, the other rubbing his jawline, staring out to sea. Tension tightened his shoulders. Cassie waited.

'I'm sorry I walked out,' he said, coming back and sitting next to Cassie again.

'I'm sorry I told Guy about the auction.'

'Don't apologise. I'm not *him*. You don't ever have to apologise to me. I hate that I did something that made you think you should. I promised myself that I would never make you feel that way.'

'I know you're not him. And I'm not Nessa. I would never do what she did.'

He nodded.

'Is that why you've come?' she asked. 'To apologise?'

'Not only that.'

Barney pulled a paper out of his pocket. She recognised it at once as the copy of the agreement she'd signed with Guy.

'Why have you done this? I know what this money means to you, and how hard you've been saving. You can't give it away.'

'Yes I can. Frances called it my freedom fund. It gave me the freedom to do what I needed to do.'

'You didn't need to buy the land for me just because you'd mentioned the auction to Guy.'

Cassie didn't answer. She hadn't done it out of guilt, or not entirely. She'd done it out of love. She wanted Barney to be happy, to have everything he wished, and she had seen a way to achieve that. Barney pulled another paper from his pocket and held it out to her. It was a cheque for thirty thousand pounds, payable to her, signed by him.

'I don't want that,' she said. He looked at her, searching her eyes, drawing out goodness knew what secrets.

'You can take the cheque and let me pay you back,' he said. 'Or there's another option.' The cheque wobbled in his fingers. 'You keep the land, join it to mine, and we can be partners.'

'Partners in the farm?'

'In everything.' Barney's eyes didn't lose contact with hers. 'I'm no good with fancy words. I don't want to do it without you. I need you. I love you.'

Did he mean it? She wasn't interested in fancy

words, only true ones.

'You've never mentioned love before,' she said.

'No. That was deliberate. You've heard the words before and they let you down. I wanted to show you what they could really mean. Surely you saw that?'

Cassie shook her head.

'I thought you were fussing about my health, like you did with Frances.'

Barney watched her, as if waiting for her to work something out. And she did. She remembered what he had said on the day Frances died.

'You told me you made a fuss of Frances because you loved her.'

'Yes.'

The tips of his fingers were white, he was holding the cheque so tightly. He was blinking more than she had ever seen him blink before. Cassie reached out and pulled the cheque from his hand. The devastation that crumpled his face convinced her beyond any reasonable doubt. She had never been so sure of what she was doing in her life. She went to the edge of the cliff, tore the cheque into pieces and tossed it, letting the scraps of paper fly out to sea on the breeze.

Barney was at her side in an instant.

'I love you too,' she said. It felt strange to say it out loud, after weeks of trying to keep it secret. She didn't want to stop. 'I don't care about the money. I love you. Nothing else matters.'

Barney stepped nearer, and Cassie thought that at last he was going to kiss her. Instead, he cradled her face between his hands, and looked into her eyes: that familiar Barney stare, no longer searching for information but revealing it. It was intoxicating.

'I'm going to spend every second of my life loving you,' he said. 'You're safe now.'

Cassie believed him. The right words from the right person had the power to heal as much as the wrong words had the power to harm. And when Barney wrapped her in his arms and kissed her, she felt the scars on her heart knit together, burying the years of pain.

'It feels wrong to be so happy,' she said, some time later, as they lay together on the grass. She rested her head against Barney's chest, hypnotised by his heartbeat.

'Because of Frances?'

Cassie nodded. Barney seemed to enjoy the sensation. When he had finished kissing her again, he sat up, pulling her with him.

'The day I arrived back from Malta, Frances summoned me when you were out for your walk,' he said.

'What did she want?'

'To tell me that I'd made the right choice at last and that I had to look after you or answer to her.'

Cassie laughed. Barney kissed her. She laughed again, and it had the same effect. She would have continued with the experiment, but he put his hand over her mouth.

'Stop it.' His eyes and his smile wore matching twinkles. 'This is important.'

He rummaged in his pocket – there seemed no end to the things he was hiding in there – and pulled out some tissue paper. He opened it to reveal a gold bracelet.

'She gave me this to give to you at the right moment. She said you would understand the significance of it.'

Cassie picked up the bracelet. It was made from linked gold loops, similar to the infinity symbol, and the clasp was a heart in two pieces, one on each end of the chain, so that when the bracelet was fastened the heart was complete. She had seen it on the portrait of Amelia Smallwood, and Frances had told her the story.

'It belonged to Amelia Smallwood,' she said. 'It was given to her by her husband. According to Frances, it was the happiest of Smallwood marriages, a true love match.'

'And it was specially made for her,' Barney continued, picking up the story, 'because she was his second wife. But he wanted her to know that she had made his heart whole again. She would be his forever wife.'

Taking the bracelet from Cassie, he fastened it on her wrist. He kissed away the tears on her cheeks.

'Why are you crying?'

'Frances wrote me a letter. I understand it now.'

'Good. But you know what she would say, if she was here, don't you?'

Cassie smiled. She could easily guess.

'Stop making such a fuss,' Barney said.

And when Cassie laughed, he pulled her back down into the grass, and made a fuss of her in such a delicious way that she didn't think she would ever tell him to stop.

Acknowledgements

Thanks to all at Accent Press for making a secret dream of over thirty years a reality. Special thanks to Rebecca Lloyd for sympathetic editing, and for understanding exactly how I wanted *The Magic of Ramblings* to be.

The RNA is a brilliant organisation for writers, providing advice, support, opportunities and friendship, and I would still be wistfully reading acknowledgements, not writing my own, if I hadn't joined the New Writers' Scheme. I'm grateful to everyone involved.

Thanks to Catherine and Julie, extraordinary friends, writers, cheerleaders and advisers. I could go on – and as you know, I usually do – but for once I'll be brief. As Frances says, friendship isn't measured in years. You have both been amazing.

Finally, to Stephen and Molly, for regular hot Ribenas, and simply for letting me get on with it.

This Large Print Book for the partially sighted, who cannot read normal print, is published under the auspices of

THE ULVERSCROFT FOUNDATION